PERFECT COVER

Linda Chase and
Joyce St George

BANTAM BOOKS

LONDON · NEW YORK · TORONTO · SYDNEY · AUCKLAND

PERFECT COVER
A BANTAM BOOK : 0 553 40795 3

Originally published in Great Britain by Bantam Press,
a division of Transworld Publishers Ltd

PRINTING HISTORY
Bantam Press edition published 1994
Bantam edition published 1995

This book is set in 10pt Palatino by
Phoenix Typesetting, Ilkley, West Yorkshire

Bantam Books are published by Transworld Publishers Ltd,
61–63 Uxbridge Road, Ealing, London W5 5SA,
in Australia by Transworld Publishers (Australia) Pty Ltd,
15–25 Helles Avenue, Moorebank, NSW 2170,
and in New Zealand by Transworld Publishers (NZ) Ltd,
3 William Pickering Drive, Albany, Auckland.

Reproduced, printed and bound in Great Britain by
Cox & Wyman Ltd, Reading, Berks

Critical Acclaim for
PERFECT COVER

'I enjoyed it immensely. It has that rare sound of an authentic voice – the voice of a woman working in a man's world, with all the damage and dirtiness that implies'

Liza Cody, author of *The Anna Lee Mysteries*

'Investigator Tina Paris is a genuine heroine and *Perfect Cover* is a page turner with a sure-fire surprise ending. It's a perfect read'

Michael Connelly, author of
The Black Echo and *The Concrete Blonde*

'Ingenious, scary, and crammed with the fascinating details of a life most of us couldn't imagine daring to live . . .'

Rosellen Brown, author of *Before and After*

'Only someone who has been there could have written this novel. *Perfect Cover* brings the reader into the real, dangerous, unexpected world of the special investigator . . . An exciting story'

Dorothy Uhnak, author of *False Witness*

Also by Linda Chase

HYPERREALISM

RALPH GOINGS

HOLLYWOOD ON MAIN STREET

To all the women and men who bring
honesty and integrity to the law
enforcement profession.

J.S.

And to a wonderful aunt, E.G. I wish you
were still here to read this.

L.C.

Acknowledgments

We would like to thank Evelyn Brown, Bill Cash, Bill Doyle, and Joe Schneider for sharing recollections of their lives and times with Joyce at the Office of the Special State Prosecutor. Also, Marie Simonetti Rosen and Peter Dodenhoff of *Law Enforcement News* for providing access to their archives, and Pat Eaton, Ed McHugh, and Collette Franov for their insight into other aspects of policing. Special thanks to Tina Mohrmann, whose friendship and assistance were invaluable.

Thanks also to our families and friends for their encouragement and support, especially Sandra Scoppettone and Dwight Kinsey. And finally, our appreciation to our friend and agent, Charlotte Sheedy.

Author's Note

The events in *Perfect Cover* are inspired by actual experiences and cases that Joyce St George encountered during her six years as the first female special investigator for the Office of the Special State Prosecutor, an arm of the New York State Attorney General's office formed in the early 1970s in response to the Knapp Commission's findings of widespread police corruption in the New York City Police Department. The mandate of the office was to investigate and prosecute cases of corruption and brutality within the criminal justice system of New York City.

Deceive boys with toys,
but men with oaths.

Plutarch
Lives 'Lysander'

Chapter One

The call came in at 4:46 p.m. I should have been out of the office by then but Vince, my Chief, was sending me undercover to a hundred-dollar-a-plate political dinner in Queens, and I was waiting around for the ticket, catching up on paperwork. 'Special Investigator Paris, can I help you?' I said, picking up the phone on the third ring.

'Who? Who is this?' an irate female voice responded.

That should have been my line, but I'm used to it. The Women's Movement aside, people still expect a man when they call the Special Prosecutor's Office. And when they hear my voice they assume I'm a secretary or a desk clerk. God, it used to make me mad. Those early years, right out of college, the first female investigator with the SPO, I was on the lookout for every slight. And there were plenty, in and out of the office. The very first thing the Chief Investigator said to me after the swearing-in ceremony wasn't 'Congratulations', but 'Can you type?' It was a useful anger, though, the fury a kind of fuel that gave me courage and made everything possible. Now I sometimes wonder where it's gone. Righteous indignation seems to be one of those things that fades with all the other attributes of youth.

'Special Investigator Paris,' I repeated patiently. 'Can I help you?'

'I called the precinct,' she said. 'They told me to call you; said there was nothin' they could do.' Her voice was wary, hysteria edging her words like lace.

'Would you like to file a complaint?'

'I don't want to talk about it.'

I didn't ask why she had called if she didn't want to talk. I had long ago given up the idea that these calls would follow any conventional conversational logic. A lot of the complainants we got were just crazies anyway, paranoids who saw conspiracies in everything; or wronged women, men too, who wanted to make trouble for whoever had spurned them; or nosy old ladies who spent their days with their elbows propped on the sills of apartment windows. Still, every call had to be logged in as a possible allegation of corruption, the gist of it jotted down, and if there seemed to be even the slightest basis in fact, it had to be checked out, at least on a rudimentary level. Corruption came in an infinite number of guises and it wasn't always easy to know who to take seriously. Even dotty old ladies sometimes saw things that were useful. To a certain extent you just had to trust your instincts. If the caller had something real to say, the conversation usually had a logic of its own.

'Does this have something to do with corruption?' I asked.

'He kicked me like a dog. In the street. Punched and kicked me like I was nothin'.'

'This is a police officer you're talking about?'

'Of course it's an officer. Big black bastard who thinks he owns Nostrand Avenue. Thinks he can beat up on anybody.'

I sat up straighter and rummaged for a pencil to start making out a report. 'Were you able to get his name?' I kept my voice matter-of-fact. I knew his name but needed to hear her say it.

'Get his name? I didn't need to get no name. I *know* his name. Calvert. Ed Calvert. Seen him hurt a lot of people. He's crazy. He's goin' to kill me. Said he would.'

'When did you say this assault took place?'

'What assault?' Her voice was suddenly wary, as if I was trying to trap her.

'I believe you said he kicked you and hit you.'

'Yeah, that's right.'

'When did the assault take place?'

She sighed. 'Sunday morning. Round six a.m. He must've been waitin' for me.'

'What did you say your name was?'

'My name? What do you need *my* name for?' Surprise mixed with outrage.

'For the complaint. We've got to have a name.'

She was silent for a few seconds. 'My name's got nothin' to do with it.'

'If you don't file a complaint, there's no way I can help you.' I felt rotten saying this. Her voice told me she was young, black, off the street – the kind of witness who wouldn't have much credibility even if the allegation developed into a case. There was little chance I could help her no matter what she said. But I said it anyway, out of habit, out of the hope that this would be one of the rare times things would work out differently. Anyway, it was my job.

'He said he'll get me if I open my mouth. He will, too, he'll do it again. Do worse. He don't fool around.'

'Why don't you give me your address so I can come see you?'

'What you want to see me for?'

'We need to talk.'

'We are talkin'.'

'Listen, if I can't see you, I can't help you. You want to stop this guy, don't you?'

'He's mean. He's buggin'. *He* need help. Need to be put away. That's what he need.'

'We can't do anything without a complaint. If you let me come see you we can talk about what you want to do.'

'Not now. If you come here now, I won't open my door.'

'Tomorrow,' I said.

'He's gonna kill me.' Her tone held equal measures of conviction, resignation, and fear, but she gave me her name and address just the same.

That was Lenora Terrell. Just like a lot of callers I get, but with something a little different. At least that's what I hoped. I knew what Vince would say. 'Go out there, get the report. File it and forget it.' And he would probably be right. We had a file as thick as a meatball sub on Ed Calvert. Two arrests on assault, probably drug-related. A list of allegations as long as the penal code, and we had never been able to make one good case. Complainants withdrew their complaints, witnesses disappeared or changed their stories. If he couldn't scare them off he paid them off. There wasn't anyone in Calvert's world that couldn't be bought or beat. The street had it he had even killed a guy, a skell dumb enough to beat him at cards and expect to be paid.

This was a man wearing a badge. If there was anyone I wanted to nail it was Eddie Calvert.

It was after six when the ticket finally arrived, which didn't leave me a lot of time to get home, get myself done up, pick up my undercover car, and rendezvous with the team. I finished up my notes and went to the tech room to sign out my pulse beeper. Vince was the only one around when I left. I glanced through the glass partition surrounding his office and saw he was on the phone, scowling as usual, the grip strengthener he always kept on his desk squeezed tightly in his fist. I have one of these devices myself, which I use to build up my shooting hand; Vince uses his as a surrogate for the necks he'd like to strangle. Obviously the conversation wasn't going well.

A compact bullfrog of a man, with a massive head and chest and vocal cords to match, Vince had risen through the ranks of the NYPD before being brought in as Chief Investigator at the SPO. He subscribed to what I think of as the Neanderthal style of management, very popular in law-enforcement circles. Communication consisted of a variety of barks and croaks interspersed with expletives, occasionally livened by off-color humor. Someone could write a bestseller about it – *Minimal Communication: How to get your message across in the least number of words while impressing everyone with your macho importance* – except that these guys don't read. Maybe I could turn it into an adult ed course at the Learning Annex. God knows I'd taken enough of them. 'How to Talk Cop' wouldn't be any weirder than 'Getting in Touch with Your Pet's Biorhythms', and might be more popular.

Actually, I sympathized with Vince. Like almost everyone in the office, he was tired, and he was spending an awful lot of energy pretending that he wasn't, that we all weren't. We were still chipping away, making cases, getting indictments, once in a while a conviction, doing what we had always done, but it was tough to run a citywide anti-corruption agency when the issue was no longer sexy. We all reminisced about the glory days in the Seventies under Maurice Nadjari after the Knapp Commission focused so much attention on police corruption and the Special Prosecutor's Office for Anti-corruption was formed. The office was a radical new concept with citywide jurisdiction and an expanded area of operations that included not just police corruption, which the NYPD's own Internal Affairs Division had so clearly failed to root out, but the entire criminal justice system as well. We were the knights on white horses primed to slay the dragon. Grand jury indictments came in fast and furiously and almost everything we did hit the papers.

Nadjari was impatient, though, and it didn't take long to realize that the indictments he wanted wouldn't be forthcoming if he didn't step on some toes. We were all upset when Judge Murtagh started throwing out some of the cases for lack of evidence, but it didn't make things any less exciting. And when Governor Carey ousted Nadjari because of a supposed lack of public confidence, and rumors started flying that the 'Super-prosecutor' was on to something that involved high-ranking people in the Democratic Party, well, those were heady days. It didn't make the work any different – you could still spend seven hours in a car parked outside a house waiting for someone who never showed, or endless evenings undercover in low-rent bars picking up tidbits from Mafia nobodies, positioning yourself to make the good connection when it came. But the mood was sure different.

There have been four special prosecutors since, and none of them has had Nadjari's charisma or his high-handedness either. There would never again be anything as big as the French Connection theft, when the infamous SIU (Special Investigation Unit) was implicated in the disappearance of 398 pounds of heroin and cocaine worth seventy million dollars from the Police Department property clerk's office. And we might never convict another DA like we did Tom Mackell, even if he did win on appeal. It would be nice to think the big guys in criminal justice are more honest now, but maybe they are just smarter.

There's no doubt the public zeal for fighting corruption is gone, though. After Watergate and Oliver North and talk of Reagan making a deal with the Iranians to hold the hostages till after the election, and every kind of character you can imagine on TV on the take, maybe it all just seems like business as usual. Cynicism on a national scale – maybe even global, who knows?

Even the recent scandal at the Seven Seven Precinct

with twelve officers indicted on various drug charges hasn't elicited any deep outrage. As far as the public is concerned, it's just normal venality, I guess. Part of the 'go-go eighties'. So why am I still here? I could move on to the FBI, or into the private sector, but the truth is, in a way I wouldn't even admit to anyone else in the office, I still believe in the mission. I keep remembering something Nadjari said in his statement to the press when they were trying to oust him – something about the little guy and the integrity of the criminal justice system, how the Office of the Special State Prosecutor was established to serve the interests of the disenfranchised and ensure that the law would be applied with an even hand. Maybe it comes from growing up in the projects, from seeing the 'little guy' getting hurt every day.

Harry, my ex live-in, used to say I had a martyr complex. That with my Puerto Rican mother and Italian father I had no choice – if I wasn't going to be a nun, I had to be a saint. There may be some truth to what he said; I can be a self-righteous jerk sometimes. And I certainly wasn't going to be a nun. But the real thing is the chase. The damn job still gets my blood up. And I'm still fool enough to believe that the good guys can win, at least some of the time.

Traffic over the Brooklyn Bridge wasn't bad, in spite of the hour, but the Brooklyn Queens Expressway was backed up near Queens Boulevard where they were working on the Woodhaven exit, so by the time I got home to Rego Park I had less than half an hour to make my transformation. I pulled off my turtle-neck, slipped off my shoes, unstrapped my ankle holster, and pulled off my slacks. I rummaged through my crowded closet until I came up with a slinky long-sleeve backless dress I had bought on sale at the Norma Kamali boutique in Macy's for just such an occasion. It was one of those 'little black dress' things made out of some kind of stretchy material, and 'little' was definitely the operative word. I don't get much time for shopping, but I keep my eye out for these numbers.

Anyone who looked in my closet at the odd combination of slacks and sweaters and jeans and *femme fatale* dresses would think I had a room-mate or a split personality, or that I was a high-priced hooker on the side. Or maybe that was just my take on it. There were probably perfectly ordinary women who wore these things on dates, but I wasn't one of them. I could hardly remember the last time I had that kind of a date. The few relationships I'd had since joining the SPO had to be fit in between investigations and undercover work. Harry had moved out three years ago. We had tried to make it work for over a year. He loved me, he said, but he needed someone who would 'be there' for him. Wherever 'there' was, I was usually somewhere else. Living together was supposed to make my odd hours easier to take, but let's face it, watching your woman get all done up in one of these outfits for a night on the town can't be pleasant, even if the men she meets are a bunch of sleazeballs and losers. And then there's the danger factor. If he wasn't worried about me making it with someone, he was worried about me getting shot. Just like a wife. It's not that I've given up on romance exactly, but New York is pretty much a wasteland when it comes to available men, anyway.

I glanced at the clock and figured if I was quick about it I could just squeeze in a shower. The stale grime of the office at Two Rector Street seeps into your pores and I hated to go out on a job without washing it off, but it probably had as much to do with washing off one role before I put on another. Undercover was like going on stage, and my preparations weren't too dissimilar from those of a method actor getting ready for a part. The difference was I had to write the script as I went along.

I toweled off, ran a razor quickly over my legs, and

eased on a pair of black panty hose. Then I took the beeper out of my purse and taped the small plastic casing to the inside of my thigh with surgical tape and ran the thin wire around to the side, up under my armpit and down to my wrist, fixing it with small pieces of tape on my waist, side, and elbow. I squeezed into the dress and made sure the seams of the arms concealed any hint of a bulge the wire might leave. The sleeves had buttons at the wrist, perfect for hiding the tiny button at the end of the wire, but I added a thick gold-cuff bracelet for extra protection. I pulled my hair into a loose bun, letting a few curls tendril down to soften the effect. Eyeliner and mascara, iridescent mauve shadow, powder blush, and plum-red lipstick Tina Paris would never wear. Everything I had on was something I would never wear as me, including the black suede spike heels I slipped on my feet and the simple pearl clip ear-rings, which were the only other touch I added. I studied myself briefly in the mirror. I wasn't the best looking woman in undercover, but whatever I had it was enough to distract your average man-on-the-make, and I had definitely gotten the sexy-but-nice-girl effect just right.

Considering my outfit and the kind of affair I was going to, I decided to leave my gun at home. I would have a team outside and mostly I would be there for a look-see. The kind of evening that might be boring but probably wouldn't be dangerous. Still, there was always the risk of being ID'd, especially when you've done as much undercover as I have.

I put my gun on its hook in the back of the closet and grabbed the keys to the Nissan. I had two cars, a run-down Chevy Citation with 102,000 miles and the dents to match, issued to me by the state, which I drove to the office and when I was out on investigations. It was reliable enough and had the advantage of not attracting attention in the kind of neighborhoods the job usually took me to. The Nissan 300ZX was mine, or rather Julia Cipriani's. It was my undercover car, bought by me and registered with confidential plates listed to my primary undercover persona. Vince had the plate number, but no-one else, not even other investigators in the office, had access. Working in anticorruption teaches you caution – you learn early you can't take chances, even with people you think you can trust. My first car chase had pitted me and the Citation against two guys in a Mercedes 500SL, and it was clear that the state issue gave all the advantage to the other guys. The Z was my baby. I could keep up with just about anyone and do it in style.

I drove down Queens Boulevard toward Astoria, driving by Crescent Manor on my way to the meeting place to scan plates and assess how and where possible 'dirty' cars might be parked. The front of the Manor was well lit and there was valet service and a parking-lot in the back. A few of the darker side streets looked like good candidates for organized-crime cars, and I made a mental note of them as I drove on to Thirty-third Avenue and Crescent to meet the team. It is an easy neighborhood for parking. I found a spot around the corner, locked up, and walked toward the waiting car.

Whistles and catcalls greeted my approach, a ritual the guys never seemed to tire of. There were three men doing backup: Bud Ryan, the senior investigator, and the two young bucks of the team, Terry O'Hanlon and Lloyd Whitten. Lloyd, a rangy Texan we all called Stets, was a good investigator but a little too hooked on action and excitement and inclined to be reckless. Like a lot of the younger recruits, he had grown up watching too many cop shows and believing too much of what he saw. Terry was both more serious and more ambitious. A real electronics buff, he had come to us from the Nassau County DA's office six months before with a specialty in computer crime. It was no secret that he was looking to make the FBI by thirty.

Bud, one of the first blacks to reach the rank of First Grade Detective in the NYPD Homicide Squad before retiring and coming to work for the SPO, was the office mainstay – intelligent, clearheaded, and totally together. He was the one I would look to if things went wrong, and I would make sure he had the other beeper. It was my lifeline. A signal from the team would be the only warning I would have if anything unexpected came up.

'Hey, Terry,' I said, getting in the car, 'we missed you yesterday.' There had been a christening party at Dan O'Keefe's house in Mineola. Dan was our tech officer, in his early forties, with a young wife and first kid, and just about everybody from the office had put in an appearance. 'Terry's got better things to do with his off-duty time,' Stets said, chuckling. Terry caught my eye for a minute but I couldn't read his expression – embarrassed maybe. Bud proceeded to go over the plan.

The dinner was a fund-raiser for Neil Dandrell, son of State Supreme Court Judge John Dandrell, up for his second term as assemblyman but with sights definitely set on Washington. The Dandrells' ties to organized crime were well known. We had four different allegations of case fixing and bribery from four different sources – three known, one anonymous – but they were difficult to prove. You don't go after a Supreme Court Judge unless you are sure of an indictment. We had to keep watching and making connections. The Donald Manes parking-ticket scandal had shaken things up in Queens, and we were still trying to sort out who the new players would be. It was a constant quest to find out who in the justice system the mob had turned and who they might be after. My job was to stay close to the Dandrells, gather overhears, and help the guys outside check plates.

The beeper system we used was something I had worked out years ago as a young recruit, updated now with improved technology. It was based on beeps from my signal to the receiver in the team's car and beeps from them to me. But instead of noise, my beeper emitted tiny electric pulses. I could feel it but no-one could hear it. It was simple, and except for the pulse, not too sophisticated, but I liked it because it didn't require speaking into a mike, or depend on the outside team listening to and interpreting conversation. I would keep an eye on movement in the room; if I saw someone with organized-crime connections talking to the Dandrells, or to anyone else from the criminal justice system who might be there, I would take note of it. If I wanted the person's identity checked I would press the button on my wrist as they started to leave. One buzz meant check out the plates. If I learned that a group of people were leaving and were planning to meet elsewhere, and I wanted them followed to the new location, I would signal with two beeps. If I had to leave in a hurry I would beep three times. If I needed assistance I would beep like crazy and hope they could get to me.

We tested the transmitter – the signal came across clearly on the receiver in the car. It was time to move. A few off-color remarks followed me as I got out of the car, rounded the corner, and got in the Z. I drove to the Manor, going around the block one more time, checking out the cars again and trying to decide where to park. I didn't like valet parking – the car park was one more person who might remember the car and me, and it limited my ability to make a quick exit if necessary. On the other hand, I couldn't walk up to an affair like this, so if I parked on the street I would have to be able to get a cab. I went for a side street around the corner from a bodega on Crescent where I knew cabbies often stopped for coffee.

The cab-driver, an Indian, took me the few blocks

with reassuring indifference. A uniformed doorman reached for the door as we pulled up in front of the wide marble steps, and another attendant ushered me into the mirrored and marbled lobby and indicated the red-carpeted staircase that led to the mezzanine, where the Dandrell dinner was taking place. An immense crystal chandelier hung in the centre of the twenty-foot ceiling, and the refracted light glittering off the marble floor had a disastrous effect on spatial perceptions. I had to place each spike-heeled foot carefully and hoped I wouldn't need to make a quick exit across it, especially after a few drinks.

The thick padding on the stairs was designed for the maximum contrast to the brilliant hardness of every surface in the foyer, and I had to hold on to the banister to keep my heels from permanently sinking in. More chandeliers greeted me on the balcony, this time set off by a gold-and-black-flocked foil wallpaper, which continued into the banquet room. Your basic Mafia school of decorating, where nothing is spared in the attempt to inundate the senses and outlavish your previous concept of opulence.

A line of people in front of me waited to hand in their tickets and I could see that some were stopping to write out additional contribution checks. The mob inside the banquet room was bustling and noisy. I judged the crowd at two hundred or more. Clearly the room would soon be full to capacity – it was the place to be tonight if you had any hopes in connection with the local political machine.

I glanced at the people taking tickets and moved toward one who was middle-aged and male. My target was usually the same, one that was depressingly reliable if you liked to think the best of human nature – particularly the masculine variety. He was true to type, with a thinning hairline, a tan that was too even, and a suit that was too shiny and too tight. A large gold Rolex emerged from his cuff as he reached for the tickets. His body looked firm yet padded, as if he worked out in the gym a few times a week but couldn't lay off the pasta.

I smiled as I handed him my ticket and introduced myself as Julia Cipriani. 'Al Randazzo,' he said, offering a brief handshake, his gaze fixed past my shoulder on the groups coming in the door.

'Any relation to Sonny Randazzo?'

This time he looked at me and his smile was more genuine. 'Yeah, sure, cousins,' he said. 'You like to dance?'

Sonny and his brother Gus owned a couple of clubs out on the Island known for lively music, exotic drinks, and Mafia-related clientele. They were friendly types and I spent a fair amount of time hanging out in the clubs, storing up names and faces and bits of information I could use to shore up my undercover persona. I nodded at Al, smiling again. 'Actually it's my boss's ticket,' I said. 'He couldn't make it but I decided to come anyway. I've been working for an insurance company out in Manhasset where I live, but it's a dead-end kind of job.' I handed him a card with my undercover name and the name of the fictitious County Insurance Company. 'You know it?' He glanced at it, shaking his head, and handed it back.

'I'd really like to work in government and everyone says the only way to do it is to get out and circulate. So here I am. The trouble is, I don't know a soul.' I let our eyes lock briefly and added what I hoped was a touch of winsomeness to my smile.

Apparently I had managed the right combination of candor and flirtatiousness to pique his interest. 'What do you drink?' He gestured to a younger man chatting in a group behind the table. 'Ricky, take over for me for a few minutes. I want to show Miss Cipriani around.'

Al was an enthusiastic host, taking me from table to table, introducing me to all his cronies – various guys in the Brooklyn and Queens political machines, someone from the Community Board, a lawyer for the Board of Elections, and, interestingly, a couple of lawyers who work for the Roselli crime family. One of our allegations against Dandrell involved a gambling and racketeering case against Roselli and six of his henchmen that the judge dismissed for lack of evidence, causing near apoplexy in the DA, who was absolutely convinced the case was solid. Finally, Al maneuvered me over to Neil Dandrell, who was greeting well-wishers with his father's law clerk, Timothy Mitchell, by his side. The judge himself was surrounded by a phalanx of cronies too thick to get through.

Being at the banquet was no crime. It was ostensibly an up-and-up fundraiser, but I made a mental note of everyone I saw and tried to keep an eye on who was connecting with who. The guys were mostly standing up talking in groups, or moving from group to group the way Al and I were. A tired-looking combo was doing a cross between Italian wedding and top-forty Muzak, but no-one was dancing. The wives were there, done up to the tips of their false eyelashes, but this wasn't their event, and they sat dotted around the white-clothed tables in their bright-coloured satins and taffetas like so many taxidermied exotic birds.

Al arranged a seat for me at one of his friends' tables – one of the lawyers' wives hadn't come – and, with assurances he would return shortly, went back to cover the front desk. The waiters had started bringing out the fruit cocktail but it wasn't enough of an incentive for the men to sit down. The two women on my left had moved their seats together and were chatting about nursery school. Directly across the table, another woman picked at the fruit in the iced bowl intently, delicately pushing aside sections of canned grapefruit and mandarin orange like an archeologist on a dig.

I was thinking I'd better get up and circulate when

I noticed Smatters, the new Kings County Assistant DA, across the room by the bar. I had never met him, but I'd seen his picture in the papers. Interesting that he should be here. I didn't recognize anyone he was with but needed a closer look. I took a cigarette and lighter out of my purse and lit up. I don't smoke but I can see why other people do; it's a crucial device for getting through these functions. When I'm doing undercover it's an essential part of my stage business. I stood up, smiling in a general way to the other women at the table, and mumbled something about refreshing my drink. I was moving toward the bar when I felt the beeper pulse against my thigh, a small but jolting sensation something like being caressed by a vibrator.

I kept walking, careful not to change the expression on my face, but scanning the crowd now. My eyes followed a waitress crossing the room with a tray of empty glasses. The exit to the kitchen had to be behind Smatters to the left. The ladies' room, I knew, was down the hall outside the banquet room. To get there I would have to pass Al and risk running into whoever it was Bud's signal was telling me to avoid. I looked back toward the bar. Smatters was looking straight at me, his ear cocked to the conversation of the man next to him, but his attention definitely in my direction. I didn't acknowledge his stare or turn away. I didn't think he knew me. I didn't remember meeting him as an investigator, or in any of my other guises, but I didn't like that look. It was possible he had been in court sometime when I was testifying and had picked me out now in spite of the outfit. Whether his presence here was on the level or not, I didn't want my cover blown. He said something perfunctory to the guy he was talking to and moved toward one of the tables where the Election Board lawyer I had just met sat in a huddle with two other gray-suited men. Shit. I usually had a good memory for faces. Why didn't I remember seeing him?

I had to move before Smatters had a chance to point me out. Whoever Bud was warning me about might be lingering by the front door, so I had to avoid going down. I found myself wishing I'd brought my gun. Maybe I was losing my edge. It was so easy to get lulled. You've seen it all before – and before that. What is it Bud always says? *Every call, every stakeout, every undercover is unique. The number-one rule of police work. If you let yourself get hung up on the patterns, it can kill you.* I joined the office a rookie right out of college. Over the years, Bud's advice has gotten me through a lot of tough times and tight situations.

Trying not to make it obvious, I ducked behind a waiter whose tray was piled with prime-rib entrées and moved along with him toward the band. The number they were playing was building to a crescendo, and if I was lucky they were about to take a break. The music stopped, more waiters started appearing with trays of food, and there was a general commotion that I hoped was obstructing Smatters' vision as the men made their way toward their seats. The lead singer announced the break and stepped down off the stage area. I walked over to the drummer, who was just getting up, and started talking about the equipment. I had played with a band briefly in college, and at least I knew a few of the right things to say. I asked him what he had paid for his Zildjian cymbals, said something vague about his touch, and asked what kind of music he liked to play on his own time. This got him animated and I walked along with him as they all made their way toward the front. I could see Al Randazzo coming toward me now, but he was surrounded by a coterie of young thugs in silk suits and barely glanced at the band walking out.

As we made our way toward the top of the stairs I looked over the railing to the main hall. Henry Zinc was standing below, about to start up, a haughty-young-model type on his arm. Zinc was a current SPO case, another wise-guy lawyer who had been playing with the system for years in ways that we couldn't prove – bribing court clerks to switch Parts so he got the judge he wanted, paying a cop off to 'amend' his UF61 report. This time we had him. A corrections officer he had tried to bribe to do some special favors for a client who was inside had come forward and was willing to testify. Zinc had seen me outside the grand jury room last week and there was little doubt he would recognize me. I stopped mid-sentence with the drummer, told him I'd forgotten something, and made a quick detour to the Ladies.

It was empty but I went in the john, waited a couple of minutes, flushed, came out, did the comb-powder-lipstick number for a few more minutes, smiled vaguely at two women who came in deep in a conversation they continued through the walls of their separate stalls, and pressed the beeper button three times to tell the guys I was coming out. I hoped Zinc and the girl hadn't met anyone on the stairs to delay them, but I didn't want to wait any longer. I still had Smatters and Randazzo to worry about. I opened the heavy-paneled ladies'-room door, glanced toward the banquet room, didn't see anyone, and moved toward the stairs. I could just hear the sounds of polite clapping and then someone starting a speech. The stairs were clear and I started down.

The sound of my high heels clicking seemed deafening as I crossed the empty marble hall. The doorman ogled me across the whole expanse and let me out with a flourish. I gave him a nod and a half-smile and started down the front steps. The musicians were standing off to the right by their van, smoking; otherwise the parking-lot seemed clear. But the valet wasn't around. Parking someone's car probably. It didn't seem likely anyone would leave with the dinner just starting, but I couldn't take a chance. I decided I'd better not wait around for him to get me a cab. I walked down the driveway, made a quick turn down the side street, spotted the guys in the undercover car, and made sure they saw me but kept on walking the seven blocks to the Nissan, cursing my tight dress and those damn stiletto heels every step of the way.

Chapter Two

She had a little red Chevette. He had been following it for about five minutes, hanging back, seeing if he was right about where she was going. He was sure she hadn't noticed him. Why should she, driving home on a clear, crisp October afternoon, a hint of frost in the air, the neighborhood suffused with the glow of golden leaves. She looked like she didn't have a care in the world. That was why he noticed her.

He had been cruising by the campus, just taking things in, when he glimpsed her coming down the steps of the Science Building, a shoulder-bag swinging by her hip, a couple of notebooks in her arm. She had a nice little hop to her step, as if something had just gone well, or maybe she was glad to be out of class, done with school for the day. She had on a loose padded car coat that hid her shape, but he liked her hair, straight and shiny, parted on the side and tied back at the nape of her neck with a ribbon or a barette, he couldn't see which yet. He liked the fresh look of her face, too – good features, not too much make-up, maybe nineteen or twenty, maybe a little younger.

She was walking straight toward him down the path like a gift when she turned her head and saw a couple, a boy and a girl, coming across the lawn. Her face lit in recognition. He felt himself tense up. She stopped where she was, smiled and waved at the other girl, and waited for them to reach her.

He looked away and drove on, catching them in the rear-view mirror laughing and gesturing, and then, before he lost sight of them, walking on together deep in animated conversation. Damn. He turned the corner, his hands involuntarily gripping the steering wheel, his jaw clenching. He hated it when things didn't go the way they were supposed to, but he forced himself to relax, rolling his shoulders under his jacket and leaning back into the seat. From the direction they were going, they were probably walking toward the student parking-lot. He turned left to circle around the block, breathing easier again, getting into it.

There was a stop sign at each intersection. He drove slowly and came to a complete halt each time, letting any cars coming in the opposite direction go by. It was partly out of caution. He wasn't about to risk a ticket, much less an accident, or even a close call, nothing anyone could remember. But more important, it was part of the game. If he went too slowly and found she was already gone, then she wasn't the one. Either things worked out or they didn't. He had to follow the rules.

When he got that feeling, when everything inside and outside clicked and he knew it was right, it was like a dance choreographed from beginning to end. Maybe it was getting too easy. So now he was teasing himself, dragging it out a little. Testing. Playing with the feeling, giving it a chance to fade. Playing with fate, or whatever the hell was out there working the strings.

Maybe she would get in a car with her friends, or maybe they would turn left at the corner before the parking-lot and go into the Student Union for a cup of coffee. He had been checking out the campus on and off for a couple of weeks now and he knew every building: the classrooms, the dorms, where the students might hang out. There were any number of places she could go – the library, the drugstore, the bookstore, a room at the dorm – but she wouldn't. He didn't pick the girls, they picked themselves. They were there at the right moment, poised to catch his eye, attracting his attention with their bland innocence like a doe who stops in the hunter's path and looks straight at the blind with its wide, dumb, unseeing eyes.

When he saw the three of them up ahead they were entering the parking-lot. He pulled over and watched them through the chain-link fence. They talked for a few more minutes and started to separate, the couple and the girl moving toward different cars. He smiled to himself. She would go toward the red Chevette – one cursory glance at the cars in the lot and he had picked it out as hers – get in, and drive off alone. He watched with satisfaction. That moment of panic when she ran into her friends had been totally unwarranted. Everything was falling into place. There were no hitches – there would be no hitches. He knew that now. He felt confident. Alert.

Sometimes he thought this was the best part. All his senses honed to a fine edge of awareness, primed like the cocked trigger of a gun; anticipation and assurance welded into a steely sense of power as cool and hard as the blue metal barrel. He was in control, yet part of something larger, too. That was why he never planned in advance. It had to just happen. It had to be right – to prove that destiny was on his side, or was acting through him, or both things at once somehow. Like he was in a movie someone was filming. Or like watching some guy on TV. You knew what was going to happen and you could enjoy watching it play itself out. Only you were the guy you were watching; it was you playing it out. And her.

He was playing his part. She was playing hers.

She made one stop at the dry-cleaner's, coming out with an armload of hangers encased in their sheer, filmy plastic, which she draped over the back seat. More clothes, it seemed, than one college girl would have cleaned at one time – maybe she had a room-mate. He didn't allow himself to worry about that. The clothes

34

would work to his advantage. She would be trying to get them out of the car carefully, to carry them and her books and not get anything wrinkled. She wouldn't notice him pulling in after her. Packages were always an advantage. In fact, the girls rarely noticed anything until it was too late. Even when he was standing before them. They never saw him for what he was, always those smiles, that wary encouragement, that sweet span of time when he knew everything and they knew nothing.

After the cleaner's, she circled back toward the campus and slowed down in front of a row of modest brick garden apartments, pulling into the driveway and around back to the parking spaces in the alley that ran behind. The place had the bland, bedraggled air of cheap student housing. No plantings, no amenities or embellishments. Most of the windows had makeshift curtains. Some had books piled along the sills, and he could see rock-star posters tacked up on some of the walls. He had noticed the place when he checked out the neighborhood earlier in the week. He knew the alley ran the whole length of the block. He continued to the corner, turning left and then left again, so he would be coming in from the opposite side and she wouldn't know he had been following her.

He entered the alley slowly and drove hesitantly, stopping a couple of times to look at the backdoors of the buildings as if he were trying to find something. She was already out of the Chevette, reaching into the back, when she heard his car. She looked up briefly and went back to her efforts, showing no concern. He pulled up next to her and got out. She looked up again, grappling with an armload of clothes. Their eyes caught. He smiled and said, 'Hi.' She smiled briefly and went back to trying to gather her books and purse. He walked toward her.

'I'm looking for a friend of mine. I think she's supposed to live here.'

She got everything out of the car, slammed the door with her hip, and looked up.

'Her name's Sally. Sally Bronfman.' Sally was number nine. But they didn't print the names in papers.

She thought for a minute. 'Doesn't sound familiar,' she said, hefting the clothes to a better position. The thin plastic bags billowed in the breeze.

'She's a senior,' he said. Coming closer.

She shrugged. 'There's a building manager somewhere around here if you can find him. Maybe he can tell you.'

By now he was standing in front of her. She started to walk toward the back door and he moved along with her. The ground was bumpy with cracked pavement. She couldn't see well because of the clothes draped over her arm and stepped gingerly.

'Here, let me help you,' he said, reaching for the hangers with his gloved hand. She looked at him a little more closely this time, as if it finally dawned on her she wasn't supposed to be talking to strangers. But there was nothing threatening in his handsome open face, in his easy-going manner or affable boy-next-door smile. There was always this point where any one of them could have closed him out.

'They ought to fix this driveway,' he said.

'They never do much around here. But the rent's cheap so no-one complains.' She relinquished the bundle and he followed her to the back door. She rummaged through her purse for a key, opened it, and let him in. The heavy metal door slammed with an ear-splitting clang behind them as they ascended a short flight of stairs to the first floor. 'I live on the third floor,' she said, with a small apologetic laugh, and they continued up. Rock music blared from somewhere down the second-floor hall. Jim Morrison, it sounded

36

like. He remembered the music from his own college days, its rhythms of sex monotonous and compelling.

Her apartment was the first one at the top of the third flight of stairs. She put the key in the lock, opened the door, and reached for the clothes. 'I really appreciate your help,' she said, smiling. 'I wish I could tell you where your friend lives. Like I said, you could try the manager. He's in the apartment to the right at the bottom of the stairs. If he's home.'

She had the cool, confident, artificially friendly smile of an actress trying to sell you something on TV. Very soon he would have to wipe that smile off her face. For now, he smiled back, handing her the clothes by the hangers bunched together on top. She was grasping them and pushing the door open when he managed to let the hangers drop. The clothes fell in a heap in the open doorway. 'Gosh, I'm sorry. What a klutz,' he said. He bent down, gathered them up, and carried them past her inside. They were in a small living-room – a cheap futon couch, some bookcases, a kitchenette along one wall with a round table and a couple of chairs next to it. An open door led to the bathroom, another to the bedroom beyond. It was perfectly quiet – no room-mate. He knew there wouldn't be, but he found himself almost disappointed. It would have been interesting.

She stood at the door, surprised and wary, now that he was actually in her house.

'Not bad,' he said.

'Well, like I said, the rent's cheap. My room-mate and I split it so it comes out cheaper than the dorm.' He chuckled. She was probably about to tell him the room-mate was due home any minute now. These girls are so fucking dumb, always playing tricks, never giving him enough credit. As he moved toward the open door, he could hear her sigh of relief – a small unconscious animal sound that tickled the hair on the back of his neck. He got to the door, reached for the knob, and

37

instead of going out, closed it behind him. He turned the bolt on the lock, a brand-new Medeco, he noticed, a safety feature her parents had no doubt insisted upon. By the time he turned back to face her, relief had turned to shock. Her eyes were wide, her lips parted, as if she wanted to say something but didn't know what.

'Your friend,' she finally stammered.

He came toward her. 'There is no friend.' His voice was cold now, insinuating. 'You know that.' He walked past her to the window and closed the drapes. She was still in shock; he didn't have to worry about her screaming or trying anything. Not yet. He turned and they faced each other. He could see her mind starting to work, trying to figure if she could outsmart him. Her eyes darted around the room, looking for a weapon, something she could hit him with, or a way out. He laughed and her eyes fixed on his. She tried for a smile, as if she figured maybe the best thing was to cooperate. Try to act like it was just a friendly little encounter. Let the guy screw her and maybe it wouldn't be so bad. Fucking slut. She didn't know who she was dealing with. He'd make sure it was bad.

'Take your clothes off,' he said.

'What?'

'Your clothes.' He pulled his gun from his waistband and pointed it toward her head. 'I like to see what I'm getting. Every inch of it.'

Her eyes grew wider. She stared at the gun. A .38 Colt. His preferred weapon. A gun with some size to it. A classic, with good heft in your hand and an impressive six-inch barrel. Slowly she shrugged her coat off her shoulders and let it fall to the floor, her eyes riveted. She was wearing jeans and a baggy pink sweater. 'Please,' she said.

He waved the gun toward her chest. 'The sweater.'

She pulled it off, revealing a plain white bra. He waved the gun again, and she reached behind and unhooked it. Her face looked less shocked now, more like she was going to cry. She hesitated, her hands at her sides like a little girl being scolded. 'Let's go, bitch. The pants, the shoes. I don't have all day.' He took off his own jacket, slipping the sleeves over the tight black driving gloves, keeping the gun pointed at her head.

She unzipped her jeans and started to pull them down, then thought better of it and backed up to the sofa, sat down and started to untie her shoes. Hightop Reeboks, he noticed. When the shoes were off she stood up and, still watching the gun, pulled down the jeans. She wasn't fat, but her hips and rump were round. She had a hard time wriggling out of them and hopped around in nervous embarrassment pulling off the legs. He watched dispassionately. A red glow of shame rose from between her breasts, along her neck, and up to her face. Her nipples stood erect. It was interesting how the effects of fear and shame mimicked arousal, the way the sounds of fucking mimicked the sounds of pain. He could feel himself getting hard and stood up. He pointed the gun at her flowered cotton panties and she took them off, and then last, her white cotton socks.

He walked around her, studying her body. It was round but firm, with a nice biblical quality about it – ripe for the plucking. He was pleased. He had been right about her, of course. He reached out and ran the cold butt of the Colt down the vertebrae of her spine. She jumped and gasped at the same time. He laughed, coming around in front of her again, and pushed her down on the couch. Tears started to run from the corners of her eyes. With the gun against her neck he undid his belt buckle and unzipped his fly. Suddenly, he grabbed her hair where the ribbon was tied behind her neck and jerked her head back.

Her eyes registered absolute terror now. He pulled the hammer back firmly to the first notch, turning the cylinder with a distinct click. A shudder of fear shook her whole body, but his hold on her hair was too tight for her to move even if she had dared. He carefully pulled the hammer in a quarter inch more, and the cylinder made another half-turn. Click. Her eyes darted wildly. He gripped her head more tightly and pulled the hammer one more notch. Two successive clicks a hair's breadth apart lined the bullet up in the chamber. Nothing moved. Even her breathing seemed to have stopped. He played the hammer back and forth, staring into her face, almost blank with terror now, enjoying the feel of the narrow metal ridges under his thumb and the pressure of the trigger, fully cocked, against his finger. It wouldn't take much, no more than a cough, a sneeze, a hiccup.

'Not yet,' he said finally. He held the hammer all the way back, pulled the trigger in, and slowly released the hammer forward.

'Please don't kill me,' she said. 'I'll do whatever you want.' Her voice was tiny and thin and didn't seem to belong to her, as if she were a puppet and a ventriloquist was throwing it from far away. It reminded him of a mouse he had once heard. The cat had it trapped under the bed in the middle of the night and in its death throes it let out a horrible, frail, high-pitched squeal. He was only a boy of nine or ten, and it had never occurred to him until that moment that a mouse could scream, that every creature will find a way to communicate the vividness of its pain.

He looked down at her smooth white flesh. With the tip of the gun he drew a line from her neck, around each breast, across her stomach, and through her pale pubic fuzz. A stippling of goose bumps followed his path. Then, turning the gun so the front sight blade pressed against her, he carefully etched the number eleven in the soft skin of her belly.

'It's time for a little game,' he said, pulling himself astride her, his knees clamping her thighs. With one quick motion, he yanked the ribbon off, pulling strands of her hair with it, grabbed one of her wrists, wrapped the ribbon around it, and demanded her other hand. She offered it up, totally compliant in her fear. Tying her probably wasn't necessary, but there was no point in taking a chance. He bound the wrists together, pushed the end of the ribbon through, pulled it tight with his teeth, and sat back to look. It was a good effect. Childish white grosgrain ribbon.

Taking the gun in both hands, he opened the cylinder and dropped the bullets on to her stomach, counting each one out loud as it fell. 'Six rounds,' he said, 'six chambers.' He picked up one round and held it in front of her face. 'Thirty-eight copper tip. Leaves a nice clean wound.' He loaded it back into the chamber, left one chamber empty, loaded another round, left another empty, and loaded the third. 'Fifty-fifty,' he said. 'Excellent odds.' He closed the gun and gave the cylinder a twirl. 'Ever see that movie *The Deer Hunter*?' She managed to shake her head, following his movements with the blank avidity of an entangled fly focused on the approaching spider. 'Robert de Niro. Great film. All about games. And guns. But I guess you were too young.'

He contemplated the gun for a second, then held it sideways and rolled it slowly down her body so the cylinder rotated along with her contours, each revolution aligning a different chamber with the barrel. 'She loves me, she loves me not,' he recited, laughing his strident, hollow laugh. A thrill of urgency rushed through his veins. He pushed her legs apart, put the gun to her head and shoved himself against her unyielding flesh. Her bound hands started to reach up toward the gun. 'No, don't, please don't.' It made him furious that she would protest at this point, when everything was

41

already decided, the game set. He grabbed both wrists with his free hand and wrenched them above her head. Pressing the barrel harder against her temple, he thrust again, forcing himself inside.

As her flesh gave, he pulled the hammer in, one click. Power ran through every nerve like a heroin high. He thrust again and pulled the hammer a little tighter. The second click. She was whimpering now with a sound that was no longer even human. Off in the distance the beat of the Doors drummed like the thudding of his heart. He shoved his body harder and harder into her, and groaning, pulled the trigger. A bright emptiness exploded behind his eyes. He collapsed momentarily against her. But he felt disorientated. Some part of him was still expectant, suspended. His mind grappled with the awareness that something was wrong. The sound. There had been nothing but a small, dull, hollow clang; he had been primed for the blast of a bullet discharging. He had been sure this time it would happen. He shook himself back to reality, pushed himself off her, and stood up.

She remained just as she was, her eyes squeezed tightly closed, her bound wrists above her head, her body shuddering spasmodically in the grip of terror's chill. A creature reduced to nothing more than her fear – life's most basic, all-encompassing emotion. She was no longer even a woman really. The sight of her filled him with disgust. He did up his pants and felt around and under her for the three rounds that had rolled off her stomach into the folds of the couch. She opened her eyes.

Moving swiftly now, he put on his jacket and then did a tour of the room to assure himself he had left no clues. Her purse was lying on the floor next to her coat and the pile of cleaning. He picked it up, rummaged for her wallet, took out her driver's license, read the name – Mary Alice McGuire – dropped it, and took out the few bills. 'Slim pickings,' he said with contempt, tossing the wallet toward the couch, where she lay staring, uncomprehending, in his direction. He stuffed the money in his pocket, unbolted the Medeco, and went out.

Chapter Three

7:45 a.m. Although my late-night undercover work exempted me from the necessity of arriving at the office at a particular time as long as I put in my thirty-seven and a half hours, I tried to be there by eight most mornings. Except for Vince and Bud, few of the guys felt compelled to show up before nine. Ten wasn't unheard of. The thirty-seven-and-a-half-hour working week was a joke; we all put in much more than that, but after all these years I was still playing the same game – trying to be better than the big boys so they would keep me on the team. Then, too, if I arrived early enough there was at least a chance of parking in one of the Dey Street spaces.

Typical of the Kafkaesque New York City bureaucracy, twenty-five official parking spaces had been allotted to thirty-eight official cars. The narrow, congested streets of lower Manhattan's Financial District afforded virtually no street parking, and far from receiving special treatment because we were cops, any car parked illegally that displayed the insignia of the SPO was guaranteed a ticket and ran a good risk of being towed. Cops who investigate other cops are definitely not popular with the boys on the force. Maybe we were slightly less despised than Internal Affairs – at least we went after lawyers and judges, too – but I didn't count on it.

I pulled into one of the last available spaces, locked the car, turned up my collar, and braced myself for the walk to the office. The rain that had been falling gently for the last hour was turning mean, and as I approached the World Trade Center plaza the wind created by the huge towers drove it against my face. When I signed on, the Special Prosecutor's Office was located on the fifty-seventh floor of the World Trade Center and my desk faced a window with a magnificent view of the Statue of Liberty. Now we occupied the twenty-third and twenty-fourth floors of the modest office building at Two Rector, and while Vince still had a commanding East River view, all I got to see was the white-shirted backs of the insurance adjusters in the building across the alley. I tried not to dwell on the implications of this comedown, though my daily buffeting by the Twin Towers' mini weather system didn't make it any easier. But what the hell – that was then and this is now, as the saying goes.

I waved to the guard on duty at the desk in the lobby and yelled 'Hold it' to the large, gray-suited back of someone just entering the elevator. It turned out to be Mickey. 'Meeting,' he said, in response to my surprised look. He is not usually one of the early birds.

'Did you hear about the good-looking rapist?' he asked as the doors closed. He was a big bear of a man with an unruly crop of mad-scientist hair that contrasted disconcertingly with the fine tailoring of his habitual three-piece suit. Maybe the hair was his way of announcing that, in spite of a sartorial elegance unusual in law-enforcement circles, he was no dandy.

'Is this one of your sick jokes?'

'No, this is for real.' He handed me the *Daily News* he was carrying under his arm. PRETTY BOY RAPIST STRIKES AGAIN, the front-page headline screamed.

'You wouldn't think a handsome guy like that would have such a hard time getting laid.' It was hard to tell whether he was sincerely perplexed by this or just trying to bait me. Mickey Rakosi, a retired NYPD detective who had been with the SPO since its inception, was famous for his tasteless but generally good-natured jokes. I refrained from the usual lecture on how rape was about violence, not sex, and glanced at the paper to try to get the gist of the story.

'What do you get when you cross a donkey and an onion?'

My mind was still on the paper so I just stared dumbly.

'A great piece of ass that will bring tears to you eyes.' He smiled and looked at me expectantly, waiting no doubt for my disgusted but tolerant look. Disgusted because of the chauvinism, tolerant, he assumed, because of the wit it was couched in. I probably complied. Being a good sport was another part of my job, or another accommodation I made, depending on how you looked at it, and I liked a good bad joke as much as the next guy. The elevator opened on twenty-four, and with a show of mock gallantry Mickey let me step out. One of these days I will come across the perfect female chauvinist joke – one that will put men in their place for ever, or at least give Mickey a run for his money – but it hasn't happened yet.

The elevator opened onto a long hallway. On the left was the tech room with a window to sign out equipment. The various surveillance devices and cameras were kept locked up, and only Dan O'Keefe, the tech officer, and Vince had access. A pair of double doors to the right opened into the main squad room. Stacey, the receptionist, sat at a desk in the front. Vince's office was in the far right-hand corner. The rest of the room was taken up with the desks of the twenty remaining SPO investigators set in pairs back to back. The number went up and down as people came and went and hiring freezes were instituted and lifted, but after the cutbacks of the early Eighties that's basically what we were down to.

Mickey's desk butted up to mine, so we headed in the same direction. I threw my coat on the back of my chair and went straight for the coffee machine, ensconced, like an altar, on its own table in a corner of the room, poured myself a cup, black, checked out the remains of an Entenmann's coffee cake that had definitely seen better days, and went back to my desk to make a plan for the day.

The jolt of excitement I felt when I realized who Lenora Terrell was talking about had stayed with me through the night, making up for the disappointing results of the aborted undercover operation. I knew it could be a dangerous feeling. It was important to force myself to be methodical, to do everything by the book. If possible, I should run a check on both Edward Calvert and Lenora Terrell before I went to see her. It would be useful to know if either of their names came up in any investigations being carried out by other departments – any division of the NYPD, Narcotics, or the Major Case or Vice Squads – or if there were any new complaints against Calvert listed with IAD or the Civilian Complaint Investigation Bureau. Any information I could get on Calvert would be helpful, but even more important, I wanted to know if there was any information tying Terrell herself, or the address she gave me, to Calvert or any of his known associates. Before I went out there, I wanted to have some idea who I would be dealing with. On the other hand, if Lenora Terrell was a known crackpot complainant, it would save a hell of a lot of time to know that.

I typed their names onto a request form and took it down the hall to Mary Lee in Intelligence. 'Hi, honey,' she said. 'What can I do for you today?' Her bright white smile flashed in her large black face like burnished silver on polished mahogany. Many a recruit over the years had been shocked to discover that Mary Lee's southern charm and

Alabama drawl, which a lifetime up North had failed to diminish, hid a core as tough and tenacious as a knot in an aged tree stump. But Mary Lee and I had always gotten along. She had joined the office as a receptionist back in the days when I came on as a rookie investigator. She commiserated with my isolation in that male bastion, and I supported her for an intelligence and integrity that went way beyond her job description. I wasn't the only one who encouraged her to move on to better things. When she had been with the office close to ten years, and her salary as a receptionist had reached the civil-service ceiling for that job category, the bosses finally got together and circumvented the issue by moving her into Intelligence, which gave her both a higher rating and pay scale and a domain better suited to her skills.

'When do you need this stuff?' she asked, as I handed her the request. 'Yesterday?' The usual harried reply. There was always a backlog of information investigators were waiting for. Mary Lee guarded computer time the way investigators guard the identity of their informants. If you were new, or someone on Mary Lee's shit list, you could wait half a day for the simplest data and, of course, all cases heading for trial had first dibs. But if she liked you she could usually manage to fit a request in. I asked her to run the names through NYSPIN (New York Statewide Police Information Network) for the usual – criminal records, aliases, etc. – and told her I needed it by afternoon. Then I told her what I really needed to see was the information in our own files.

For my purposes, NYSPIN was just the tip of the iceberg. More comprehensive in some ways, and certainly far more unwieldy, was our own card file – over 175,000 index cards wedged tightly into wall-to-wall metal cabinets, categorized by name, case number, aliases, government or business affiliations, known gambling and after-hours joints, organized-crime families and their associates. There was a category for practically everything, and cross-referencing was a nightmare. This might be the Age of Computers, but our office has not gotten much past scratching hieroglyphics in stone. We have been begging the state for a computerized system for years, and since his arrival Terry O'Hanlon has stepped up the campaign, putting in for several terminals in the name of efficiency. He has even persuaded Vince to request a fax machine. Hardly unreasonable, but contingent, of course, on funding. Fifty thousand dollars was reportedly set aside in this year's budget to update our equipment, but it hadn't been allocated yet. Until it comes through we have our fingers to do the walking, or Mary Lee's, anyway.

There was nothing under Terrell, and the Calvert files I knew all too well. Still, I asked Mary Lee to pull them out and went through them again to see if her name had ever been mentioned. When I was finished I checked with Mary Lee, but the NYSPIN reports weren't back yet. I knew I should do my own report for last night's undercover but the headline Mickey had shown me was gnawing at the back of my mind. I got another cup of coffee and opened the paper. From a police point of view, rape is usually outside my realm, but from a woman's point of view it is gut central. I glanced down the page and noticed my friend Maddy Keitel was quoted in her role as Police Department spokesperson. A Queens College coed was assaulted at gunpoint and Sex Crimes investigators had reason to believe there was a serial rapist at large. To date, they had five other cases with similar MOs, each involving a good-looking white male who appears to befriend the victim and then rapes her at gunpoint. Yesterday's victim was in shock and had not been able to supply a more precise description.

I got a sick, sinking feeling in my stomach as I read it and instinctively looked at my watch to see if it was a good time to call Maddy. I wanted to know if there was anything more she could tell me, but mostly I just wanted to connect, to see how she felt. Maddy and I had met our freshman year at John Jay. Two scared little girls behind our bravado, each needing somehow to crack the male domain of policing in order to propel ourselves out of the poverty of expectation to which we were born. After graduation we shared an apartment for a while until our jobs and our boyfriends got in the way. She was the only person who understood where I had come from and where I was now, and whenever I felt vulnerable, or compromised, or misunderstood, I thought of her.

Before I could reach for the phone, Vince opened his door and called me into his office. He had called Bud, Mickey, Terry, and Stets in, too, so I thought he wanted to discuss last night's surveillance, but when I saw the look on his face I knew he had something else on his mind.

'I've heard some news that I wanted you to hear first from me.' His usually stony face showed the strain of emotions he was trying to control. This was going to be bad. He looked around at us. 'Where's Monk?' he barked, as if suddenly remembering something. 'He was on the phone,' Stets said. 'I'll get him.' Stuart 'Monk' Carlin was one of the original old-timers at the SPO, a confirmed bachelor with an apparently celibate lifestyle. He had spent most of the last year working closely with IAD on a group of officers involved in an embezzling ring, a case I was not assigned to, so our paths rarely crossed.

The rest of us waited nervously. The big fear, the fear that came most readily to mind, was that the state was finally going to withdraw our budget and close the office. Governor Cuomo had commented more than once that he didn't see the need for a Special Prosecutor's Office, and there were frequent rumors of our demise. Our ability to handle the sensitive racial issues in the Howard Beach case – which we'd been assigned precisely because we were an investigative and prosecutorial body independent of the NYPD and the DA's office – along with our work on the Seven Seven, had put the rumors to rest for a while. But if the guys were anything like me, they were wondering how soon they would be looking for work. We certainly avoided each other's eyes.

Monk finally came in and Vince repeated his statement that he wanted us to hear the news from him. He looked down at a folder on his desk as if he were going to read something, then looked up. 'You know the trial for the officers indicted for embezzling began a couple of weeks ago.' We nodded. He went on, avoiding Monk's eyes. 'Artie Silverstein didn't show up in court. The brass sent a couple of his buddies up to the family camp in the Catskills to look for him. They found him all right. He'd put a bullet through his brain.' A muted groan circled the room, reverberating like wind in an empty bottle. Vince closed the folder. 'At least it wasn't the wife and kids that found him.'

We all looked at Monk, catching each other's eyes as we quickly looked away. He sat down, stunned. He had worked the case longer than anybody, and Silverstein had been his particular baby.

'Look, it happens, it was nobody's fault,' Vince said.

There were murmurs of agreement. We all knew how Monk was feeling. Silverstein was basically a decent guy who had made a mistake; a family man. It was one thing to expose a bad cop: no-one wanted to be responsible for another person's death. All of us at the SPO were there because we believed corruption destroyed the system, but we were cops too. We knew what they were up against out there, how easy it was to get talked into taking a little something here, fudging the evidence a little there, especially now that the streets were flooded with drug money and the 'war on crime' seemed so hopeless. And when they got caught, it was often the ones who had tried the hardest to stay clean who couldn't handle the exposure.

Vince allowed for a moment of silence, whether of prayer or reflection or simple shock. 'OK,' he said, by way of dismissal, 'we've still got a job to do.'

Commiseration, as usual, took the form of humor. 'Hey, one less report to write,' Mickey said, slapping Monk on the back as we walked to our desks. 'Yeah, sure.' Monk tried for a laugh. Neither of them sounded convincing. None of us was taking it lightly, certainly no-one expected Monk would, but police are notoriously lousy at dealing with feelings. The most sensitive response a cop ever gave to another cop's pain was to try to cajole him out of it. I guess it's something like the studied detachment of surgeons – with a layer of street macho for added insulation. Still, understanding it and sympathizing with it are two different things. I had no patience for their infantile avoidance. I grabbed my coat and bag and left the office.

Whether housing projects are a social experiment designed to fail, or whether they are only doomed to fail, is a difficult question. With the homeless wandering the streets of virtually every New York neighborhood, the necessity of government-sponsored low-cost housing is clear, but a tour of any of the projects built in the Fifties certainly makes you question the wisdom of past experiments. Enormous complexes of red brick, at first glance they seem to resemble their middle-class cousins. The windows are smaller and there are no terraces, only the wired-in open hallways between double buildings that mark the center of each pair. There are no gracious lobbies or spacious carpeted hallways. But these differences do not seem so crucial – certainly not crucial enough to explain what they have become. Maybe it's only the isolation – stuck away in marginal neighborhoods where land was cheap, they quickly became ghettos of poverty, of race, and eventually of crime. When the projects were new, families put their names on waiting-lists, dreaming of getting into the apartments. Now they put their names on waiting-lists and dream of getting out.

The Brooklyn address Lenora Terrell gave me, 395 Pulaski Street, was in the Eleanor Roosevelt projects, three blocks of six-storey brick buildings separated by patches of weedy, garbage-strewn earth and bumpy, cracked concrete paths. Driving down Lewis Avenue away from the honky-tonk bustle of Bushwick, I passed the larger Sumner and Tompkins projects, their monolithic forms brooding over blocks of empty lots and row upon row of boarded and burned-out abandoned buildings. I hadn't seen a store for eight or ten blocks, not even a corner bodega, and wondered how far the tenants had to go to do their shopping. There was nothing, not even one of those ubiquitous store-front 'Flats Fixed' that seem to spring up every few blocks in these neighborhoods.

I drove around the perimeter of the project. The locks on most of the gray metal entrance doors were hanging loose and broken, the squares of wired glass smashed. There is no-one to fix them, and not much point anyway; there is probably as much crime inside the buildings as out. The benches that had been placed for the tenants' convenience along the paths between the buildings had all been stripped of their wooden backs and seats. It wasn't haphazard enough to be vandalism, so I assumed it was the result of some public policy aimed at preventing the homeless from turning the benches into beds. The thick, denuded concrete supports had an odd, sad dignity, like relics from another age, as disconcerting and poignant as dinosaur bones. Poor Eleanor Roosevelt, I thought. This could not be what she had envisioned when she staunchly championed good works.

The back of Lenora's building faced Lewis Avenue, the main street, as good a place to park as any. Not that I had any illusions about traffic inhibiting dedicated car thieves and vandals. The sidewalks glittered with the glass pebbles of shattered car windows; the curbs were dotted with the burned-out hulks of stolen and abandoned vehicles. Fortunately, the Citation is not such an appealing mark. I pulled in behind a shockingly new, .bright white Jeep Cherokee – even the skells are going yuppie these days – and hoped for the best.

Although the back door of the building was hanging open, I walked around to the front. There was no point spending any more time than necessary wandering the halls. When I was growing up in the Wagner projects on 125th Street in Manhattan, the halls and stairwells were our indoor backyard, a place where kids, especially on rainy days, could play and run. Now the respectable families that are left barricade themselves behind the metal doors – except at mail times, when they wait in the hall by the post boxes for the mail carrier. Anything of value put in a box will be stolen the second he walks out the door.

There was no-one in the hall when I came in. Either the mail had already come or no-one was expecting anything. It wasn't the first or the fifteenth of the month, so no welfare, social security, or unemployment checks would be due. The elevator was directly in front of me, but it wasn't worth the risk of being trapped so I went for the stairs. You can meet up with anything there, too, but at least you have some mobility. My gun was tucked into my belt in the small of my back but I hoped I wouldn't have to pull it. In a building like this, there were probably several people better armed than I was.

Usually you go out in the field with a partner, but my gut feeling in this case told me I would do much better one on one. The Chief used to have a fit at the idea of my going into a place like this alone, but he's learned I'm going to do it anyway, so why get aggravated? Frightened as Lenora seemed on the phone, I didn't want to call any more attention to my visit than necessary. If someone saw me in the hall, they wouldn't necessarily assume I was there on police business. Two of us would be a dead giveaway. It was one of those situations when I hoped my Puerto Rican blood showed; it would be better for both me and Lenora if I were picked out as a social worker or someone from immigration rather than a cop.

I passed one guy nodded out in the third-floor hallway, a pool of piss spreading around his legs. The smells of old and new urine, rotting garbage, and burning crack hung in the stale air like vapor. Maybe that's why the first thing I noticed about Lenora's apartment when she finally opened the door was how clean it was – clean and lifeless.

I had to ring the bell three times before I heard even a rustling. Then there was a moment of silence when I knew she was standing on the other side, deciding what to do, and then she called through the door, asking who it was. I told her my name and reminded her of our phone conversation. There was another pause, which seemed to stretch out interminably, but then, a few minutes seem like eternity when you're standing in one of these halls. Finally, I heard the sound of the bolts as she began to open the four locks. The door opened. She glanced at me, her eyes darting quickly to the hall behind me, and then stood aside, staring at the floor, waiting for me to come in. Her feet were bare and she had a worn terry-cloth robe wrapped tightly around her.

She closed and locked the door behind me and I showed her my shield and identification. 'I let you come cause you seemed to believe me,' she said, handing them back. 'Those other cops at the precinct made me feel like garbage, like it was me was the criminal.' I tried to explain to her that I was a special investigator, not a regular police officer, and that my office only handled allegations of corruption involving people in the criminal justice system, like hers against Calvert. I'm not sure she understood it all, but she nodded and invited me to come sit in the kitchen, which she said was the brightest room.

The apartment I followed her through was spotless and sparsely furnished. I noticed several cardboard packing boxes stacked in the living-room. A dog-eared comic book was spread out on a chair – the only sign of activity anywhere. She offered me coffee, and while she filled an old-fashioned glass percolator and set it on the stove I took out my notebook and tried to decide what the best way to get to this woman might be. When she turned back, her eyes immediately focused on the tiny spiral pad, so I left it sitting there and went for an informal approach, commenting on the sunshine streaming through the white-curtained windows. 'It's a pretty nice apartment,' she said, 'as long as you don't have to go out.'

I nodded. 'It's a rough neighborhood.'

She stiffened noticeably. 'I can take care of myself.'

'You seemed pretty upset when I spoke to you on the

phone yesterday,' I reminded her. If she was going to be that defensive about everything, I was wasting my time.

She looked away, staring out the window. 'He should be locked up is what,' she said finally.

'You mean Officer Calvert.'

She nodded. 'He kicked me and hit me like a dog. He had no right.'

'Was Officer Calvert on duty and in uniform at the time?'

'No. Like I told you, this was early in the morning. A bunch of us were playing cards till about five-thirty. He was waitin' when I got home like he knew I was comin'.'

'Why would he be waiting for you?'

'He's been doin' that. Got so I'm scared to go out.'

She seemed to be avoiding the question, and I was beginning to think she had something personal going with Calvert. While that didn't give him the right to abuse her, it would make her story much harder to sell to a jury. If she even had a story.

'So you arrived home and Officer Calvert was waiting?'

'He wasn't standing right there. He was back in the shadow, by the building. See, I got out of the car and was tryin' to find some money I had stuck away to get home with, and something made me turn around and I see this shape in the shadow behind me. Big square man like a truck. I knew it was him right away. Wasn't nothin' I could do about it, though, so I paid the driver and started walkin' toward the front door. "Don't you be walkin' past me, bitch," he say, real low and mean, so I stopped. Be worse trouble if I didn't. "What's up, Eddie?" I asked him, thinkin' maybe I could chill him out, but he came up real close and I could see in his eyes he was too far gone for that. "Where you playin' the game, whore?" he say. "Around," I said. "You ain't been at Mom's for more than a week," he say. "You puttin' your money down on someone else's table, bitch?"

'I told him it don't mean nothin', the other game's just closer to where I live, that's all, but he grabs my wrist and starts twisting till it hurt real bad and then he gives a jerk and pulls my arm up behind my back. "You runnin' from me, bitch?" he say. I told him it was nothin' like that and that's when he took out his gun. Pointed it at me like he was goin' to shoot. Then he started to laugh, took it and smacked me with the handle, cross my arm and shoulder. Hit me so hard I was on the ground, and then when I'm down he starts kicking me. He got no call to be treatin' me that way.' The aroma of perked coffee filled the room and she got up to get the cups.

'So what you're telling me, he beat you up because you were playing cards someplace new?'

She nodded.

'Why does that bother him so much?'

She looked surprised by my question, started to answer, then turned away and busied herself with the coffee.

'Does Officer Calvert have a stake in the other club – what was it, Mom's – or get a percentage of the winnings, or anything like that?'

She shook her head. 'Not like you mean. He don't own it or nothin' like that. He just take what he wants.'

'Is that why you stopped playing there?'

'I just didn't feel like going for a while.'

It was clear I was losing her and decided to change the subject. 'Do you work?' I asked.

'I used to. Before Danny, that's my husband, left, things were real good. I was working regular, saving up to leave the projects. But with him gone it's just too much. I can't seem to keep hold of myself. Everything just fell apart. He's in the Army. They sent him to Texas this time, but we split up before that. Been over a year now. Seemed like we was always moving. I told him I had it, living on bases, never knowing where you're gonna be next year. When he reupped I stayed here. Told him I would, but he signed the papers anyways. He said it'd be better. All we were doing was fighting anyway. He says it's me always picking on him, but I don't know.'

She blew on the hot coffee in her cup and took a sip, her hands shaking, but her voice stayed composed. 'Like I said, things was going real well for a while. Now Danny's gone. He's got the GI bill. He's going to college, he says.' She told me this with evident pride.

'I noticed the comic book in the living-room. Do you have children?'

'Just my boy, Kari. He's a good boy. Nine years old this month. Takes after his daddy.' Her eyes brightened with a different kind of light, and a hint of a smile passed over her lips, then she looked away out the window. When she turned back to me there were tears where the light had been. 'It's hard on him. His daddy gone and his mama out all night. I don't know what I'm gonna do.'

I asked if the father sent any money and she said he did, but not as often as he used to. 'See, I got to do my gamblin'. Better doin' that than goin' on welfare. But how am I going to face Eddie? He finds out you were here he'll kill me.'

'There's no reason for him to know. Not at this point. But if I'm going to help you, you've got to be straight with me.'

'I am being straight.'

'You've told me Officer Calvert was waiting for you when you came home in the early morning and that he assaulted you because you had been playing at a different club. But it just doesn't add up. There must be another reason. Why was he waiting for you?'

'He's tryin' to scare me. He been doin' that. Like I look out the window and I see a police car goin' round the block. Or I see a uniform leaning up against this car. Can't see a face, but it's him. This is Bushwick. We don't get no cops hangin' out here. I know it's him. He want me to know. Get so I don't like to go out my house.'

'So you believe he's harassing you then?'

'He been harassing me all right.'

'But you still haven't told me why.'

She sighed. 'Cause I don't go to Mom's no more,' she said slowly, as if she was speaking a language I didn't quite understand.

'Why is that?'

'I don't like the way he play. He act like he one of us, but soon as someone starts winnin' he waves that gun around. When Eddie's around, winnin' don't mean nothin'.' She leaned back in her chair, her arms crossed in front of her chest, her lips in a tight line.

We stared at each other this way for a moment. 'He the Law,' she said finally. 'It ain't right. I told him, "You a police officer, what you doin' this for?" and he just laugh and say that mean he can kill me and get away with it. "You think you can tell me what to do, bitch? You're no better than a whore and don't ever forget it." That's what he say. "And don't you tell nobody about this. You try to dime on me I'll come back here and kill your ass." That's what he say and that's what he'll do.

'I told the other cop, the one at the precinct, 'bout Eddie sayin' that. He laughed too. Said he wouldn't take the complaint unless I had bruises and came into the station house and showed them.'

'Do you have any bruises?'

'Did have, from the gun. Had a lump, but I wasn't goin' to show them down at no station house. It's gone now. Eddie can hurt people so it don't show much.

He can do what he wants. If he finds out I'm telling you this, he'll kill me for sure.'

She looked straight at me, defying me, what? To disagree? To take her seriously? It wasn't clear.

'You believe that and yet you called the police anyway.'

'I'm no whore,' she said. I nodded. I wasn't totally convinced about her motivation, but there didn't seem any point in prodding her any more. There were enough details in her description of the assault to give it validity, and the part about Calvert being a sore loser and intimidating people was certainly borne out by other allegations we had. I thought about trying to add theft to the assault allegation, but theft of illegal winnings at an after-hours card game wouldn't carry much weight in court, and besides, we would have to have corroboration. I couldn't imagine anyone else coming forward. I still wasn't sure why Lenora had. Something didn't ring true.

I asked her if she went to the hospital after the assault. She said there wasn't any point; she knew nothing was broken. Then I asked how long she had known Calvert, and she said about five months. After her husband left, when things started to fall apart and she got laid off from her job, she started playing the numbers. It didn't take too long before one of her numbers came up. The payoff was supposed to be fifteen hundred dollars, but when she went to collect, the numbers man had disappeared. That's when she learned she had to run with a crowd. If she was going to be gambling, her friends told her, she needed protection. Everyone had to know she wasn't someone you could welsh on. So she started playing poker at Mom's and met Calvert. He was the meanest, she said. If you stay on his good side nobody will mess with you. There was a certain logic to it.

I asked if she had ever had intimate relations with him. 'You mean sex?' I nodded. 'No way,' she said, flashing me a look. 'I told you, I'm no whore.' I looked in her eyes trying to read the truth. She looked away, her mouth set.

In spite of her frowzy, unkempt appearance, she was an attractive woman, thin and small-boned with high cheekbones defining the lines of her dark face. But tension pinched her features, and her eyes flashed a wild, hidden look I couldn't read. Her terror and her determination were both too big for the story she told. There was more to the incident, or to the relationship. Maybe it was sex. Maybe it was drugs. Maybe it was something else. I just didn't know, and I wasn't sure it mattered. At best, this was looking like a case for IAD. It didn't have the scope necessary for the SPO to get involved, in spite of Calvert's reputation. I had to get out of there; I had wasted too much time already.

I read over my notes with her, going over her story, checking the facts. That's what would go into my report – the facts. In my journal, the unofficial notes I kept for myself on every case, I would write about my misgivings, about the deep sense of disappointment that was knotting my stomach like a bad meal. So this is your hot new witness, your big breakthrough, a nasty critical voice was saying in my head. Grow up, kid.

I closed my pad and put it in my purse, getting ready to leave. Lenora stood, holding her robe tightly around her, suddenly embarrassed again at not being dressed. 'I appreciate your comin',' she said, as if it had been a social engagement. I gave her a card with the office number and address on it and told her to call me if she thought of anything else.

There were odd things about this woman. Her language, which veered from street lingo to proper grammar almost from sentence to sentence. The timid pleasure she had when she spoke of her son and her guilt at leaving him alone. The obvious pride she took in her husband's aspirations in spite of his leaving her. Things that made me want to trust her. But then I reminded myself she made a living gambling with pros. She was a poker player.

It was only later I remembered the boxes.

Chapter Four

Sergeant Maddy Keitel enjoyed the night-time shift at the Department of Public Relations. After twelve years on the street at the Sixth Precinct she was happy for a desk job, relieved to have confronted her last bloody shooting victim, to have rushed down her last reeking hallway to the hysterical, unpredictable fury of her last family dispute. The family stuff was the hardest; she never got tough enough to let it roll off. She still dreamt about them sometimes – the bruised and bleeding wives, the children cringing in corners, and the others, the ones found abandoned or abused. And the endless stream of perps, back on the street before you could finish the paperwork. Everybody burns out eventually; then you hang in for retirement.

With no husband or kids waiting at home, she could enjoy the perks of working at night – peace and quiet on the job and less brass to deal with. The sixteen-hour shift – 4 p.m. to 8 a.m. – was long, but after four double tours of duty she had three precious days off. Hard on the digestion and sleep patterns, but great for the head. Usually she shared the early part of the shift; after midnight she was on her own. Some nights, when things on the street were quiet, there was hardly anything to do. If the solitude didn't get to you, it was an incredibly easy way to go.

She would sit at one of the desks in the large room on the thirteenth floor of One Police Plaza in front of the four overhead video monitors with one or two tuned to MTV and another to one of the seemingly interchangeable cop shows that were always good for a laugh. If one of the guys was staffing the office with her, he would probably tune one to a sports channel. If something newsworthy was going on, they would switch to CNN. And there were a few sitcoms she was loyal to, so all four sets might be tuned to different programs at once.

It was Tuesday. Not bad. *Matlock* followed by *Crime Story*. She was alone, and so far, thank God, it was a quiet night. It could all change in an instant. If a big story broke, dealing with reporters would get hectic. The phone rang. Someone wanted info on a rabid dog running loose in Central Park. Another call came in about last week's police shooting. She watched the antics on *Matlock* for a few seconds and decided it was time for a Lean Cuisine. She had lost twenty-three pounds so far. The slacks of her dress uniform were getting loose. Last week she had tried on her gun belt; it slung so low on her hips it almost slid off. If she ever went on patrol again she would have to get a new one. She had always been athletic. At five-ten, with short curly blond hair and a healthy-looking Germanic face, she salved her hunger by telling herself she was on her way from sturdy to statuesque.

She went over to the compact kitchen area, took a chicken cacciatore out of the freezer and popped it into the microwave. On the way back to her desk, she heard a job come over on the police radio. She pressed some buttons on the Finest System computer and waited for a printout of the incident.

Incident 58 C, 945 63 ST. FT Hamilton PKWY – 10 Ave. 68F 10–93. CRIME 0517. PERP—UNK DESC—NFI—FC HYSTCL—CALL.

She automatically decoded it in her head: 58 C, the patrol sector, the address of the incident, the crime number, the perpetrator, unknown description, no further information, the female complainant was hysterical when she called it in.

Her eyes ran down the sheet full of numbers and codes to

MALE SHOT DOA. LOOKING FOR A M WHITE – FLED POSS IN A SMALL WHITE AUTO JAPANESE TYPE MODEL.

The fourth shooting tonight, still considered quiet in a city this size. The victim dead on arrival. The complainant too hysterical to give a description more precise than white male, the description of the getaway car equally vague. Score one for the bad guys.

As she waited for the paper in the computer to advance, she heard the phone ring, and then the fax machine on the desk behind her began printing out a message. The fax was a new addition – barely two months old. They didn't get many faxes on her shift, didn't get many at all, as far as she knew – sometimes requests for information concerning traffic closures. The fax was used primarily to send information out to the news media, including the papers and news services. It was set up with twenty buttons, one for each of the major local papers – the *Times*, *Newsday*, the *News*, the *Post*, *USA Today*, *El Diario*, *The Village Voice* – radio and TV stations, and the wire services, and one button to send to all of them at once.

She pulled the male DOA report out of the printer and wandered over to the fax machine as she tore off the serrated holes to separate the copies. The paper was still advancing. The microwave dinged in the background and she went to retrieve her dinner, which she took back to the desk. Eat slowly, she admonished herself. Then she laughed. How do you spell 'fat chance'? Before the end of the three-minute commercial, the pathetic portion had disappeared. She did not feel her strongest dietwise. It was only later, during the news, that she remembered the fax and decided she had better check it out.

The cover sheet indicated the address of a copy shop in Brooklyn. It was addressed to the Public Relations Department, NYPD. The sender was listed as John Doe. Another wise ass. Or maybe a loonie. Usually, the nut jobs would limit themselves to phone calls and letters, but even the lunatics are up on the latest technology nowadays. She looked at the fax itself. The message was neatly typed, short and to the point. When she read it, the hairs on the back of her neck prickled. It was a small sensation, not instantly recognizable.

To the NYPD, Public Relations

YOUR NUMBERS ARE ALL OFF.

You think I have only bagged five!
Closer to a dozen!

Talk to Denise Levenson. Female, white,
21–3 yrs, 5′4″, 120, bld/blu. 194 Bleecker
Street. She had fun Labor Day weekend.
Ask her if she wants to play again.

If you don't, I will.

I want accurate coverage from now on.
Tell the Press to show some respect.
YOU ARE RESPONSIBLE.

This is no boy and there is nothing pretty
about what I do but the targets.

My aim is true.

Maddy read it again, her hand unconsciously rising to
rub her neck. Most faxes that came on her shift just got
stamped with the date received, given a number, and
put in the out basket to be sent to the right department,
or more usually, filed away the next morning. This was
different. She knew instantly what newspaper story he
was referring to; it was one in which she had been
quoted as Police Department spokesperson. The last
rape had been reported during her shift. She took the
fax back to her desk and dialed the fifteenth floor.

Chapter Five

The Chevy seemed to be the way I left it – more or less intact and looking depressingly like it belonged parked among the other beat-up and abandoned vehicles. Some kid had scrawled his handle in the grime that was always accumulating on the back window. RAGE LIVES, it announced in an aggressive graffiti pseudo-script that had become the trademark of the underclass teenager. It made me think of the time after Charlie 'Bird' Parker died, when you'd keep coming on the words BIRD LIVES scrawled on subway platforms and tenement walls all over the city. The current pronouncement was all anger and doom, with none of the mystical optimism of the earlier slogan. It seemed a depressingly accurate portrayal of the times. At least the writer hadn't used a spray can.

It wasn't quite four yet. I could have gone home but I wasn't anxious to be alone, and there was always paperwork waiting for me. I got on to the BQE and headed back to the office. I was kind of hoping to see Bud – I felt like I'd let him down at the Dandrell dinner, although I knew he probably wouldn't view it that way, and wanted to see if they had gotten any leads – but he was already gone by the time I got there. He had left a copy of the case report from the night before on my desk, though, with a note to add any information I might have forgotten to give them. I read it over and was interested to learn that the team had checked the registration of the limo that dropped Zinc off at the banquet. It was registered to Mario Panzerella.

Panzerella is the owner of a known mob hang-out, the Roma Restaurant in Maspeth – the kind of businessman whose suspected mob ties are about as much in doubt as an eight-month pregnancy.

Mickey had the phone glued to his ear, as usual, tufts of hair puffing out around the receiver, so I couldn't ask him to fill me in further. 'You can do better than that,' I heard him say, probably to one of his cronies on Wall Street. But whether he was complaining about a stock deal or the latest bad joke was impossible to tell. Like Bud, Mickey was old enough to be my father, and his relationship to me veered between a protective gallantry and a provoking and often raunchy humor. I chafed much more at the former than the latter.

Mickey and Bud and I were all that was left of the original FYGs (Fuckin' Young Guys and Gals) and the FOGs (Fuckin' Old Guys). Names we gave ourselves back in the old days to reflect the enormous disparity in age and experience between the two types Nadjari recruited to make up his investigative force – high-ranking retirees from the NYPD and hot-shot young graduates from John Jay and other criminal justice colleges.

Like many of the FOGs, Mickey had originally joined the agency as much for the excitement and commitment to the ideal as for the money. These were guys who knew the criminal justice system inside and out and knew how much it needed cleaning up. But now they were hanging in for that second retirement pay-off. With less than five years to go, Mickey considered himself semi-retired already. He had made a killing in Bally Casino stock on a tip from a questionable source when Atlantic City first opened to gambling, and now he spent most of his spare time on the phone to his broker buying and selling, or trading tips and black-humor jokes with the Wall Street crowd. On the street he was still incredible, though, with an uncanny ability to size up a situation and act decisively, so that any of us was glad to be partnered with him on an investigation. Add to that the hundreds of informants he had collected over the years, and his presence in the office was invaluable.

'What's the latest in Wall Street humor?' I said when he hung up.

'The Dow just dropped fifty points and it's still falling.'

'That's not very funny.'

'Tell me about it.' He reached in his pocket and pulled out his ever-present pack of Tums, peeling off three and dropping them in his mouth.

'You really mean it, don't you?'

'I wouldn't joke about a thing like that.'

'Are you going to be OK?'

'Yeah, well, at least I still have my police pension.' He laughed without humor and picked up the phone. I still wasn't sure if he was putting me on, or at least exaggerating, but there wasn't much consolation I could offer in any case. I had never owned a share of stock and didn't believe I ever would.

I put a piece of paper in my IBM and started the allegation report for Complaint #1/1349, Lenora Terrell.

On this day, at 1310 hours, this investigator visited the home of Lenora Terrell at 395 Pulaski Street, Apt 5C. The visit was in response to an allegation called into this office by Ms Terrell on the previous day, alleging that she was assaulted by POM Edward Calvert, Shield #82196, 18 October 1987. Preliminary intelligence reports reveal that Officer Calvert was arrested by this office on 17 September 1985, Case #K287/85, for Assault 2 and official misconduct and was acquitted. Calvert received a two-day suspension following

an NYPD disciplinary hearing on this matter. No
information on Terrell.

I typed in the substance of the interview, double-
checking my notes, and concluded: *Based on the above
information it is the recommendation of this investigator
that this case be opened.* Policeeze. That it was more than
likely another bullshit case which would go nowhere
was something I kept to myself.

The report took longer than it should. They always
did because I still hadn't learned to type well. The
more my mother had tried to convince me that it was
important for a woman to learn to type, the harder I
had resisted. Some part of me was still resisting. Typing
was like cooking – once people found out a woman was
good at either, they would never let her do anything
else. I did them both only well enough to get by.

I was really feeling the need of a double Scotch,
and the camaraderie I would find at the Bull and
Bear was tempting me. But what I needed more
right then was a sense of accomplishment. Last night
had been a wash and today didn't look much better.
Neither was my fault, but somehow that simple
fact rarely provides much consolation. Maybe it's
those early doses of Catholicism, original sin and
all that. I decided to check out the Roma on my
way home, maybe grab a bite.

Before I left, I went over my schedule for the next
day. My expense report for the month was due three
days ago. If I didn't fill it out I wouldn't get reimbursed
again, so it was high on my list. I was supposed to show
one of the new recruits how to take a witness through a
pretrial, though I wasn't sure where I would fit him in
because I had to pick up Amando Vasquez, the fifteen-
year-old kid who was our only witness in the Muehler
arson case. Investigators were constantly being laid off
and then new ones recruited as the commitment to our

office and therefore our budget rose and fell with the lawmakers in Albany.

Which reminded me that the quarterly case report was coming due. I needed to work on that. With the constant political pressure the office was under to prove our value and hang on to our funding, we all did our part to make the quarterly look good. Not that we had to do anything more than report what we were actually doing, but without wanting to admit it, we were starting to operate on the defensive. It wasn't just a personal thing – worry about our paychecks – we had a lot of important ongoing investigations we all knew would be lost if the office was ever closed. We all believed in the importance of a separate Special Prosecutor's Office that wasn't beholden to anybody and could operate freely among the other branches of law enforcement. There are cases that just wouldn't get pursued if the NYPD and the DA's office and the courts all had to be responsible for policing themselves.

The Roma was on Grand Avenue and Fifty-ninth, a pseudo-Tuscan castle surrounded by an asphalt moat. I toured the parking-lot scouting for cars that didn't seem to belong – Mercedeses, Lincolns, Caddies – and checking for cars with official plates. There was a new-model Olds with what appeared to be an official parking permit stuck in the visor. I read the plate number into the recorder on the seat next to me and drove around to the front again. A navy blue Mercedes with tinted windows was double-parked by the front entrance. I pulled by slowly and noticed the Supreme Court shield mounted on the back fender. A space several cars ahead on the same side of the street opened up and I parallel parked, adjusted the side-view mirror for a better view, and turned off the engine. I could see the short flight of steps that went up to the Roma's glass door and the whole length of the sidewalk down the block. Nothing much happened for fifteen or twenty minutes, and I had to fight the temptation to lean my head back and close my eyes. Staying awake was always the hardest part of surveillance. It's like driving in the dark when you're exhausted. You keep thinking if you could just close your eyes for one minute you'd feel fine, but that one minute can be crucial.

A light-blue vintage Caddie pulled up and a blonde with a beehive to match got out. She gave the Mercedes a curious look and then headed for the steps. Her sheath was so tight I wondered how she was going to make it up, and she sported one of those waist-length mink jackets I didn't think anybody even had in mothballs any more. I didn't know if it was the latest 'married-to-the-mob' retro look or just bad taste. By the time she reached the door, her boyfriend had parked the car and mounted the steps behind her. Just as they were about to go in, another man pushed his way out, nearly knocking her over.

I couldn't make him out at first, but as he started down the stairs he turned back toward the door. I sat up and looked closer. I hadn't seen him too many times before, but it was clearly Timothy Mitchell, Justice Dandrell's clerk. There was more confusion at the door as the couple tried to get in and Al Randazzo came barreling out. He yelled something at Mitchell, who turned without answering, took a few more steps, stopped, turned back, and yelled something in reply. I couldn't hear what they were saying, but there was no doubt it wasn't friendly.

Randazzo raised his arm in a classic 'fuck-you' gesture. Mitchell continued down the stairs, got in the Mercedes and peeled out. I let him get about a block ahead and then followed him up Grand Avenue to Queens Boulevard. He turned right and sped through Rego Park, running a few lights along the way. I figured he wasn't going out to the Island or he would have gotten on the expressway by now. As he got to Forest Hills, he cut across the three lanes and took the turn-off to Continental Avenue, but there wasn't any indication he knew he was being followed; he was just another lousy, impatient driver.

By now I was pretty sure where he was going but I followed anyway, past the busy shops and the Midway Theater, down a few side streets into Forest Hills Gardens, an exclusive enclave of million-dollar private homes set off by large, professionally landscaped lawns and fifty-year-old maples just starting to turn a rich orange-gold. A little bit of old-money suburbia preserved like a secret garden within a forest of red-brick middle-class apartment houses. I didn't particularly want him to see me, so I pulled over and waited a few minutes and then drove the few blocks to 41 Puritan Avenue. The Mercedes had pulled into Judge Dandrell's driveway. Nothing unusual in a clerk going to a judge's residence, but Mitchell's haste in getting there after the argument with Randazzo indicated a connection. Another 'seen with' to add to the file. I decided to call it a night. At least I wasn't far from home.

I passed my favorite Szechuan restaurant on the way back to my apartment on Saunders Street and stopped for some takeout. The aroma drove me crazy. I deposited the bag in my galley kitchen, pulled out the carton of sesame noodles, and dug in. When I'd polished those off, I grabbed a spare rib and a beer from the fridge and wandered into the living-room to confront the answering machine. It was ensconced like the Holy Sepulcher on the only piece of antique furniture I owned, an imposing, if somewhat battered, walnut secretary I inherited by default from Maddy's grandmother when no-one in her family wanted it. It wasn't exactly the epitome of style and grace, with its urnlike finial and pawlike feet, but it reigned over the Door Store functionalism of everything else I owned like a dowager queen and made me smile. I admired its staying power.

I pressed Play and prepared myself for the verbal onslaught. Like most modern conveniences, the answering machine creates its own imperative while offering no graceful escape. People know they've got you; you can claim you didn't get the message, that the machine was broken, but we all know how lame that is. 'This is your father,' the first message began, as if I wouldn't recognize his voice. 'I just wanted to see how you're doing. Your mother was worried. Are you coming over on Sunday?' He still sounded nervous talking to the machine after all these years. Maybe he sounded that way all the time and I just didn't notice. My mother was too nervous even to call. They weren't so old, but everything new frightened them. It was as if all their adventurousness, all their risk-taking ability, had been used up in getting married. After that one big step, all they could do was hunker down and pray for safety. To me it always seemed mysterious how people who had so much courage at one point in their lives could become so timid later. Even harder to fathom was how my father, who was open-minded enough to defy his Italian family and marry my Puerto Rican mother, could live with her all those years yet remain so bigoted that he wouldn't let us learn Spanish or hang out with Puerto Rican kids, or even allow mention of the Puerto Rican side of the family. We were Italian, he insisted, and my mother, with her silence, seemed to acquiesce. As far as I knew when I was growing up, his relatives were the only relatives I had.

My parents' insecurities affected every aspect of my upbringing – they wanted to raise a proper little girl who would never take any chances. I learned to deal with it by hiding my real self. They didn't know I had been working for the Special Prosecutor's Office until

I had been at the job over a year, and then I said I was just doing research. They wanted me at home, or better still, safely married with kids, not out on the street doing surveillance and undercover work. There was no way they could ever accept the thought of me carrying a gun.

'Hey, kid. Sorry I missed you. Things were pretty freaky around here last night. Where the hell are you when I need you? Just kidding! Catch you later.' That was Maddy. Between her crazy schedule and mine, we were always missing each other. It seemed like we hardly ever had a chance to get together any more. I tried her number. Of course, she wasn't in, so I had a chat with her machine, took a shower, and fell into bed. It was almost midnight when the phone rang, and I thought when I picked it up that it might be her. It was a male voice I heard though.

'I'm downstairs at the pay phone.'

'Yeah, so?' It had been a few weeks since Steve had called, and the sound of his voice jolted me with more anticipation than I liked to admit – to myself or him.

'I'm coming right up.'

'I'm already in bed.'

'Good.' He hung up before I could protest, but to be honest with myself, I probably wouldn't have protested much anyway, even though I knew this was a relationship increasingly on a collision course with reality.

I had given up going out with married men long before I met Steve, had never intended to start going out with them in the first place. But the trouble is I never know they're married until it's too late. In my intermittent quest to meet interesting new people – read *men* – I had signed up for a course on film developing at the Learning Annex. Steve was the instructor: good-looking, intelligent, charming, and open-minded. We started talking after class one day, and unlike most of the men I meet who would just as soon date Attila the Hun as a female cop, he was fascinated by my line of work. We had coffee. A week later we had drinks, and then I invited him back to my place. He was warm and loving and sexy, and when I asked if he was married he said, 'Not any more.'

Was he lying then? And lying when he told me several months later that he and his wife had been on the verge of divorce and then decided to reconcile for the sake of the kids? Probably. 'For the kids' is one of those phrases, like 'I can explain everything', that a single woman in her thirties has heard enough to make her ears ring. Now we were in the push-me-pull-you phase. I told him if he was reconciling with her he would have to *un*reconcile with me. But whenever I work up the determination and willpower to stick to my edict, he starts telling me how the marriage still isn't working out, kids or no kids, and that anyway, it's me he really wants. What woman doesn't want to believe that?

I got out of bed and went into the bathroom to comb my hair. I was thinking of taking off the oversized T-shirt I wore as a nightshirt and replacing it with the silk kimono he had given me for my birthday when the doorbell rang, which saved me from having to decide which would make me feel more uncomfortable, greeting him the way I was or vamping myself up.

I opened the door and started to say, 'Hi'. He took me in his arms and that and every other issue instantly became moot, as the prosecutors like to say. Steve's embrace has always communicated the perfect combination of sexual passion and pleasure at being with me, a combination that invariably makes me feel desired, desirable, and full of desire.

I reached my mouth up to meet his. Soon his hands were roaming sensuously under the shirt and we managed to get his coat off and move into the bedroom. 'You look cute,' he said as I was undoing his tie. I smiled, although it was a word I usually despised, and he started nuzzling my neck. 'I'll never get these buttons,' I said. Undressing each other was part of our ritual. He moved to my mouth and we spent several minutes just kissing. Steve's kisses were wonderful. Gentle and slow and sweet on the tongue, tantalizing like the flavor of a spice you can't quite identify.

I finished the buttons and moved down to his belt, every step making me greedy for more. I didn't let myself think about how lonely I had been or how much I had wanted to be held. I didn't think about love, whether I loved him now or had loved him before, or whether he loved me. Every nerve ending just told me that I loved him touching me, me touching him, that the boundaries were melting, that we were both going where we wanted to go.

Chapter Six

It was six thirty-five when Detectives Ann Gallagher and Joe Moskowitz pulled up in front of Denise Levenson's building on the corner of Thompson and Bleecker Streets. It was a neighborhood that thrived on the magic of night-time, and everything looked tired and a little seedy in the early-evening light. Vestiges of its beatnik hey-day hung on as tenaciously as a hangover. The Figaro, now relocated and modernized, and the other sidewalk cafés advertising espresso and *cappuccino* were today's versions of the intimate Parisian-style coffeehouses of the Sixties where avant-garde artists and writers had once gathered. 'European' postcard and print shops, funky beer joints and rock clubs, vendors of ethnic clothing, jewelry, and leather vied for the attention of the crowds that would soon be jostling each other on the sidewalks and lining up to catch the shows at the Village Vanguard and The Bitter End.

Joe Moskowitz was an insomniac. It started during his wife's illness and became a permanent way of life when she died two years ago. Work was the only way he could cope. He had come into the office early after another lousy night's sleep the morning Sergeant Maddy Keitel called about the fax and was the first member of the Sex Crimes unit to see it. It had been in his mind ever since. Everything about it bothered him, but particularly the reference to the Levenson woman. It was too specific to be completely arbitrary, right down to the description of the girl. If the sender was responsible for Monday's rape at Queens College, they had a dangerous situation on their hands – a serial rapist who had pulled off close to a dozen assaults by his own count without getting caught and was looking to up the ante. If he was a crackpot inspired by the Press coverage, and the incident referred to in the fax involving Ms Levenson never happened, he was still someone they would have to watch out for – someone *she* would have to watch out for.

Joe was almost certain no report of a sexual assault in that neighborhood on Labor Day weekend had come to his office. It was only six weeks ago, and he was sure he would have remembered it, but he had run the name, date, and address through their office computer anyway. There was no record of a complaint. A check with the Sixth Precinct had also come up blank, as had inquiries to all the local hospital emergency rooms and the St Vincent's Rape Crisis Program. Denise Levenson was not listed in the phone book, but a check with the phone company had revealed she had an unlisted number at the address given in the fax, and a subpoena of postal records had confirmed that a Denise Levenson was receiving mail at the Bleecker Street building, Apartment 4C. They were going to pay her a visit, but they didn't know if it was to gain information on an assault that had already occurred, or to furnish a warning.

The entrance to the seven-storey red-brick structure was around the corner on Thompson Street. The building had been recently renovated, and the resulting pastiche of flashy modern and pseudo-colonial was harshly out of sync with both the nineteenth-century town houses on Thompson Street and the neo-classical façade of the Bleecker Street Cinema that abutted it on the other side. The front door opened into a small glass-walled vestibule through which the fake brick walls, brass chandeliers, and black leather couches of the small lobby could be seen.

The two detectives studied the names by the intercom. They made an odd pair. Everything about Joe sagged with a careworn benevolent tiredness – his shoulders, his face, his rumpled corduroy jacket – while Ann stood pressed and proper, giving off the scent of disapproval like bathroom disinfectant. The rabbi and the nun, Joe used to think sometimes, although the analogy was too pat, and he didn't in the least think he had the wisdom to carry his part. There was no name next to the buzzer for 4C. Ann looked at Joe, who nodded, before she pushed it. No-one answered. She waited and then pushed it again. 'Yes?' a tentative voice came over the crackling wires.

'Miss Levenson?'

'Who is this?' The use of her name by a stranger made her instantly suspicious.

'This is the police. We'd like to talk to you.'

'Police?'

'Yes. Could we come up please? This might be important.'

'Is there some kind of problem?'

'That's what we'd like to talk to you about.'

She was silent for a moment, considering. 'I'll have to see some ID.'

'Yes, of course.'

As they got off the elevator on the fourth floor and looked up and down the hall, they could see that the door to 4C was slightly ajar. A thin young woman with long blond hair watched them warily through the chained opening, but there was no way to tell whether this was the normal, even healthy, wariness of the city dweller or something more personally based. Ann continued to take the lead. She always spoke to the women first; it was easier for them that way. 'Miss Levenson?' The young woman nodded. 'I'm Detective

Ann Gallagher and this is my partner, Joe Moskowitz.'
She showed her ID and badge through the door.

Denise scrutinized the ID, checking the picture against Ann's cropped red hair and prim, forthright features a couple of times.

'Can we come in? We need to talk to you.'

Denise hesitated another moment and then undid the chain. They stepped inside and looked around the apartment. The room they were in, a living-dining-room arrangement, was compact and neat but seemed crowded. It was sparsely furnished – a modern sofa, a couple of chairs, a bookcase unit with TV and stereo along one wall – but almost every piece had stacks of clothes, folded sweaters and shirts and underclothes, piled on it. There was no sign of eating or of dinner cooking. Magazines, books, and newspapers took up most of the tabletop. A crumpled blanket and pillow lay across one end of the sofa.

Denise watched them taking it all in with an expression that appeared perfectly neutral – or was it only trying to be?

'I think maybe we should sit down,' Joe said.

She shrugged and then looked at the chairs as if noticing for the first time the things piled on them. She lifted a pile of clothes from one and put it on top of the books. Then she sat down on the couch near the blanket and pillow, gesturing for Ann to sit on the other end. Ann sat on the edge with her usual erect posture; Joe took the chair. He couldn't think how to begin. Interviewing a rape victim who had come forward was difficult enough, but at least there was a protocol to follow. What was the etiquette in a case like this, where no crime had been reported? If the weirdo who sent the fax had raped her, she obviously didn't want to talk about it. And that was her right. And even if it had never happened, even if he had just gotten her name somehow, he had singled her out in a way that would be terrifying to her once she knew.

'Has there been some problem in the building?' Denise asked when neither of them said anything. She spoke calmly, but her voice was high-pitched with tension.

'We don't mean to alarm you,' Ann began. Denise's body tensed another notch.

'The thing is,' Joe interjected, 'you could just be the victim of a cruel joke. It's possible there's no basis for any of this, but once something like this is brought to our attention, we have to ask you.' He could hear himself going around in circles.

Ann cast him an impatient look. 'What Detective Moskowitz is trying to say is that we have information that a woman with your name, at this address, may have been assaulted.'

'You mean mugged?'

'Not exactly,' Joe said.

'We mean sexually assaulted,' Ann stated.

Denise glanced briefly at Ann, her eyes wide, and then looked away. 'It's very important for us to know if this information is correct,' Ann said more quietly.

'I can't imagine where you could get such an idea,' Denise said. And then her mouth twitched, as if in making that statement the answer became all too clear.

'Have you been assaulted, Ms Levenson?' Ann asked.

Denise pulled the pillow onto her lap. Several minutes passed. 'We wouldn't be here if this wasn't important,' Joe said finally. 'We need your help.'

'Have you caught him, then? Is he in jail? Is that why he told you about me?' The hopefulness in her voice was more heart-rending than her fear. Joe and Ann exchanged glances.

'I'm afraid not,' he said. 'We believe the same man is out there assaulting other women. We need you to help us find him.'

She looked from one to the other, her eyes wide. There was no taking back what her questions had revealed. She looked down at her hands, twisting in her lap. 'I've been reading the papers, the stuff about that girl at Queens College. The one today, "Russian Roulette Rapist Shoots Blanks", did you see it?' She looked up at them, questioning. They both nodded. 'It couldn't be true, could it? I mean, whoever wrote that just doesn't understand. It wasn't some kind of game; it was real. Everything he did was *real*.' She clutched the pillow to her, staring straight ahead now. Tears welled in her eyes and ran down her cheeks. 'I kept hoping that if I didn't tell anybody it would be like it never happened. Every morning I thought I'd wake up and it would be like I just had a bad dream. A terrible nightmare.' Her body rocked gently back and forth as she spoke. 'But he was here all the time, wasn't he?' Pulling herself together, she wiped her eyes with her hand and tried for a laugh, as if she were the butt of some foolish joke and she had just caught on.

'I've been sleeping out here,' she said. 'I can't even go in that room.' She gestured toward the bedroom door. 'I haven't been in there since it happened. Just to get my clothes. I had to.' Then she broke down completely and started to sob.

Ann moved next to her, handed her some tissues, and put a tentative arm around her shoulder. 'I don't sleep; I'm afraid to sleep. In my nightmares he always comes back. And now he is back.' She leaned into Ann's shoulder and cried. 'He'll always be here.'

Ann stroked her awkwardly. She did what she had to do, but she wasn't really the maternal type, Joe thought, watching. He had worked with Ann for three years, but he still didn't know if she was really a cold person or one of those women who felt they had to repress their feelings to make it in a man's world. In either case, she didn't seem particularly well suited to the kind of job they did. Warm and empathetic by nature, he would have been much better at giving comfort, but the type of situation and the relation of the sexes in general made it impossible for him to be much help, or to even offer the kind of consolation he felt. Not physically, anyway; he was stuck with awkward verbalizations.

After a few minutes, Denise became calmer. Ann eased her away. 'I can see this is hard for you, but we need you to tell us what happened.'

'Just take it slowly,' Joe added. 'Begin at the beginning.'

She blew her nose and wiped her eyes but didn't answer.

'When exactly did the assault happen?' Ann pressed.

'September fifth, Labor Day weekend,' Denise said surprised. 'I thought you knew. I mean, you knew it happened, I thought you knew when.' She frowned, confused. 'If you didn't catch him, how *did* you know about me?'

'It's not important right now. We'd like to hear your story.' Joe hoped she wouldn't press it; hearing about the fax would only add to her fear, give her one more thing to have nightmares about.

She looked to Ann. 'Labor Day weekend,' Ann said, prompting.

Denise nodded. 'I was supposed to go to Fire Island with this guy I'd been dating, but he'd been acting like a jerk, and at the last minute I decided not to go.' She looked from one to the other of them for corroboration that this had been a reasonable thing to do.

'Was the assailant someone you knew?'

She shook her head. 'I didn't know him, but I let him in. That's what I can't believe. I mean, how could I be so stupid?'

It was a question she had clearly asked herself a thousand times. She shot Joe a pitiful, imploring glance and tried to repress the sobs that started to well up again. 'He rang the buzzer and said he was supposed to be staying with Gordon Jaeger, the guy who lives next door. He said he and Gordie must have gotten their signals crossed because Gordie wasn't home. Gordie and I keep each other's keys for emergencies and stuff. The story made sense, I knew Gordie was away, so I buzzed him up. I talked to him through the door, and then I opened it with the chain, and he seemed like a real nice, clean-cut guy. I don't know. It was such a lonely, empty weekend, I needed someone to talk to, and I figured if he was one of Gordie's friends he must be safe, so I let him in.'

She looked down and concentrated on the pieces of tissue she'd been shredding in her hands. Then she looked up again. 'That's why I didn't tell anybody. How could I tell anybody when it was my own fault?' Her gaze moved from Joe to Ann and back, as if expecting to see in their stares confirmation of her own harsh judgment.

Joe leaned forward. He wanted so much to reach out and console her. 'It certainly wasn't your fault,' he said, but though he believed this completely, it came out sounding hollow.

'Do you think you would recognize him if you saw him again?' Ann asked.

Denise shrugged. 'I think so. I don't know. I mean, I've tried so hard to forget him but I can't. He's always here. But if I close my eyes and try to picture him, nothing comes.' She was staring into space, as if trying to conjure his image, and then turned toward the bedroom door. 'Just this smile,' she said, turning back to the detectives, 'this horrible, knowing, evil, little-boy kind of smile.'

Chapter Seven

My disappointment with the Terrell interview had stayed with me all night, disturbing my sleep like indigestion. Or maybe that was Steve's surprise visit. He had a bad habit of showing up just when I was getting used to being alone and reminding me how much I liked him and how much I disliked the kind of relationship we had. Maybe it was waking up and finding him already gone that had put me in this mood. God, I hated that. As I drank my coffee alone, I tortured myself with images of him smiling across the table at his wife, who I knew was happy to believe whatever story he came up with to explain his hours. But then, she wasn't any more gullible than I was.

I know I have to end it. But what can I say, to myself or him, to make it sound convincing? *This time I really mean it?* As trite as *I'm really going to leave her, I promise,* and just about as convincing. I don't even want him to leave her. I hate this home-wrecker role. I don't want somebody else's husband. I'm not even sure I want one of my own. A real relationship with a guy who is crazy about me and not attached to someone else would sure cover it, though.

I didn't quite make my usual eight-thirty and was lucky to squeeze my car into the last space on Dey Street a little before nine. Stets was sitting at the front desk, filling in for the receptionist, when I came in. 'Hey, Parisi,' he called in his southern drawl as I walked in. The Italian version of my name, which my father's family discarded the moment they landed in America, was one of the less-offensive things I was called around here. A lot better than Spic-ghetti, for example. Crude ethnic humor seemed to be endemic to policing. Along with crude sexist humor and every other kind.

'You've got a visitor waiting downstairs,' he said.

'Shit.' I couldn't imagine who it could be. I was tempted to get a cup of coffee first but decided to just get back on the elevator, go down to twenty-three, and find out.

The twenty-third floor was where MacCallister, the current Special Prosecutor, had his office. It also held the offices of the SAAGs (Special Assistant Attorney Generals) and other administrators, the Grand Jury room, and an official reception area where all visitors were sent by the guard in the ground-floor lobby. Lenora Terrell was sitting in the corner by the receptionist's desk, head against the wall, eyes closed, obviously exhausted. When I walked over she opened her eyes, startled, as if she had forgotten where she was, and stood up. 'Sorry,' she mumbled, embarrassed. 'I came straight from the game.' She smoothed her hair, which had been combed and sprayed into a real 'do'. Her black suede spike heels and red wool coat were stylish, if a little dressy for the morning.

'You left me that card.'

I nodded. 'It's fine. I'm glad you came.'

She leaned closer to me. 'We got to talk,' she said, her eyes darting around the room to see if anyone was listening. 'I can't make no complaint.'

The waiting-room wasn't the place for this and the office with all the other investigators around would just freak her out more. 'Have you had breakfast yet?'

'He'll kill me if he finds out I came here.'

Something must have happened since yesterday. Her voice was hoarse with fear and lack of sleep. 'We'll go have coffee,' I told her. 'I just have to arrange something in the office. You wait here. I'll be right back.'

I was supposed to pick up Amando Vasquez in an hour and bring him back to meet with Charlie Wing, the SAAG on his case, to give a deposition. Amando was a nervous, quiet fifteen-year-old Puerto Rican kid who happened to be taking a shortcut through the alley just when Ed Muehler was throwing a lighted match into an oil drum full of kerosene-soaked rags at the back door of his own bar. It would have been just another insurance-fraud case except that Muehler was a corrections officer at the Manhattan House of Detention with suspected underworld ties. The money for the bar definitely came from questionable sources, and after Muehler took it over it quickly changed from a quiet neighborhood hang-out to a popular drug drop. Muehler had apparently gotten word of an impending raid and decided to raise some cash and destroy the evidence in one stroke. If it hadn't been for the Vasquez kid he probably would have gotten away with it.

I looked around the office for someone who could take my place. Most of the desks were still empty. I could see Mickey and Bud through the glass door conferring with Vince, but I knew it would be a mistake to hold out for one of them. In the state she was in, Lenora could not be counted on to wait long. I picked on John Bremmer, a pugnacious bull of a guy who thought white skin and a male appendage entitled him to an easy living – usually my last choice for anything. He had only been with the office for eight months and did what he could to let me know what he thought of spics, dagos, and cunts, not to mention someone who was a combination of all three. Bud claimed Bremmer was just baiting me, that he was a decent investigator and not a bad guy. I had my doubts.

When I walked up to his desk he was munching a cheese Danish. 'Hey, Bremmer, I need a favor.'

'I'm busy.'

'Busy stuffing your gut. This is important.' I told him what I needed.

'You want me to go into Cuchifritoland and pick up some roach-chasing spic. You must be kidding.'

I resisted the impulse to squash the rest of his breakfast into his face. 'Get out there and do it. And keep your racist mouth shut or I'm going to go into MacCallister's office and tell him you've been tying up the VCR jerking off to that rented porn of yours.' Office scuttlebutt I took the liberty of embroidering on. The usual sexist and ethnic jokes I could handle; Bremmer's bigotry was something else. How he got picked for the SPO was a mystery. He was the kind of scumbag we were supposed to be trying to get rid of. I hated subjecting the Vasquez kid to him. 'Tell Amando I'll call him later. If I find out he had to take any racist shit from you, Bremmer, I swear I'll call your wife. I could talk to her for hours, and you know it.' I walked away before he could say anything. Thank God I had seniority. I couldn't count on Lenora waiting too long; I just had to assume Bremmer's purported professionalism would take over.

Lenora was already standing by the elevator when I went back down to twenty-three. She looked like she was about to say something but then thought better of it, and we got back in the elevator and rode down in silence. When we stepped out of the building she hesitated and looked up and down the street quickly before starting down the steps. I wasn't sure where to take her, but decided the Plaza Coffee Shop on the corner of Cedar and Greenwich would be OK. It would be a madhouse at lunch-hour but was probably deserted at this time of the morning. The waitress, methodically arranging plastic-wrapped donuts in a glass case, glanced up as we came in. I led Lenora to a booth at the far end, away from the windows. 'He's going to kill me,' she said again as soon as we sat down.

The waitress approached, coffeepot in hand, and filled the cups already set out on the table. 'Did Officer Calvert threaten you?' I asked when she had gone.

'He didn't need to. He just look at me with those icepick eyes. Didn't say a word to me all night. Then, just when I'm leavin', "Hear you had some company." He says it real casual like. How he know that?'

'Wait a minute. Are you telling me you saw him last night?'

'I told you he was mad cause I wasn't playin' at Mom's, so I had to go. Didn't count on him knowing I talked to you.'

'I'm sorry about that. We don't want to see you hurt. But it certainly wasn't from our office. Someone in the building must have seen me.' Calvert up to his old tricks. I felt, like shit. I hated to see witnesses intimidated. I didn't know if she would feel better if I told her that it didn't matter if she withdrew her complaint, that we really had no case anyway, or worse. Still, even in these circumstances, her fear seemed extreme.

'I know you're frightened. That's what he wants. But he's not going to kill you over a simple assault charge.'

'You don't know him; he's buggin'. I told you.'

'Yet you went to play cards with him . . .'

'Sure I did.' Her tone was belligerent. She took a sip of coffee and then stared sullenly across the room. Finally she turned back to me. 'He sees me in the game, he figures he knows where I am, what I'm doing. You understand? When he don't see me, that's when my real trouble starts.'

'If someone told him about my visit, if he already knows you talked to someone from the police, I'm not sure what we can do about it.'

'I just want to drop the whole thing, all right?'

'That's certainly your prerogative,' I said, annoyed, although God knows why. I had already decided the case was bullshit, and I didn't want to see the woman get hurt. I really wanted that bastard, though. 'Did anyone see Officer Calvert attacking you the other night? Anyone passing by on the street, or coming in or out of your building?' Writing up the report, I'd realized I'd forgotten to ask her that.

She shook her head, still sullen. 'Wasn't nobody around that I could see.'

She didn't offer anything else. I took a couple of dollars out of my wallet to leave with the check and slipped into my coat. It was time for me to get back to the office. Then I glanced at her across the table and something stopped me. I guess it was the look on her face, stricken and frightened but also fierce. She had a lot to be afraid of in the life she led, but violent as Calvert was, he wasn't likely to do anything worse to her than he already had. Not unless there was a lot more to the story than she was letting on. I couldn't throw off the feeling that her fear was bigger than her accusation warranted.

'There's something you're not telling me,' I said, winging it. 'Edward Calvert is one bad cop. If you know something you're not telling me, you're just helping him to get away with doing the things he does.'

She looked startled. 'I don't know nothin'. He hit me, like I said.'

I shrugged and stood up.

'You don't understand,' she blurted. 'He's gonna do something. I know it. I'm so scared.' Her hand holding the coffee cup started to tremble. 'You got me into this. Now you just gonna leave?'

'Wait a minute. It was you who called me, remember?'

'I can't take it. I just can't take it. I'll kill myself.' She was trembling all over now, tears welling in her eyes. I sat back down.

'Lenora, what's this all about? You haven't told me anything to make it worth the risk to Calvert to kill you, certainly nothing serious enough to make you want to kill yourself.'

'What do you know? Killing me be nothin' to him. I've seen him do it.' She looked quickly away from me, surprised herself by her sudden revelation. Then she turned back and we stared into each other's eyes. Rumor had it Calvert had been responsible for at least one death, but rumor was no use to me. Maybe Lenora Terrell was going to provide the break I needed to nail Calvert after all. 'What was it you saw?' I asked, keeping my voice calm.

'Saw more than I want.' Her voice was suddenly very quiet. 'Saw him take the gun and shoot. Saw the man's brains on the wall.' She didn't say anything else.

'Lenora, talk to me.'

'I wasn't the only one saw it. Why's it got to be me?'

'I don't know, you're here. Maybe you're the only one who cares, or the only one with enough courage.'

This brought a nervous laugh. 'The only one dumb enough, more like.'

'The person who was killed, was he a friend of yours?'

'No. He was from out of town. From Atlantic City, I think. Played poker with us one night.'

'At Mom's?'

She nodded.

She didn't say anything more for a few minutes. She was so skittish I didn't want to push her. If she was going to make any kind of a witness, she was going to have to decide to tell me the story herself.

'If I tell you, then what?'

'Then we'll try to corroborate your story, and if we

can get enough evidence, we'll take it to the grand jury, and if they indict him, we'll arrest Calvert and he'll go to trial.'

'Will they put him away?'

'I hope so. It's something I can't promise, though. Ultimately, it's up to the jury.'

'Don't know what I'm more scared of,' she moaned. 'What Eddie's gonna do to me or what my own mind is gonna do. I wake up at night cryin'. My little boy asks me, "Momma, what's the matter?" I see Slick's face, and the bullet goin' through his brain. I got to tell somebody, but I'm so scared. What kinda world is this? He's the Law.' She looked at me earnestly, as if I could offer some kind of explanation. 'I keep thinkin' about that. My Kari's growing up. I'm scared to let him out on the street with all the killing keeps goin' on.'

I took out my notebook. She sat up straight, her eyes suddenly full of alarm. 'What you need that for?'

'I have to take notes on what you tell me.'

'I didn't promise to make no complaint.'

'If this man Slick is dead like you said, there has to be an investigation. It doesn't matter if you make a complaint or not.'

'I can't take no more,' she said, slumping. 'I'll just kill myself, that's all. Eddie's going to kill me anyway. I'll beat him to it.'

I was getting tired of the histrionics. 'You can't kill yourself. I need you. You told me this much, I need to know the rest. There's no turning back.'

She didn't say anything, just shook her head back and forth, bemoaning her fate more than refusing. 'The shooting took place at Mom's?' I asked.

She sighed dramatically and gave me a look. Then she took a deep breath, like she was about to jump into a pond she knew would be icy. 'We were playing cards like we always do,' she said finally. 'Me and Eddie and my friend Auletta and this guy Sweet Thing. And another guy, Money, owns a bar, and Slick. And Gato, too, but what Gato sees nobody knows, he's so gone.'

'Did Slick have another name?'

'Not that I ever heard. Only met him that one time.'

'Did Ṣlick and Calvert have an argument?'

'Weren't an argument really. Slick owed Eddie some money, for cocaine, I think. See, the game was going along OK till Eddie starts losing. He hates losin'. And this guy Slick, he's doin' OK and gettin' real happy about it. He was a real cheerful, easy-goin' type. Seem like he thought he was winnin' enough to pay Eddie back. But Eddie didn't like it. Pretty soon Slick just have this grin sitting on his face and Eddie getting meaner and meaner.

'Everybody's getting nervous, looking at each other out of the corner of our eye, ya know. Then Eddie takes a hundred-dollar bill out of his wallet, rolls it into a straw, takes out a packet of cocaine, spills it onto the table, snorts it, and says there's more if anyone's interested. That's the kind of thing he do – real slow, so everybody got to stop and notice. Eddie sold a couple of packets, a hundred a bag, so he was feelin' better. Money in his pocket and snort up his nose.'

'Do you remember the names of the buyers?'

'Sure. Auletta and Sweet Thing. They always the ones.'

The names didn't sound familiar from the file.

'Trouble is, Slick kept on winning. It got real late and the game started to break up, I think it was about five. Slick picks up his money and offers to buy breakfast for anyone wants to come to the Apollo Diner down the street. So me and a few of the boys start to get up. Eddie don't like this one bit. He jumps to his feet, grabs Slick by the collar and tells him he don't like his attitude, that he ain't leavin' the room till he pays back what he owes. Slick still tryin' to chill, says that just what he was plannin' on doin'. He starts to count

96

out the money from this wad he won. Eddie starts buggin' then, shoving Slick against the wall. Calls him a cheat. "You hear this shit?" he says to all of us. "Wants to pay me back with my own money." Then he starts to laugh his big bad awful laugh and takes out this gun. He say if he let Slick dis him, he'd have no juice on the street. Slick tries to talk him down. Tells him to chill, he can have the money and he'll get the other money too, just give him a couple of days. Eddie just shoots. Slick don't even have time to stop smiling. Bullet went right through his head. Me and Auletta both start screaming. I grabbed her hand and we run outta there, got us a gypsy cab and got as far away as fast as we could.'

I knew there were questions I should ask, but I could hardly absorb what Lenora was saying. It was an amazing story. Calvert shoots someone in cold blood with five witnesses – over a drug debt. I could feel my blood racing and forced myself to calm down. Amazing, I reminded myself, if it was true. I didn't need any more investigator's fool's gold. I signaled the waitress for more coffee and went over it all with her again. She hadn't seen what kind of gun Calvert had, but from her description it sounded like an automatic. She thought the bullet was in the wall. Calvert had taken her back to Mom's and into the same room a week after the shooting to see if she'd be cool, and she saw the hole in the wall then. Not very big, not very obvious, unless you were looking for it, but it had drawn her eyes like it was lit by a two-hundred-watt spot. About a month after, they'd played cards in the room again, and a picture was hanging over the place where the hole was. I asked her about the other witnesses, but she didn't know any more than she first told me. 'So Calvert beat you up to keep you quiet,' I said finally.

'You don't drop no dime on Eddie and live. Everybody knows that.'

'Yet here you are.'

'Someone's got to stop him.' I looked in her eyes, where a fiery stubbornness seemed to war with the fear, and wondered if she was brave enough and stable enough to be the one.

After a few minutes, I told her she would have to come into the office so I could type up a statement for her to sign, but the idea started freaking her out again so I didn't push it. We could do it tomorrow. I assured her that there was no reason for Calvert to know she had spoken to me, that he wouldn't have to know there was an investigation until we were ready to make an arrest, which wouldn't be for a while. He'd hear about it once we got a search warrant for Mom's and maybe before, when we started asking questions on the street. But there was no point in getting into that now. She probably knew that already. She might be a little emotionally unstable, but Lenora wasn't stupid. I told her my office would do what it could to protect her and to let me know immediately if Calvert threatened her in any way. Her best defense was to act as normally as possible. She agreed to come into the office the next day and left the coffee shop ahead of me so we wouldn't be seen on the street together.

I needed to fill Vince in on this new development, but when I got back to the office he was in another closed-door session. I went over my notes and decided to see what I could find on this guy Money. If he owned a bar as Lenora said, he would be the easiest of the alleged witnesses to trace. I knew Vince was going to want some corroboration of her story before he let me run with it, so I might as well run a check on the other names as well.

I typed out the five names Lenora had given me – Money, Auletta, Sweet Thing, Gato, and Slick – and took it down the hall to Mary Lee. I asked her to run the names through the usual channels and to see what she could find in a quick check on Money's bar.

She plugged into the State Liquor Authority and found that Leon Simms owned a bar called Money's Inn at 192 Clermont Avenue. So far, so good. I didn't think Lenora was lying, but I knew I didn't want to think so, and any corroboration of her story was a relief. I asked Mary Lee to run a check on the bar. The printout that came through was a couple of pages long. A suspected drug hang-out, so many 'frequented-bys'. The local precinct had filed a couple of reports based on call-in allegations. Now the SNU (Special Narcotics Unit) was watching the place. There was a recent report filed by a Detective Jeff Collins.

Vince's office was empty now – he was probably out to lunch. I went back to my desk and killed an hour doing the goddamned expense report – a lot of work to be reimbursed $67.59, but over the year those outlays added up. By the time I had it ready, Vince was back in his office, his ear glued to the phone, a beleaguered look on his face. All head and chest, he looked much larger seated behind his desk than his five foot seven inches. The close-cropped steel-gray hair, like Italian Brillo, and street fighter's nose completed the effect. I knocked on the open door and he waved me in. 'Did you read my report?' I asked when he hung up.

'Which one?'

'Terrell.'

'Yeah, I read it. No obvious bruises, no hospital report, no witnesses. What have you got? Nothing.'

'She came in this morning.' I sat down and gave him a quick summary of what Lenora had told me.

'First it's assault, now it's murder. What's with this woman?'

'I know how it looks,' I said. 'But I believe her. Look at all the information she gave me. The location of the shooting. The name of the victim plus four witnesses. She told me she went back and saw the bullet hole in the wall.'

'So there's a bullet hole in the wall of some social club. There're bullet holes in all those places. What does that prove? Only that someone fired a gun. And those names. Slick? Sweet Thing? Could be every other asshole on the street. Maybe she's Calvert's old lady. Maybe he's trying to dump her, and she made the whole thing up to get even.'

'You were busy so I ran a check on this guy Money. He's for real. Runs a bar on Clermont.'

'OK, so one of the names is for real.'

'Listen, we know Calvert is dirty. We've spent a lot of time and manpower trying to nail him, *I've* spent a lot of time trying to nail him. This is the biggest thing we've got yet. If we can make this stick, we've got him. For life. I know we've had a lot of witnesses turn, but this one is different.'

'Why?'

'I don't know. I just know she's stand-up. I can't explain it. I just know she is.'

'You're talking about a cop murdering someone over drug money. This is not some bribe or something. A black cop, too. We haven't had enough this year with the Eleanor Bumpers business and then the Tawana Brawley thing? The black community will have a field day. We would have to be 500 per cent sure there was real merit to the case before I'd even go to MacCallister with it.'

'It's easy enough to check out the basic story. Let me play around with it.'

'OK, but we have to bring in IAD.'

'Muñoz will want it for himself.'

'Maybe.' His attitude infuriated me. I can't say I'd hoped he'd be as excited as I was. I had never seen Vince excited about anything. But a little mild enthusiasm would have been nice. I stood there, barely restraining myself from making some sarcastic comment I would certainly regret.

'Anything else?' He was already reaching toward a pile of folders on his desk.

'No.'

He nodded. A tiny dose of approval along with my dismissal. What else did I expect?

Chapter Eight

The shift started out quietly enough. Maddy had the TV monitors down low. She was tired of the usual Thursday night programs and was trying to study for the lieutenant's exam that was coming up next month. Two of the sets were tuned to CNN, and ESPN was playing a late-season baseball game. She got out her review book and was flipping to the chapter on Patrol Unit Morale when all hell broke loose. She heard it first on the police radio: a multiple homicide on West 110th Street. Then the phones started ringing and all the lights seemed to go into action at once, flashing their frenzied insistence to be answered.

For the next several hours she fielded calls from reporters who had picked up the news on their radios, at first giving out 'no further information' and then, as details from the crime scene were called in to her, passing on the official word.

There was a blessed lull in the action around 2 a.m. She went to the refrigerator and got out the container of chicken soup she had brought from home, remnants of last night's dinner she had looked forward to as a respite from her usual frozen-diet delight. She put it in the microwave and pushed the buttons, but the phone started in again before the three minutes were up. She would definitely be losing weight tonight.

'Sergeant Keitel,' she said wearily into the receiver.

'Oh, really.' The voice on the other end registered an exaggerated skepticism.

She immediately perked up. 'Hey, kid. What are you doing up at this hour?'

'You know me,' her friend Tina replied, 'your basic workaholic.'

'Everything OK?'

'The usual. How's the big bad city?'

Maddy launched into a few bars from the theme song from the TV show *Car 54*: '*There's a holdup in the Bronx, Brooklyn's broken out in fights. There's a traffic jam in Harlem that's backed up to Jackson Heights . . .* Add to that a multiple homicide.'

'That kind of night, huh?'

'That kind of job. This place is nuts.'

'Yeah, I saw your name in that piece about the rape in Queens.'

'WINS picked it up. I was all over the radio. I don't know why they never quote me when it's good news.'

'No such thing in your job.'

'No, I guess not.'

'What do you think? Are the papers blowing this serial-rapist stuff up?'

Maddy paused for a second. In spite of their friendship and Tina's position at the SPO, her job constraints prevented her from revealing much more than the official department line. 'It's hot,' she said finally.

'I hear you. Listen, when do you swing off again? If we don't make a plan, we'll never see each other.'

'At least I know when my time off is. When the hell do you get off?'

'Let's aim for Wednesday.'

'Sounds good.' The second phone on Maddy's desk started ringing. 'I gotta go,' she said. 'Talk to you soon.'

After an intense car chase through upper Manhattan, a suspect had been apprehended. The news was picked up on the police radio and the phone madness began again and lasted almost to the end of her shift. She had no time to think about the fax machine during the night, but she went over to check for messages before she left. Her heart sank as she tore off the incoming sheets; there was no mistaking the look and feel of those terse, aggressive words. Another fax from the rapist had arrived.

To the NYPD

YOU ARE PUSHING ME.

Who the hell are you to challenge
my game? You don't even know the rules.

I asked for accurate coverage. You're
giving false info to the Press.

Who says I'm shooting blanks? You're
forcing me to prove what's in my piece.

You won't be satisfied until one is wasted.

I'm in combat load.

Chapter Nine

The boundaries between the SPO and IAD were not always clear. A case like Calvert, that involved a member of the NYPD, would be under their jurisdiction as well as ours. Sometimes, if the charges weren't too serious and there was indication of wider involvement, we would turn the case over to IAD completely: more likely it would become a monitor, a case they investigated but which our office kept an eye on. Often we worked together on a case. Now that our manpower had been cut, we often used IAD and other arms of the NYPD to help with investigations.

The power of the SPO superseded IAD. We were statewide and investigated corruption outside the police department as well as in it, and had our own prosecutorial arm. In fact, we had almost as many SAAGs as we had investigators, most of whom thought they were more important than we were. The more arrogant of them treated the investigators as hired flunkies whose job it was to gather evidence and serve subpoenas on 'their' case. But that's a whole other issue. Sometimes we were given jurisdiction on a particular case by the DA if it seemed either too far-reaching or too sensitive to be handled within the NYPD. That's how we got the Seven Seven Precinct scandal and the Howard Beach case. Those cases, and the whole concept that the criminal justice system could not be counted on to police itself, were what the SPO was really about.

Every morning Vince went over the reports from IAD and decided which cases the SPO had an interest in. IAD didn't always like his decisions, and there were constant turf wars. Hector Muñoz, an extremely polite, overly correct little Latino IAD captain, was usually our liaison. Everything with Muñoz went by the book, down to the letter, and though I respected his intelligence, I often found his fastidiousness a pain in the ass. Vince also sent any case reports we had on the NYPD to IAD, partly as a courtesy, partly because the two branches helped each other and kept an eye on each other. The morning after the Terrell report on Calvert went through, Muñoz came hurrying into the office and caught me by the coffee machine.

'Just got in your C #1/1349. How come you're keeping the case?'

'I love the guy, what can I tell you?' I tore open a packet of Cremora. Sometimes my stomach just can't take it black.

'You lost the last one. What makes you think you'll get him this time?'

'Hey, when was the last time you lost a case? No, better still, when was the last time you won one?'

Muñoz feigned surprise. 'You know what, Paris, you're too thin-skinned. But then you're not pure Puerto Rican, are you? Too much *pasta fazule* in the brain, huh?'

'Hey, you hear that?' Mickey chimed in from behind us. 'Muñoz tried to make a joke. One of these days he might try to make a case.' It was Mickey I was glad to see capable of humor; this stock-market business was hitting him hard. He popped a handful of Tums in his mouth as he poured his coffee, flashing a sheepish grin when he saw me watching.

Muñoz forced a smile and turned back to me. 'Seriously,' he said, 'this is not a case for the SPO. We're not talking a few bribes here; this is murder. I know your obsessions, but I'm surprised Vince is backing you on this.'

I gave him a look and walked back to my desk. He followed me, picked up a stack of files from the metal chair next to it, and sat down.

'With all due respect, Captain, IAD is hardly doing any surveillance any more, you have no undercovers, your informants suck. You guys have had your *cogliones* cut off and you think we're going to let this case go to you. You've got to be kidding.'

He looked genuinely offended and I didn't think it was my off-color remark. Policy at IAD had changed in recent years. They were getting a lot less aggressive in gathering evidence, and stories were circulating about cases that had dropped through the cracks or hadn't been pursued forcefully. I knew that Muñoz, for all his politeness, was not one to hold back in an investigation. In fact, ridding the police force of its bad apples amounted to almost a personal crusade for him. 'Listen,' I said, softening, 'I'm not saying IAD won't have some involvement. We need your help. But Vince will never let go of this one.' Or so I hoped. I knew I'd have to make a much better case than I had now if I wanted Vince's full support.

'In actuality, I came this morning because I think I have something that will be of help.' He opened one of the folders he was carrying. 'I noticed in your report mention of a bar, Money's Inn, I believe. It would seem this Money Miss Terrell mentions would be our best chance for a corroboration of her story. I did some investigating, preliminary of course.' He looked up and smiled to assure me he hadn't intended to step on my toes. 'It appears that the bar has been under surveillance by our narcotics people for some time.' He looked up again and I nodded. I'd read the reports too.

'It just happens that one of the detectives on the narcotics team is an old friend of mine; actually we came on together in seventy-two and worked the Two

Four Precinct. Jeff Collins. I think he could be very useful to our investigation.'

'I noticed his name on the report.'

'He's a good man, one whose integrity I can vouch for myself, and one who really knows the territory.'

'If he's got an ongoing investigation, he isn't going to want us moving in on his turf.'

He nodded. 'Another reason I thought I should speak with him before we – or you – try to bring in this Money for questioning.'

'It's OK by me. We could use a good street guy. Just understand one thing, this time we're going to get Calvert. I want this guy nailed once and for all, whatever it takes.'

He nodded but his lips formed a tight prim line. He probably didn't like the sound of 'whatever it takes', or else it was just too clear I wasn't giving it up.

'I'd better run the Collins business by Vince,' I added. 'He really sees this one as a ticking bomb.'

With Muñoz to deal with narcotics I decided to pursue some other avenues myself. I checked back with Mary Lee to see if she'd made any progress with any of the other names I'd given her. Slick was such a common sleazeball name that it would take a while to go through them all. Forty-nine had come up, and NYSPIN will only give info on six at a time. Mary Lee had brought up eighteen so far, but none sounded even remotely like the guy we were looking for. Since he was an out-of-towner it was possible the New York system wouldn't have anything on him anyway.

I checked with the Communications Division to see if there were any 911 calls logged in around the time of the Terrell allegation for 1350 Myrtle Avenue, the address she had given me for Mom's, or for the immediate area, but nothing of interest had come in. I also put in a request with the Personnel Unit for information on Calvert's tour of duty for the time indicated as well as a record of all firearms registered to him. I hadn't gotten those back yet.

I decided to scoot over to the County Clerk's office in the basement of the Kings County Supreme Court Building and pick up a copy of the building plans for Mom's. Lenora was due in later that afternoon to give a formal statement. I wanted to see if she could point out exactly where in the building the shooting occurred. It was the kind of detail that would provide an excellent point of comparison if one of the other witnesses did corroborate her story, and it would be a big help in getting a judge to sign a search warrant.

The building, Block #79, Lot #15, was a four-storey walkup built in 1917 with two apartments on each floor. The plan showed a storefront on the ground floor with a side entrance leading to the back apartment and staircases to the upper floors. The registered owner was a Mrs Juanita Thomson. I made copies of the papers and grabbed my favorite lunch, a Sabrett's smothered in onions.

When I got back to the office, there was a message on my desk that a call had come in on my undercover phone from Al Randazzo. Apparently he was taking the bait. Monday's undercover was not such a total loss after all. I decided to give it a couple of days and then call him back; a girl like Julia Cipriani wouldn't want to seem too anxious.

Lenora arrived on time, her son in tow, and I was more relieved than I like to admit. I had impressed upon her that the murder charge changed everything. It was no longer a case of a simple assault that she could decide to pursue or not; as a witness to an alleged murder she could be forced to testify. We both knew it would be dangerous for her if I had to go to her apartment again to bring her in. Even so, witnesses have a nasty habit of disappearing, especially those testifying against Calvert.

She apologized for bringing Kari but said she thought she had better follow her normal routine of picking him up at school. She felt more secure coming into my office than going to one of the precincts, she said, but even so, she had changed trains three times in case she was being followed. Calvert knew our office had investigated him in the past, but I didn't get into that with her. In any case, I doubted he had the manpower to follow her every move, and he probably assumed, pretty correctly, that she was scared shitless after the assault and would keep her mouth shut. Why she had come forward in spite of his threats and her fear remained a mystery. But that's the trouble with this job. You get so used to the scumbags that only decency has the capacity to surprise you.

Lenora had made a distinct attempt to pull herself together. She wore a simple dark cotton dress under her red wool coat. Her hair was carefully combed, her make-up discreetly applied. Although clearly tense, she appeared much less overwrought than the two times I had seen her before. Perhaps her decision to speak out had brought her some peace. I met her on the twenty-third floor and took her directly into the grand jury room. We set Kari up in one of the large leather chairs at the far end of the room, where he sat quietly turning the pages of a schoolbook on his lap. He was neatly and conservatively dressed – no jeans or unlaced hi-tops – and displayed the timid politeness and terror of misbehaving in public that seems to be the hallmark of well-brought-up lower-class children.

Charlie Wing was the SAAG assigned to the case – definitely a relief. Charlie, a second-generation Chinese American with a serious, dignified manner, had joined the office in '85. He was a tenacious prosecutor who would worry every detail out of a case like a Mafia thug chewing on a toothpick, but he was one of the few who actually viewed the investigators as partners rather than flunkies or adversaries. I had typed up a statement for Lenora to sign, but he wanted to hear her tell the story himself. I thought he might want to interview her alone, but as soon as I started to leave the room she looked up in alarm and insisted she wouldn't talk unless I was present. I sat down opposite her, next to Wing, and she began her story.

Her manner was a great deal more subdued than the first time she described the shooting, but the facts came out the same. The social club was nothing more than an apartment on the first floor used regularly for gambling. The card room, as she called it, was in the apartment at the back. I showed her the floor plan, and she immediately pointed out the room and the spot where Slick was standing when he was shot. Because of the lack of a body, Wing wanted corroboration from another witness before he went for a search warrant, but Lenora could tell us no more about the other players than she already had. She thought Money, Sweet Thing, and Gato were buddies of Calvert's, but she only saw them at card games. She had no idea what their real names might be and didn't have a last name for Auletta, the only member of the game she considered a 'friend'. She did tell us Auletta worked at a check-cashing establishment, which she thought was on Bushwick Avenue near Cedar or Stockholm. I asked her if she knew Juanita Thomson, the listed owner of the building, and she said she didn't know for sure but thought she was 'Mom'. She opened the front door when you rang the buzzer and let people into the backroom with the large ring of keys she wore on her waist, but that was all Lenora ever saw of her.

The three of us went over the statement carefully, double-checking every detail, and then had it retyped by the secretary for Lenora to sign. Things were going well. Maybe we would have a case after all.

* * *

When the phone rings in the middle of the night it's like a buzzer right to my brain. Maybe it's something about the job, but I'm instantly awake and alert no matter what the hour or how long I've been asleep. I looked at the clock, 2:34 a.m., and for a moment thought it might be Steve, but the voice I heard was both too jovial and too businesslike. 'Hey, Shorty, thought you were gonna sleep tonight, didn't you?' Bud said. 'I just got the call on the beeper from Muñoz. There was a raid on Money's. They took Money into custody. He's on his way to our office.'

'Who's bringing him in, Muñoz?'

'It's that narcotics guy.'

'I can be there in twenty minutes.'

'Good. I'll call Wing and get him over. We don't want any problems from the legal side. Why don't you call Muñoz and let him know what you're going to do.'

I rolled out of bed and headed for the john. There wasn't time for a shower, but a little cold water on the face would help. The temptation at that hour was to throw on a pair of jeans and a sweatshirt, but I'd be interrogating a witness, I'd better look official. I reached for the slacks and sweater I'd been wearing earlier and added a good tweed jacket. Shoulder-pads always made me feel better – well tailored, fashionable, and, let's face it, more important. Probably some chauvinism deep in my, and the fashion world's, psyche. You can't grow balls, but you *can* beef up the silhouette.

Wing arrived at the office right after I did. I filled him in on what Muñoz had told me while we waited for Detective Collins to bring Money in. The raid had gone well. Sixteen people, including two known dealers, were arrested along with Money. Except for Money, they had all been taken to Central Booking. It sounded like we should have enough to get Money to turn on Calvert, but we wouldn't know for sure until we had more details. We were discussing the tactics of the interrogation when the buzzer rang.

I definitely got off on the wrong foot with Collins. When I went to open the door I saw a black man in cuffs who I knew was Money escorted by an undercover cop I assumed was him. 'Detective Collins,' I said, putting out my hand as a third man walked in behind them. 'I'm Collins,' he announced, his voice full of strained patience at my stupidity. 'This is my partner, Hal Beringer.' How was I supposed to know what he looked like? In fact, the two men were around the same age, mid-thirties, and had the same type of slim, athletic build. One was blond, the other had light-brown hair. Straight noses, square jaws, a couple of all-American boys – even if I'd had a description I wouldn't have known which one was which. Just what I needed, I thought, a narc with a star complex.

'We're doing the interrogation in the grand jury room,' I said, and started to lead them down the hall.

'Hold it a second,' Collins barked. I stood aside and waited while the partners conferred.

'You can have it,' I overheard Hal say. 'I'll get back to Central Booking. You don't need me to hang around here for this bullshit.'

'Some attitude,' I said, as Hal stepped back on the elevator. Collins didn't react.

'Where do you want this mutt?' he said, giving Money a shove in my direction.

'It's this way.'

I opened the door and indicated seats at the end of the large conference table to the left of Wing, who was already seated with a tape recorder in front of him. I sat opposite them on his right. Collins took the cuffs off the prisoner. Wing turned on the tape recorder and read in the date and time and the names of all of us present. Money was identified by his real name, Leon Simms, along with his street name. It was 3:19 and everyone in the room looked drawn and tired except Money, who was wired on coke and fear and kept darting his eyes around, tapping his fingers on the table, and twitching in his chair.

'My prisoner wants to know why he's here,' Collins said, 'and I'd like to know that myself.'

Wing ignored the question and asked Collins if he had advised Mr Simms of his rights. He stated he had and then Money was asked if he understood his rights. He nodded and was told to say it out loud for the tape recorder. 'Do you know why you have been arrested, Mr Simms?' Wing then asked him.

He seemed startled every time Wing called him that. 'It's some kinda mistake,' he said, his eyes making a quick circle of the room. 'If somethin' was going down at my bar, I didn't know nothin' about it.'

I signaled to Wing and he turned the recorder off. 'Rather than getting into that, I would like you to understand something about our office and why you are here,' I said. 'Do you know anything about the Special Prosecutor's Office?'

'No.'

'The New York State Special Prosecutor's Office is a branch of the state government. We investigate corruption in the criminal justice system.'

'What's that got to do with me? I didn't do nothin'. I don't know what you want.' His eyes did another canvass of the room and then he retreated back into himself.

Wing switched the recorder back on and turned to Collins. 'Detective Collins, are you a detective assigned to the New York City Police Department's Special Narcotics Unit?' Collins said yes and Wing went on. 'Detective Collins, have you and your narcotics team been conducting an investigation concerning possible narcotics activities at a bar and grill known to the State Liquor Authority as Money's Inn?' Collins said yes, bored by these legalities, but understanding the necessity for them.

'I have been advised that you and your team made a massive number of arrests this evening at said Money's Inn. Mr Simms here, the licensed owner of said bar and grill, has indicated that he has no understanding of the circumstances surrounding the arrest. I would like to help Mr Simms gain a greater appreciation of his situation. Would you please advise him of the alleged crimes for which he has been arrested?'

Collins took out a three-by-four spiral notepad and read from the narcotics team's preliminary report in the practiced way of an old hand for whom the exciting part was already over. There was no doubt he was an attractive guy, but there was something a little too studied in the contrast between his blond, boyish good looks and the tough-guy narc outfit of jeans, T-shirt, and leather bomber jacket, and he had too much of an attitude to be appealing, at least to me. I watched Money as he read.

'At 2300 hours the SNU set up a van outside Money's bar and began videotaping people entering and exiting the bar and eyeballing the activities inside with infrared binoculars. Two officers from the TARU, that's the Technical Assistance Response Unit, oversaw the technical end of the surveillance. Three undercover officers from the SNU entered the bar, one male, two female. The undercover officers were all wearing wires. Two additional plain-clothes police were also on the premises.

'At 0112 hours a known cocaine dealer was observed entering the bar, where he spoke with the subject, Leon Simms, a.k.a. Money, and was observed to hand him a brown paper bag, which the subject then placed behind the bar. Simms was observed removing several glassine envelopes from the bag and placing them in his shirt pocket. At approximately 0127 hours undercover detective Gene Davis joined several known drug users and pushers in a line that formed in the hall outside the men's room. Each individual in turn approached a black male, known by this team as Thomas Blondale, a.k.a. TB, and handed ten dollars to Blondale. Blondale then advised them to go see Simms at the bar. A black female stood by the end of the bar watching Blondale and indicating to Simms with a nod when someone approached the bar who had paid his money. The defendant then handed the buyer one of the glassine envelopes, which were later ascertained to contain eight balls, packets of cocaine of one-eighth of an ounce. The defendant sold cocaine to three undercover officers and in addition was observed selling cocaine twenty-seven times in a three-hour period. A felony quantity of cocaine was found on the premises. At the time of arrest a Walther PPK was removed from the defendant's person. Sixteen subjects were taken into custody, one of whom was found in possession of half a kilo of cocaine.'

Wing stopped the tape. 'So, Mr Simms,' he said, 'it looks like you are about to be charged with multiple counts of Article 220.43, criminal sale of a controlled substance in the first degree; Article 265.03, criminal possession of a weapon in the second degree; Article 105.17, conspiracy in the first degree.'

Silence followed this recital until Money, who had continued to stare at the table, realized it was over. 'I'm being set up,' he said. He glared at Collins for as long as he could keep his eyes focused in one direction. 'Some dudes were standing in line to take a piss. I can't keep track of everything goes on in the place.' Even in the state he was in he could hear how lame that sounded. 'I wanna call my lawyer,' he said.

We let that float for a couple of minutes. No-one said anything. Money's eyes did their tour. Soon his shoulders started twitching and rolling like he was wearing a hair shirt. I glanced at Wing, who nodded imperceptibly. 'I don't think you understand the situation, Mr Simms,' I said. 'You can have a lawyer right now if that's what you want, but I think it's in your best interest to listen to what we have to say first. Is that all right with you?'

'I don't know nothin' about corruption. I ain't payin' off no cops. What do you want?'

'Detective Collins, what kind of time are we talking here?'

Collins rattled off the numbers. 'Fifty-four counts of twenty-five to life, and a 265.03 Class-C weapons charge. With a mandatory, that's another five to fifteen. I'd say we're looking at some real time here.'

It was impressive. Money's eyes darted. His shoulders jerked. 'I told you, I don't know nothin' about no corruption.'

'I think you do. I believe you can help us and our office can help you.' I stood up, taking my Styrofoam cup and pouring a refill from the coffeepot that was sitting on the cabinet against the wall behind Wing, buying a little time and working on Money's nerves. I wanted to do this right. I knew there would be only one chance. Once the lawyer got into it it would get complicated beyond recognition. He might not be averse to a deal, but he'd want to talk to Money first, finding out what he knew that we wanted and controlling just how much of it came out. I needed to get what I could about Calvert while Money was scared and up against it and too rattled to edit his thoughts. And Money's interests right then really weren't too different from ours. If the lawyer messed things up there would be no deal – we'd get nothing and Money would do serious time. I just had to make sure he understood that.

I walked around behind Money and leaned against the table next to him. 'As we told you, you're not dealing with the NYPD here. Our interest is not in drug pushers like yourself. There are enough fine officers like Detective Collins here to take care of that end of the system.' I couldn't help glancing over at Collins when I said this. He looked me straight in the eye, his expression deadpan. 'What my office is interested in is the officers who are not like Detective Collins – those who abuse the law rather than enforce it.'

Money gave me a quick look and shifted uncomfortably. Out of the corner of my eye I saw Collins flip his notebook closed and put it in his pocket. 'Do you understand what I'm saying, Mr Simms?'

'I don't know nothin' 'bout cops.'

'Maybe I'm going too fast for you.' I stood up and went back to my seat opposite him. 'Do you understand that you're going to be doing some serious time and that we're offering you an opportunity to help yourself?'

'What are you gonna cut me?'

'The choice is yours. We believe you have some information that will be helpful to us. We can do right by you, but we need to know that you're giving us full cooperation. Do we understand each other?'

He sighed and said, 'Yeah, I understand,' and for some reason looked at Collins. Then he looked back at me. 'What do you want to know?'

Collins stood up. 'I'll wait for the prisoner outside,' he said, his jaw tight, and left.

'Tell me about Edward Calvert,' I said as soon as the door closed.

'I see him around.' If he was surprised by the direction of the questioning he didn't show it.

'Do you know he's a police officer?'

'That's what he says.'

'Where do you see Officer Calvert?'

'We play cards every now and then.'

'Have you ever known Officer Calvert to be violent?'

He reached behind his neck and scratched under his collar. 'The man's got a bad temper. He don't like losing.'

'Then maybe you can shed some light on what happened at Mom's Social Club on September seventeenth?'

His eyes darted around the room and came to rest on the door. Tiny beads of sweat sprouted on his brow. Bingo.

'Our information tells us you were playing cards at Mom's that night.'

Money stared at the table. 'I don't know . . .'

'Twenty years, minimum,' Wing said. 'Even with the best lawyer.'

His head jerked up. 'I tell you, how do I know you gonna help me?'

'This is a very important case. All you have to do is tell the truth. If you can help us, I can assure you this office can be instrumental in how the courts view the charges against you. Before you sign anything we'll bring your lawyer in to go over everything with you.'

He thought about it for a few minutes, adding and subtracting the pros and cons of cooperating with us, like a bookie doing odds. Even after he agreed to cooperate it was a slow, difficult process. Wing turned the tape back on and we did it for the record. Each question had to be asked over and over again to elicit the information. It wasn't my favorite hour in the morning for playing games and it sure wasn't my favorite game. I kept wondering why he couldn't just give me the information he knew I wanted. It was fear of Calvert he was balancing against fear of the time he would do, and he weighed and reweighed them with each question. The harder it was for him to go along with our deal, the more I knew we were on to something important.

In the end, he reiterated Lenora's story. He placed

the same people at the scene and confirmed that the victim, Slick, was an out-of-towner. He said he didn't know Lenora, Lee he called her, too well, either. He had only played with her a few times. I asked if he had arrived with Calvert that night. He said he was the first one there, that Calvert came in around one-thirty. After a lot of prodding, he revealed that while they were alone in the room Calvert brought out a new gun. When he came in, Calvert said he had just gotten a new insurance policy and pulled out a 9mm automatic he said he had taken off some basehead. Slick was the last one to show up that night. Money said Calvert seemed surprised to see him, and it was obvious Slick didn't plan on seeing Calvert there either.

After a lot of circling around the subject, he finally admitted to witnessing the shooting. I asked him what happened immediately after the shots were fired. He said everyone was stunned for a minute, then the women ran out. Calvert kept his cool. He told Sweet Thing and Gato to take care of the body and handed Sweet Thing the wad of bills he'd gotten from Slick, saying, 'Let the motherfucker pay for his own funeral,' and laughing. Money said he left right after he heard that and was adamant that he didn't see them remove the body.

'How come Calvert asked Sweet Thing and Gato to take care of it and not you?' I asked him.

'Listen,' he said. 'I got me a bar. I may mess around a little with drugs, but I don't do none of that cuttin' and shootin' shit and Eddie knows it.'

'Then why did they find a loaded Walther PPK on you?'

'That's for protection. I don't want no trouble.'

'Have you seen any of the people at the card game since that night?'

'Sweet Thing came into the bar a couple of times, like he wants me to know Eddie's watching to see if I'm doin' right. I ain't seen no-one else.'

I asked if he had told me everything he knew about the shooting. He said he had. I asked if he had any idea where they had taken the body, and he said no. 'No idea whatsoever?' I reiterated.

'Well,' he said, 'I did run into Gato about a week after. He was messed up on crack so I didn't pay much mind to it, but he said something about Slick bein' in the freezer.'

'Do you know where the freezer he was referring to is?'

This caused Money to twitch as uncomfortably as any question I had asked him. 'I know there's an old freezer in the basement at Mom's,' he said at last. 'That's probably what he meant.'

The interrogation had taken almost three hours. I was absolutely wiped out. But in spite of the exhaustion I was elated. Money had corroborated Lenora's accusation, and while he hadn't actually been involved with the disposal of the body, he had given us a good lead on its location.

I left Wing to wrap things up and went to look for Collins. He was sitting on a wooden bench in the hall leafing through a *New York Post* I knew had been lying there at least two weeks. 'I really appreciate your helping us with this one,' I said.

'Don't make me laugh.' He dropped the paper and stood up. 'Your office gets what they want whenever they damn well want it.'

'I'm sorry you feel that way. This is a very important case we're working on.'

'It ought to be since you're helping one of the biggest suppliers in Fort Greene.'

'Listen, I'm sorry if we got in the way of your case, but the way I understand it, you got your two big catches. Money's just small change.'

'Oh, yeah? Where'd you hear that?'

'Muñoz. The way he laid it out, you agreed to turn Money over. You knew what was up.'

'That sounds about right. IAD and the SPO stick together and the rest of us get fucked.'

'I'm sorry you're getting bent out of shape about this.'

'Hey, don't let it bother you. I just hope it was worth it for this big investigation of yours. I mean what have you got, some cop taking a sandwich he didn't pay for? Worth springing a dealer any day.'

Before I could answer he had gone back into the grand jury room to retrieve his prisoner.

Chapter Ten

OK, so what did they have? Detective Moskowitz laid it out for himself one more time. Two faxes from the rapist baiting and berating the Press and the police. The last victim, the college girl, Mary Alice McGuire, was still in shock, apparently suffering from hysterical amnesia, and could offer very little information about her attacker. She remembered talking to a man in the parking area who was looking for a friend. He helped her carry her dry-cleaning upstairs. She remembered being frightened, being cold suddenly, shivering violently as if the window had been thrown open in the dead of winter, as if someone had run an ice cube down her spine. She thought she remembered a gun but she could remember nothing about the rape itself.

As a result of the coverage this case was getting, another victim, Sally Bronfman, had come forward. It was the headlines about the Russian Roulette rapist that caught her eye. She had been raped during lunch-hour at a two-man law office on lower Broadway where she was a receptionist. The rapist had posed as a client who had made a mistake about the time of an appointment. Both lawyers had been in court. He had known enough about the workings of the office to gain her confidence, and enough to know that she was alone. He had forced her into the backroom at gunpoint and taunted her with the gun, opening the barrel to reveal five empty chambers and one with a bullet. Then he had held it to her temple as he raped her, pulling the trigger at climax.

When she reported the rape at the time, she had stuck to the most cursory description of the incident, mentioning the gun but leaving out the Russian Roulette aspect. It was too terrifying to dwell on, she explained. This wasn't so surprising. For rape victims, the need to deny the experience was often so intense that they were unable or unwilling to report it at all, much less to methodically relive it. Joe read her case file; he could see the connection now – the attractive, clean-cut subject who was able to insinuate himself into the victim's confidence. How many others like that had he overlooked? He was going over the files from the last year again, looking for other descriptions or situations that would match up. Maybe one of them would contain a crucial piece of evidence that had been overlooked.

The trouble was, the descriptions provided by the victims, including the three roulette victims and the victims of the other 'Pretty Boy' rapes, varied enough to allow for the possibility of more than one perpetrator. The hair color and style ranged from blond to light brown, and from slicked back to tousled. Eye color varied, too, from blue to green to brown. Sally Bronfman described a man with glasses, as did two of the others. One woman described a man with a mustache. Were they different men or one man with a knack for altering his appearance? When you really came down to it, the general description – good-looking, clean-cut white male, medium height, medium build, mid-thirties – fit thousands, probably tens of thousands, of men.

Since Mary Alice McGuire was not emotionally ready to do it, Denise Levenson, as the second-most-recent victim, had been asked to work with the police artist on a composite. The gap of time since the attack was a handicap, but as she worked with the artist, the details of his face came back. Of the seven rape victims shown the completed drawing, only one had been positive her attacker was the same man. The task of comparing blood types and doing DNA workups for those cases where semen samples had been taken was just beginning, so as yet they could neither confirm nor deny the existence of more than one man.

Another issue was venue. Where had the other assaults the rapist was claiming to have committed taken place? And when? The known cases were in Manhattan, Brooklyn, and Queens. One of the faxes had been sent from the Borough Hall area of Brooklyn, the other from the West Village. Joe decided to stick to the five boroughs for now, but maybe put the word out to the Long Island units in case any similar cases came to mind.

Which sent him back to the faxes. No matter how clever he thought he was, it was here the subject would reveal himself. Joe stared at the two copies in front of him. He knew them almost by heart, but he read first one and then the other again, wanting to absorb them, to make them part of him so he could read all their messages, the implied as well as the stated, the intended and the unintended. But he felt himself getting stale. Taking out a yellow pad, he decided to jot down some quick impressions, a kind of free association of words or feelings the faxes called up. The police psychologist was busy coming up with her profile of the personality type they were looking for, but while the official version was sometimes useful, Joe liked to do his own, based not on psychology books but on gut reaction. And street experience. Sometimes he thought he'd seen enough sickos to write a book himself.

He scribbled what first came to mind: anger, egotism, swagger, literate, gun imagery. Not a hell of a lot. Except for maybe the literate part, it described most of the men he knew, certainly most of the men on the force. He looked at the two faxes again. Something was bothering him and now he knew what it was.

There were places in both messages where the guy sounded like a cop. The description of the Levenson woman – female, white, 21–3 yrs, 5′4″, 120, bld/blu. Exactly the way you would describe a victim or suspect in a police report. The use of the term 'piece' in the second fax, and 'combat load'. Although that could be Vietnam. Could be a cop, or an ex-cop, who was over there. Or a police groupie – there were plenty of those who listened to the police frequency, showing up at crime scenes and hanging on every piece of jargon. But that didn't feel right. This guy didn't use enough jargon. It wasn't like he was trying to sound like a cop, it was like it just slipped in.

And then there was the business of the faxes themselves. The NYPD Department of Public Relations had only had the fax setup since September, and it hadn't been advertised to the public. Only high-ranking cops and members of the Press had been informed. But even this didn't exactly narrow the field when you really thought about it; any one of them could have mentioned it to countless other people. Every lead seemed to take him back around in a circle.

The only thing to do was to keep checking all the facts and gathering information. Sooner or later it would fall into place. Or not. He hated that possibility. This guy made him nervous. If he hadn't already been up all night, he'd be losing sleep over it. When you read the two faxes together, what jumped out at you was the level of the hostility in the second compared with the first. The guy was very controlled. Both messages were carefully worded, succinct, and thought out. But the second was definitely, distinctly hotter. Joe had seen this before. The guy was on a short fuse and it was getting shorter. Sometimes the control freaks were the worst, almost worse than the out-and-out psychos. Worse because they were more effective – for longer. If this one wasn't lying, he'd been at it a long time. The faxes were a sign he was upping the ante, and the emotional state of his last victim seemed to indicate the assaults were getting uglier. Joe had a bad feeling about this guy and hoped he was wrong. He called in to IAD for information on any cop who had been arrested on a sex offense, and since his old friend Vince Bruno was heading up the SPO, he decided to put in a call to him as well. He dialed the number, thinking of Bruno's retirement dinner from the NYPD. What was it, five or six years ago? He heard the familiar bark of a greeting come over the phone.

'That you, Bruno?'

'Who's this?'

'Joe Moskowitz.'

'Moskie, you old fuck. How the hell are you?'

'Could be better. How about you?'

'I was sorry to hear about Miriam. Rotten break. She was a good woman.'

'It's not the same without her, that's for sure. At least the job keeps me busy.'

'You still protecting those girls from us perverts?'

'I'm trying. We've got this serial rapist on our hands.'

'Yeah, the papers are full of it.'

'I've been put in charge of the investigation citywide, and I've been piecing some things together. We don't have a lot to go on, but we have reason to believe the guy may be a cop.' He laid out the case, filling Vince in on the other rapes they had tied to the same subject, and on the existence and general content of the first two faxes.

'So why are you bringing it to me? Shouldn't IAD take it?'

'They're putting it through their computer, but it could be anyone in the system – a parole officer, some-one from corrections. Maybe I'm grasping at straws, but there seems to be some insider knowledge. Does what

I've told you ring any bells? Fit anybody you can think of?'

'Not offhand. It's not our usual kind of case.'

'This isn't an official request, you understand, we don't have enough to go on for that yet. But if you could do some quiet checking, look through old records. Anyone in law enforcement picked up on a sex charge with a similar MO, I'd like to know about it.'

'Sounds like this slime's got your ulcer up.'

'That's what they pay me for.'

'I'll see what we can come up with.'

There was nothing more Joe could do in the office; he decided it was time to pay Denise Levenson another visit. Maybe working on the composite had jogged her memory. He would feel more comfortable pushing her for details now that she had had time to get used to the idea that the police knew about the rape. And that guy Gordon Jaeger, her neighbor. He had been away on a business trip but should be back by now. There was no directory in the lobby of their building and no name next to his buzzer on the intercom, yet the assailant had used his name. Joe wanted to hear what he had to say.

Denise was tense and aloof but clearly more in control than the first time Joe had visited her. Her clothes were no longer piled on the furniture, which seemed to indicate that she was sleeping in her bedroom again. Ann had provided her with referrals for rape counseling and he hoped it was helping. He got right to business, explaining the trouble he was having pinning down an exact description of the rapist. She stood by her composite, though, reiterating that the man who raped her did not have a mustache or wear glasses. She seemed distressed that the drawing wasn't more help, but perked up when he asked if she had remembered anything new. There was one thing, she said. A few minutes after her assailant left the apartment she had gone to the window to see if she could catch a glimpse of him coming out of the building. She wasn't thinking of identifying him, she just wanted to make sure he was gone. There was no-one on the street, but she did see a car door close and a gray hatchback pull away from the curb. She didn't know if it was foreign or domestic, but it looked new. Joe jotted this information down, thanked her, and rang the buzzer of the apartment next door.

Gordon Jaeger was in. He was tall and slim with curly black hair, intelligent eyes, and a cautious, patrician manner. He wanted to be helpful but could think of no-one he had told he would be away that weekend except for his close friends. Of course, a lot of people did go away Labor Day, he offered, so the attacker could have just been playing the odds. Somehow Joe didn't think so. He showed Jaeger the composite and asked if it reminded him of anybody he might have seen around the building. He studied the drawing carefully and then shook his head. It looked like a hundred fellows he saw every day in the Village, he said.

'You and Denise know each other pretty well?'

'We've been neighbors for a couple of years, help each other out once in a while.'

'Are you dating her?'

Gordie laughed, shaking his head. 'Nothing against Denise, I'm just not into women.'

Joe studied the man's face; Jaeger's sincerity and good humor seemed real enough. He gave him the number at Sex Crimes and told him to feel free to call either him or Detective Gallagher at any time if he happened to remember anything that might seem even remotely useful.

Back in the office the next morning he checked the incident reports for the Village for the night of the rape, in case a gray hatchback was involved in anything, and put in a request for traffic summonses issued in the area. He was trying to figure out what to do next when he got a call from Jaeger. He was surprised. He always gave that rap about people remembering anything even remotely relevant, but very few people took it seriously, and he couldn't even remember the last occasion it had produced any results.

Jaeger's car, a brand-new Honda Prelude, had been stolen early in August and found miraculously untouched in a raid on a chop shop a week later. When he was loading his luggage in front of the building before taking off the Friday of Labor Day weekend, a man came up behind him and made some comment about the car's being found and what a lucky break it was. Jaeger had agreed, saying he was especially glad to have it back for the long weekend since he had been planning a fishing trip to Montauk. The man made some small talk about sport fishing, they chatted a few minutes about the weather, and Gordon took off. He hadn't thought much about it at the time. The man didn't look familiar, but he was a nice-looking fellow, well dressed in a sports coat and tie, not the kind of person you would be suspicious of at all, and the way he approached from behind, Gordon had just assumed he had come out of the building. Maybe he was a new tenant, or visiting somebody Gordon knew. He didn't question at the time how the man knew about the car, it all just seemed so natural. Now, when he thought about it, with the rapist using his name and all, it just didn't seem right. He couldn't remember the man's face exactly, but there did seem to be a resemblance to Denise's composite.

Joe thanked him for calling and said he would look into it. When he hung up the phone he realized he was smiling. Maybe he was getting a break on this one at last.

Chapter Eleven

I went home to grab a few hours' sleep and was back in the office by noon to get my report done and make sure Wing had everything he needed to go for the search warrant on Mom's. Money would be out on bail that day, and there was no way of knowing whether he would lay low and avoid Calvert or tip him off. If the body was in Mom's basement, we didn't want to give Calvert the chance to remove it or to tamper with any other evidence that might remain from the shooting. There was no time to lose.

Vince had been apprised of the situation immediately, and even he had to agree that with signed statements from both Terrell and Simms we had good cause to go for the warrant, although his predictions on my nailing Calvert were no more sanguine than before. 'OK, Paris, run with it. But don't get your hopes up,' was all he said. He assigned Terry the task of hand-delivering the petition to Judge Brock, one of the three justices assigned to handle the needs of our office, and Wing put in a call to the judge first to explain the situation. Hopefully Brock wouldn't ponder it too long. It was Friday and we needed that warrant fast.

In spite of Vince's apparent lack of enthusiasm, he gave the case priority, assigning Bud to work with me on the search because of his homicide experience. It would be a joint effort of the SPO and IAD, with IAD coordinating the participation of other divisions of the NYPD. Muñoz went through department channels and lined up a team from the Crime Scene Unit to conduct the search, including a photographer, a fingerprint person, two forensic technicians, and a supervisor, along with an officer from the Ballistics Unit. He would also bring two detectives from IAD, since we were so short of investigators ourselves, and he arranged to bring Jeff Collins in because of the allegations of drug sales. Everyone had to be put on alert in the hope that the judge would come through by morning.

I was notified a little after 11 p.m. that Judge Brock had signed the warrant, and I fell gratefully into bed. If I hadn't been so tired from the night before I probably would have had a hard time sleeping, but in spite of my excitement about the search I knew Vince was right, there was no percentage in getting my hopes up about what we would find. With that in mind, I fell into a deep sleep and didn't so much as turn over until my alarm went off at 7 a.m. The teams convened in front of 1350 Myrtle at 0830 hours. The local precinct had been notified and two officers, grunts, as the detectives liked to call them, were assigned to guard the premises while the search was going on.

The storefront of the four-storey building was boarded up with plywood, the front door padlocked, but the door on the side was a solid metal job that looked like a fairly recent installation. There was a row of buzzers with no names listed, not unusual for this kind of building or for an after-hours gambling club. Bud pushed the bottom button, and after a few minutes we could hear someone move the metal shield from the peephole. To any halfway experienced eye, it would be clear we were cops. 'What do you want?' a female voice said.

'Police, Mrs Thomson,' Bud replied. 'We have a warrant to search the premises.' Nothing happened for a couple of minutes. 'You'd better open up. We're going to get in there one way or another.' After another pause, the door was opened part way by a tiny dark-skinned woman who, from Lenora's description, had to be Mom. Bud handed her the warrant, which she read quite carefully. 'Basement stairs at the end of the hall,' she said, handing it back to him and standing aside to let the team in. 'And mind you stick to where it say on that paper.'

She led us down a dark, foul-smelling hall. 'I gots to unlock it,' she said, unhooking a key ring from her waist and peering at the bunch of keys. She went through them one by one until she had studied them all, and then went round again, picking one out. 'Don't go down here much,' she said.

'Does anyone else have access to the basement?' I asked her. She shook her head. 'What about the Con Ed man, doesn't he have to read the meters?'

'He got to ring the bell like everyone else.'

Either she was lying about the key, or else she had to let the men into the basement to dispose of the body. If there *was* a body in the basement. She didn't seem particularly nervous about us down there or about our presence in the building, but that didn't necessarily mean anything – a stone face was an essential survival tool in her line of work.

Muñoz turned to me as we started down the stairs. 'Tina, it might be a good idea if you stay up here while we peruse the area.' As the sole female on the team, it was not surprising that I was the only one asked to stay upstairs, but if I got angry every time somebody tried to protect me for my own good on this job I would be dysfunctional.

'Thanks for your concern,' I replied calmly. 'I'll chance it.' I glanced back at Bud before starting down and noticed him glaring belligerently at someone behind me. I turned to see Jeff Collins giving me an appraising look. Our eyes caught for a second and he smiled slightly, but it wasn't clear whether it was approving or patronizing.

I led the way down to the basement, where Mrs Thomson opened the door. She flipped a switch on the wall, which lit a single bare bulb hanging from the ceiling. It illuminated the room just enough to reveal an oppressive jumble of debris – piles of broken furniture, ancient discarded building materials, old oil and paint cans – things which hadn't had a name, much less a use, for more years than I had lived. Some of the junk appeared to be stacked in an attempt at order, other stuff was strewn about like it had been thrown through the open doorway, or perhaps someone had bumped into the piles in the near darkness and sent them sprawling. Immediately to the left of the door was a mound of dark-green plastic garbage bags, their putrid contents spewing forth through gaping holes undoubtedly made by gnawing rats. The stench of rotting food was almost strong enough to conceal a body, if there was one.

I switched on my flashlight and ran the beam around the room. There was no freezer immediately visible, but several large shapes around the perimeter were obscured by piles of trash or covered with filthy drop cloths. I hesitated by the doorway, caught between anticipation and disgust, my breath coming in shallow gasps as I unconsciously tried to avoid inhaling the dank, disgusting air. Forcing myself to breathe, I moved forward, stepping carefully through the debris. I had pushed to make this search happen, I was closer than I had ever been before to nailing Calvert, and I was the only woman on the search team – it was no time to be squeamish. I don't know what I'd expected, really. I've been at searches and in undercovers in some pretty scuzzy bars and grimy alleys. But even though I knew better, Money's story of a freezer in the basement had reminded me of my Uncle Tony's neat Long Island cellar, where the huge freezer chest contained a hoard of Good Humor ice-cream pops. I was glad I had worn jeans and an old jacket.

'Let's see what's under that stuff back there,' I said. Bud, Muñoz, and the other two IAD detectives started to follow me toward the back, where we fanned out to investigate various large piles of junk, which could be obscuring the shape of a freezer. One of the IAD guys who had arrived in a suit started bitching at Muñoz. Apparently he'd been commandeered for the search at the last minute when someone else called in sick and was dressed for a buddy's retirement dinner after work. I approached a likely-looking pile covered by a blanket so old and dirty it was impossible to tell what color it had once been. I pulled a pair of old gloves from my pocket, put them on, gave the corner of the blanket a tug, and uncovered a large battered steamer trunk, certainly large enough to hold a body, but not a freezer. I gave it a shove anyway, but it was light and apparently empty.

As I looked around for the next likely object I heard Muñoz' excited voice to my left. 'Over here. I think I've got something.' My flashlight caught the dull sheen of a yellowing enamel door below a pile of cardboard boxes. Muñoz shoved the boxes off, kicking up a fog of grimy dust that in this filth could as easily have been accumulated in three weeks as three years.

Junked refrigerators and freezers are supposed to have their doors removed; this upright was firmly closed with a padlocked bicycle chain linked through the handles. Whatever was in there was not being kept cold. The fingerprint guy moved in to start taking prints but Umansky, the supervisor, told him to hang on until we found out if anything was in it. He sent his tech man back to the van for some tools to cut the lock. We waited while he got them, standing stiffly, trying not to lean on anything. 'Five'll get you ten it's full of nothing but garbage, just like this whole case,' one of the CSU guys quipped. There were a couple of laughs, but the lock and chain had disconcerted even them. No-one locks up their rotten food.

The tech man came back with a large wire-cutter, which snapped the lock after a couple of good tries. 'I think she ought to do the honors,' he said, giving me a look that was somewhere between a challenge and a leer. I didn't answer. Umansky nodded to the other two CSU guys, who put on paper masks and plastic gloves and approached the door. There was a collective holding of breath. I was torn between needing to watch and not being able to, and wondered why I still felt I had to prove myself every goddamned time? I could have taken Muñoz up on his suggestion and avoided all this. I kept my eyes on Bud, who stood a little in front of me. He'd spent years with Homicide and I assumed he'd gotten used to this stuff. 'Cover your nose,' he said to me quietly. I pulled my cotton turtleneck over my face. It didn't help much. As soon as the door was open we were hit by a wall of hot, putrid gas, sweet and thick and sickening. We all stepped back – were pushed back – by the intensity of it.

I took a quick glance. Whatever was in there, it was certainly dead, and it was just as certainly not a human body, or not a whole one anyway. It was wrapped in plastic and took up only one shelf. There was no reason for Sweet Thing to have dismembered the body we were looking for – it just didn't fit the MO of the crime. Disappointment clutched at my stomach with a different kind of sickness, but at least it prevented me from throwing up. I looked around. Everyone was waiting to see what it was. Three IAD guys, six from CSU and Bud. Everyone but Collins, who never did come down to the basement.

One of the CSU guys removed the package with his rubber-gloved hands, put it on the floor, and slit it open with a knife. 'Definitely not human,' he said. 'Canine,' he pronounced shortly after. We all moved closer. Four stubby legs, a short compact body, long thick snout. 'There's your body, Paris, fucking pit bull.'

'Gang-style execution,' the ballistic guy offered, 'bullet straight to the brain.'

The laughter was immediate. 'Another case goes to the dogs, huh, Paris,' the guy with the suit piped in. 'And to think I'll have to have my suit cleaned just to wear it to the trial of a degenerate cop who killed Spot.'

'You guys from the Special Prosecutor's Office are sure into some heavy-duty stuff. Maybe we should call the ASPCA.' They all had something they found unbearably witty to say. Even Muñoz piped in that he'd never arrested a cop for dog abuse before.

'Let's check out the card room upstairs,' Bud said. The one person who had refrained from a joke at my expense. 'You think there could be another freezer down here?' I asked him as the others started to leave.

'If we find something to corroborate the story, we can come back and do a more thorough check. Without that there's no way these guys are going to look around here any more.'

I turned and made my way to the stairs. One of the older CSU guys started singing, 'How much is that doggie in the freezer, the one with the wagging entrails.'

'Just how much of the taxpayers' money does the state waste to uncover these atrocities anyway?' one of his buddies interjected. CSU had to be there to help us, but like the rest of the department, they were happy to believe the SPO picked on innocent cops. I'd be getting razzing about this one for a long time. Still, the way the freezer was locked up was weird, and though it apparently had nothing to do with our case, they had to feel as strange about it as I did.

As we climbed the stairs, I was all business. I didn't want the guys to know how much either thing had gotten to me – not finding Slick's body or looking at the body we did find. I hoped against hope that my faith in Lenora, my trust in her story, would turn out to be justified.

When we got to the ground-floor hall, one of the uniformed officers who had stayed with Mrs Thomson led her to the back apartment, and she opened it without comment. We stepped into the first room, which held an old green plastic couch and some beat-up chairs like a cut-rate dentist's waiting-room. The card room, which Lenora and Money had both pointed out on the building plans, was to the right in the back. Bud was leading the group then, and as we approached the open door he held out his hand to stop us from going in. Bud had become legendary at Homicide for the sixth sense he had about crime scenes, and I'd seen it in action a few times myself. It had nothing to do with observable evidence. It was a feeling he would get, a feeling that something had happened, as if a room, like a person, held secrets it could never forget.

The room was almost dark, the two windows on the back alley covered in cheap translucent shades that let in only a dim glow. Bud flicked the light switch near the door but didn't let anyone enter. In the center was a large round table covered in green felt surrounded by an assortment of straight-backed wooden chairs. Everything was neat, and cleaner than you would expect from having seen the basement and the halls.

Bud called Umansky over, who ordered one of his men to make notes as first Bud, and then he, called out descriptions of the room. Approximately twelve by fourteen feet with two windows on the east wall. Walls light green, appear to be newly painted. Floors covered with a brown tweed low-pile rug. I trusted in Bud's intuition more even than in Lenora's story, and my sense of anticipation rose as they catalogued the scene. The table and chairs, an old orange tweed couch on the west wall adjacent to the door; a painting on velvet of a bullfight on the north wall; the wall where I hoped the bullet would be.

The photographer was brought in to shoot the scene and then the CSU specialists came in to start their work. The north wall was the immediate target of their attention. They removed the painting and studied the surface. It appeared perfectly smooth, but after running his hand over it, one of the forensic technicians announced that a thin ridge seemed to indicate a spackled area under the paint. He eased his fingers gently back and forth over the section and discovered two round indentations he believed to be the holes that had been filled. With a small knife he gently pried the spackle from the first hole, which was in exactly the place the bullet would have hit if it had gone through Slick's body, provided Slick had been standing where Lenora and Money both said he was. I just hoped the bullet was still in there.

The officer worked carefully. After some initial flaking, he was able to remove a cylindrical chunk almost the size of a wine cork. He looked into the hole with a flashlight and then delicately removed a few more pieces of hardened plaster with a rubber tweezer. He stated for the record that there was a change in the appearance of the hole behind the spackle, that it was narrower and smoother. The tension was killing me but I knew he had to be precise, that everything had to be done with the greatest care so that any evidence we found would remain untainted and unassailable in court.

He looked again with the flashlight and observed a blackish dot approximately one-quarter inch in diameter. With a small brush he removed the tiny particles of spackle that remained, then reached into the hole with the tweezers and pulled something out, announcing that he had extracted what appeared to be a spent bullet. He held it up and I could hear Bud, standing next to me, let out a sigh of relief that matched my own. Umansky told the ballistics officer to initial the bullet. 'Looks like a nine millimeter,' he said as he placed it in an evidence bag and proceeded to the next hole.

'OK,' Umansky said, his tone entirely different now. 'We're going to go over this room with a microscope. We've got a long haul ahead of us, so let's get going.' The fingerprint expert started dusting, beginning with the inside doorknob and moving to the chairs. One of the forensic officers started an inch-by-inch inspection of the wall, while the second measured the exact location of the bullet holes.

Umansky stood next to Bud as they worked. 'Do you think you'll find anything useful after all this time?' Bud asked him.

'If the information you have is correct, there's been over a month since the shooting. The integrity of the crime scene has definitely been compromised during that time. The walls have been painted. The carpet has probably been washed.' He looked down at it. 'It looks too worn to have been replaced. They probably wiped for prints and God knows how many people have been in here since then. But if a killing occurred here and they left anything, a hair, a skull fragment, a remnant of a bloodstain, we might be able to ID it. It's amazing what we can do in the lab these days.' He thought for a couple of minutes and then added, 'Of course, there will be the difficulty of proving anything we collect is connected to that particular event. We can only see what we get and take it from there.'

In spite of these very real reservations, my mood had gone from despair to something pretty near elation. The bullet had been found; somehow I would make everything else fall into place. It would be tough, but I was going to make this case. Bud and I watched the forensics team for a few more minutes, and then we went to the front room of the apartment, where he gathered the IAD detectives and suggested that in view of the finding of the spent bullet in the prescribed location we should return to the basement and continue the search. We all went into the hall, but I decided I needed some fresh air before facing the basement again and headed to the front door.

The bright sunlight was a shock. The squalid world inside the building had wiped out all sense of time, all sense that a daylight world existed. Collins was by the curb, leaning against the squad car in his jeans and leather jacket, drinking takeout coffee, exuding a kind of energized languor – the Marlboro Man with a Styrofoam cup. I wasn't surprised to see him; I guess maybe I had hoped to find him there. I was still bothered by his attitude at the interrogation the other night and I wanted to straighten things out. I wanted him to understand that I wouldn't have offered Money a deal if I hadn't believed Muñoz had squared it with him first. I wasn't in the habit of horning in on other people's collars or blowing other cops' cases. What I really wanted was for him to respect me. And I didn't want him to think we'd turned Money for nothing. He had never actually gone into the basement but I was sure he had heard about the dog, and now I wanted to make sure he knew about the bullet.

He watched me noncommittally as I walked over.

'Ballistics extracted a spent bullet out of the plaster in the north wall of the card room one point nine meters from the floor. Almost to the millimeter where your prisoner said it would be.' It wasn't what I thought I was going to say and it sounded obnoxiously defensive.

'Congratulations,' he said.

'Look, Detective Collins, I'm sorry about the other night. I thought Muñoz told me you two had worked it out. I guess I just figured you were bringing him to the SPO, you must have known what it was about.'

'I was just doing what I was told.' The way he said it, the way he stood there, made it clear that was rarely the case.

'This is not some cop on a petty bribery charge. This is murder we're talking about. Money's testimony is crucial.'

'He's your baby now.'

'Yeah, well, thanks.' I had started out annoyed at myself, but now I was getting angry with him; he did not have to make this so damn difficult. I should have trusted my first instinct: the guy was a prima donna. I gave up the idea of getting some coffee myself. 'Now that they found the bullet, there's more of a reason to search the basement. I'm going to head back down.' I turned and walked back to the building. I opened the door, stepped inside, and paused to give my eyes a chance to readjust to the dim, murky light. Collins had followed me and opened the door behind me.

In the stairwell above I heard the sound of someone coming down. The steps were quick and uneven. Whoever it was was in a hurry, taking two at a time. I looked up. A glint like metal flashed from under the jacket of a man on the landing above. The only light in the stairwell came from a grimy skylight four floors above, so I really couldn't see much. Maybe it was just the way he was moving. Maybe it was an instinct like Bud's about the crime scene. My senses went into overdrive like a junkie with a shot of meth. I reached for the gun in the small of my back. Collins saw the motion of my hand, looked up and saw the guy coming down. 'Police,' he said. The man apparently hadn't seen us. He stopped for a second, and the next thing I saw was the flash from the gun as he fired.

Before I fully registered what had happened, Collins was up the stairs in pursuit. I found myself running behind him, not completely understanding why. I hadn't yet reached the third-floor landing when I heard an apartment door slam, and, as I got closer, running feet and the sound of glass breaking. There was no longer any sound on the stairs. Collins had apparently followed the guy into one of the apartments. I couldn't tell which one it was, but figured from the broken glass that the guy had gone out the back fire-escape and that Collins had probably followed him. I decided to continue up the stairs and try to intercept him on the roof. I made the last two flights in record time, my heart pounding. There was a small landing at the top littered with crack vials and empty Jim Beam bottles. I turned the knob and pushed at the rusted metal door, but it didn't budge. The lock was hanging loose, so I figured it was blocked from the other side. I kicked away the debris so I could get a better purchase, leaned against it with my shoulder, and pushed as hard as I could. It gave a few inches. Taking a deep breath, I stepped back and then rammed my shoulder forward. This time I was able to push whatever was blocking it about a foot – enough for me to squeeze through. I didn't know if the guy had gotten to the roof before me or if he had heard the door, but I had to get out there. I squeezed myself through, my gun at the ready, flattened myself against the wall and looked around.

The door opened onto the left side of the roof. The structure of the skylight was on my right, and a small building that looked like an abandoned pigeon coop was in front of me, blocking my view of the fire-escape. I ran across the tar, pressed myself against the back of the coop, eased myself over to the corner, and peered around it. A wiry black man was just climbing over the railing onto the roof. He stopped, looked down, and then ran toward the opposite side and looked over the edge of the building. The next building was too far to jump and apparently he didn't see any way down because he turned, glanced at the fire-escape, and ran back toward the coop. I kept myself flat against the wall out of view and concentrated on his footsteps. He ran around the coop and stopped on the left side. My heart was pounding and my breath was coming in gasps from the exertion of the door and the stairs. I forced myself to quiet it, gulping air and holding it. I wasn't sure what I was going to do, but I knew I couldn't risk him hearing me.

Slowly I inched my way along the back to the corner, held my breath and took a quick look around. The man was by the front corner of the coop, his back to me, his gun aimed at the fire-escape. I could hear Collins on the metal steps, and I knew as soon as he showed his head above the roofline he'd be an easy target. I pressed myself back against the wall and tried to think. But there was no time; I had to act. I had to disarm the guy. He was so close that if I didn't get him with the first shot he would almost surely get me. If I shot, I would have to shoot to kill. I was shaking so badly I was afraid I'd miss, but I was just as afraid I wouldn't. I had never killed anybody, and I didn't want this to be the first time, no matter who this skell was. I stepped around the corner, my gun in front of me. He was concentrating so hard on the fire-escape he didn't notice me behind him. I could just make out the metal railing. I was about to scream, 'Police, freeze,' when Collins's head rose into view. The guy took aim. I raised my gun in the air and leapt at him, my arm bringing it down on his head as my momentum brought him to his knees. I was on top of him now, and with one continuing motion I grabbed his gun hand at the wrist and pulled it back. For once, being a lefty had worked to my advantage. I had swung the gun with my left hand, leaving my right hand free to grab his. I heard a distinct crack as his forearm crashed against my knee.

I held him down as Collins climbed onto the roof and rushed over. He pulled his cuffs from his belt, cuffed the prisoner, and pulled him to his feet. 'Take it easy, man,' the guy started to scream in a thick Haitian accent. 'My arm is broke. The fuckin' broad, she broke my arm.'

'Shut up, motherfucker, you tried to kill me,' Collins said. Then he mirandized him, the guy still blubbering about his arm.

'He's right, it is broken,' I said.

Collins shrugged, looking at the prisoner's face. 'I know you,' he said after a minute. 'Kibodeaux. We've had a warrant on you for six months. Henri Kibodeaux.

'This motherfucker killed some poor schmuck who happened to get in the line of fire in a bar down on DeKalb,' he explained, turning to me. 'Fucking drug wars.'

I followed as Collins walked Kibodeaux down the stairs. My shoulder and knee throbbed; my right hand was scraped all along the side where I had slammed it against the graveled tar. My breathing still hadn't returned to normal. We took Kibodeaux outside and turned him over to the precinct officer, who was still on guard there, and Collins told the officer to wait a few minutes. Then Collins went back in and I could hear him call down the basement stairs. 'Hey, Muñoz, get up here. I've got something to show you.' They came back out, and while Collins told Muñoz about the bust I went over to the state car Bud had driven that morning, got the first-aid kit, and cleaned up my hand.

Muñoz went back into the building, Collins gave some instructions to the patrol officer, told him he would meet them at Central Booking, and came over and looked at my hand.

'You OK?'

'I'll live.'

We stood there in silence for a moment. 'I want to know one thing,' he said finally. 'Why the fuck didn't you shoot the bastard?'

'I'm not into carving notches on my gun.'

'He had his gun pointed straight at me.'

'He didn't shoot, did he?' We stood and stared at each other.

'No,' he said finally, 'he didn't.'

Chapter Twelve

He was taking a detour, trying to avoid the traffic on Broome Street, when he first noticed the store, and the girl. Ever since they'd put in the one-way toll going to Brooklyn on the Verrazano-Narrows Bridge, Broome Street had become a main artery for motorists trying to avoid paying the five dollars as they went from Brooklyn or Staten Island to Manhattan and Jersey. The truck traffic was unbearable. He tried to avoid being down there at rush hour, but rush hour on Broome Street now extended from three till almost seven and all morning till noon.

Just as the light was changing and the traffic began to inch forward, he made a quick turn on to Greene with the idea of zipping over to Houston. He had forgotten about the bone-jarring potholes caused by years of truck traffic on the ancient cobblestone street. Between that and the stop signs at every corner he was moving at a snail's pace – still, he was moving. The store was on the right tucked between the columned entrance to a renovated professional building and a showroom for Italian designer furniture. He had been coming to this neighborhood for one reason or another for years and had watched with bemused fascination as it turned from Hell's Hundred Acres into the chic boutique-land of SoHo. He could sort of understand why artists would want to take over the industrial loft spaces, but why the rich would want to follow them here was a mystery. There wasn't a tree or a park. Trucks still made deliveries to the commercial spaces that remained and to the pretentious new showrooms that replaced the sweatshops as they went out of business, often blocking the sidewalks where boxes of debris and barrels of garbage tended to proliferate. He preferred it out on the Island, where at least a person could have a plot of grass and a little privacy and a man could feel his house was his own.

Still, he liked to check it out once in a while. There were always splashy new places opening up and the jazzy young women that went with them. Cleaner than the girls in the East Village, richer, not as weird. He hated weird women. He hated these women too. Thought they were such hot shit with their hundred-dollar haircuts and shoes that cost more than his week's pay. But he liked to look at them.

What caught his eye was a glint of sunlight on something satin. He glanced in the rear-view mirror. There was no-one behind him so he slowed down to a stop and checked it out. Some kind of flimsy little top with a tiny pair of bikini panties to match laid out on a very modern chair – all iron and angles that would not be inviting to sit on. The underwear was purple satin, absolutely inviting. A long string of pearls was draped across the angular metal back of the chair. One of those stores that sold silky underthings he thought of as French. The aggressiveness of the chair accentuated the delicacy of the lingerie in a way that gave the display an S & M flavor. Some fag window-dresser thought it was kinky, he supposed. It irritated him to look at it. He peered deeper into the store to see what kind of a person ran it and, as if she could read his thoughts, the girl behind the counter looked up at just that moment and turned her head toward him. A good sign. He could not see her features clearly because of the reflections on the plate-glass window, but he could see she was pretty in the honest, simple way he liked. Dark wavy hair, in her early twenties, he thought. A car was coming up behind him. He moved on, needing to get uptown anyway.

It was over a week before he was back in the neighborhood again. He hadn't allowed himself to go out of his way to go there. If he was right, it would work out without him pushing it. It always did. Watching it happen, being alert to the possibilities, was part of the game. But he had been anxious all week. That stupid piece in the paper had put him off balance. He knew he would make the papers eventually, but hadn't counted on what they would say, hadn't expected that fucking snide attitude. The Press. They never got anything right. Bunch of assholes. And the jerks in Sex Crimes weren't much better. He would straighten them all out. He found his pulse racing in a way he didn't like as he made the turn off from Broome, and he forced himself to take it easy on the potholed street.

This time there was a car honking behind him as he slowed to a near stop when he approached the store. He gave the driver the finger, stopped, and looked through the display into the interior. A different face turned to look at him. Long, straight blond hair, exotic made-up eyes. Damn. Not that she wasn't pretty too. All these girls were pretty; it was part of the job. But she wasn't right. Her lipstick was too red – a slash in her face. Harsh. Like the spiky iron chair next to the lingerie. He would not have been drawn here for her. He peered deeper into the store, trying to see if the other girl was inside.

The horn behind him was blaring. He stepped on the gas pedal, moving forward with an angry jerk and then slowing again, looking for a place to park. All the spaces on the block were taken with trucks unloading. He couldn't find a place to pull over until he crossed Prince Street. He watched the guy pull by him, turned off the ignition and took out the key, his hand forming a fist around it. He squeezed it tightly in his palm, letting the serrated metal edge dig into his flesh. How could he be so stupid? Leaning back against the seat, he took several deep breaths. He knew better than to call attention to himself that way. Control was the key. Never let them see anything. He had learned that lesson long ago.

Control was power. He had learned it in the mountains as a boy, his back against a tree, the rifle resting across his lap, waiting in the bitter cold for dawn, for the deer, whose sense of smell and hearing was thirty times more acute than his, whose awareness of movement was so keen it could register the flicker of an eyelid from thirty yards. He had learned to keep his limbs still and his mouth shut, his stomach a hard knot of hunger and cold, fear and anticipation; he had learned not to complain. If he moved, or spoke, his father's wrath would be worse than the pain gripping his numb legs and stiff fingers. The whole day would be ruined, the hunt over; he would be ashamed and banished from his father's sight, forced to make his way back to the truck alone to wait for the others.

He had experienced it as mere cruelty then, gratuitous and impersonal – the killing itself and the harsh discipline imposed on him to accomplish it. But now he knew it was a gift. Once he had found that calm in the center, the place where nothing hurt any more, once he had learned to retreat there at will, he could do anything. The Captain's only legacy.

He took a sip of coffee from the Styrofoam cup he always had next to him. He had picked up the coffee at a deli in Brooklyn, and it was already cold. He fought the desire to spit it out. He wanted to drive around the block and check again if the blonde was alone in the store or if the brunette was there too, but he knew it wasn't a good idea.

The next time he drove by, taking a detour this time on his way home to the Island, he was surprised to see a green shade pulled down covering the plate-glass window. Shit. It was only six-thirty. This was SoHo – stores didn't close until seven or eight. Could they have gone out of business? Maybe they were closed for vacation. He had to know. He turned left on Prince and lucked into a parking space.

He got out slowly and held himself to an easy stroller's pace as he rounded the corner, forcing himself to pause in front of the furniture showroom next to the lingerie store. A pale green leather sofa floated starkly on a huge expanse of cool black marble. The leather exuded a tactile sensuality he found both thrilling and repellent, like the flesh of a voluptuous woman. Casually, he moved a few steps farther down the block. 'Pardon us while we change,' the message in script said on the dark green shade over the lingerie display window. He let out a breath he hadn't realized he was holding. Walking slowly, he looked through the lace-curtained door to the interior of the shop. It was deeper than he expected, with racks of robes and nightgowns and underthings on hangers, and a seating group of hi-tech chairs and tables toward the rear. The blonde was at the counter talking to a customer. The other girl had her back to him, hanging something up, but he had no doubt it was her. He looked at the store hours posted on the door – 11 a.m. to 8 p.m. Closed Monday.

The week was busy, but he managed to drive by a couple of times between eleven and twelve. The store appeared to be opened by one or the other girl each day, and whoever opened it seemed to be alone the first hour. It made sense; there was very little activity in SoHo until two or three in the afternoon. The last time he drove by, the blonde was entering the store. The brunette was inside, looking toward him it seemed, or maybe she was watching the other girl. He looked at his watch. It was just twelve o'clock.

Everything was working to his advantage. It would soon be time. But he had to be sure, going with his instincts but checking and double-checking everything. All of the lunch-hour encounters had required this element of extra caution. The time frame was extremely limited, and other workers and passers-by were a factor. The limitations changed the tone of the game, adding constraints but lending their own layer of excitement. There were a few that had been close enough to the office to take lunch orders for the guys – stop at Sam's Deli, put in the order, tell him he had a couple of errands to run, do the girl, and be back while the pastrami on rye was still hot. It made him chuckle to think about it.

But this was different. He could feel it in his gut, and his loins – a sharper edge to his anticipation. Everything was more thrilling, more frightening, more compelling now that he had made contact. They had probably spoken to Denise Levenson by now; they thought they were on to something. They didn't know the half of it. That crap about him shooting blanks – maybe he had started out that way, but that had changed too. It felt good: it was what he needed. The stakes were getting higher.

When he got the call that he had to do a tour on Sunday, he decided to do a drive-by on the way in, not expecting anything in particular, not even sure why he was doing it. Sunday was one of the biggest days in SoHo, the streets full of tourists and strollers, as busy gawking as shopping. And it was a day he was rarely in the city. A day he hadn't even considered. But when he drove by, the street was surprisingly deserted. The green shade was down again. He put his foot on the brake and peered into the dark interior. Then he looked at his watch. Not quite eleven. He continued to the corner, where the early brunch crowd was starting to collect outside of Food. Turning left on Prince, he circled back around the block. As he approached the shop a second time he saw the dark-haired girl coming toward him down the street, moving purposefully, her expression fixed in a light scowl, maybe annoyed to have her Sunday morning interrupted by work. He pulled ahead of her and eased into a vacant parking space, watching through the rear-view mirror as she stopped in front of the store, searched in her shoulder-bag for the key, and opened the door. He leaned back against the seat to collect his thoughts. He had to be sure he was ready. Sometimes you waited, preparing yourself, keeping calm until the wait became an end in itself; other times the prey walked across your path before you had time to settle into the blind.

He checked his watch again: 11:06. He looked up the street. No-one was coming this way. He reached over to the glove compartment, took out a can of Stiff Stuff Hair Lacquer, closed his eyes, and with a few short sweeping motions, sprayed the front of his hair. He replaced the can, took a comb out of his pocket and slicked his stiff, darkened hair away from his forehead, then pulled a pair of black leather gloves from their place next to the can and put them on. He was about to open the door of the car when he turned to look behind him. Suddenly, a pair of buff-colored Afghans came bounding up the block, stopping abruptly like children playing statue to stand immobile in front of the building that housed the furniture showroom. He turned to see their owner, ambling slowly up the block, hefting a Sunday *Times* in one arm and a bag of groceries in the other.

It threw him at first. The empty streets were a bonus, but not if it caused some damn dog-walker to remember seeing him here. Not that a description would make that much difference. None of the descriptions furnished by the girls had done the cops any good, none of them ever would. He smiled as he thought about it, feeling better. The dog owner walked past the car and entered the building without even a glance in his direction. He checked the street again, got out of the car, and walked back to the store.

Timing is all, someone had said. Julius Caesar, or maybe Shakespeare, he couldn't remember. It struck him as a funny idea, funny that he should recall it now. It had something to do with history, the quote. But it was true for hunting too. Being at the right place at the right time. But that wasn't enough. There was timing and there was readiness, a kind of anticipation that was still at the center. The big trophy hunters, the ones that shot the fourteen- and sixteen-point bucks, planned in advance, hiking the deer runs all summer, learning to psyche out their prey – learning to be quiet, to sit and wait, but knowing, too, when to move. Skill and instinct honed so that you could cock your gun and fire in the split second before your brain could even register the rack of a buck appearing suddenly out of the tangle of bare brown branches.

As he approached the store, he pulled a pair of wire-framed aviator-style glasses from his pocket and put them on. A bell tinkled as he entered. She was standing in the back, removing her coat, looking up, watching him, as if she, too, had been waiting for this day. 'Hi,' he said, closing the door behind him. 'How're ya doing?' His voice was louder than usual, his motion in flicking the lock so quick she didn't even notice it.

He stood by the entrance for a second, taking everything in, and then moved nonchalantly to the racks on the right, running his hand along the slinky fabrics the way a little boy will run a stick along an iron fence. When he got to the end he turned and approached the counter.

'Nice store you have here.' He smiled his most disarming smile.

'Can I help you with something?'

'I hope so. I'm looking for something really sexy, but classy, you know?'

She nodded, uncomfortable but trying not to show it. 'A gift for your wife?'

'My wife?' She had looked at his hand to see if he was wearing a ring. Her gaze lingered on his glove, which he didn't remove. 'It doesn't matter who's going to wear it, does it? It's really for me, if you know what I mean. That's the reason men buy this stuff, don't you think?'

'We have many items of fine-quality intimate apparel. Perhaps you can give me a better idea of what you have in mind.' She had become noticeably primmer, a layer of professional haughtiness distancing her like a film of smoothly applied make-up. It was useless. Hers was a soft face. The eyes, as he expected, vulnerable in spite of their armor of mascara and eye-liner. For now that he was close to her he could see that, like the blonde, she was elaborately made-up. Who did she think she was fooling?

'Maybe if you could model some of them for me, I'd have a better idea.' He said it with a smile, but she took a step back from the counter, instinctively wanting to put as much space between them as she could. Usually the game was different – it depended on making the girl feel comfortable at first so she would let him in her apartment, or car, or wherever it was he wanted to be. But he was already there. This time the fun was in seeing her squirm, playing with her like a cat with a mouse, letting her think she could get free, letting her think he was just some bore, pushy and coarse, but ultimately in her power to dismiss. Then watching her face as the truth dawned.

'Hey, don't get me wrong. It was just a joke.' He shrugged and gave her a boyish grin. She didn't smile or comment. He picked up a pair of white satin panties draped over a heart-shaped pillow on the side of the counter. 'These are nice,' he said. 'Innocent.' He gathered the silky fabric in his hand and used it to stroke the side of his cheek. Then he reached across the counter and very gently feathered it across hers. She jumped back and pushed his hand away. 'If you don't leave the store, I'll have to call the police.' She was still trying to be haughty, but her voice was tremulous.

'Don't you want to wear these for me?' he asked in mock surprise.

'Rachel, the other girl who works here, is coming right back,' she said. 'She just went around the corner to Dean and DeLuca for *cappuccino.*' He looked in her eyes. She was lying, of course. He hated it when women lied. Stupid cunts think they can fool you. They lie all the time. Her make-up, with its soft 'natural' colors was a lie. Her demure little dress with its flowered print and lacy front was a lie. He reached out and grabbed it where the lace made a V at the neckline. His knuckles grazed the skin of her thin chest. He could feel her breastbone underneath. 'We definitely need a fashion show,' he said, yanking downward. The silk fabric tore with a tender papery sound that made his body shudder like a sudden chill. It was amazing how easily it ripped. She grasped the fabric to hold it together and tried to move farther back, away from him, but the aisle was narrow and she was already pressed against the wall.

Pulling her to him, he pushed the flimsy fabric aside. He reached his hand into the cup of her lacy lavender-flowered bra and fondled her breast, his eyes on hers, pressing against the small girlish nipple, kneading the smooth, pliant flesh in a cruelly sensual motion.

'I bet your cunt's as round and soft as your tits.' He saw the flicker in her eye and grabbed her wrist with his other hand as she reached below the counter to press the alarm button. Before she knew what was happening he had twisted her arm up behind her back.

He took his hand out of her bra, pulled his gun from his holster, and pressed it against the back of her neck. 'You're going to come out from behind the counter now,' he said. 'And we're going to walk over to the door. It's already locked, so don't try anything stupid. I want you to put the closed sign up and pull down the shade. Walk calmly and hold your dress together so everything looks normal. And don't make a sound. I'll be right behind you.'

'Rachel . . .' she started to say.

'She doesn't come in till noon.' He looked at his watch. 'It's only twenty-five after eleven. We've got plenty of time.'

'Why are you doing this? What do you want?'

He laughed a cold, sneering laugh. No-one walked by as they approached the door. She hesitated, still trying to think of something, and he shoved the nose of the Colt into her back. She quickly turned the sign and pulled the shade. He grabbed her around the front, his free hand cupping her breast again, pulling her tightly against him so she could feel his growing erection through the thin fabric of her dress. He leaned his lips against her ear. 'Now we're going to have some fun,' his whisper insinuating, caressing.

'Please, no. Just let me go. I won't say anything. Please.'

'I told you to be quiet.' He squeezed her nipple between his fingers until she gasped in pain, propelling her in front of him toward the back of the store. He shoved her into the small stockroom and turned her to face him. 'Get this thing off.' He ripped at her dress, pulling it off her shoulder. She started undoing the belt, but he couldn't wait. With his free hand, he pulled the bra off the breast that was still covered. The nipple he had pinched was red and sore looking, the other a soft pale tan, the color, he noticed with an amused smirk, of those pampered overbred dogs next door. Carefully, he ran the nose of the gun down the rounded ridges of her ribs, following their contours through her thin bluish flesh. She finally got the belt open, and he tore the dress the rest of the way.

She was crying now. Trembling on fawn-thin legs like a new-born learning to stand. What the fuck did she expect? They were all the same, stupid cunts underneath the flowers and lace. Did themselves up like birthday packages and started to cry when you ripped open the wrapping. It would have been so easy to make her want him, it almost made him laugh to think about it – the earnest gaze, the boy-next-door grin, the nice words, the gentle touch. They all fell for it. Born suckers. They were so dumb he was tempted to feel sorry for them. There wasn't a woman he had met yet he couldn't have had if he turned on the charm – but then there would have been no game.

He ran the gun down her flat stomach into her bikini pants, rubbing the muzzle in the fuzz over her padded mound of flesh. Then he eased the barrel through the strip on her hip and, with a swift pull, snapped the elastic. Releasing himself from his pants, he pushed her onto a stack of cardboard boxes. 'Open your legs,' he commanded. The gun against her neck, his free hand kneading her breasts, he forced himself in. He was stunned by the pleasure he felt; he hadn't expected to want her this much; he didn't usually want them that way at all. The contrast between her ripeness and fragility was maddening. He had better slow down. He was forgetting the game. He should never forget the game. Or the gun. Especially not now when they had made him raise the stakes. He pulled back on the hammer with his thumb, freeing the cylinder, listening for the familiar click.

Concentrating on the gun, he wrenched himself out of her, took her hand and placed it around the cylinder. 'You know what this is?' She nodded dumbly, her pupils blank with fear. He held her fingers under his and rotated the chambers. She felt the metal turning and tried to pull her hand away. 'The cylinder,' he said. He removed her hand, pressed the release and the cylinder rolled out. 'Six chambers.' He held the open cylinder up to her face. 'Three empty, three with rounds.' He rotated the cylinder, one chamber at a time, demonstrating. 'Life. Death. Life. Death. Life. Death.' He snapped the gun closed and pulled back the hammer, hearing the first click. Wrapping her hand around the cylinder again, he rolled it with her palm. 'Life, death. Life, death,' he whispered. 'It's up to you.'

'Stop, please stop,' she wailed, struggling to pull her hand away. He wrenched her hand from the gun, pulled it behind her back, and rammed himself into her again. 'Life, death, life, death,' he chanted to the rhythm of his motion, the gun against her temple now. He moved faster, pulling the hammer, listening for the second click. It was too much. He couldn't wait any longer. 'Three clicks and you're out,' he said through gritted teeth. He held his breath, pulled his thumb back on the hammer, and then, pulling the trigger, let everything go.

The explosion when he came echoed through his brain like a cannon. It took a second to register what had happened. His ears rang, his breath came in gasps. He had never been so close to the barrel of a gun going off; his head reverberated with the sound. He pulled himself off her and turned away to do up his pants. Still clutching the gun, he ran his hand over his stiff, slicked-back hair and surveyed the tiny room. Her pocketbook was sitting on a table in the corner. He found her wallet and pulled out her driver's license. Annabelle Ross, 244 East 75th Street. He put it back, took out the bills, dropped the wallet, and moved to the front of the store. Cautiously he pulled the shade aside and looked out the door. There was no sign of commotion, the boxes that padded the stockroom must have muffled the sound like sandbags in a bunker. He took a deep breath, holstered his gun, and stepped calmly out into the street.

Chapter Thirteen

After Collins took off for Central Booking, I went back down to the basement to join in the search. He had given Muñoz a pretty fair idea of what had happened on the roof and Muñoz had passed it on to the guys. The razzing I got now had a whole different tone – a lot of jokes about how they didn't know I had a gun, but then, of course, I didn't know what it was for. I didn't mind; it was hard for them to accept a woman, one from SPO no less, bringing down a tough nut like Kibodeaux without actually firing a shot. I was probably more surprised than anyone.

A couple of hours mucking around in the trash didn't reveal anything more. A few of us tried a canvass of the other apartments in the building, but either no-one was home or they weren't answering. Still, I was satisfied. Money's information about the body had proved to be a bum steer but, in spite of that, the day had clearly been a success. We cleaned up as best we could at the basement sink. We were all starving and one of the CSU guys said he knew a good diner not too far from where we were. After a burger and a few beers I could think of only one thing – getting home, stripping down and standing in the shower till my skin shriveled or the hot water ran out, whichever came first.

When I got in I made the mistake of listening to my messages. My machine blared forth the usual reminders that I was not holding my own in the regular world. Two messages from my dad: Was I coming tomorrow? Why hadn't I called? My mother was worried about me. One from Maddy: 'Are we still on for Wednesday night? If you don't get me, tell my machine what time.'

Even Steve had tried to reach me. 'Working on Saturday again? Too bad. You missed a great brunch. We'll do it tomorrow. See you around ten, coffee and croissants on me.'

I flipped on the tube, got in the shower, and resolved to call my folks first thing in the morning. If I'd let myself, I could have worked up a good head of annoyance at Steve's assumption that I would be there waiting for him when he showed up in the morning, but I was so tired and wired at the same time I couldn't trust my feelings about anything. I kept seeing Henri Kibodeaux' back in that second before I leaped – the glint on his gun as he took aim at Collins – going over it in my mind, trying to figure out how I had had the guts to do it, and maybe even more important, if I would ever be able to do anything like that again. I poured myself a Scotch and tried to find something I could watch, but nothing held my attention, and I just kept flipping through the channels. Maybe I needed some exercise. Some way to burn up the excess adrenaline that was still coursing through my body like my veins were an Indy 500 track. I flipped off the sound of a *MacGyver* rerun, rummaged through my tapes for my favorite Janis Joplin, put it in my Walkman and hopped on the stationary bike. The bike is the most boring, grueling, and unpleasant form of exercise ever invented. After twenty-five minutes at my peak aerobic heart rate I was sweaty and exhausted but no more relaxed.

Another shower, another Scotch, and the thing I still couldn't get out of my mind was Collins's question. Why the fuck hadn't I shot the creep? Was I really so moral, or was I just too scared I'd miss? Certainly what I did was a lot riskier for me, and potentially for Collins, than pulling the trigger. Who the hell did I think I was anyway, Ms *Machette*? The jokes of the CSU guys about having a gun but not knowing how to use it kept running through my head. Maybe they were more right than they knew. Or was I overreacting? I couldn't shoot the guy in the back – it was as simple as that. Still, my annual marksmanship test on the range was coming up in a couple of weeks, and I figured I'd better start practicing. I'd always scored a perfect 100; I didn't want anything less this time to fuel their doubts, or my own.

The last movie I watched, *Bride of Frankenstein*, didn't even come on till 2:30 a.m., so when Steve rang the buzzer a little after ten I was still sound asleep. True to his word, he arrived with croissants from Jon Vie, one of his favorite French bakeries – three flaky, buttery varieties, plain, almond, and chocolate; two jars of imported cherry and blueberry preserves; a dozen eggs; and a pound of the best Jamaican Blue Mountain coffee, beans that were as rich and strong and went for almost as much as the grass from the same country. He knew me well enough to know what he was likely to find in my refrigerator. There was also a bunch of rose-and-cream-striped tulips he had picked up at one of the Korean markets, which were also no doubt imported from somewhere, Mexico perhaps, and gloriously exotic for that time of year. I wondered if all this pampering indicated something was up but was too tired to ask. Whatever it was, I might as well enjoy it.

I scrambled up some eggs, which is just about the range of my culinary abilities, and after a leisurely breakfast we ambled back to bed. Steve was in a lazy, affectionate mood. We made love in a friendly, languid way, after which I promptly fell asleep. When I woke up a few hours later Steve was in the living-room engrossed in the Sunday *Times*. A pleasant surprise. I'm used to waking up alone.

'Your father called,' he said.

'Did you talk to him?'

'Sure.'

'Oh, God.'

'It was fine. We had a nice chat. He said he hadn't heard from you in days and your mother was worried. I told him not to worry, you were fine, just working very hard on a case. He asked if I thought you would be coming for Sunday dinner and I said I didn't think they should expect you. That you'd been up all night and had just gotten to sleep.'

'Who did he think you were?'

'Someone from work, I guess. We didn't discuss it. You *are* a big girl now.'

'Yeah, and he's still an Italian father.'

The idea of this conversation between Steve and my father flipped me out. 'What right do you have answering my phone, anyway?'

'I was just trying to be helpful.'

'Yeah, well, I'll never hear the end of it, between a guy answering my phone and you telling him I've been working late. I never talk to my folks about stuff like that. God!' The more I thought about it, the angrier I got. 'What if I called your wife? Do you think that would be helpful?'

'I didn't call him, I just picked up the phone. You were asleep, remember? Besides, what's my wife got to do with it?'

'I don't know, something. Everything.'

He looked sheepish and I relented a little. 'How'd you know I was on a case?' I asked.

'You've been out almost every night. Saturday, too.'

Which meant he had tried to come by, since I only got one message on the machine – a nice thought. What was not so nice was the idea that the only thing that would keep me so busy was work and that he knew it. I went in the bedroom to get dressed, trying to squelch my growing irritability. Our lovely, lazy Sunday together was taking on an edge I didn't like.

I threw on some jeans and a sweatshirt and ran a comb through my hair, and we hung out for a while reading the paper and toying with the idea of a walk but never quite getting up the energy to leave the apartment. Neither of us made any reference to our situation or showed any inclination to discuss our relationship. I was still seething about my father's call, pretending I wasn't, not sure how rational my anger was, trying to be fair. A couple of times he had the look of someone about to say something and thinking better of it, and I didn't press him. We were sitting in the same room, but I didn't feel the kind of closeness I always thought would be there if we just had time to spend together. I tried to bridge the gap by talking about work. Without going into any details of the case, I told him what had happened on the roof the day before, but it came out sounding like Wonder Woman and I couldn't quite get across what I found disturbing about it. He was fascinated. He loved it when I talked about police work. Men either love the idea of a woman holding a gun or hate it. I'm not sure what makes the difference, but Steve was the 'love it' variety. Before I knew it, he was leaning closer, nuzzling me behind the ear and kissing my neck.

His interest didn't have the effect he wanted, though. This was my dream, unhurried time to be together like a real couple – so why wasn't I enjoying it more? I chalked my mood up to exhaustion and the pressure of the Calvert case. I couldn't feign a responsiveness I didn't feel, and after a while Steve gave up and went to take a shower.

I decided to put the time to good use and got out my gun to start practicing. I sat down at the table, emptied the rounds on to the tablecloth, inspected the empty cylinders in the chamber, closed it, balanced a dime on the barrel, and pulled the trigger. The trick was to fire without displacing the dime. No mean feat. You had to squeeze the trigger with an even pressure, holding the gun steady, fighting the recoil and your own tendency to pull up as you fired. I shot several times, the dime steady, and then stood up and aimed at the cactus on top of the TV. I wanted to make sure my nerves weren't getting to me, that I still had my edge, and I checked my breathing, making sure that when I fired I held my breath.

I fired once, cocked the gun, and fired again. It felt good. Better than I remembered. I raised my arms and aimed again, wishing I was at the range firing real rounds. I craved the noise and the rush of power when the bullet explodes from the gun. I wanted the satisfaction of hitting the target, of seeing the bullet holes form a pattern dead center.

Steve came out of the shower and must have been watching me, but I didn't hear him. Suddenly he grabbed me from behind. 'Gotcha,' he said, reaching for the gun.

My reaction was a combination of instinct and training. I whirled and pointed the gun straight at his head. 'What the fuck is wrong with you?' I said. 'What if it was loaded?' His face went white with alarm.

Then he laughed and everything inside me exploded. It was all a sham. Us as a couple. This cozy domesticity. Our whole relationship was as empty as the gun I was pointing. There would never be a me and him without her in the background. Even his interest in my work, his fascination with what I did, was just a game. Steve stood there in a towel, his mouth open, confusion passing over his face like a cloud over the sun. I turned away and aimed one last time at the cactus. My hand shook violently. I forced myself to steady my arm, closed my eyes, and envisioned Steve's head. I had no idea I had that much anger inside me. I pulled the trigger, blasting him finally, with that gesture, out of my life for ever.

On my way to work Monday morning I stopped at the Police Academy at 235 East Twentieth Street, where the police lab is located, to pick up the preliminary report from Mom's. The bullets both came from the same gun. A 9mm, the same type Money claimed Calvert had been showing him, but the gun had not been traced, and because of the weekend the rest of the forensic work had not yet been done.

I didn't get back down to Rector Street until after nine-thirty but miraculously still found a space I could squeeze the old bomb into. At least it had the virtue of being small. By the time I got upstairs Mickey, Stets, and Terry were already at their desks. I got a few nods and waves – no big deal. I don't know what else I expected. I guess I assumed they would have heard about Saturday, but everyone was business as usual, only more so. Then I reached my desk and saw why. Spread over the surface was an array of 'wanted' posters, the kind you see hanging in the least-conspicuous corner of the Post Office. There was an amazing assortment that must have gone back several years; a more dismal collection of sullen, ugly mugs would be hard to imagine. Added to these beauties was an old movie poster featuring Jack the Ripper and an extremely aggressive 'Uncle Sam Wants You', with a scowling Uncle pointing an index finger that could bore a hole through your chest. Draped across the whole display was a large computer printout that read 'Tina Paris, Bounty Hunter'. I was totally overwhelmed. Where had they gotten all this stuff, and on such short notice? I stared at the display on my desk, trying to pull myself together. When I looked up, the guys were all grinning at me. 'Go get 'em, Spaghetti,' Mickey said.

Stets handed me a stack of pink slips. 'Here're

your telephone messages.' Among the regular calls, one from Lenora I noticed, were messages supposedly from Geraldo and Donahue, Oprah, and *America's Most Wanted* – even one from the FBI Warrant Division. Mary Lee came over with Stacey, both beaming. 'You showed 'em, girl,' she said, reaching out to shake my hand.

It was all a little too heady. Then Mickey reached into his desk drawer. 'I've got something for you.' He handed me a box from one of the local candy shops. I opened it up and there, wrapped in tissue paper, was a chocolate gun. 'Since you're not going to use it anyway, we thought you ought to have one that's good for something.' I laughed, feeling more relaxed. Things wouldn't seem right without the usual razzing.

Everyone wandered back to their own desks and I looked around for Bud, who hadn't joined in, and noticed the door to Vince's office was closed. 'What's going on?' I asked Mickey, indicating the door.

'Big powwow,' he said. 'MacCallister came in to see Vince first thing in the morning. Now Bud's in there with Muñoz and Wing.'

My good mood left me instantly. 'They're talking about my case.'

'Word is, Muñoz doesn't want it to be your case.'

'It's not up to him.'

'No, but it looks like he's got the big brass on his side,' Stets said in his Southern drawl. 'I guess you could say you're somewhere between a dog and a fire hydrant on this one.'

I turned scowling at the door, and just then it opened. Bud stuck his head out, saw me, and gestured for me to come in. Vince was seated behind his desk, framed by his expansive view of the East River. Inside the office, space was cramped. Bud, Muñoz, and Wing were seated on wooden chairs clustered in front of the desk. A straight-backed chair had been placed by the side of the door for me, but I remained standing. 'Tina,' Vince said, 'I heard about the bust on Saturday. Good work.'

'Thank you.'

He waited a minute, but when it became clear I wasn't going to say anything else he went on. 'We've been talking about the Calvert investigation.'

'I can see that,' I said, with more sarcasm than I should have allowed. 'If you were going to meet on one of my cases, Vince, I should have been told.'

No-one spoke. I could hear Bud shifting in his chair, but I didn't turn away. I knew I wasn't supposed to use a tone like that with the Chief, but I was too angry to care. Vince and I stared at each other and I knew he was surprised when I didn't back down. The only other time he'd seen me this angry and determined was when someone in the office blew my cover before a meet and I wasn't told. Then my life had been at stake. Now I felt it was my life as an investigator that was on the line. I wanted him to know that this one was mine and I was going to fight for it. He turned away first and looked out of the window at two pigeons that had landed on the ledge and were pecking at each other, fighting for their little bit of turf.

'I'm sorry we had to do it this way,' Charlie Wing said, breaking the tension. 'Since the search at the social club substantiated some of the statements obtained from two separate witnesses, it has become clear that the case is stronger than was originally thought. Captain Muñoz has come here today with that knowledge and has raised several significant concerns.'

Wing's tone and demeanor were absolutely calm and reasonable. I looked over at Muñoz, who sat staring straight ahead. His suit looked newly pressed, his white shirt gleamed, his discreet dark blue striped tie was perfectly knotted. His hands rested on the Calvert file conspicuously placed on his lap. I knew I wasn't expected to say anything. Bud quietly cleared his throat and my eyes immediately went to his. He was watching my hands, which I realized were trembling. Silently thanking him for the tip, I clutched my own folder more tightly to steady them and sat down. Why I could be absolutely calm confronting a room full of Mafia thugs and yet have no control over my emotions when faced with police politics was a paradox I had contemplated before. It had something to do with being female, but I wasn't sure what since we were the ones who were supposed to be so good at human relationships.

Vince took over from Wing, expounding on the political implications of the case. 'He's a black cop. One we've arrested before, and we've never convicted him of anything serious. Now we all know that doesn't mean shit, but there are elements in the community that would love to call it harassment. And if we're not careful in the way we handle this, that's just what it will look like.'

'The Press would love nothing more than to have all the community groups screaming,' Muñoz chimed in.

'I don't see race as the issue here,' I said. 'But if it is going to be a problem, then this office is uniquely situated to deal with it. We were handed the Howard Beach case for that reason. The same with Tawana Brawley.'

'This whole case could blow up on us,' Vince said. 'We don't have a body, number one. And number two, you've been on this guy for years with no success. On top of that, you've got a shaky witness. Who knows what this Terrell woman is going to do. We don't want to be blindsided. You read the papers, Albany's ready to pull the rug from under us. We don't need to give them a reason.'

'We don't have a body *yet*,' I said. 'And the two prior cases on Calvert weren't just mine, they were IAD's as well. If we failed, we both failed. And anyway, those cases were Mickey Mouse compared to the gravity of the current allegation. As for the witness, if you think she is going to be less shaky with Captain Muñoz running the investigation, good luck.'

'For all it's worth,' Wing interjected, 'I said it before Tina was in the room, and I'll say it again. I question the wisdom of changing horses in mid-stream. Tina's point about the witness is well taken. She has established a strong rapport with the woman. I'm the one who has to trust that the witness will give me what I need while she's on the stand.'

'This is a homicide investigation. How many homicide investigations has she been on?'

'Hey, Hector,' Vince fired back, 'if that's the hair up your ass then Bud will take the case. He's a seasoned homicide detective, he's black, and he's a former member of New York's Finest.'

'If you want me to I will, boss, but I can't match the rapport with the witness that Tina has, and I don't see anything in the investigation to this point that calls into question Tina's capabilities.'

A strained silence reigned again, with a lot more tension radiating from Muñoz now, and again it was Wing who broke the deadlock. 'If the case is transferred to IAD, everything would be transferred to the Kings County DA's office. With all due respect to IAD, I've put too much effort into this already to see it taken out of my hands.'

'Hector, is that what you're asking?'

'I think it's appropriate, Vince. We have a situation. I'm catching a lot of heat from Police Plaza because Officer Calvert is still on the job. The whole department knows he's dirty and they're laughing because we can't nail him.'

More politics. I should have known. 'We have the same concern, Captain Muñoz,' I said. 'If my performance is the question, if there's anything I've missed, or anything I should have done differently, let me know. Otherwise, I'll keep you informed the way I have been.'

I was furious, but this time I kept my voice in control. He should have come to me directly, instead of engineering this whole circus. Now it was turning against him and it served him right. *You anal-compulsive little hump*, I thought, *I'll bury you with paper*.

'It's your decision, Vince. I just needed to inform you of IAD's concerns.'

'Thank you, Hector. We appreciate that, but I don't see any need to make changes at the current time. Charlie's concerns are well taken. Our legal arm is the best in the city and particularly well suited to handling difficult, sensitive cases like this one. He deserves a chance to run with it.'

Muñoz stood, nodded to everyone in the room, the picture of polite fury, and left. Vince turned to me when he was gone. 'I want to see all the reports. Everything by the book. Remember my motto, Paris, No Surprises. Don't break my heart or any other part of my anatomy.'

I nodded. It was really Charlie he was supporting, not me, but I had gotten what I wanted and wasn't about to complain. 'Make sure you take her other cases and spread them out,' he said to Bud. 'But don't give Bremmer the Muehler case. I'm tired of him crying in his beer every time he has to deal with Puerto Ricans.'

'Anything cooking with Randazzo, Tina?'

'Randazzo. Right.' I had totally forgotten about his call. 'I was just about to call back to arrange a meet.'

He turned back to Bud. 'Keep Tina in the loop with Randazzo but give Nydia everything else.' There was no missing the smirk on Bud's face. 'Yeah, I know, the guys will love that. She looks like a five-dollar special. Mickey's wife sees him with her, he's dead meat.'

He laughed at his own joke. Nydia Zapata was the only other woman investigator left at SPO, a gorgeous, flashy twenty-five-year-old Puerto Rican with a modeling career on the side. She had a certain talent for undercover, but her taste in clothes and her dedication to the job were both questionable.

'OK, Tina,' Vince said to me, 'tell me what you need.'

'I've got Calvert's tour-of-duty schedule. Number one, he was off duty the night of the murder. Number two, he's doing an eight-to-four today. I want to get on him. Who can I take?'

'Take Terry, everyone else is loaded.'

'Terry called in. He's taking a personal,' Bud said.

'Again? What's with this guy?' He looked at us, shaking his head, not really expecting an answer. 'Can you take tonight, Bud?' Bud nodded. 'And I want Terry in my office first thing in the morning.' We both turned to go, but Vince stopped me.

'Tina, there's something else.'

Bud closed the door behind him and I sat down in front of Vince's desk. He picked up the grip strengthener and gave it a few slow, deliberate squeezes before going on. 'You been reading about this latest psycho?'

'You mean the roulette guy?'

He nodded. 'You know he killed the last one?'

'I didn't see that.'

'Happened yesterday.' He shoved a copy of the morning *Post* across the desk. SEX KILLING SHOCKS SoHo, the front page headline screamed. It was an ugly development, but I didn't see what it had to do with me.

'Didn't you handle some sex offenders in the early days of the office?'

I nodded, thinking back. It had been a while since we'd had anything like that.

'Do you remember any cases we've had that might be related, anything to do with someone in the system raping women at gunpoint?'

'Not that I remember. Why?'

'They think this Russian Roulette guy might be someone on the job or in the system.'

'What's the connection?'

'Not much that I can see. They've got some faxes that were sent to Public Relations. Not too many people outside know about the fax setup. Seems the psycho sounds like a cop. What can I tell you? I got a call from Joe Moskowitz over at Sex Crimes. I know the guy and he's no alarmist, but he was worried about this one, and now I can see why. They've got no clues, and he thinks the guy's going to do a lot more damage.'

I immediately thought of Maddy and wondered if that was why she sounded so tense on the phone the other night.

'I'm gonna run it through our intelligence, but if there's anything you remember, let me know. And keep this conversation under wraps.'

It was a disturbing conversation, but I didn't have time to dwell on it. If I didn't call Randazzo right away I would probably forget about it again, so I picked up the file and headed for the tech room. 'Phone,' I said to Dan O'Keefe's enquiring glance, and he buzzed me in. The undercover phone has a Long Island number, but sits hooked up to an answering machine on a battered wooden desk in the back corner of Dan's preserve. I opened the folder and took out the message slip from last Monday with Al Randazzo's phone number. I would have to think of something to explain the week it had taken to get back to him. I glanced over my notes from the Dandrell dinner. It seemed a thousand years ago. Somehow I had to get back into the role of Julia Cipriani, aspiring Mafia moll, at least enough to have a convincing conversation. I closed my eyes and tried to focus. I had to rid my mind of Edward Calvert and everything to do with that case; I had to remind myself that getting close to Randazzo was laying important groundwork that could lead to something potentially even more significant for the SPO.

I closed my eyes, pictured myself in my black dress

and upswept hair, tottering on those damn spike heels, smiling at Al, and picked up the phone. I realized as I dialed that I didn't even know what kind of an office I was calling. Because of my hasty departure the night of the dinner, Al and I had never actually exchanged numbers. The card I gave him only had my undercover work number on it, and he had handed it back, anyway. He had found me in the Manhasset phone book, which was actually better in terms of Julia's validity. Still, it made me a little nervous that he had bothered; I had expected to have to pursue him. Maybe Julia was more attractive than I realized.

A secretary answered. I gave her my name and Al picked up. It struck me suddenly that apologies and explanations would not be Julia's style and I let him do most of the talking. 'You still interested in a job?' he asked after a warm greeting.

'Sure.'

'I think I might have something for you. We can talk about it over dinner. How about it?'

I paused, letting the silence reverberate a little. 'I guess I could manage that.'

'How about Thursday night then?'

'Let's see.' I looked at my calendar. 'Sure, why not?'

'Busy girl, huh?'

I didn't answer.

'Maybe we'll go out to my cousin's, try a little dancing.'

I could see this becoming a problem already, but I'd have to see what he was offering before I turned him off. We agreed to meet at Luna's in Little Italy and take it from there. It was a work night so I would have a ready excuse for cutting the evening short. Fighting off men I am trying to learn something from doesn't exactly suit the tone of high moral purpose this job is supposed to have. I hate using my sexuality that way, but the bitch of it is, it works.

Bud was black; I was white. That violated one of the three cardinal principles of surveillance. The first is patience. That was the hardest to learn and I guess I'm still learning it. In the years I've been with the SPO I've spent hundreds, maybe even thousands of hours peering through windshields and rear-view mirrors watching doorways some subject has entered and may or may not come out of in my lifetime. It is not only boring, it's an infuriatingly passive activity, sort of like sitting on an egg and waiting for it to hatch, only there is no guarantee it ever will. Add to patience strong bladder control. Whereas it might seem that surveillance is a job women are uniquely qualified to do, with all the training we get in waiting and watching, it is simply not true. A man *in extremis* can almost always find someplace to get out of the car and take a leak. With the dearth of public bathrooms around, women simply have to hold it.

The second cardinal rule of surveillance is to look and behave in such a way as to meld into the environment, so neither the suspect nor anyone else who might knowingly or unknowingly tip them off will suspect your presence. In that sense, it's a passive form of undercover.

And the third rule is never to do anything to compromise rules one or two.

An interracial couple is not the norm in any neighborhood I know of, and Bud and I only did surveillance together in situations where we wouldn't be seen. Add to that the fact that Calvert had probably seen both of us at different times at various arraignments, and we were not the ideal team for this assignment. But we didn't want to let another night go by without seeing what he was up to. While Money had probably kept quiet after his own arrest, news of the search at Mom's would certainly have reached Calvert by now. The duty roster had shown him off over the weekend, so if he had been out of town, or otherwise unavailable, it was just possible he would have gotten the news today. We decided to do a loose tail.

Bud and I left the office at the same time and drove out to Rego Park, where we both left our state cars and picked up my Z. The Ninth Precinct is in the East Village on East Fifth Street between First and Second avenues. It's one way going west, and cops park in diagonal spaces along the street in front of the station house. We arrived a few minutes before the change of tours, double-parking past the precinct near the corner of Second. We could watch for Calvert out of the rear- and side-view mirrors, but even if we missed him, he would have to drive past us when he left.

We only had to wait a few minutes before he lumbered down the steps in front of the building and made his way to the driver's side of a new Lincoln Town Car. 'Not bad for a cop,' I said. Bud laughed. 'They might say that about you, driving this jazzy little number.'

I made a note to subpoena Calvert's bank records again. We had done that each time we had a case on him and hadn't found anything yet. I doubted he would put drug money into his account, but I've seen dumber things. It was always worth a look.

The Lincoln pulled past us and turned left on Second Avenue. I let a few other cars go by and then pulled out after him. He crossed Houston and took Allen over to the Manhattan Bridge entrance. He didn't make any fancy moves and the car was easy to spot. We followed him over the bridge on to Flatbush Avenue, where he made a quick left. I'd staked out Calvert's place before and it was pretty clear by now that he was on his way home. We hung back, letting several cars pass us and watched as he turned into his street. We pulled up by the corner in time to see him exit his car and walk up to the front door of his building.

Now came the part I hated; the killer wait. He could be out in ten minutes or in there all night. It was a five-storey brick building, and we knew Calvert's was the front right apartment on the third floor. We watched and in a few minutes the lights came on. I noted the time in the log and then suggested to Bud that he get behind the wheel so we would look more like a traditional couple to any passers-by as we settled in for the wait. The key is to stay alert. It would be a mistake to assume that the lights indicated Calvert's presence in the apartment in any conclusive way. People often went out and left their lights on, and if he had heard about Mom's, Calvert might well assume he was being watched, in which case he might deliberately do just that. I turned on the radio, WNEW Top Forty. Good for passing the time without being too distracting.

'You come down from your big bust yet?' Bud asked after a few minutes.

'The guys were sweet to get together the posters and all that, but it really shook me up. I'm happy to leave that stuff to the hot shots.'

'Like your friend Collins, you mean?'

That took me by surprise. 'He's not my friend, just another detective,' I said, maybe a little too quickly.

'That's good to hear.'

There was an edge to his voice that went beyond the usual kidding and caught me up short. 'You know something about Collins I don't?'

'No.'

'You sure?'

'You can do a lot better, that's all.'

'I get it. This is Big Daddy Bud Ryan talking.'

'OK, so it's none of my business. There's just something about the man I don't like. He's just too full of himself.'

I felt myself blushing and looked out the window. There *was* something about Collins, but not the way

178

Bud meant, although there was that, too. 'Listen, thanks for taking my part this morning,' I said, changing the subject.

'I know what it would mean to you to get Calvert, but everything I said was true. You think your witness will stick?'

'I don't know. I sure hope so. She's a strange woman, but I feel I can trust her. Maybe it's just that she had the guts to come forward. I've got a good feeling about this one. I think we're finally going to get him.'

'Maybe. But don't let those feelings fool you. Nothing takes the place of good solid police work. That's why I pushed for you. I know you can do it. But I also know you can get carried away.' He paused for a minute but I didn't contradict him. 'And we both know we've got nothing until we've got a body.'

'Right. And all we have to do is sit here and wait for Officer Calvert to lead us right to it.'

Bud chuckled. 'I've seen weirder things.'

'Sure. Right after he gets a sex change.'

We pondered what we were up against in silence. Usually I enjoyed working with Bud, but tonight we were both snappy and on edge. Fortunately, it didn't take long for Calvert to emerge. He came out of the front door of the building, stood for a second on the stoop surveying the block, and then turned toward his car, a little more swagger in his step. I noted the time in the log; he had been upstairs a little less than an hour. Then he surprised us. Instead of getting in the Lincoln, he walked past it and continued toward us. Bud grabbed me in a mock embrace as Calvert approached, his face covering mine in a fair imitation of passion. We had no way of knowing if Calvert looked in our car as he went by. We disengaged in time to see him opening the door to a beat-up green Bonneville. He got in, turned on the engine, and pulled out.

'He didn't adjust the seat or the rear-view mirror,'

Bud noted. Either it was his car or one he had been the last to drive. We let him get a couple of blocks ahead before pulling out ourselves. We didn't allow ourselves to get any closer until we were out in traffic. As soon as I could read the plate I put the number in the log. I'd run it through tomorrow. The plate number and description of the Lincoln fit the information I had from Calvert's MVD; this one must be registered under another name.

We followed Calvert onto the BQE going toward Long Island and got on the Long Island Expressway. He drove at a fairly consistent speed in the far left lane. We stayed in the middle lane so it would be easier to make a move if we had to. We followed him this way for over twenty minutes.

Suddenly Calvert made his move, darting across the three lanes just in time to take the Springfield Boulevard exit. We were pretty sure he hadn't spotted us but equally sure it was an avoidance maneuver. In Calvert's situation, you didn't have to spot a tail to take pains to avoid one. Bud was still behind the wheel. Calvert had made his move on a sharp right turn. Bud cut right to try to follow him and the Z started to shimmy alarmingly. Bud immediately slowed down. We made the exit but not in time to see where Calvert was going after the ramp. Bud sighed. 'I know, I know,' I interjected before he could say anything. 'I'll get it fixed.' The Z was a sports car, designed for fancy maneuvers, but it had recently developed an annoying propensity to go out of control when the wheels were turned sharply to the right.

We drove around for a little bit, taking a right, then a left, then another right, but didn't see him anywhere. Then we doubled back onto the expressway toward Calvert's neighborhood hang-outs in case he was doing the same thing.

Bud was too much of a gentleman to do much

cursing, at least in front of me, so *damn* was all he said. We knew we had done the right thing, hanging back, giving him room, and we also knew we had lost him for the night. We drove up and down Broadway, Myrtle, and Flatbush, checking out the likely local bars, then parked down the street from Mom's for a while, but it was dead as that dog we had found in the refrigerator downstairs. I made a note to myself to check on the plates of the Bonneville, and we called it a night.

Chapter Fourteen

Sunday brunch was a ritual Joe Moskowitz forced himself to continue in order to give some focus to his barren home life since Miriam's death. Ritual was important, his sister, the analyst, was always telling him: routine, structure. He needed something besides work to hang his life on. Blueberry pancakes were probably not exactly what she had in mind, but it was the best he could do. Sunday brunch had always been his meal – Miriam snuggled in the living-room wing-chair with a mug of dark, rich coffee and the Sunday *Times* crossword puzzle while he measured the flour, cracked the eggs, added the milk. Fresh berries when he could get them, real maple syrup – everything from scratch and only the best ingredients. Now he felt he honored her with these preparations, and cooking had become one of the few activities that gave him any pleasure.

He was just finishing the dishes when the call about the SoHo murder came, and he was at the scene in half an hour. He had been called in because of the sexual nature of the crime, and the moment the sheet was pulled aside and he saw the slim, exposed body collapsed against the boxes like a discarded doll, he knew it was the work of his man. The clean, dark hole at the temple consistent with the roulette MO, the youth and attractiveness of the victim, the time of day, and the type of establishment all supported this conclusion, but it was strictly a gut reaction. He would have to question it, but he knew he would never doubt it. He looked at the floral pattern of her torn bodice, the pallor of her bare breast, and felt sick with horror and pity. He realized that he knew nothing of her life, but the artless innocence of her appearance tugged at his heart. She was so very young, and the terrifying last moments of her life were so heartbreakingly apparent. There was no sign of a struggle; the only indication anything had been taken was the empty wallet discarded on the floor. He didn't want to imagine a scenario in which she had acquiesced quietly to her slaughter, too terrified to fight, or perhaps hoping until the last second that her attacker would leave and let her be free. How would her parents be able to go on living, haunted with images like these? It made him briefly glad he and Miriam had never had children. *You are forcing me to prove what's in my piece*, the rapist had asserted in the last fax. Was this the first time he had used live rounds? Or was she just the first loser in a game of Russian Roulette for real? Why hadn't he prevented it? He was overwhelmed with a sense of his own inadequacy.

On Monday he decided to pay a visit to Sergeant Maddy Keitel. The answer, he still believed, was somewhere in the faxes – it had to be. Maybe he had been asking the wrong questions. Sergeant Keitel had been on duty both nights when the faxes arrived; maybe there was something in that. He had checked with Public Relations and learned she had come in at four but he decided to wait until seven before going down to the thirteenth floor. By that time the afternoon shift would have gone home and, hopefully, things would be relatively quiet. He called to let her know he was on his way and she met him at the glass door, introducing herself and shaking his hand firmly.

Tall and athletically built, with short blond hair, she had the kind of open face and blunt, forthright manner that seemed to preclude anything untoward ever happening to her – an asset, no doubt, when she was working on the street. It wouldn't preclude some nut fixating on her, though. There was another officer still on duty, answering phones at a desk in front of the bank of TV monitors. Joe suggested they speak in private, and she escorted him into the plushly appointed Deputy Commissioner's office.

'This is probably about the faxes, right?' she said, as they seated themselves in a pair of imitation-leather armchairs.

'Yes, especially in the light of yesterday's murder.'

'Which one?'

He raised his eyebrows, but then realized that, of course, it wasn't the only murder in the city that Sunday. 'The girl in the SoHo lingerie store.'

'I didn't realize you were making the connection. The subject never murdered before.'

'We think it's him, and we need you to help us with some information. On the two nights you received the faxes, were there any unusual calls?'

'That's like asking if the post office receives mail.'

'Anything particular that you remember?'

She shook her head. 'I don't think there were any tied to your guy. If there had been, I think I would have made the connection right away.'

'What about anyone you knew? Personal or departmental?'

'You mean like friends?'

'Friends, colleagues, co-workers.'

'My girlfriend Tina called. I remember because it was the night of that triple homicide and I had to hang up on her. Departmentally, let me think. A couple of guys out on the street, the usual calls from reporters, fishing expeditions for information. I don't think there was anyone else.'

'What about someone you didn't know but whose voice maybe sounded familiar?'

184

'Run that by me again.'

'The situation is this: both of the faxes came on your shift. The first one was logged in at ten p.m., the second a little after two. Unusual hours to be sending faxes. The subject, it seems, was willing to risk sending them at hours when the copy shops would most likely be deserted and he had a much greater chance of being ID'd. We have to wonder what made it worth the risk.'

'Maybe he just likes taking chances. Or maybe he works late.'

'That's always possible.'

Moskowitz gave her time to absorb the impact of what he was suggesting before going on. She watched him, apparently unperturbed.

'Ever date a police officer?'

'I make it a point to stay away from them.'

'I understand you answer personal ads.'

'I didn't know that was in my personnel file.'

He was glad to get a reaction, even if it was just huffiness about her privacy; maybe now they could get somewhere. 'I'm sorry, Sergeant, I don't like this any more than you do, but we're honestly stuck, and now he's left one dead. We've got to cover all bases.'

'There are plenty of perverts out there for the picking and I've met my share through the ads, but trust me, none of them is capable of what this animal is doing.'

'I appreciate your feelings, but I still need a list of all the people you've dated in the last year.' He took a pad and pencil from his jacket pocket.

'With all due respect, sir, it's none of your business.'

Moskowitz sighed. He couldn't grasp why she was making this so difficult. 'You read the faxes, you know what he's done. We've got to get this man off the street.'

'Great. I finally have a social life after all these years, and you're telling me I'm dating Ted Bundy.'

'I can't believe you can be so flippant. He faxed *you*.'

Their eyes caught for a second and he saw the spark of fear her joking banter was meant to conceal. She looked away and then back. The possibility the rapist could be someone she knew was sinking in. 'A bunch of losers mostly,' she said, reaching behind her head to the soft hairs on the back of her neck. She stopped herself mid-gesture. An odd expression crossed her face. She quickly put her hand in her lap, studied it briefly as if it had suddenly become a strange and willful object, and then looked up at him. 'When do you need the list?'

'It probably won't lead to anything, but we need it as soon as possible.'

Chapter Fifteen

The Calvert investigation had reached the stage where it was necessary to regroup. Last night's surveillance with Bud was important to show Vince I was actively on the case, but now it was time to slow down long enough to go over the files, reread everything, and make sure all the bases were being covered. And I needed to focus myself as well. After the satisfaction of my angry outburst at Steve began to fade, a dull emptiness was taking over. I didn't regret what I had done, but memories of the sweeter moments crept up on me unawares, sabotaging both my sleep and my dreams.

The first thing I did was run a check through intelligence on the plate from the Bonneville Calvert was driving last night. Then I reread my notes from the search at Mom's. During the second search of the basement I had gone back upstairs to interview Mrs Thomson in her apartment. I realized I wasn't likely to get much more out of this woman, although she was one of the few people who could probably tell me everything I needed to know, but I had to try. I asked who paid the rent on the back apartment, and she said it was a man named John Goode. When I asked when she had last seen him, she said she never did, he slipped the rent under the door on the first of the month like he was supposed to, and it suited her fine. She claimed to know nothing about the regular card game being held in the apartment, or about its being used as an illegal gambling club. 'Long's they pay the rent and don't keep me awake nights, it don't matter to me what they do,' she told me. 'I mind my own business and I 'spect they do the same.'

She also denied any knowledge of the recent paint job in the apartment, reiterating her tenant-noninterference policy. Taking another tack, I asked her if she knew why we were searching the apartment and basement. She said no. I told her there had been a shooting and asked if she knew anything about it, and again she said she didn't. I asked her what she was doing on the night of 17 September, and if she remembered hearing anything unusual. She thought for a minute and then said she had been visiting her daughter in South Carolina at that time. I could have pushed it, asking for proof, telling her she could be brought in as a material witness, but it didn't seem worth the trouble. It was clear I wasn't going to get anywhere with this woman. She was a pro. Whoever had dubbed her 'Mom' definitely had a sense of humor.

Getting up to leave, I asked her again if anybody else had a key to the basement. Well, she said, she did give a key to some Spanish fella sometimes because he took down the trash. She thought he was called Gato. A small, skinny Puerto Rican who maybe had a mustache, was all she could, or would, give for a description.

Gato's real name was one of the missing pieces in this puzzle and he seemed to be getting more important. Official sources had turned up nothing. I'd have to ask the guys to check with their street contacts. Mickey was going through his own channels in Atlantic City to see what he could find out about Slick. We still had no information on the whereabouts or true identity of Sweet Thing, either.

I looked over the forensic report from the search. There were twenty-six clear prints lifted off various surfaces in the card room, and they were being checked for matches through the NYSPIN system. Because of the time lapse since the shooting, a person's presence in the room wouldn't prove much, but it would sure help to place Calvert at the scene. The minuscule blood, bone, skin, hair, and brain samples that had been scraped off the walls and from behind the floor molding had all been run through DNA tests. The DNA matched so we were talking about one victim; another confirmation of our witnesses' story. Now all we needed was the rest of the body. Hundreds of other fiber and hair samples had been vacuumed off the carpet, upholstery, and card-table felt, but none was strikingly unusual, and they were too numerous and diverse to indicate anything even if they could be checked against the clothes of possible suspects.

I got up, got my fifth cup of coffee for the day, and came back to my desk and read everything I had from the beginning: Lenora's allegation, Money's interrogation, the works. What we needed first and foremost, of course, was the body – we needed to find it and follow its trail, to learn how it got wherever it was. And it would help to have an outside source, someone aside from the people at that game, who could place Calvert at the scene. A canvass of the neighborhood was one way to go, but the gap of time since the shooting and the type of neighborhood we were talking about made it extremely unlikely we would come up with anything that way. It would be a waste of personnel, and our office was short as it was.

It would be more useful to narrow the field by sitting on the place for a while, see who passes by and who goes in and out of the building. I could do that tonight, I thought, but I needed to stay on Calvert. He was still our best hope for locating Gato and Sweet Thing.

I thought about it for a while and then decided to call Muñoz and get him to put someone from IAD on it. I was still furious about the end run he had tried, but I might as well use his interest in the case to some advantage. After all that speech-making in front of Vince, he could hardly refuse our office the help we needed.

The seventh person at the card game, and one we did have a lead on was the other woman, Auletta. According to Lenora she worked at a check-cashing establishment on Bushwick and I decided to make that my next stop.

Bushwick Avenue is a busy place, lined along both sides with stores of striking ethnic variety sporting names like *TEJADA GROCERY* and *PRODUCTOS TROPICALES*, which, if not exactly thriving, are hanging on, serving the needs of the black and Hispanic population. But the thing that really gets your attention is the potholes, several of them so large that wire garbage drums have been taken off the corners and placed in the craters, where they sit to a depth of one or two feet, blocking entire lanes of traffic. Others are merely foot-deep dents in the asphalt, large enough to lose a wheel in, if not a whole car. Traffic moves at a good clip, the locals having memorized where the worst obstacles are. For a stranger it's like negotiating a minefield. Euphemistically dubbed the 'inner city', ghetto neighborhoods like Bushwick have the deterio-rated infrastructure and lack of basic services of a third-world country.

And close to the same level of danger found in war zones. Any establishment dealing in cash is fair game. Merchants operate at constant risk. The cashiers of take-out Chinese restaurants stand like bank tellers behind counters covered by bullet-proof Plexiglas with slots too narrow for a gun barrel. The setup at the check-cashing place at Bushwick was not too different, with the added assumption that those behind the counter counting the cash were either armed themselves or protected by someone who was.

When I arrived a little after eleven, there was a waiting-line snaking out the door. Behind the Plexi window a tall, knobby black woman was methodically checking IDs and counting out money. Many of the people seemed to be regular customers. They called Auletta by her first name and there was a good deal of sassing back and forth with a distinct edge on Auletta's side. She wasn't taking any guff from anyone and made sure they all knew it. I waited in line with the rest.

'Are you the Auletta who goes to Mom's?' I asked when my turn finally came up.

'You here to cash a check?'

'No, I want to talk.'

'You don't want cash, you better move on. I got a line here.'

I showed her my shield. That silenced her for about half a second. She tossed her head with a clicking sound of disgust and viewed me from the corners of her eyes like I was something too repellent and too trivial for notice. 'I don't talk to no *police*.'

'Your boss won't be too happy when that line is down the block, but I'm not moving until we talk.'

'I don't need no honky bitch comin' in here fuckin' me up.'

'You want to see fucked up? Just keep up the bullshit. You know what's going down. You know I've been asking around, and right now you're not looking good. You can talk to me now, or you can wait until I bring you into the office as an accessory to murder.'

'What murder? I don't know nothin' 'bout no murder.'

'Then you're dumber than I thought. All I'm asking is for you to help me put some pieces together, and you're looking to do time.'

The people in the line behind me had just about had it. 'What you up to, girl? I got things to do,' someone called, and several other voices joined in. Auletta sighed and did another of the head-shaking numbers she used to convey distaste, impatience, and a heavy dose of attitude. 'Hadley,' she said to a man working at a cluttered desk behind her. 'Take over for me will ya?' Then she opened the heavily bolted door at the side and beckoned me in. We moved to a back corner.

'I've got plenty of people telling me you were at Mom's the night Slick was shot. That implicates you in a murder. You can either be a witness or a suspect. It's your call.'

She nodded slightly, which I took as her agreement to answer some questions, but she still didn't have much to say. She admitted to playing cards at Mom's the night of the shooting but insisted she had left before it happened. She said she heard about it after and that's how she knew what night I was talking about. I asked who was there when she left, and after some more prodding she gave me the same names I already had, calling Calvert 'Big Eddie'. Like the others, she said she had no information on anybody's real name or whereabouts and wouldn't even admit to knowing which player had been shot. I tried riling her up. 'You keep telling me you weren't there at the time of the shooting, but that's not what my witnesses say.'

'I don't know who's rattin', but if it be that bitch Lenora, she's a whore and everybody know it.' She stared at me coldly, daring me to contradict her. I didn't give her the satisfaction. We glared at each other in silence for a couple of minutes. Before I left, I told her she'd better not go anywhere because she would be wanted as a witness.

When I got back to the office, Mary Lee had put the report on the Bonneville plate on my desk. The registration was under the name Carlos Perales, with an address listed as 815 44th Street in Brooklyn. It wasn't a name I recognized from any of the Calvert files or from the files on Money's Inn. Still, when I got the chance I would have to ask her to put it through to see if the man had a record.

The interview with Auletta had taken up a lot of time and hadn't gotten me anywhere except to confirm that if we chose to call her she would definitely be an unfriendly witness. It was already two-twenty. I was supposed to hook up with Terry at two-thirty so we would have enough time to get over to the Ninth to pick up Calvert at the end of his shift, but O'Hanlon was nowhere around. Muñoz had returned my call. I called him back, and he reluctantly agreed to put a couple of officers on Mom's. By the time I was done with the call it was after three and still no Terry. I could feel myself starting to fume. I went to the ladies' room, but when I got back to my desk he still wasn't there. I sat down, trying to figure out how long I would give him before leaving. I was too irritated to accomplish anything so I just sat there tapping my fingers, looking at my watch every couple of minutes. Mickey sat at his desk across from me, talking intently on the phone. 'What's the Italian word for suppository?' he said when he hung up.

'Just don't start, OK? I'm not in the mood.'

He raised his eyebrows, but one look at my face told him I wasn't kidding. I looked at my watch. It was three-twenty. I stood up and headed for the door.

'Inn-u-endo,' Mickey called after me. I didn't even smile. When I got to the lobby, Terry was barreling in, looking like an errant choirboy. With his easy Irish-American good looks he could have passed for one of the Kennedy boys. 'Hey, look, I'm sorry,' he said in response to my glare. 'I got hung up.' I didn't answer, and he followed me to Dey Street, where we got in the Chevy. The traffic in lower Manhattan was hellish, as usual, with angry drivers crawling up West Broadway. Canal Street looked even worse, so after waiting through two lights to make a turn, I pulled out of the right lane, barely missing a collision with a delivery truck, and crossed Canal, figuring I could go east on Houston. 'West Broadway turns one-way up ahead,' Terry said, somewhat reluctant to criticize my choice. 'There's bound to be a tie-up. You'd better go right on Grand and left on Greene.' He was obviously more familiar with the streets of SoHo than I was. I caught the light making both turns, slowing us down even more, and when I saw the garbage truck holding up traffic between Spring and Price, I thought I'd scream.

By the time we finally made it to East Fifth Street it was ten after four. I drove slowly down the block past the station house, but neither the Lincoln nor the Bonneville was there. We had missed him. 'I shouldn't have waited for you,' I said through clenched teeth, screeching my tires as I turned sharply on Second Avenue. I took the route Calvert had taken yesterday, and when we got to his house found the Lincoln parked down the block. There was no way to know whether Calvert was home or had simply parked the car and gone somewhere else. Or even if he had taken that car to work. I drove around a little and saw no sign of the green Bonneville.

I pulled past the Lincoln and parked on the other side of the street a few spaces ahead to wait. There was nothing else to do. I sat there fuming for a while, so angry at Terry I could kill him, but trying to force myself to calm down. The guy was relatively new, and seemed to be having a hard time; I didn't want to lay into him. On the other hand, I couldn't tolerate anyone compromising my investigation of Calvert, especially not with Muñoz breathing down my neck, ready to push me out of the way. I turned on the radio, fiddling with the dial to try to find something that wouldn't irritate me. The Bangles were singing 'Walk Like an Egyptian' – all about cops in donut shops saying *way-oh, way-oh*.

A song that usually makes me laugh. Now it didn't strike me as even vaguely entertaining. I knew Terry wasn't completely to blame; I'd been in a funk since Sunday. I tapped my fingers on the wheel more to vent my frustration than to keep time to the music.

It must have given Terry the idea I had cooled down. 'How do I play Vince?' he asked. 'The guy is ripping me apart.'

That did it. I flipped. 'Do you know how long I've been after Calvert? Four years. Do you know how close I am to a murder indictment? And thanks to you we don't know if we're on a surveillance here or just playing with ourselves. If Calvert doesn't come out that door, you're not going to have to worry about Vince, I'm going to tear you apart myself.'

He stared at me in silence for a moment, surprised I was still so mad. 'I told you I was sorry I was late,' he said finally. 'I tried to call but I couldn't get through.' His voice was icy.

'You know, Terry, it's not just today. Vince is on your case with good reason. What's going on with you?'

He didn't answer.

'When you first came to the office I had a lot of hope for you. You were the first one they'd hired in five years that wasn't a cowboy. You were focused, you were methodical, and you seemed committed. What happened to all that?'

'I've got a lot on my mind. Not that it's any of your business.'

'Is it Sarah? I saw the two of you at the Labor Day picnic and you were hardly talking. Are you two OK?'

'I just told you, it's none of your business. Don't push me.'

'OK, fine. Then keep it out of *my* business.'

After that delightful interchange we both retreated into silence, Terry staring out the window distracted and sullen, me trying to fight off a lethal combination of depression and anger. Last night Bud had been touchy and now this. What was it with everybody lately? I kept expecting Terry to relent and start telling me his troubles. I had had that experience a million times before, guys telling me their problems with their wives, their kids, their girlfriends, and sometimes all of the above. The surveillance vehicle often took on the aura of substitute confessional – or analyst's couch. But it didn't happen.

Calvert didn't show until nine-thirty. I would have called it off before then if I could have thought of anything else useful to do. When he came out, he paused on the stoop to survey the block, precisely as he had done the night before, but it seemed a gesture of habitual caution rather than an indication he suspected he was being watched. Apparently satisfied, he walked directly to the Lincoln.

We gave him some slack and then followed as he retraced his earlier route back to Manhattan. Instead of the East Village, though, he went west on Houston Street, over to Hudson, on to Eighth Avenue, and over to Tenth at Fourteenth Street. We were close enough behind him to see him slow down and cruise by the El Caribe, a club between Twenty-third and Twenty-fourth streets. He turned left at the corner and pulled over to park. We drove past and pulled up further down the block. Calvert got out, locked his car, and started back toward the corner. Terry jumped out of the Chevy and followed him on foot, reaching the corner in time to see him entering the club. I drove around the block and pulled up on the other side of Tenth near the corner, where we could watch the entrance plus keep an eye on the Lincoln in case there was a back way out of the club.

We sat and waited, the air between us still crackling with tension and ill will. It seemed clear Calvert was going to hang out there awhile. We hadn't had dinner and normally I would have sent Terry down the street to one of the hundred or so 'Original' Famous Ray's pizza joints for a couple of slices, but I didn't want to push it. After we had watched the club for over two hours, I decided to call it a night.

I drove Terry back downtown to his car and then pulled up to a phone booth on the off chance that Maddy would be home. I sure could use the sight of a friendly face. She sounded kind of down, or maybe tired, when she picked up the phone, so I told her to forget it, we would meet tomorrow night as planned.

'Hey, no way,' she said. 'I'm glad you called. I could use a little moral support myself.'

It was about twenty minutes to Maddy's apartment in Elmhurst, Queens. She lived on Justice Avenue. I found a space around the corner on one of the side streets and walked back, already more cheerful, chuckling to myself about the jokes we used to make when she moved to that oddly appropriate address, making up other locations – Illegal Avenue, Felony Lane, Plea Bargain Boulevard – and laughing about how crowded those places would be. I had to ring her buzzer twice to be heard over the strains of 'We Are the Champions' that were emanating from her third-floor window, drowning out all other sounds of the city. I figured my call must have gotten her in the middle of her workout.

Maddy answered the door in her sweats, but when I got inside I saw the driving beat was supplying the momentum not for her exercises but for one of her periodic cleanathons. Maddy was an intermittent but avid reorganizer. The sectional couch was covered with the kitchen drawers, which had been removed from the cabinets and lined up on the cushions. All the contents from the shelves were scattered about on the tables and chairs, in the process of being sorted.

'I got white or red. What'll it be?'

I threw my coat over the back of a chair while Maddy lifted a drawer containing various-size Tupperware containers and placed it on top of another holding assorted boxes of plastic Baggies so I would have somewhere to sit down.

'You got Scotch?'

'That bad, huh?' She stopped and looked at me. 'Just so happens I have Johnnie Walker Red.'

The place she had cleared for me on the couch looked a little precarious so I removed a couple of baking pans from the rocker and sat down. It was the perfect vantage point for viewing the painting over the couch that I had bought for her birthday a few years ago. It was a bucolic country scene – rolling fields, white farmhouses, picturesque barn, grazing cows, puffy clouds in the distance. It wasn't great art, but I knew why she loved it. You wanted to crawl right in and live there for ever.

Maddy came back, handed me a hefty glass, and sat in the spot intended for me. 'So how long have you been on the hard stuff?' She knew I switched from wine only when the going got tough.

'I told Steve to take a walk,' I said. I didn't think it was uppermost in my mind, but it was the first thing that popped out.

'As in long walk off a short pier?' She had never liked Steve, and liked even less the idea that I was dating a married man. Not that she didn't understand the difficulty of finding the right single one. Her current solution was the personal-ad route.

We both sipped our drinks and contemplated our single state.

'He was a real jerk from the start,' she said after a while. 'I'm glad you finally caught on.'

'It was me that was the jerk. I got taken in by all that tender, caring bullshit. It took me a while to catch on, to see how deceptive it really was.'

'You mean he was good in bed?'

I laughed. 'Yeah, I guess that was it, but somehow I thought it was more. All that waffling, on-again, off-again stuff with his wife kept me off balance. He had the technique down pat. Never promised me anything in so many words, but his lips and hands promised it all. I'm through with married men. Absolutely, for ever.'

'I'll drink to that.' We raised our glasses a little grimly. 'Not that it leaves us a hell of a lot to choose from.'

'C'mon, you've got guys answering your ads all the time. I have to wait weeks to make a date with you myself.'

Maddy laughed but looked uncomfortable. Since her first personal ad appeared she had gone on a constant stream of dates. There weren't many she wanted to see a second time, though. You weed out the Jack the Rippers on the phone, she liked to say, but her psycho detector wasn't always as good as she thought, and she had had some pretty unpleasant experiences. 'Listen to this one,' she said, forcing herself to be more upbeat. 'Last week this guy calls up. He answered my ad and looked OK from the picture he sent so I gave him my number. We're talking on the phone, having a nice conversation about skiing in the White Mountains, and all of a sudden he asks where I work. When I tell him I'm a sergeant in the department he says, "I don't do cops," and hangs up. Give me a break. *I don't do assholes.*' She mimicked his haughty tone of voice and we both burst out laughing.

'Yeah, well, Steve loved the fact I was in policing, so what does that tell you?'

'You just can't win, I guess.' We laughed some more. I'd forgotten how good it was to have someone to laugh with.

'Personally,' I said, 'I'm signing up for celibacy.'

'I'm right behind you, kiddo. I figure I'm going to lay low for a while, especially with that Russian Roulette guy out there.'

The thought of the rapist sobered us both. With everything else going on, I had pretty much forgotten about my conversation with Vince. Now I thought about Maddy's office getting those faxes. The faxes hadn't been made public, so she had no way of knowing I knew about them. Talking about work was touchy for us, and we usually avoided it. Our relationship involved a certain amount of consorting with the enemy, but even when there was no conflict of interest, we were intensely aware of how much police work involved classified information. We forced ourselves to stick to the emotional rather than the factual content of our professional problems and rarely asked each other work-related questions. But the newspaper coverage opened the door a little on this one.

'The department got any leads on this new guy you can share?'

'He's one sick fuck, I can tell you that.' She looked away and started fiddling with the stack of plastic tops next to her. The subject was obviously upsetting, but she didn't seem to want to say anything more, and I didn't push it. It was getting late, we were both tired. It was time for me to go home, but I wasn't ready to leave yet. Maddy got up and poured herself some more wine, offering me a refill, but I was still nursing my first drink. 'It's not Steve,' I said, after she sat back down. 'This case I'm working on is a real bitch. It's really starting to get to me. We have a great case of murder except for a small thing like the body, which I can't seem to locate. There's a bunch of witnesses with names like a losers' *Who's Who*, most of whom I can't find either. My prime witness is scared to death and could go off the deep end at any moment. I'm keeping up a good front with Vince, but I'm afraid I'm losing it.'

'It'll break.'

'I sure hope so. This is a big one. I don't want to let everybody down.'

I was surprised when Maddy started to laugh.

'What's so funny?'

'I'm sorry, I just had this picture of you as patron saint of the SPO.' I frowned, not taking it well. 'Come off the martyr trip, Paris,' she said, cocking her head and studying my appearance as if she was trying to envision it. 'Halos don't go with your outfit.'

I wanted to be annoyed at her for taking what I said lightly, but I laughed too. Maddy always had a genius for making me laugh at myself. It didn't always solve things, but then neither did taking yourself too seriously. I got up to go.

'Want to stay over?' Her way of saying she would see me through the night if I needed it. I shook my head. 'I'll walk you out then. I need milk for the morning anyway.'

'You know a narcotics guy named Jeff Collins?' I asked as we were putting on our coats.

'You want to indict him or marry him?'

'Don't get smart. He's just a guy I'm working with.'

'You work with guys all the time.'

'That's right, I do.'

'So how come he's the first one you ever asked me about?'

'Don't give me a hard time.'

She narrowed her eyes and fixed me with a look of exaggerated scrutiny. Then she shrugged. 'There's a whole shitload of Collinses in the department. If he's the one I'm thinking of, then his father's a captain with Special Ops. I think he has a couple of uncles on the job too. But as for the guy himself, I can't say I know him.'

The streets of the working-class Queens neighborhood were quiet. We walked along Justice and then turned the corner to where I had left my car. We walked slowly in a companionable silence, each lost in our own thoughts. Vehicles lined both sides of the narrow street, parked tightly. Instinctively, I looked toward the end of the block to make sure the Chevy was still there. As my eye traveled the row of automobiles something up ahead on the right caught my attention. It was one of those bits of visual information so small it tends to get lost before it registers. A tiny glowing orange spot on the driver's side of a silver hatchback. I almost dismissed it, but I couldn't figure it out, and when I looked again, I saw it move. We kept walking, my eye focused on that car. The dot flickered and then I knew what it was. I put my hand on Maddy's arm and she stopped, her eyes instinctively following mine. After a minute I heard a soft intake of breath, and I knew she had seen what I saw and had come to the same conclusions. Someone we couldn't see was in the car, wearing dark clothes, scrunched down in the seat, smoking a cigarette. Except for the tiny flame, whoever it was was doing a damn good job of concealing himself.

'You packing?' I asked.

'No,' she said, deadpan, 'I figured I'd pay for the milk this time.' My laughter broke the tension. 'I don't carry all the time any more,' she said. 'I'm just an office cop now. You're the undercover.' Her comment made me think about my upcoming dinner with Randazzo. Maybe he was having me followed, checking me out. It wouldn't be that unusual. If so, I'd led him right to the apartment of a sergeant in the Department. What an idiot I was.

We hesitated on the sidewalk, not quite sure whether to go forward or back. I was lost in my own thoughts, not really thinking about Maddy and how she might be reacting to the possibility we were being watched. 'Maybe it's him,' she whispered, suddenly squeezing my arm. There was a palpable fear in her voice.

'Who?'

'The Russian Roulette guy.'

I stared at her worried face in the darkness. 'Why would it be him?' Then I remembered the faxes to her office.

She looked away. 'I don't know. No reason, the case has just got me spooked, I guess.'

I looked back at the car. Vince had told me to keep it quiet, but it was information we both had, and Maddy clearly needed to talk. Maybe this was one time I could bend the rules. 'I know about those faxes,' I said.

She turned back to me, her eyes registering surprise and relief. 'They came on my shift. Both of them. I handle a lot of weirdos, but this was different. It was like he knew I was there. Did you see what he wrote?'

I shook my head.

'Short, cryptic, and nasty. Both faxes mentioned stories in the papers that quoted me as Department spokesperson. He didn't like what we said about him. Then yesterday Moskowitz from Sex Crimes came in and asked me about my dates. They think maybe it's one of those scumbags I went out with – you know, from those ads. Maybe he saw my name in the paper and made the connection.'

'I heard they thought it was someone in the system. That's why they came to us.'

'They're checking everyone I've had dates with. They want copies of all the replies I got when I answered the ads. I keep thinking about those guys, remembering the most innocuous things they said or did, but now they all seem scary. I'm so afraid, Tina. Maybe that's him watching me. Maybe they're right; maybe he is singling me out.'

'Listen, if this bozo in the car up there is watching us, more than likely it's someone from one of my cases. Like you said, I'm the one in undercover.'

'I didn't think I'd let this dirtbag get to me, but

you don't know what it's like. When one of those faxes comes in it's like he's in the room. I can feel his eyes staring; I can almost hear him breathing. Like someone's sick soul can come right through the machine.'

I put my arm on her shoulder and turned her around. 'I think I'll take you up on your offer to spend the night. We could both use another drink, and that way I won't have to drive.'

She accepted my lame excuse without argument, a barometer of how frightened she really was. We both knew it could be anyone in that car. Someone waiting for a friend, or spying on a lover. A PI doing divorce work. A Randazzo henchman. Or the Russian Roulette rapist. It could be one of her dates, or someone who had glimpsed her name in a newspaper. She didn't need me to tell her that these things happen. Her fear was far from outlandish.

Chapter Sixteen

DON'T BLAME ME, BLAME THE NYPD

I warned them and they failed.
They had the truth and turned a blind eye.

I demand accurate coverage. The burden
is on you.

Tell the quarry to beware.
Only fools are fooled by what they see.

I'm setting my sights.

The *New York Post* published the fax in full on the front page under the headline RAPIST TURNS KILLER/ BRAGS ABOUT IT IN FAX. Joe Moskowitz stared at it, trying to stifle his anger. You couldn't expect the Press not to take advantage of such a stunning piece of sensationalism, not when the rapist had dropped it right in their laps, which, of course, was what he was counting on when he sent it. But they were reveling in it, and the gleefully prominent coverage was guaranteed to fuel the hysteria in the city, already at fever pitch after Sunday's killing. The existence of the previous faxes was not public knowledge, and the papers were having a field day lambasting the police for ignoring the 'warnings', whatever they might have been.

Monday's story, SHOCKING SEX KILLING IN SOHO, had surmised a connection between the murder and the Russian Roulette rapist. Now, with the fax in hand, the *Post* had pulled out all the stops. Actually, despite their headline, the fax contained no confession of murder, but the link was clear. Joe's own certainty that it was the same man had been confirmed by the ballistics report. The bullet, which had entered the victim's left temple, exited behind her right ear, and become embedded in the side of a carton containing a shipment of lace camisoles, was fired from a .38, the same type of weapon described by both Levenson and Bronfman. In fact, Sally Bronfman had been able to identify the weapon used by her attacker quite specifically. During one of their interviews she had suddenly remembered that the rapist, after using the gun to stroke various parts of her body, had held it up for her to admire and identified it as a single-action Colt .38, touting its power and accuracy before putting it to her head.

Not the usual weapon of choice in this age of automatics, but perfectly suited to the psychological profile of the rapist-murderer. It had to be cocked by hand before each firing, slowing firing time – definitely considered a drawback by both cops and criminals, but possibly an appealing feature to the subject, an enhancement to the psychological games he played with his victims. It was a revolver often used by hunters of medium-sized game because of its reliability in the field, and it was more powerful than a semi-automatic of the same caliber. It offered a great deal of control and play in the trigger, plus it had the old-fashioned macho appeal of a six-inch barrel. A perfect weapon for a cowboy or a 'hot dog' – or a psycho who apparently saw himself as part poet, part avenger, and all powerful. The fact that it wasn't a typical police gun did not alter Joe's belief that the killer was in some way connected to law enforcement. The new fax confirmed one thing for him above all. This was a man who would only become more dangerous.

The two news stories had brought an avalanche of calls to the Sex Crimes Unit. Reporters called from all over the country hoping for a quotable tidbit. People called claiming to have evidence or to know someone who looked like the composite, which had been featured along with both articles. Twenty-three women called reporting what they believed to be similar attacks. None of the incidents seemed to be connected from the information supplied, but all would have to be investigated further. The father of one young woman who had been raped, although not necessarily by the same man, wanted Joe to promise to call him when they captured the guy. 'I want to be there with the meat cleaver when you get him so I can cut it off,' he announced in righteous fury. Joe was too exhausted to find it offensive or funny. He hadn't been able to manage even his usual three or four hours of morning sleep since the murder.

The fax to the *Post*, like the first two, was sent from a commercial copy shop. In spite of Joe's feeling that the subject was taking risks in sending the night-time faxes, neither incident had produced a witness who could ID the sender. In the first instance, the harried clerk had been experiencing a rush in spite of the hour; in the second, the clerk who sent the fax had picked up his check the next day and disappeared without explanation. The manager expressed no surprise – that's the kind of job it was. All the faxes were paid for in cash. This time the sender had sandwiched the actual message between two other sheets of paper, which contained copies of the previous articles on the rapes. The cover sheets seemed to be intended to reinforce the rapist's message that he was not happy with the reporting, but also served to make the document he was sending innocuous. It demonstrated a level of caution somewhat at odds with the impulse to reveal himself. On the other hand, it wasn't unlike his seesaw method of taunting the police with clues in the faxes while carefully leaving none at the actual crime scenes. The fax had been taken by a college kid who noticed it because it was going to a newspaper but didn't pay any attention to the contents. He described the sender as an older guy who looked sort of like Dan Quayle. When Joe showed him the composite he shrugged and said the drawing was weird. It could have been the same guy, but he wasn't sure.

All roads seemed to be leading nowhere; it was hard not to get discouraged. He had checked out the officers involved in the raid on the chop shop where Gordon Jaeger's Prelude was found and none in any way fit the description of the rapist. But you didn't get anywhere in policing believing in coincidence – there had to be some connection. It was possible someone on the force who had access to crime records and incident reports was involved, but that would include half the Department. The gray hatchback Denise had observed outside her building immediately after the rape had become his most promising lead. Ann had been assigned the task of going over the computer printouts from Motor Vehicles, checking the colors and makes of cars receiving tickets that day.

Two desk officers were checking on possible suspects whose names or descriptions were being steadily called in. An awful lot of people had it in for someone in this city, or thought their neighbors looked suspicious, or were just overzealous in their desire to help. But in among the morass of irrelevant leads the identity of the killer could be lurking. He really couldn't afford to dismiss any possibility out of hand. And then there was Sergeant Keitel. He had just received her list, all the names she could remember. There were over thirty. He would run them all through the computer to see if any had records, then begin the laborious process of locating and checking them out.

He got up and went to the cooler for some cold water and popped a couple of Bufferin to take the edge off the dull headache that had become his constant companion. When he got back to his desk Ann was standing there, a printout several pages long in her hand. 'All the tickets given in the Bleecker Street area on September fifth,' she said. One entry in the barely legible list was circled in red. He put on his reading glasses and looked at it closely.

PLATE ID: 308 MZO. MAKE: TOYOTA. COLOR: GRAY. TYPE: PAS. OWNER ID: 0120246161234207938. EXP DATE: 4/5/88. OWNER NM: O'HANLON, TERRANCE P. DMV ADDR: 234 HOLLIS AVE.

'Any connection to the Department?'
'SPO,' she said.

Chapter Seventeen

I had tailed Calvert two nights now and was getting nothing but frustration. It didn't do much good to know where he was going unless I could find out what was happening when he got there. It was too soon to know if the El Caribe was a regular hang-out, but I put in a call to Jeff Collins anyway and asked if the SNU had anything on the club. He said he'd get back to me. Among the pile of papers on my desk was a message that Lenora had called yesterday afternoon, but there was no answer when I called. I wrote up the report on last night's surveillance and was trying to decide what to do next when the phone rang.

'Paris, it's Collins.'

'That was quick.'

'I've got something for you. Meet me at Junior's.'

'Why Junior's?'

'I'm hungry.'

That didn't answer why not Mo's Deli or Vinnie's Pizza, but Junior's is just over the Brooklyn Bridge and serves a mean hot pastrami sandwich, not to mention cheesecake to die for, so I was game. I looked at my watch. It was just after eleven. By the time I got there it would be just about time for lunch. I told Collins to give me about forty-five minutes.

The restaurant was filling up when I arrived, and the long deli counter at the entrance was already packed with workers handling takeout orders. A good proportion of the customers and most of the waiters were black, reflecting changes in the neighborhood that housed this bastion of New York Jewish cuisine – if that word can be applied to great deli food. I told the hostess I was meeting someone. 'Yeah, he told me to look out for you,' she said, giving me a once-over that made me wonder how I had been described. She led me past the lunch counter through the large first-floor room and around a divider. Collins sat at a booth against the far wall looking natty in a gray tweed sports jacket and French blue shirt that definitely did something for his eyes. He looked up from the plate of blintzes in front of him as I approached. 'I told you I was hungry,' he said between bites. I sat down and the waitress handed me the huge laminated menu she was holding. I gave it a cursory glance. 'I'll stick with the hot pastrami,' I said. 'On rye. And an order of onion rings.'

'Make it extra lean,' Collins added. I tried not to be annoyed. He had an assurance that verged on arrogance, which I guess was why Bud took such a dislike to him, but it was so offhand it was almost tongue-in-cheek. But maybe that was something only a woman would see.

'The onion rings are lousy,' he confided between bites when the waitress had gone. He definitely wasn't the type I would have picked out to be a deli maven, but obviously he was a regular here. The restaurant wasn't far from the Brooklyn courts so it really wasn't so odd – a lot of cops and lawyers frequented the place. 'I've done my time in Brooklyn,' he said, as if reading my mind.

I nodded. He had a way of making me feel awkward and tongue-tied.

The waitress came back with bowls of pickles, pickled green tomatoes, and coleslaw. She poured coffee for me and a refill for him. 'Don't wait,' I said, indicating his half-eaten order, 'it'll get cold.' It sounded more sarcastic than I intended. As for what we were there for, I had to wait for him to tell me that. I stirred milk into my coffee, staring longer than necessary into the cup. God knows, I spent most of my life with men – investigators, detectives, cops, SAAGs – in every kind of situation imaginable, and I rarely thought much of it, but the simple act of sitting opposite Jeff Collins in a restaurant was making me nervous.

My sandwich finally arrived. I slathered the bread with their classic, tangy, bright gold mustard and took a large bite. Meat slid from the sides. It was delicious, and impossible to eat with any finesse. The pastrami, trimmed of all visible fat, was wonderfully tender. 'You were right about the extra lean,' I said, wiping my mouth. The onion rings arrived – large, artificial-looking circles – and I could see he was right about that too.

'I don't want a repeat of Money's,' he said, when he was finished with his blintzes.

'What's that supposed to mean?'

'You know, we set the trap and you guys at SPO get to make the kill.'

'I thought you knew . . .'

'Yeah, yeah, you told me. I'm just saying this has got to be different. We have a man in there and I don't want it blown.'

'I've been tailing Calvert and I think it's one of his hang-outs. The office has no interest in the club. I just need to get someone in there to get close to him.'

'My man's already there. Let him do it.'

'Calvert's a cop. It has to be SPO or IAD, you know that.'

'There are exceptions.'

'Listen, we have to get close to Calvert fast. It's just going to compromise your guy. And a woman undercover has a much better chance getting near him without being obvious.'

'There's a lot of heavy dealing going down in there. Maybe your man Calvert is involved.'

'It's not the angle we're going for right now, but I don't see why our interests can't coincide. I send someone inside with a wire. You and I can monitor together. Whatever SNU gets out of it is gravy.'

He leaned back against the booth and looked me steadily in the eye. Not exactly staring down, more like taking my measure. 'What are you in this for, anyway, Paris?'

'The guy's a scum. You know that.'

'I didn't just mean Calvert.'

'You mean policing? The SPO?' I shrugged. There was something compelling about the guy, but I wasn't ready to wear my idealism on my sleeve. 'What about you? What are you in it for?'

He laughed, but gave me no more of an answer than I had given him. 'I guess you're OK, Paris,' he said finally. 'Anyway, after Kibodeaux I owe you.'

Bud and I tailed Calvert again that night; a repeat of the events of the night before. Same club, same time. We sat outside the El Caribe for a couple of frustrating hours and went home to bed. I had to get someone inside. Vince's door was open when I came in Thursday morning. 'Hey, boss, you got a minute?' I said, standing in the doorway.

'If it's about your expense report, if they kicked it back it's not my fault.'

'I need something on Calvert.'

'You mean you haven't got him in cuffs yet?'

'C'mon, Vince, don't break my heart, or any other part of my anatomy.'

He laughed, enjoying the repetition of his own wit.

'Listen,' I said, 'we've tailed Calvert two nights in a row to the same club at the same time. We don't know if Sweet Thing and Gato are in there with him, we don't know what he's doing. We have to get someone inside. You know it can't be me.'

'You have someone in mind?'

'How about Zapata?'

'Am I hearing right? I thought you hated Nydia.'

'It's the El Caribe. I need someone Caribbean who can get close to him. Do you have a better suggestion?'

'Two nights isn't exactly a trend. How do you know he'll even show up?'

'We'll tail him, and if he goes somewhere else we can send Nydia wherever he ends up.'

'Did you check the place out?'

'I ran it by Detective Collins. The place is definitely dirty. They've got a man inside now but I don't think it's a good idea to try to use him, even if he would agree to give evidence against another cop.'

'If I give you Zapata you'll need someone else with you on the outside. What are you trying to do, empty out the whole office for this one?'

'Somehow I knew you'd say that. Collins is going to ride with me. If he picks up something SNU can use, all the better.'

'You two are really getting cozy. First you save his ass, then he gives you a tip. What do they call that? A symbiotic relationship. Sort of like a rat and a python.' He chuckled at his own image. 'I don't want to hear any complaints about Nydia. You know the way she is.'

'Yeah, I know, brain dead. It's going to be very low risk. All she has to do is observe and wear a wire. I'll hear what's going on. If it doesn't sound right I'll bring her out.'

'All right. I'll make the arrangements. How long do you want her? She's not going to sit on this thing every night.'

'Tomorrow and Saturday should do it.'

'Just because you don't have a date on Saturday night, you think she doesn't?'

I didn't bother to answer.

*　　*　　*

There wouldn't be any case without Lenora, so I decided I'd better try to reach her again. I dialed and waited while the phone rang eight or ten times, hung up and tried again. This time I let it keep ringing, more out of annoyance than because I expected her to answer – she called and left me messages, but was never there when I called back. Although, in fairness, with everything else going on, I hadn't tried as often as I should have. After what must have been fifteen rings, someone apparently picked up but gave no greeting. 'Hello,' I said, into the silence. 'Lenora, is that you? This is Tina Paris.'

There was no immediate response. I almost hung up, when I heard a faint voice. 'I'm here.'

'I'm sorry I didn't get back to you sooner,' I said. 'How are you doing?'

'You said you'd be there,' she said weakly.

'I told you I was sorry. Is everything all right? Did something happen?'

'The word is out. He know I been talkin' to you.'

'We've been interviewing several people in regard to this case. You're not the only one we have contact with, and I'm sure Officer Calvert knows that. He wouldn't be stupid enough to do anything to you now.'

'So how come my phone ring all night long? I pick up and they hang up, or I hear this breathin'. I know it's Eddie makin' sure I don't sleep, tryin' to scare me.'

I should have known Calvert would try something. Compared to the other things he'd done it didn't seem like much. But he knew his people, and the implied threat was apparently enough. 'If you want, I'll help you get your phone number changed. We'll get you an unlisted one.'

'I don't want my number changed,' she said, her voice stronger, her innate orneriness perking her up.

I took a deep breath and tried to muster my patience. After all these years, my tolerance for this kind of witness was just about tapped out. 'Lenora, how can I help you if you won't take my suggestions?'

'I don't want your help. I want you to leave me alone.'

I could hear sobs welling in her voice. She was building up to a nice head of hysteria. 'You know I can't do that. We have to work together on this.'

'I ain't workin' with you no more. You ruinin' my life.'

I could feel my pulse quickening. I was building up to a nice head of anger myself, but I forced myself to maintain a reasonable tone. 'Lenora, at this point we're too far into the case. I need you to stay calm so you can testify.'

'Then I want a lawyer. Any criminal can have a lawyer, right?'

'If it will make you feel better to have the advice of an attorney, that's fine. But you are not a criminal. You're a victim and a witness in this case. No-one is accusing you of anything.'

'Yeah, then how come it's me gets treated like trash out on the street? I was wrong. I should never have called no police.'

'You did the right thing, Lenora. You witnessed a murder, you were assaulted yourself. Pretending those things didn't happen wouldn't change anything. You don't want to walk around scared of him the rest of your life.' She didn't say anything so I pulled out all the stops. 'Remember what you told me about how he was the Law and shouldn't be able to act that way; how you didn't want your little boy, Kari, growing up in that kind of a world?'

'I remember,' she said, quiet again. Her son seemed to be the one sure way to get to her.

'Let me call the phone company for you.'

'No, I can do it.' I heard her sniffing and blowing her nose.

'OK, but do it today. And call the new number in to me. Let's try this and see how it goes.'

Al Randazzo was already seated at a round table at the back of Luna's small narrow main floor when I arrived at seven. I was a little surprised by his choice. It was one of the old-time originals of Little Italy, but it had long ago become a tourist attraction, with people lining up outside on weekends waiting for tables. The décor featured crude murals of the Tuscan landscape, Chianti-bottle candlesticks, and checked tablecloths – Italian restaurant clichés, forgivable because it was one of the prototypes. Flashy as Randazzo was, I would have expected him to choose one of the fancier places that had sprung up on Mulberry, one with an indoor fountain, maybe, and marble floors.

He nodded to me as I sat down and offered a glass of Chianti from a bottle he already had open on the table. The waiter came over almost immediately with a basket of bread sticks and hot garlic bread. 'You like seafood?' Al asked. I nodded. That was the last I was consulted. He gave the order in Italian, and I just had to wait till the food came to know what I would be eating. 'You're gonna like the food here,' he said. 'Just like your grandmother used to make.' I smiled. He took a piece of garlic bread, bit into it and passed the basket to me. 'So, you got something to tell me?' he asked.

'Like what, Al?'

'Like why'd you cut out on me like that. I introduce you to the best people, try to do right by you, and you split out. You embarrassed me.'

He kept his eyes on my face as he waited for the answer. I did my best to look wide-eyed and candid. 'Do you know the band?'

'Nah, I didn't have anything to do with that. The union sent them over.'

It was the answer I was counting on. 'I used to go

out with the drummer, Nicky Caruso.' Al was giving no eye contact now. 'You know him?' I asked, making sure, thanking myself for finding out the guy's name.

'No. So what?'

His tone was not encouraging; I knew I had to make it good. 'Nicky and I . . . well,' I looked down at the cloth, moving some crumbs around with my finger. Then I looked up into his eyes. 'He was kind of rough on me. He liked to get physical, you know. It took me a while, but I finally got away from him. It was a shock to see him at the dinner. And I figured if he saw me with you, he'd start in. Instead of waiting around for him to do something stupid, I split.'

He poured himself another glass of wine and took a sip before saying anything, giving himself time to process my story. 'You should have said something. I would have taken care of it.'

'I know the guy,' I said. 'I didn't want trouble. I knew it would be better if he just didn't see me. Better for everybody.'

Al shook his head. 'A nice girl like you, you don't let some *sfaccim* fuck with you. Excuse my mouth.' I nodded, my expression earnest; I knew I had played it right. 'You got protection?' he asked.

'Like what?'

'Like what?' He shook his head with a look of fond amusement, at my *naïveté* this time. 'Like a gun. There's lots of nuts running around out there, and I don't mean just your friend.'

I looked thoughtful, taking my time with this, needing to make sure the tape would pick it up clearly. 'You know my dad tells me the same thing,' I said, 'about getting a gun.' I hesitated. 'I just don't know.'

The innocence I was spooning out was about as subtle and authentic as Cool Whip on a cannoli but Randazzo didn't seem to notice. He leaned back in his chair and pulled his suit jacket open just a fraction. 'You see this?'

His hand uncovered a small automatic attached to his belt. 'This is like my American Express card. I never leave home without it.' He sat back up, chuckling at the joke.

A steaming plate of hot antipasto arrived. We sat in silence as the waiter served out the portions. 'I just don't know what to do,' I said when he was gone. 'Where would I get one? Don't you need a license?'

Al laughed out loud. 'Listen, doll, you say the word and I'll get you one. And don't worry about no license. Ninety per cent of the guns on the streets don't have no licenses. Just don't tell anyone your Uncle Al is doing this for you.'

'Sure, Al,' I said, smiling into his eyes, 'as long as you teach me how to use it.'

After this it was smooth sailing. Randazzo's male ego had received the right massage and was in rare form. He bragged through the rest of the meal, which included exquisitely tender fried scungilli, paper-thin veal scaloppini with spaghetti on the side, and spinach sautéed in garlic, claiming to know every political and judicial bigwig in the city. First names spewed from his lips like cheese from a grater – including Neil and Timothy, Dandrell's son and law clerk – and I didn't push for anything more. This was our first private encounter. I wanted him to stay relaxed, to get more and more comfortable with me. There would be plenty of opportunities for him to incriminate himself – and others.

We wrapped up the meal with espresso and anisette, and he told me he was going to help me find work in the city system. I said I was hoping for something that would let me use my experience with lawyers, I'd had a lot of contact with them in the insurance business. 'You want a judge in Queens,' he said. 'That way you won't have to travel. Let me see what I can do.'

I didn't see the check but Al must have tipped

heavily, judging by the profusion of thank-yous from the waiter as we left. Out on the street, he asked me back to his apartment. I refused as nicely as I could. I let him walk me to the Z, which was parked around the corner. As I reached in my purse for the key, he put both hands on my shoulder and stepped toward me. I turned my head aside so his kiss became a brush on the cheek. I quickly thanked him for dinner and moved around to open the driver's side. 'Call me,' I said with a smile, and got in, knowing the surveillance team would be torturing me tomorrow with reminders of this moment.

When I saw Nydia's undercover outfit on Friday I didn't know whether to laugh or cry – a Lycra miniskirt with a bare-midriff sleeveless top, not enough fabric to cover a baby's bottom. The finishing touch was a pair of sky-high black platform shoes. Using her sexuality did not create any moral conflicts for Nydia. Compared to her, Julia Cipriani looked like a nun. 'What can possibly be going on in your head?' I asked her. 'I told you you're going to be wearing a transmitter. Where do you think you're going to put it?'

'You said you wanted me to get close to Calvert. Believe me, honey, this will do it.'

'Come with me,' I said. I walked her over to the tech room, where we signed out the kel for the night. I handed her the metal device and told her to put it on. I was sitting at my desk about fifteen minutes later when Stacey came over and said Nydia wanted to see me in the ladies' room.

'I don't know where it can go,' Nydia said when I walked in. I turned her around, inspecting her more closely. The kel, a micro transmitter, was smaller than a cigarette pack, but there wasn't enough give in that top or skirt to hide an ear-ring. Something devilish came over me. 'I know just where to put it.'

She looked at me dumbly. 'Take off your skirt,' I told her.

She gave me a funny look. 'You nuts?'

'Don't go ballistic on me, Nydia. You knew you were going to have to wear one. Now pull down your panty hose while I get the surgical tape.'

'You're a sadist, you know that?'

'You bring out the best in me.' I couldn't help smiling as I taped the kel to her crotch.

Chapter Eighteen

Joe Moskowitz sent over to Motor Vehicle for a copy of Terrance O'Hanlon's license photo. *Face forward, focus on a point midway up the wall* – no-one ever looked their best in these. Everyone looked harder, a little like a criminal – the resemblance to a mug shot was inescapable. He told himself this as he stared at O'Hanlon's picture, trying not to read character into it, just deciding if the face could fit the descriptions provided by the victims. Good, even features, a little on the boyish side, hair color listed as blond but looking more brown. Not strikingly handsome, but certainly a man who might be described as good-looking. Nothing in the photograph ruled him out.

Joe sighed. He could hardly say he was sorry to have a suspect, but though it fit his theories on the case, he was sorry to have it be a law enforcement officer. If O'Hanlon was their man, the Press would have a field day. An investigator with the élite Special Prosecutor's Office, sworn to rout out the crooked cop, the immoral judge, the breach of public faith. Not that the Press was the point, it was simply a reprehensible idea, totally insupportable. And then there was his old friend Vince. Bruno would take it hard, something like this happening in his agency, under his stewardship, tarnishing a distinguished career as it neared the end. He wouldn't feel any personal blame; Joe knew him better than that. In the days when they were young hotshots together, Vince had kidded him unmercifully about his own tendency to take responsibility for everything –

'Hang on to your hats, or better yet your yarmulkes,' Vince would say. 'We're going into Jewish guilt mode.' No, Vince would simply see it as unfair, a rotten break. Vince was a much more political animal than he was. Which was why, Joe couldn't help musing, Vince was Chief Investigator at SPO while he was still a detective, albeit a respected one.

He pushed back his chair, got up, went into the men's room, and splashed himself with cold water. Then he rubbed his skin vigorously with a paper towel and stared in the mirror. Faces. What did they tell you? His looked rumpled but not unfriendly, like a well-worn couch. Everything he had lived was there, Jewish guilt and all. He smiled ruefully. Vince was right: now he was feeling guilty for having to foist this news on his friend. If O'Hanlon was their man, what he ought to be feeling was relief. But it was too soon for relief – or for laying it on Vince. A traffic ticket proved nothing, really. Denise's observation gave weight to the connection, but the guy could have been on that street for any number of reasons. He didn't believe in coincidence as a principle but, of course, it existed; he had nothing he could bring the guy in on, certainly not enough evidence to charge him; he couldn't even, in good conscience, show his picture to the victims yet. But if this was their guy, he would never be able to live with himself if another assault occurred while he pussyfooted around. He decided to put on a twenty-four hour tail.

Terrance O'Hanlon lived in Lake Success, just over the Queens border in Nassau County, not far from Queens College. Joe noted this with a pleased sense of things falling into place as he arranged for the surveillance team, but again, he reminded himself that it proved nothing. Most cops lived somewhere on the Island or in the less affluent towns of Westchester. They weren't allowed to live out of state, so Jersey was out, and few chose the city itself. The first team picked O'Hanlon up after work Friday afternoon and tailed him from Dey Street onto the BQE and from there to the Long Island Expressway. He made one stop at a mini-mall near his home, went into Price Chopper, came out with a bag of groceries, then went into Blockbuster Video and emerged ten minutes later, having apparently chosen the evening's entertainment. After that, he drove directly to his garden-apartment complex, parked the car, entered his apartment, and remained there the rest of the night.

The second shift took over in the early hours of the morning. Terry did not leave the apartment until 11 a.m. Saturday, when he drove to the Fitness First Health Club on Northern Boulevard. He entered the health club with a gym bag, remained an hour and a half, and then drove directly back to his apartment.

Joe listened to the reports. Nothing unusual, certainly, except that O'Hanlon had spent all his time since leaving work alone. Even in the health club, where one of the men had followed him, he did a solitary workout and was not observed communicating with anyone. Was it the strange behavior of an alienated and possibly psychopathic individual, or the normal actions of a man who simply wanted to relax on his own after a hard week? It was impossible to read, but Joe was too nervous to sit home waiting for the men to call in. The three most recent incidents had occurred on or immediately after a weekend. All the assaults appeared to have been carefully planned, with indications the rapist had scouted the locations and possibly the women as well. He decided to take the afternoon-to-evening shift himself and called in Ann Gallagher to partner him.

When they took over at four, the subject had been in his apartment for over three hours. As they sat and waited, Joe considered the possibility that O'Hanlon could leave without being seen, but they had a clear view of his car and of the driveway entrance to the complex. He believed he would recognize the man if he left in another vehicle, and the previous teams insisted they had been careful and had given him no cause to suspect he was being followed.

It was almost five when O'Hanlon finally left the house again. He was neatly, even nattily, dressed, a tan trenchcoat open to reveal wool slacks and a tweed sports coat. They followed him on to the Northern State Parkway, keeping several cars back. He exited shortly after the Northern ran into the Grand Central and drove through Forest Hills to Queens Boulevard. He appeared nervous, tapping the wheel as he drove; several times they noticed him checking his watch as if he were late for an appointment. He took a left turn off the Boulevard on to Sixty-fifth Road. They had to wait for the light to make the turn themselves but were able to catch sight of his car turning left onto Saunders Street. Joe drove slowly, not wanting to lose him but more afraid of calling attention to their car.

O'Hanlon's Toyota was parked up ahead. Joe pulled past, but there were no other spots on the block. He double-parked about ten cars ahead. Ann adjusted the mirror for a better view and made a pretense of primping in front of it as she watched. O'Hanlon sat, his hands gripping the wheel. He made no move to get out but looked over at the entrance to the red-brick apartment building on his right every couple of minutes. After a while, he got out of the car and walked up to the entrance. Ann immediately jumped out of the car and walked back toward the building, but before she reached the doorway he had turned and was coming out. She continued in, observed nothing unusual and pretended to ring one of the buzzers while she read the names. None of them was familiar.

O'Hanlon was already back in his car when she emerged. Almost immediately, however, he got out again and started walking back to the corner of Sixty-fifth. She paused, gave him a minute, walked to the corner herself, and observed him entering the deli at the end of the block. In a few minutes he started back up the street, gingerly sipping from a takeout coffee. She got back into the car with Joe and watched in the mirror as he got in his own car. He sat for several minutes sipping the coffee. After a while he lit a cigarette, took a few drags, then suddenly rolled down the window, tossed the cigarette, started the car, and pulled out.

Joe did not like the idea of him driving by with the two of them just sitting there. He saw another car pulling out of a space near the next corner and pulled up to it so that he appeared to be parking when O'Hanlon went by. They watched as he took the next left back to Queens Boulevard but didn't follow immediately. They had to give him slack or he would almost certainly pick up on the tail. By the time Joe reached the junction, there was no sign of the gray hatchback. Joe turned to Ann. 'East or West? Toward the city or back toward the Island?'

'Pull up a bit.'

He pulled out as far as he could without imperiling the oncoming traffic. Ann leaned forward and peered intently, first to the left and then to the right. 'I don't know. Try right. The road curves a bit and I can't see as far.'

Joe made the turn, speeding up. There was no sign of O'Hanlon's car for several blocks. Then he spied a gray hatchback double-parked up ahead, but as he slowed down he could see it wasn't a Toyota. He moved into the middle lane, out of the way of the local traffic. 'Keep an eye on the side streets,' he said to Ann as he speeded up again.

They were almost to Kew Gardens by the time he

saw the gray hatchback up ahead. O'Hanlon was in the middle lane but moving to the right, apparently preparing to turn. Joe eased up behind him, made the next turn with him and followed him through a warren of back streets until he slowed down, looking for a space. He parked and walked toward another anonymous-looking red-brick building. Joe did not want to risk being in front of him again. 'Take the driver's seat,' he said to Ann as he pulled over. Grabbing the folded newspaper he always kept next to him in the car, he got out and followed nonchalantly as O'Hanlon entered the building.

O'Hanlon had apparently pushed one of the buzzers and was waiting for a reply. As Joe reached over and pushed a button at random, a female voice came over the intercom. O'Hanlon leaned closer. 'It's me, Terry.' The buzzer sounded immediately and Terry pushed the door open. Joe entered along with him and ambled behind him to the elevator. O'Hanlon gave a brief backward glance but registered no suspicion. In the elevator, Joe waited as Terry pressed '4' before stepping up and pressing the floor above.

As he got out of the elevator on Five, Joe could hear a door opening and the murmur of voices. He ran down the stairs in time to see the door of the apartment across from the elevator closing. He didn't stop but checked the letter of the apartment below it. 'D'. Back in the vestibule he looked at the name beside 4D. S. Olitsky.

'A friend, female,' he informed Ann back in the car. 'She let him in almost immediately so was apparently expecting him. Or else he drops by often.'

'None of the Roulette victims knew their assailant.'

'None so far.'

They sat in silence for a long time. They had been on stake-outs together before, but they weren't the kind of partners that responded to the womblike intimacy of the surveillance vehicle by sharing confidences. The longer they waited the more likely it seemed they were there for the evening – perhaps for the night. 'You want a sandwich?' Joe asked. His own stomach was growling, but he didn't really want to risk one of them leaving the car and was relieved when she shook her head. 'We're too far from anything to take the chance.'

Joe turned on the radio, ran through the stations and turned it off. It was all just noise, abrasive and irritating. 'Christ, I hate this. What if we're sitting on the wrong guy and the real killer is out there stalking someone else.'

'I started checking the men on Keitel's date list,' Ann said. 'I can't believe people do that, answer those ads, go out with perfect strangers, especially a police sergeant.'

Joe grunted. 'There's a lot of lonely people out there.'

'I will say that the majority I've interviewed so far seem to be quite ordinary men. Of course, not the kind you would meet at the church supper.'

'Is that where you meet your dates?'

She didn't answer and Joe was surprised to see that she was flustered. Even the darkness of the fall twilight didn't conceal a distinct blush. He smiled. Maybe she did have a private life, after all.

She pulled herself straighter and looked him in the eye, all business. 'Back to the subject at hand. There is actually one person who stands out. George Bender, an accountant. Thirty-eight. Medium build, fits the general description. His MO is to date women in policing. Sergeant Keitel went on two dates with him on consecutive weekends in May. I interviewed him at his home, and he claims to have dated fifteen female police officers. He seems to think it's some sort of record.'

'So he's a copophile?'

Ann took a minute to register this as a joke, then scowled. 'I'm not sure it's a matter for humor.'

'Laugh or you eat your gun in this job.'

Ann's frown deepened, but she didn't reply.

'Did Sergeant Keitel say why she stopped seeing him?'

'She said, and I quote, "The last time I met someone that lively was at the morgue."'

Joe nodded, remembering Maddy's blunt, irreverent replies to his own questioning. 'Check him out anyway. He could be a Jekyll and Hyde.'

They were just about convinced O'Hanlon was spending the night when he emerged from the building, walked purposefully to his car, and peeled out with a squeal of tires that did not indicate a pleasant end to the evening. The urge to ensure that S. Olitsky was all right fought with the fear of losing the tail. Then Joe noticed the light at the end of the block turning red as O'Hanlon's car approached it. He jumped out of the car, ran into the building and pressed 4D. 'Enrico's Pizza,' he called when she answered. 'I didn't order anything,' she said, her voice strong.

'This 4C?'

'Wrong buzzer,' he heard her answering as he rushed back to the car. Ann was still in the driver's seat as they followed Terry on to the center lane going west on Queens Boulevard. To their surprise, he retraced his route back to the apartment on Saunders Street. They parked on Sixty-fifth and watched as he pulled up in front. He would certainly recognize Joe, so it was Ann who followed him in. Terry had had much less time to take in her features, and if he did remember seeing her, he would probably assume she lived in the building. She was close enough for him to hold the door open as she entered behind him. She mumbled a thank-you, her head down as she rummaged in her purse in an apparent attempt to locate her keys. As he reached for the buzzer, she glanced up just long enough to get the number. There was no response. He rang again, waited a second, and then pushed past her out the door. When he was gone, she quickly checked the name, then watched as he got in his car and pulled away before emerging herself.

'T. Paris,' she said as Joe eased the car around the corner. He thought for a minute, running reports through his head. It rang some kind of bell, but he couldn't think what. They followed Terry back to Lake Success and called in for their replacements.

Chapter Nineteen

This time it was Nydia who rode with me while we tailed Calvert from the precinct to his home and then to the El Caribe. I thought I would go mad with impatience waiting outside his apartment building, especially with Nydia spouting inanities beside me. It was like being in Dante's Inferno, doomed to a circle of hell created just for investigators. Collins was waiting at his office, and when we saw Calvert enter the El Caribe I gave him a call. We met him around the corner on Twenty-third Street off Tenth Avenue, where we could keep an eye on Calvert's Lincoln parked out front. Collins pulled up in a silver Trans Am about fifteen minutes later. We checked the sound on the kel one last time and Nydia got out to totter on her stilettos over to the club. I locked up the Chevy and got in with Collins, pushing aside several discarded Styrofoam cups that littered the passenger seat – the standard debris of a surveillance vehicle. After Nydia was inside we cruised by the club, parked on Tenth by the corner of Twenty-fourth Street, with a good view of the club entrance, and settled in for what could be a long night.

The radio in the car crackled with the transmission from the kel. The ambient noise from the bar – music, voices, laughter, the bangs and clangs of glasses on tables, chairs and bar stools being moved, the thump of dancers' feet on the floor – melded to create an indecipherable assault. After a few minutes, though, our ears started to get used to the jumble and we were able to make sense out of at least some of the sound. Nydia's voice, whenever she spoke, came through loud and clear. She made her way to the bar and we heard her order a Sex on the Beach as other voices ordered drinks around her. A male voice, thin and whiny, came through the din. 'You're sure lookin' hot tonight. Where's your old man?'

'Why, you wanna buy my next drink?'

'What's it gonna cost?'

'How much you got?'

'What in the hell?' Collins said. 'She trying to get him on solicitation or what?'

'I wouldn't put it past her.' I was already regretting my promise to Vince not to complain.

She seemed to move away from the bar and closer to the band. We heard her laughter coming over the beat but could no longer make out any words.

'She's just stupid enough to start dancing, if she could do it in those heels,' he said.

'I don't think the shoes are the problem.'

He looked at me quizzically, but I didn't explain.

The music and noise continued. If Nydia was getting anything, we certainly weren't. I looked at my watch; it was after eleven-thirty.

'You have to call home or something?' Collins asked, reacting to the gesture.

'What, to talk to my goldfish?'

'Still on the prowl?'

'Not me, I've been bitten too many times.'

'I know what you mean. I practically had to chew my foot off to get out of the last trap I stepped in.'

'Separated?'

'Divorced. Over a year now.'

'How come? You play around?'

'You think I seem like the type?'

'I think you *look* the type. Although I've known guys who didn't who played around too.'

'If I did, it was only at the end, after everything had fallen apart.'

'So what went wrong then?'

'I don't know, the usual, I guess.'

My wife didn't understand me, or, how about, *I changed but she didn't*? Or, *We got married too young*, that's always a good one. Or else there's, *Cops aren't made for marriage, too much pressure on the job.*'

'Sounds like you know what you're talking about.'

'Unfortunately, I do.'

'You want to see a player, you should meet my partner Hal.'

'I think I did.'

'He's the kind of guy cheats on his wife with his mistress, then cheats on his mistress with the waitress from the corner bar. Then he cheats on her with any skirt he can find. And they all love him. He can charm the skin off a snake or the pants off a woman faster than I can pull the gun out of my holster.'

'Whatever winds your watch.'

'Not me. Too much work. Anyway, it's not my style. I'm really a very loyal, upright kind of guy.'

'I'll try to remember that.'

'I'll try to remind you.'

We exchanged appraising looks, each trying to gauge the depth of the other's cynicism and sincerity.

I was leaning against the inside of the door, looking past Collins at the entrance to the club. A short, wiry, light-skinned black man with a tan fedora came out and got in a Mercedes parked out front.

'That might be Sweet Thing,' I said. 'Fits the description we got from Lenora and Money. Especially the hat. He's supposed to have a light spot like a reverse beauty mark the size of a fifty-cent piece on his left cheek, but I can't tell from here.'

I pulled a piece of paper from a pad Jeff had stuck on the dashboard in a plastic holder and tried to jot down the plate number, but the ballpoint I pulled out of my pocket wouldn't work. 'Got a pen?'

Collins laughed. 'Boy, they really have cut back your budget. Look in the glove compartment.'

I rummaged among the debris – bits of paper, matchbooks, spare cuffs, a screwdriver, leather gloves, a bottle of aspirin. From way in the back I pulled out a pair of wire-rimmed glasses and held them up. 'Once the eyes go, the rest isn't far behind.'

'Those aren't mine.'

'It happens to the best of us.'

'No kidding.'

I handed them over. He looked at them quizzically like he had never seen glasses before. 'They must belong to Hal; he's always taking the car.'

'Sure. And my mother sings at the opera.'

'Just get the pen.'

'I'm looking.'.

I was just jotting down the plate number when we picked up Nydia's voice coming through a confusion of sounds. Over the other noises came the unmistakable rush of a toilet flushing. She must have gone into the ladies' room.

'Great sound effects,' Jeff snorted.

'Say what, honey?' Nydia's voice suddenly came through loud and clear. We heard another woman responding, but we couldn't quite make out what she was saying.

'What you got honey? . . . Oh, that's sweet. What you want for it?'

'Shit,' he said. 'She's making a drug buy. That's Eva she's talking to. I thought you said you weren't interested in drugs.'

'Damn her. *We're* not. She's the only one in the office who is.'

I could hardly believe what I was hearing. I had specifically told her not to focus on drugs since there

234

was already an ongoing investigation being conducted by the SNU. If she saw Calvert doing drugs or dealing she was supposed to take note of it, but that was all. Her job in there was strictly to gather overhears and descriptions of people Calvert was hanging out with.

As we listened incredulously to Nydia discussing the quality and price of the woman's product my eye was caught by some activity at the entrance to the club. A large, stocky man in a navy suit was coming out, gesticulating broadly to some friends. 'Holy shit,' I said. It was definitely Calvert. I leaned forward to get a better look, as if after following him all these nights I could possibly be mistaken. Collins and I exchanged pained glances. We couldn't follow him because we couldn't leave Nydia in the club uncovered.

I started buzzing the pulser to get her out of there, but from the sounds coming over the wire she hadn't left the john yet. There was nothing to do but sit and listen to her toy with the dealer as we watched Calvert get in his car and drive away. I kept on buzzing, hoping it would turn into electric-shock therapy, and finally she got the message and came out.

'Excuse me while I confer with my associate,' I said to Collins as I saw her coming toward us. I got out and walked over to meet her. 'What the fuck do you think you were pulling in there?' I yelled as soon as I was close enough.

'Hey, I'm on to something here.'

'You're on to getting your ass kicked. Do you know where Calvert is?'

'Oh, yeah, he's in there bullshitting with all these guys.'

'You're the only one who's bullshitting. Calvert's gone. He just got in his car and drove away, and we couldn't take him because you were in there playing Miami Vice.' I wanted to kill her but murder was too kind. The only satisfaction I had was thinking of her pulling off the tape that held the kel to her crotch.

'Just get in the car. You get Saturday night off; you're off the case. And don't say a word. I wouldn't want you to embarrass yourself in front of a real narc.'

Saturday morning I was up early but forced myself to wait until ten-thirty to call Vince's house. His young wife, Dorothy, answered and informed me in her usual chirpy voice that Vince was doing his stint as coach for their son's weekend soccer league and wouldn't be home till one-thirty. This was Vince's second go around, and like a lot of fathers in that situation, he was lavishing on the second set of kids all the time he had never had for the first.

I drove out to their place on Magpie Lane in Levittown, and waited down the block until I saw Vince drive the family station wagon into the driveway. It was weird sitting there, as if I was doing surveillance on the boss, but I was just too angry and frustrated to pull off the kind of cute talk Dorothy would expect. I watched as Vince helped his six-year-old with his gear, waited a few minutes, and drove up in front.

Vince answered the bell, looking almost cuddly in his weekend sweats. 'Hey, Tina, what are you doing all the way out here?' He was surprised but apparently not annoyed to see me. 'Come on in. Did you eat? Hey, Dottie,' he called into the house, 'put another plate out.'

'No thanks, I'm not hungry, but I need five minutes.'

'Yeah, sure. C'mon out on the deck. It's still warm enough to get a little sun.'

I followed him through the house and out the back, giving a wave to Dorothy's astonished face as we passed the kitchen. The lone maple shimmered gold in the sun, but the air was brisk. I sat on the edge of a redwood lounger; Vince sank into an armchair.

'Listen, Vince, you were right about Nydia. She doesn't know what the hell's going on. I had to stop her from making a drug bust last night. She really outdid herself. She managed to compromise two investigations at the same time. We're talking package deal here. Collins was sitting next to me wondering why Nydia was screwing around with someone they already have, and in the meantime Calvert is walking out of the club.'

'Didn't you explain what you were looking for?'

'Yeah, but I guess I didn't find the right one-syllable words to get my point across.'

'You knew how she was. We went over all that. You said it was low risk, that she could handle it. She was supposed to be on stake-out with Bremmer last night. I had to fight with him to get her.'

'You said it yourself, we're sitting on a time bomb with this one. I'm not going to let some flakehead blow the whole thing. I'm going in there myself.'

He opened his mouth but before he could protest I went on. 'I'm well aware of the risks, and I've figured out how to work with them. I have get-ups that would fool even my parents. And Calvert hasn't seen me in connection with the office for a couple of years.'

'Considering how often you see your parents, they probably wouldn't recognize you, anyway.'

I didn't answer.

'You know, Tina, I've known you for a lotta years. I think you're stepping over the line this time. You're taking it too personally. The mutt was on the street a long time before you came around.' He stood up with the kind of sigh that said this conversation was making him feel old. 'You know what your problem is? You're too touchy-feely. You get too involved with these witnesses. You think you're going to make an honest woman out of this Lenora character if you convict the guy?'

'I'm going in.'

'Go ahead. Do what you're going to do, you're going to do it anyway. Do it tonight. It's Saturday. The place will be so crowded no-one will even see you. I'm gonna put Mickey on with you, and I want a full report on Monday.' He looked at me hard, but I had nothing more to say. We started toward the door. 'Let's hope this is worth it,' he said as I let myself out.

It would have been expedient to rush home and pull my closet apart looking for an outfit to wear to the El Caribe, but what I needed even more was to clear my head. I knew Vince was right about this one – I was losing my perspective. I'd complained all year that I'd been seen in too many joints by too many people, but we weren't getting any closer to finding Slick's body. My gut told me it would never be found unless we could get close enough to Calvert to see what he was up to, and with Nydia's flakiness, there was no-one to do it but me.

I took the Southern State from Vince's, heading back toward Queens, but detoured onto the Meadowbrook Parkway over to Freeport and parked at a local boat launch. I had to calm down and think, and the peaceful expanse of water and the monotony of lapping waves seemed like the right prescription.

It was the end of October. The temperature out here by the water was about fifteen degrees cooler than the city, even with the sunshine, and the breeze against my face was invigorating and oddly soothing. I walked along the shore for about an hour, letting my thoughts bounce randomly around my brain, and after a while I found my pace slowing and my pulse with it. The anxiety, anger, and frustration were slowly being replaced by a calm sense of purpose. A few late-season fishermen stood knee-deep in the surf. The rhythm of casting, trolling, reeling in the line and casting again was hypnotic. I envied their centeredness, all their gestures and movements at one with the task and with their environment. I thought about Calvert and the El Caribe. My goal was to enter the club and be accepted immediately, to blend with the surroundings, but also to use them to get close to a man I knew to be dangerous, a man I believed to be a killer. I saw the scenario in my mind's eye and knew I had to find something similar in myself if what I was trying to do was going to be successful.

When I got back in the car I turned the radio to 97.9 FM, a Latino station. I needed to think Puerto Rican if I was to be a success at the El Caribe. I didn't speak Spanish, but I had heard it occasionally growing up, and as I listened, words and phrases came back to me. If Calvert was a regular at the club, it meant he felt comfortable with Caribbean people, and Nydia had said he gave her an appreciative once-over. I decided on a mild Puerto Rican accent and a look that I hoped would play into his fantasies – one that would also completely conceal my identity.

Back home, I put in a call to Mickey to go over plans for the night and also tried Collins to let him know I was going in. After last night and that business with Money I didn't want him thinking the SPO was stepping on his toes. As usual, he wasn't around. Then I confronted my closet.

I pulled out a pair of black Spandex pants and looked for a top to go with them. One of those gold lamé mesh jobs would have done nicely, but my closet didn't contain anything quite that extreme. I had a couple of stretchy black tops but definitely wanted some color. Then I remembered I had just the thing. I went to my bureau and pulled out a red silk V-neck blouse Steve had given me last Valentine's Day. It was the kind of thing that wrapped around your body and tied at the waist. I had never worn it because no matter how I wrapped it it always ended up with a V that plunged too far for comfort. Cleavage was not my thing, but it would be perfect for the El Caribe, and the thought of putting it to such a purpose gave me a perverse satisfaction. A wide black belt, I decided, would go well with my black spike heels and also serve to hide my beeper.

With these items lined up, I dug around the top shelf of the closet and dragged out my hot rollers. If I was going to get as close to Calvert as I hoped, my appearance would have to be altered dramatically, and curls would certainly help. I plugged in the contraption, showered, dried my hair, and proceeded with the arduous task of putting the suckers in. Curling your hair is not like sex or riding a bike – when you haven't done it in a while you definitely lose the knack.

The rollers in place, I started on my make-up. Instead of my regular natural foundation I reached for a dark tan I had bought for the time I would want an ethnic look. I poured a glob into my palm and began smoothing it on. The transformation was radical and disconcerting. As my skin got darker the whites of my eyes looked lighter and more prominent. The curve of my lips looked somehow more sensual; even the contour of my face seemed to change. It took me back to a time in high school when my family finally made it out of the projects and moved to Long Island. The high school was in a very white, middle-class area, and it was a time when my mixed nationalities came to a head socially. I was under strict orders from my father to tell everyone I was Italian, but there was a small group of Puerto Rican kids who picked up on my dark complexion and welcomed me into their circle. I brushed them off, trying to stay true to my dad, and took to rubbing talcum powder into my face before I went to school so that my complexion would no longer give me away. It was one of those memories that still had the power to make my skin crawl. Now it seemed ironic how useful my mixed parentage was. I wish I could have appreciated it when I was a kid.

After the foundation I added false eyelashes – a pain, but worth it – some turquoise eye shadow, and a light coral-pink lipstick. I carefully removed the rollers, loosened the curls a bit, and lacquered the whole thing into place. Large gold hoop earrings, gold bracelets, and a few gold chains around my neck. It was perfect. I no longer even recognized myself. It would be easy to go in there and act like somebody else.

As I drove over the Fifty-ninth Street Bridge I reviewed my identity in my mind. I had decided to be Elise Perez, living with my Aunt Cruzita at 2330 University Avenue in the Bronx. I had no car and worked as a seamstress at a costume shop on West Twenty-ninth Street.

I turned the Z onto Twenty-fourth, saw where Mickey was parked, and parked across the street. I casually crossed over and walked by, 'accidentally' dropping my purse when I was next to his car. Mickey looked at me with bored indifference – until I winked. His face perked up and he rolled down his window. *'Gucci, gucci mama,'* he intoned, heavy on the phony Spanish accent.

'The Z doesn't have a police radio but I have a walkie-talkie in the car. If you have to tail him while I'm in there, I'll catch up,' I said, picking up the purse and moving on. 'I'll beep if I need you.'

Mickey nodded. 'I'll be on Channel B.'

As I approached the club, several other people were making their way to the door. It was Saturday night and the place was hot. A strong Latin beat poured out on to the street and engulfed me totally once I got inside. The place was packed. People were laughing and talking, jostling one another for a place at the bar or on the dance floor. I inched through the crowd toward the bar and eased my way onto an empty stool that was squeezed between clusters of laughing, gesticulating people.

The bartender was too busy to notice me and I took the opportunity to do a visual of the place, locate the exits, restrooms, kitchen, and any other escape routes in case of emergency. The place was different than I had expected from my drive-bys and from listening to Nydia last night, smaller than all the hubbub would indicate and less sophisticated than its large tropical-style neon sign seemed to promise. The décor, apparently meant to represent a beach bar in the islands, was confined to some fishnets draped haphazardly from the ceiling and a few sharks and sea turtles mounted above the bar.

'Yo, baby, what you want to drink?' a large, round-faced Jamaican bartender asked above the din.

I turned to him with a smile. 'I'll have a margarita, honey. No salt.'

He returned a couple of minutes later with a concoction that looked 90 per cent bar foam. 'You alone, baby?'

'Why you want to know?' I teased back, taking a sip of my drink.

He eyed me appraisingly. 'You don't come with no man, MoJo gonna make sure you don't leave with no man. You just sit right here till I get done, I take you home with me.' Then he flashed a wide grin, turned, and was back down the bar serving other customers.

I swiveled toward the room, drink in hand, and surveyed the scene. A well-made margarita is a good drink; this one was as vile as I assumed it would be. It pays to order a drink you don't like in these situations to force yourself to slow down. Undercover work often involves alcohol, but the combination is not ideal.

I watched the crowd from my perch, everyone too involved in their own trip to pay any attention to me. There had to be at least a hundred and fifty people in the place, pressing against the bar or gyrating in a trancelike state on the dance floor, and I wondered what the legal limit was in a little dump like this. MoJo came back my way from time to time to see if I wanted another drink, and eventually I forced the first one down and started on a second. We kept up the teasing tone. It was the kind of banter just right for my purposes, friendly and completely inconsequential.

After about an hour the band took a break, and the dancers cleared out of the area in the center, giving me my first view of the action on the other side. A waitress was bringing fresh drinks in shot glasses to five black men seated around a small table. The man whose back was facing me was broad-shouldered and blocky with a short, bullish neck. I could see a bulge at the waist through the fabric of his dark suit jacket. A moment later a woman with the high-style flash of a hundred-dollar hooker sashayed over. He turned and put his arm around her, his profile confirming it was Calvert.

The only way to get closer without being too obvious was to flirt with one of the other men. I looked them over, trying to pick a target, scanning the Calvert reports in my mind to see if any of them fit the description of either Sweet Thing or Gato. I hopped off the stool, drink in hand, and moved a little closer. They were laughing and joking loudly. The Jamaican accents of two of the men ruled them out. Of the other two, one was too beefy, the other too tall to be Sweet Thing, and none was Hispanic.

The taller one seemed bored with the conversation, his eye roving the room, and I was about to approach him when Calvert stood up, the woman pressed against him, and started toward the door. 'You're not leaving me already?' MoJo said behind me, and I turned back to the bar. 'This one's on the house.' He placed a third margarita in front of me. I smiled and thanked him, glancing over my shoulder just long enough to confirm Calvert's exit. If I took off after him it would blow my cover and ruin the relationship I was establishing with MoJo. I flashed MoJo another smile, my hand surreptitiously pressing the buzzer on my waist. I knew I could count on Mickey to pick up the signal and hoped he wouldn't lose Calvert.

I gulped down the third margarita and left as soon as I gracefully could. When I got in the car I radioed Mickey, who informed me he was sitting on Calvert, who had taken the woman back to his apartment. God, another night and I was no closer to the information I needed to clinch this case. I drove home in disgust. There wasn't enough alcohol in those glasses of green foam I'd been drinking to drown the sorrows of a flea. As soon as I got in, I poured myself a Scotch. I peeled off my outfit, flipped on the late movie, and tried not to think about the lonely night and empty Sunday ahead. Being an investigator hasn't been good for my drinking or my sex life – too much of one, not enough of the other.

When I woke up in the morning I decided I could no longer avoid that Sunday dinner my parents had been nagging me about. I made the usual stop at the Cinderella Bakery to pick up a dozen mixed rolls and a lemon meringue pie. We never had the rolls with dinner, but I knew they loved them and would be eating them for breakfast all week. They still lived in the house we had moved to when I was in high school, and going there was like a time warp – nothing ever changed. Except maybe my mom's rosebush, which was threatening to take over the neighborhood.

Mom had fussed, maybe because I hadn't been around for a while. We had macaroni with tomato sauce, meatballs and sweet sausages, and salad. She is still a perfect size eight but Dad has gotten paunchy.

She's always complaining that his buttons are popping, but it hasn't inspired her to change the menu.

It didn't take very long for Dad to get to the point. 'So you want to tell me anything?' It was like an instant replay of dinner with Randazzo.

'Like what?'

'Like who's answering your phone lately?'

'Just a friend.'

'Does this friend have a name? Your mother wants to know.'

'I don't want to know,' she said in her singsong Puerto Rican voice, 'it's your father. You know I don't interfere.'

'Dad, don't get the trousseau together. It's nothing.'

'Well, your friend with no name tells me you're working at night on a case. I thought you said you only work days.'

'I don't know what he told you, but everything's fine. I'm just plugging away as usual.'

'I don't want to hear that you're doing something dangerous.'

'You won't, Dad, I promise.' It was answering my father's questions that gave me my first lessons in undercover.

I was too restless to stay long after dinner, and it was still early evening when I got back to my apartment. I wasn't anxious to go into the office in the morning and face Vince's snide remarks about how little I had gotten out of my big undercover, and even more important, I couldn't bear wasting a whole day without making some progress on the investigation. This case was beginning to feel like a rock face I couldn't climb; no matter how I scrambled I couldn't seem to get a toehold or find anything to grab on to. Thoughts of Steve and last Sunday kept coming unbidden into my head. Dwelling on that affair and everything it said about my personal life would be even less productive, I knew, than harping on the Calvert case. And hovering behind Steve was Jeff Collins, whose equally uninvited image seemed to be gnawing its way into my consciousness. So what if he wasn't married? The last thing I needed was another egocentric male. Hadn't I learned anything yet?

I got out a yellow pad, wrote *Calvert* on top, and drew a line down the center of the page. Over the left column I wrote *Have*, over the right column *Need*. Probably an exercise in futility, but sometimes writing things down in an organized way sparks new ideas.

In the left column I wrote *Witnesses*, and then it hit me. Lenora. After our last painful conversation I had tried to get her a couple of times with no success. Sunday evening was probably a good time. I picked up the phone and dialed the number, prepared to let it ring if necessary. I was totally surprised when a message immediately clicked in: 'The number you have called, 555–3692, has been disconnected.' I knew she was supposed to have the number changed but didn't really expect her to do it, and if she had, I would have gotten a different message. I pushed in the numbers again, not wanting to believe what I was hearing.

Maybe she didn't pay her bill, I thought. It happens all the time. But the message hadn't said *temporarily* disconnected. I pictured Lenora's spare, antiseptic apartment, and then I remembered. The boxes. Even back then she was packed. Poised. Ready to run. I replaced the receiver and sat back, stunned. I would go out to the projects and check, of course, but in my heart I knew. She had skipped. My star witness. A minute ago I was worried about gaining a toehold, now I felt like I was in free fall.

I got up and started pacing the small living-room. I could get in the car and go over to Brooklyn, but when she wasn't there what would I do? And what would I say to Vince in the morning? The surveillance was a wash and our best witness, *my* witness, was on the lam. I could just picture the smug little smirk of satisfaction on Muñoz' face when Vince handed the case over to him. I couldn't let it happen.

If I just had something positive to say, one concrete piece of information. I thought about the El Caribe. I'd made a good contact with MoJo. Before I left he mentioned he would be working tonight. I knew what I had to do. The odds of catching Calvert there were good. I wouldn't have any backup so I couldn't follow anyone, but maybe, just maybe, I could get close enough to hear something. I went into the bedroom, sat down in front of the mirror, and started on my disguise.

Chapter Twenty

He watched from his vantage point at the end of the dark wooden bar of the International Travel Lodge cocktail lounge as she entered the room, looked around, hesitated, and then came toward him. She glanced at him out of the corner of her eye before taking the stool closest to where the female bartender was washing glasses. The two women immediately exchanged greetings. What a contrast! The bartender was short, with a pouffed bleached-blond hairdo that made her head appear too large for her body, and make-up that looked like it had been applied with a spoon. The other one, the stewardess, was tall and graceful. Definitely a class act.

The bartender wiped her hands and poured the stewardess a white wine. She took a sip, then let her eyes pass over him again as if she were just looking around the room. He pretended not to notice but could feel his blood start to race. A stewardess. It was perfect. All these months working out at the airport, he didn't know why he hadn't thought of it before. Not that he ever thought about it that way, picking a type or even a location. The women just presented themselves and he took it from there. And that's what she was doing, all right. He took a long drink from his beer before looking at her again.

She was wearing her uniform, so she must have just come off a flight. They probably didn't call their suits uniforms any more, the way they didn't call the women stewardesses. But her flight attendant's outfit, whatever they did call it, with its tailored jacket, shoulder-pads, and straight skirt, retained a military air. He didn't particularly like the effect. Too severe. He liked his women soft. But those were just clothes, like a shell you removed to reach the soft white belly underneath. And there was something kind of intriguing about the look – maybe he was changing his type. Someone more experienced might be interesting, more of a challenge. Maybe he'd even go in for female cops. There was one particular little bitch he wouldn't mind tangling with. He chuckled to himself at the thought. She was always so cool. Well, he could be cool too. He liked the idea of seeing her nervous, on edge – terrified.

There were plenty of perps who consistently sought out the same kind of victim – slim young blondes, buxom middle-aged redheads – letting their obsessions get the better of them, leaving a trail, giving themselves away with their choices. It always seemed to have something to do with getting even with women the victims reminded them of – usually their mothers. It was dumb. He didn't care about crap like that, wasn't getting even with anybody. And his mother, if he pictured her at all, was always gray, not her hair gray, but gray like in a black-and-white film, faded out and unimportant. Not really there somehow.

If the stewardess reminded him of anybody it was one of those actresses from the forties. It had to do with her hair style, parted on the side and dipping over her cheek. She reminded him of the WACs in those Second World War movies his father could never get enough of on TV. His father. The Captain! What a laugh. Even when he was nothing more than a drunk with a bottle of bourbon to obscure his view of the screen, he still insisted on being called that.

'You're no captain,' he remembered yelling once in a fit of rash adolescent rebellion. 'I bet you never made more than buck sergeant.' Before he knew what was happening, his father had grabbed his arm and flipped him in a karate maneuver onto the floor. 'I'm the captain of this fucking company and don't you ever forget it.' The old man's muscle tone was gone by then, but he still had the moves.

The lounge was quiet. He watched her for about fifteen minutes, glancing in her direction from time to time but careful not to stare. Nothing blatant. Nothing threatening. Just a little friendly interest. If he played it right, she would come to him. He just had to keep cool, stay relaxed. But he was so god-damned tense. He could feel his palms starting to sweat. Nonchalantly, he slid the napkin out from under the glass and ran his hand with it along the bar as if he were wiping condensation from the wood. Then he crunched the napkin in his fist.

He had to regain his control. Everything was different now – changing, speeding up, getting more intense. Ever since Annabelle Ross he had been on edge, wondering what would happen next, wondering if the game would change – if he would change it. He hadn't thought about how she looked after, only about the sound, and the feel under his finger, the thrill that electrified his body when he knew he had exploded a live round.

It was their fault, but what did it matter? There always had to be that first kill. After that everything was easy. He thought about that time with the Captain. He was eleven. He had been going out with the men for four years. At 5 a.m. on the first morning of the hunt, his father had roused him and told him to get ready. He had pulled on his boots and gone outside to pee. Suddenly a hand came down on his shoulder, forcing him to jump, urine splashing on his boot. His father's jibe came swiftly. 'If you can't hang on to your gun while firing, you're never gonna hit anything.' He could still hear the raucous, joyless laugh and the ominous tone of the command that followed – he was not to come back to the camp until he had taken down a deer.

He had grabbed his rifle and trudged off, resentful, but also awed by his father's omniscience. He thought it was his secret, how he watched and prayed no deer would come his way, willing them to take other paths, turning away for just a split second when he saw the hint of ruddy brown out of the corner of his eye. But his father had known, had flushed him out, seen to the heart of his weakness the way he always did.

All day he had walked and watched and waited, but he could not will toward him the deer he had willed away. He knew it was a deep failure within him, his conflicted impulses destroying his instincts, forcing him to fail. Darkness fell early in the dank November woods. His legs ached, his stomach gnawed with hunger, a cold, deeper and heavier than anything he could have imagined, pierced him to his bones. He tried not to think of going back, but if he stayed in the woods he thought he would die. He moved toward the camp almost unwittingly, taking small pride in the fact that he could find it in the darkness, that he wasn't lost, hoping, and in that same instant giving up the hope, that his father would find in this something to commend him for.

Finally, he came to the hill behind the cabin. He smelt the smoke from the fire before he saw the lights. The urge to rush down overcame him. He took a few lurching steps, catching his heel on a twisted root, pitching forward. He held his breath. A single, distinct sound broke the quiet: the sound of a rifle being cocked. He flattened himself on the ground just before his father fired.

He couldn't believe he had been so stupid, let his fear and hunger get the better of him. Once his father had proclaimed something there was no gainsaying it. There were no pleas that would be heard, no sentence was ever commuted. Somehow he lived through the night, sobbing and shivering until exhaustion overcame him and he fell into a fitful few hours of sleep. He woke at first light a different person, empty of both tears and fear. Grabbing his rifle, he pulled himself up. He didn't think, he was beyond conscious thought, but somewhere in his mind he knew where he was going. He pictured two yearling does browsing on a grassy knoll, one turning at the crackle of a twig under his foot. One turning, then the other. One leaping, disappearing in the distance, the other standing just long enough in the unearthly stillness of the early dawn for him to shoot. He would aim right for the heart.

It played out so clearly in his mind that when he got there it was as if it had already happened. There wasn't a second of hesitation; he took his shot. He expected a jolt of anguish as he pulled the trigger, or, in his current state, a nothingness. What he felt had surprised him. The moment he pulled the trigger, secure in the knowledge that the bullet would find its mark, he had felt a kind of peace, almost a joy. A warm rush of blood had flushed his body. He felt giddy. As the doe dropped, he lowered the gun and started to laugh.

After a while the stewardess got up and walked toward the ladies' room, smiling slightly at him as she passed and then immediately casting her eyes toward the carpet. God, what actresses they were. He tapped on the bar and nodded to the bartender for another beer, feeling better, in control again. He figured he would make his move when she walked by on her way back, say something easygoing, something offhand and friendly. Ask her if she was on a stopover, something like that. Once she paused to talk to him, everything else would be easy.

He sipped his beer, alert, primed but no longer tense; savoring the wait, remembering that morning so long ago. He had dragged the carcass back to camp, girded for his father's contempt. The Captain wouldn't shoot a doe, not even if she stopped right in front of them, turned her head, and peered in their direction, inviting the bullet. It wasn't out of sympathy – compassion was for wimps and fools and women. He wouldn't shoot a doe because it was beneath him. He respected the game he stalked: he wouldn't give that much respect to a female, not of any species. But the kill would be good enough, he knew that, and he knew, too, that he had crossed some crucial line; he had gone beyond his father's power to hurt him.

Lost in his reverie, he didn't immediately register the length of time that had gone by since the stewardess left. Suddenly, he looked at his watch and realized it had been at least fifteen minutes. He glanced around the room, thinking maybe she had taken a table, but it was immediately clear that she was gone. He stood up abruptly, pulling some money from his pocket for the tab. He had to get out of there. He felt suddenly exposed, vulnerable, trapped. He walked quickly into the lobby, noticed a group of travelers by the elevator, turned the other way and pushed through the entrance to the stairs. The metal door clanged shut behind him, reminding him with a jolt of that other door, the one at the back entrance to that college girl's apartment. He leaned against it and took several deep breaths. Mary Alice McGuire. He reminded himself how he had thought he was losing her when she ran into her two friends, and then how everything had fallen into place.

He shouldn't have allowed himself to think about the Captain. Feelings were dangerous; they always got you into trouble. Even desire was dangerous. You could not want anything too much. Will was different. You could will something toward you. But only if you followed the rules. What was it they used to say in school? It's not if you win but how you play the game that counts. The Captain got a laugh out of that. Don't listen to that crap, he said. It's not how you play the game but if you win. But they were both wrong. It was how you played the game that allowed you to win.

He looked around him and started to ascend the stairs. It might be a good idea to check the building out. It always paid to be prepared. He walked up three flights and then slowly pulled the door open just far enough to look into the hall. There was no-one there, so he stepped out and walked past the closed doors. It was odd, he thought, that he had been in this place having drinks at the bar any number of times but had never been in one of the rooms. He was hoping someone would come out so he could get a glimpse, but no-one did. Not that it mattered what the rooms looked like; it would just be interesting, that's all. Information to store up for the future. He pressed the elevator button, and when it arrived empty, took it up to the next floor. He got out, walked the length of the empty hall, entered the staircase again, and walked down. This time he took the stairs to the garage level and walked through the underground space to his car. By the time he was driving up the ramp he was feeling relaxed again, on top of things. It was always good to do a little reconnaissance, scope things out, analyze the lay of the land.

Chapter Twenty-one

The El Caribe on Sunday night was a different place. Without the live band it had turned from a hot scene to a tired neighborhood hang-out. The former dance floor was a vacant expanse of linoleum; most of the tables were empty, and the regulars hunkering on the bar stools were subdued to the point of being comatose. The only music came from a small cassette system wedged in among the liquor bottles. I had figured the Sunday scene would be more low key and was glad I had followed my instincts and gone for black stretch jeans and boots.

MoJo recognized me immediately. 'Where did you disappear to last night, girl? I turn around and you're gone. I think you don't love me no more.'

His lyrical Jamaican accent and obviously sweet nature brought a sincere smile. 'My friend showed up and I had to leave.'

'Margarita, no salt.'

I nodded and his grin broadened. When he brought the drink he leaned on the bar in front of me and asked my name and where I came from. 'Elise' was pretty, he thought. We chatted for a while and I mentioned the name Inez, a name I had picked up from Nydia's wire before the scene went bad, and said she had told me about the place and that she was supposed to meet me there later. It was always good to establish a connection to someone they knew if you want to be accepted. It was a little risky, since I didn't know what Inez looked like, but if MoJo had pointed her out I would have said my friend was a different woman with the same name.

It was getting close to midnight, and the place was starting to fill up with the hard-core crowd, mostly men, but a few couples and a sprinkling of single women. A couple of men who saw me talking to MoJo moved down the bar to join us, and I joked with them for a while. I finished the second margarita, which MoJo placed in front of me as soon as I had emptied the first, and decided it was time for a trip to the ladies' room.

A woman stood by the entrance and at first I thought she was a cleaning person because she lingered outside the stall while I used the john, but as I was drying my hands she came closer. 'I send you to heaven, girl. You got ten dollars?' I knew by her voice it was Eva, the dealer we heard on Nydia's wire. I told her I wasn't interested, and her sly smile turned to a scowl. Two other women entered the bathroom and she started talking to them in Spanish. I understood enough to gather I was the subject of the conversation. One of them said *'puta'*, whore, and they glanced at me sideways. The two women bought some of Eva's wares and went out. As I reached for the doorknob she put herself in front of me. 'I ask you got any money, girl?' I told her again I didn't want any drugs and she let out a stream of curses in Spanish – the only part of the language I understand well – and told me if I didn't want crack that I was either the Law or a pussy. I tried to get around her and out the door but she grabbed my shoulder. My arm automatically swung around and caught hers at the elbow and I pulled her toward me. *'Cono*, I stick with the alcohol, I don't like your shit,' I said in my best Puerto Rican accent. 'You got a problem with that?'

'No,' she squeaked.

'Then leave me alone, OK, or I tell MoJo you're a pain in the ass to everyone who comes in here.' I let her go and prayed she didn't have a gun or a knife. *'Mira,'* I said, 'you come outside and I buy you a drink. I come in here, you leave me the fuck alone. *Tu sabes?*' I stared her down long enough for her to nod and left.

Jesus, I'm losing it, I thought. There were eight different ways I could have handled that situation to defuse it and I had to go tactical. I could have blown it. This was not turning out to be the easy low-key surveillance I had planned. Much as I had gone a little crazy, she could have done worse. I was beginning to wonder about my wisdom in coming in here with no backup outside.

Several people had joined the group I was drinking with. Two black men, one dark-skinned, one light, were flanking a third whose large black-suited back was toward me but who I knew instantly was Calvert. MoJo was placing a drink in front of him as I walked over. 'Yo,' he said, 'we have a new girl here.' The men turned to eye me. 'This is Big Eddie,' he nodded toward Calvert. 'Eddie likes the little ones, so don't forget you already in love with me.' Calvert glanced at me but showed no particular interest, fortunately. I needed to get close to him, but it would be dangerous to get too close.

MoJo brought me a refill and the men went back to their conversation, which seemed to involve a new poker game they were trying to get going. They threw out a few names of men who might join, but someone had an objection to each. 'What about that little Puerto Rican used to hang with you?' MoJo asked. 'Didn't take a leak less you tell him to. Don't see him around no more.'

This struck Calvert as enormously funny. 'You mean Gato?' His cynical laugh was the opposite of MoJo's spontaneous good humor. 'He took a trip,' he said, shaking his head and continuing to chuckle to himself. No-one pressed him further. I wasn't sure what it meant. Was Calvert really arrogant enough to be bragging he had Gato killed, or had he actually been sent away? MoJo moved down the bar to serve some other customers, and the group started to move off. Of the two men with Calvert the lighter one fit the general description of Sweet Thing, but I looked at him closely and could see no hint of the birthmark he was reported to have. I eyeballed the other men in the room. Two I could see fit the basic height, weight, and age description, but neither of them had the telltale light spot either. Another man had a prominent scar that ran under his eye and on to his cheek, but that wasn't what I was looking for, and anyway, he was heavy-set and too dark.

I was so busy eyeballing the men I paid no attention to the women who came in. A big mistake. It was only when I turned back to the bar and was standing right next to her that I noticed Auletta. I tried not to let anything show on my face, and if she recognized me she didn't show it either. I prayed my disguise was as good as I thought. Moving down the bar to where MoJo was standing I told him flirtatiously that I had to be on my way but would be sure to be back soon. Then I ambled nonchalantly toward the door, using all my willpower to force myself not to look back at Auletta. I had no idea if she was watching.

I walked down the block to Twenty-third Street and picked up the pace as I headed toward Ninth Avenue, torn by conflicting emotions, half of me congratulating myself on getting the overhear from Calvert, and the other half furious at myself for almost getting my cover blown. I had left my car on the avenue near Twenty-second Street so no-one at the bar could see me park it, but now I cursed the long walk back. The wide block with the unbroken, monolithic façade of London Terrace on the left was virtually deserted. Late Sunday night was one of the few times even New Yorkers tended to stay home. A chill November wind blew steadily off the Hudson, pressing against my back and urging me forward. I was tempted to dash around the corner to my car, but something else was urging me to take stock and slow down. I didn't really know if I'd been made, and if I was being followed I didn't want to give away the Z. I stopped in front of a small florist as if I was looking at the display but concentrated instead on the reflections on the window. The street was eerily empty and quiet. A single man was reflected from across the street. He was walking slowly, not looking in my direction. It could be anyone, I told myself, but moved to the next window. His pace slowed down and he kept the same distance behind me.

I was almost at the corner when I made the decision to turn away from the direction of the car back toward Twenty-fourth. My eye did a quick search of the sparse traffic on Ninth for cabs but I didn't see any. I walked slowly but steadily, scanning the plate glass of the stores I passed; the man kept the same pace.

The window of the Citibank on Twenty-fourth angled across the corner, providing a panoramic view of Ninth Avenue and revealing the reflection of another man on my side of the street, even with and keeping pace with the first. Both men were wearing sports coats and didn't seem to resemble anyone I had seen at the El Caribe, but it was too dark and they were too far away for me to make out any details or even the color of their skin in the glass. I told myself I was probably being paranoid, but at the same time I was instinctively taking precautions, staying on the brightly lit avenue and keeping my eye out for empty cabs or even patrol cars.

I walked past a few more stores, halting twice to see what they would do. The man across the street stopped when I did, and the second time I saw his reflection turn, look directly at me for a second, then look toward the man behind me and nod. I glanced over my shoulder in time to see the second man, who had closed the distance between us considerably, nod in acknowledgment. There was no longer any doubt that I was being tailed. I studied the activity reflected on the glass to see if I could pick out anyone else on the street or in a car or truck that might be involved. The two men seemed to be alone.

I continued walking, considering escape routes. My options were limited. Avoiding the car had probably been a mistake; if I'd hustled I could have gotten in and driven off before they saw me. Now it was behind me and there was no way to get to it without passing the men. Heading down a side street would be dangerous. I continued along Ninth toward the projects up ahead. I could hear the footsteps of the man behind me getting closer. It sounded like he was wearing cowboy boots, or some other shoes with heels. At least that would slow him down a bit. It was time to book. A car was coming toward me down Twenty-fifth. I ran in front of it against the light. The man behind me started to run, too, but I knew the car would come between us. I got to the projects and hopped the four-foot fence surrounding the playground just as I had done so many times growing up in one of these places.

I ran through the playground, the sound of the two men running behind me now, dodging around the concrete animal shapes to obscure my path, running toward the parking-lot ahead. The fence around the lot was higher. I scanned it quickly as I ran toward it. The entrance was about a hundred yards away, too far to make it without being seen. Then I noticed a hole where the fence had been cut and pulled back about halfway along. I was in luck. Hedges and trees were planted around the lot, obscuring much of it from view. If I could keep low and get in before the men saw me, they would have to slow down to figure out where I had gone.

I reached the fence and prayed there was no broken glass as I dove toward the hole. I scrambled through, hunkering down, keeping low behind the cars, moving deeper into the lot, trying to catch my breath. I could hear their voices as they stopped to consider their next move and their footsteps as they started running again, going toward the main entrance to the lot. I flattened myself and eased my body under the nearest car. The footsteps came closer, and I heard the sound of their breathing, strained from running. They seemed to be moving up and down the aisles of the lot, searching between the cars. Then they stopped, not a car's length away from me, and stood looking round. All I could see was a pair of black Italian loafers and two snakeskin cowboy boots.

The feet pivoted as they surveyed the lot. Their breathing was as loud as a lover's in my ear. It took everything I had to control my own. I had no gun, no escape route, and no excuse. I tried to think how I would play it after they yanked me out, what I could possibly say. My heart pounded, ticking off the seconds that seemed like years. I didn't think I could stand it any more. I was desperate to do something, anything, to break the tension.

Suddenly there were other steps coming from the pathway and the two men started to move away. Maybe I'd be saved by some night owl coming to pick up his car. It seemed too good to be true. I didn't move. After a couple of minutes, two new sets of shoes passed me and disappeared in the direction the first men had taken.

I waited as long as I could stand it, which probably wasn't much more than a couple of minutes, and eased myself out from under the car. I felt dizzy and my whole body ached from the strain of keeping still. Slowly I headed for the parking-lot entrance.

'Close call.' A male voice came out of the darkness,

jolting me to at least the next planet.

My head spun around and I saw Jeff Collins standing in the shadows with his partner, Hal. 'We were watching the club when we saw you leave,' he said. 'I thought you were taking the night off.'

'I should have.'

'Some pretty good avoidance maneuvers,' Hal said. 'You'd be a hard one to catch. Good camouflage too.' He let his eye rove over my outfit.

'Did you get a good look at the two men?' I asked, not wanting them to know how relieved I was to see them and how utterly vulnerable I felt.

'We've seen them around the El Caribe before,' Hal said.

'I didn't pick them out right away. The jackets threw me off. Calvert was the only guy in the club dressed like that.'

'He came out after you and signaled the two jokers parked in a car across the street. That's when we put it together and figured out it was you.'

'I shouldn't have gone in there. It was stupid. I convinced myself it was OK, but too many people know me.'

'It happens, Tina. Don't be so hard on yourself,' Collins said. 'All you did was blow your cover. One day I'll tell you about the cases I've blown.'

It struck me that it was the first time he had used my first name. It seemed unnervingly intimate.

'Where's your car?'

'Over on Ninth.'

'We'll walk you back.'

I didn't protest. We walked the few blocks in silence. I just kept thinking how stupid I was, how close I'd come to blowing everything, maybe even my own life, and wondering how I could possibly face Vince.

'Nice,' Hal said when we reached the Z. We all looked at the car a minute, not knowing quite what to do next. I knew I was safe, but it was going to take me a while to come down

'You OK to drive?' Jeff asked, sensing my hesitation. 'We could drop you.'

'I'd just have to come back and pick up the car tomorrow. Anyway, I'm OK. All in a night's work, right?' My jaunty tone fell a little flat.

'Next time don't go out without a partner. I can't count the times this guy has bailed me out before I even knew I was in trouble.'

We both looked at Hal, who had started backing away down the street.

When I woke up Monday morning my head felt like the worst hangover imaginable. It wasn't the result of the watered-down swill they'd been serving at the club, and I hadn't had anything to drink after. By the time I had driven the Z back to Rego Park, my brain and body had both crashed from the fear and the adrenaline; I fell into bed and immediately slid into a state so blank it was more like coma than sleep. Now, frustration, anger, and self-loathing were fighting it out with my brain as the battlefield. I swallowed a couple of codeine-laced Tylenol I'd kept from a tooth extraction, in the hope of nipping what could be a two-day migraine. Three cups of strong black espresso later, I was as ready as I was going to be to start the day.

Before I went to the office, I took a drive out to the Eleanor Roosevelt projects to see if I could find Lenora. I climbed the four flights to her apartment, rang the bell, waited several minutes, and rang it again. I knew she wasn't there, but I stood outside her door, pushing her bell and waiting longer than seemed reasonable, long enough to eliminate any possible doubt. Then I turned and walked back down the stairs. I didn't want to knock on any neighbors' doors and risk calling attention to her disappearance in case Calvert was not yet aware of it. The least I could do was protect her as much as possible now.

When I got to the hallway by the mailboxes I saw an elderly woman pushing a shopping cart off the elevator. She didn't look like someone likely to be part of Calvert's network. I held the front door open for her. 'Have you seen Lenora Terrell?' I asked as she pulled her cart past me.

She looked me straight in the eye with a proud, saucy defiance. 'Don't see nothin', don't answer no questions. Learned that much by my age.' She nodded emphatically.

I couldn't repress a smile. 'Is there a housing manager around here?'

'Not that you'd notice,' she said and walked on.

I stood indecisively on the sidewalk for a few minutes. I could look for the manager to see if he could tell me anything, but afraid as Lenora was of Calvert, it was impossible to imagine her telling anyone where she was going. And I really didn't want to call attention to my visit. I kept thinking about our last conversation. I needed to find Lenora, but I needed to protect her, too. My anger at her leaving was tempered by an overriding sense of guilt. If I had handled it differently, if I had stayed in contact, if I'd worked harder to calm her fears, she would probably still be here.

I was relieved to see Vince's door closed when I got back to the office. I immediately put in a call to Lou Donaldson, a former investigator who left the SPO to become a postal inspector, and asked him to find out where Lenora Terrell's mail was being sent. Then I went to work typing up the reports on the two surveillances. I made up my mind that the way to face Vince was to tell him what I heard and leave out the close call. The excitement in the parking-lot was best relegated to my private journal. I knew Collins would never bring it up in front of anyone else – we didn't have to talk about it,

I just knew I could trust him. It was almost like being partners. But the feelings I was starting to have about him wouldn't get written about even there.

The loyalty and camaraderie among the investigators at the SPO had always been one of the enduring pleasures of this job. But the only person I had ever been close to in the Department was Maddy. With Collins I had gotten beyond the barrier of my office and my gender. We had been through enough action together by now, shared enough tough spots, to know we would protect each other. It was about the only good thing I could find in the mess this case was turning into – the mess my life was turning into.

Last week I had felt on the verge of clinching one of the most important cases of my career; now I felt utterly dumb and useless. I had been too impetuous; I had let my emotions rule; I hadn't been methodical. I couldn't remember when my stock with myself had been lower. I craved a good word from someone, but there was no-one in the office I could be completely honest with about what had happened. Not unless I wanted to risk having the case taken away. And no matter how low I felt, I wasn't ready to do that. I reached for the phone and dialed Maddy's number. I knew I could count on her for some emotional support even if I couldn't discuss my professional difficulties. It was a little after 10 a.m. She would be coming off her graveyard shift and should still be awake. I dialed her number, but after four rings the machine cut in, and I hung up without leaving a message.

Mickey was just coming in when I put down the phone. 'Sorry we didn't get more the other night.'

I shrugged.

'Here's something to cheer you up.' He dropped a missing person's report on my desk. It was from the New Jersey State Police and listed a Clarence Anderson, a.k.a. Slick, as reported missing on 21 September 1987.

'It's our guy,' he said. 'Adult male, black, missing. The police didn't follow up on it till a week later, and then it was just a cursory interview of the girlfriend who said he'd gone to the city gambling the week before. They figured he took off and that was that. I called her myself and got the same story. Slick used to come to the city every few weeks for a regular game. She didn't really worry until he didn't come back by Monday. She never heard from him again. He took the bus in so there was no car to trace. She was sure he wouldn't have left her, they always are. But in her case I think she's right. He left a three-year-old Buick LeSabre in her hands, a car she didn't think he would have walked away from. I don't either.'

'Did he ever mention anyone in the game?' I asked.

'This you're going to love. At first she said no, but then she said there was one guy he mentioned, she didn't know if it was in connection to the game, but she did think Slick owed him money. His name was Big Eddie.'

If we hadn't been in the office I would have jumped up and kissed him. I wasn't ready to roll over and let Vince give the case to IAD, and now I wouldn't have to. An MPR wasn't a body, but for the first time in days I felt we were getting closer. I flipped open the Calvert file. The two things weren't really connected, but somehow Mickey's information made the overhear I had gotten at the El Caribe seem more useful. Maybe it was just that my mood was improved. I hadn't remembered Bud's advice, I hadn't been methodical. Now I would be.

I read everything in the file slowly and carefully, trying to forget that I knew most of it by heart, trying to look at it like it was all new. What caught my eye, after more than an hour of reading, was the MV report on the green Bonneville. The owner's name was Carlos Perales. The address was in Borough Park, not far from

Mom's. Calvert didn't hang out with many Hispanics. I had meant to ask Mary Lee to put the name through, but in my zeal to keep on Calvert I had forgotten about it.

Vince's door was open now and he called me in as I walked by. I handed him the reports on Saturday and Sunday nights.

'Sunday?' he said, as he glanced through them, his eyebrows raised.

'What can I tell you? I didn't have a date so I thought I might as well go back in. When I saw Auletta I decided I'd better leave. At least I got something first.'

'Not much. If Calvert wasted the guy, it sure won't stand up as an admission.'

'I want to look for the Bonneville. Gato and the car are both missing. I think they're connected.'

He leaned back in his chair and gave me a long you-must-be-kidding look. Then he shrugged. 'It's your time, waste it if you want to.'

Back at my desk, I looked at my appointment calendar and realized I was slated for drinks that night with Al Randazzo and Neil Dandrell. Dandrell's secretary was going on maternity leave in a couple of months and he was going to need a replacement. Al had recommended Julia Cipriani for the job and set up the meet. An evening with these two guys was about as high on my list as going to the dentist. I had to keep reminding myself I was laying the groundwork for something important; a job in the Assemblyman's office would offer a choice vantage point for surveying the Dandrells' connections and taking in their activities.

I told Al I didn't have time for dinner, but we met at Luna's anyway – obviously one of his favorite haunts. He was sitting at his regular table in the back, pouring wine from a half-empty bottle of Chianti. The diamonds in his cuff links caught the light and threatened to put out my eyes as I approached. He looked like his usual self, only more so. His thinning hair was styled for maximum volume, his tan looked burnished, his clothes were perfectly pressed, his manicure impeccable – you had to give the guy credit for trying. I just hoped he hadn't been polishing the apple for me. He poured me a glass of wine as I sat down and was soon regaling me with anecdotes about all the city bigwigs he had seen that week. Not enough detail to give me anything, though, and I had to work to keep my eyes from glazing over. It was getting late, and no Dandrell. I hoped Al wasn't leading me on.

I gave him an hour and he was five minutes shy when Neil walked in the door. I had seen Neil briefly at the fundraiser but was unprepared for his current appearance – he looked like someone who had gone through a car wash without the car. His tie was loosened, his shirt wrinkled and opened at the neck, his suit jacket, an obviously expensive dark-blue pinstripe, sagged and buckled, the lining hanging down below the hem in several places, and the pants had lost more than their creases. But it was his face that really told the tale: this was a man on a bender. My records indicated that Neil Dandrell was forty-six years old. When I saw him now, all I could think of was the old adage, 'It's not the years, it's the miles.'

Al rose to greet him, somewhat embarrassed but clearly not shocked by his appearance. If this was typical, Judge Dandrell's henchmen must have had quite a time getting the heir apparent spiffed up for his shindig the other night. The men shook hands, Al introduced me, and then offered Neil a glass of wine. 'You know I never touch the stuff.' He laughed raucously, waving the waiter over and ordering bourbon. Neil Dandrell had son-of-the-famous-man syndrome, and he had it bad.

It soon became clear that the evening was a test. Neil's mission that night was to try to trip up Julia

Cipriani. Or maybe he was the fall guy and it was really Randazzo who had engineered the whole thing. Someone was suspicious and it didn't really matter who. The two of them spent the next hour pulling a good-guy/bad-guy routine – kind of a funny thing to pull if they thought I was a cop, but maybe their suspicions weren't that well thought out. I knew the drill, I'd done it so many times myself: Dandrell played the hard-nose, shooting questions at me – what I did at work, what kind of clients we had, where I lived, who I hung out with, what bars I went to, where my parents lived, where I bought my milk and went for coffee – while Randazzo exhorted him to lay off, intoning in his oily voice how anyone could see what a nice, honest Italian girl I was. I played the *ingénue*, earnest and cooperative and *naïve*.

Neil continued to drink steadily, but though it didn't look like his critical faculty had been on the cutting edge for a long time, I didn't let myself relax. A serious drunk can fool you. As the questioning went on, it became more intrusive and absurd. When he said he had heard something about trouble between me and Nicky Caruso, the guy in the band, and couldn't countenance that kind of thing getting in the way of work, I allowed myself to blow up. I really wanted the job, I told him, I knew it was a wonderful opportunity, but this was going too far. I had a right to some privacy. I gave Al a pointed stare, and he immediately tried to patch it up, telling Neil that it wasn't my fault and reiterating how much he admired my feistiness. A real *malandrina*, he called me.

Well, I don't know, I said. Maybe the political life was not for me after all. I mean, all I wanted was a simple office job, and look what I had to go through. I was probably better off where I was. I withdrew into a cool, dignified silence. This was all it took to turn young Dandrell around. By the time I called it an evening he

269

was frothing at the mouth to have me. It's fascinating how people tend to want you after you reject them – some kind of principle of universal masochism, or maybe just low self-esteem.

Another observation for my private journal, and another evening when the official report would be short – time, place, date, names of people present, names of officials mentioned, the gist of our conversation about the job – and most of what I really found interesting left out. I thought about why I kept the journal and, of course, that had a lot to do with it. I needed an outlet for my personal, quirky perceptions and suppositions. So much of what I did was related to work, and everything related to work was privileged information, particularly everything I did undercover. There were so many things I couldn't talk about to anyone – so many thoughts and observations that fell through the official cracks. But I think I kept it even more because I expected to learn something from it. I wanted to record my feelings and theories, and even my wise-ass assumptions, because I wanted to test them against the future, see if they added up to anything. I wanted to be able to read them over when cases were finished and see if my instincts had been good, in order to hone them and make them better. Besides, I hated waste, and you never knew when some detail too insignificant or frivolous for an official report might come in handy.

Chapter Twenty-two

Joe kept thinking the name T. Paris sounded familiar; he just couldn't remember from where. He thought maybe it was in one of the case files he'd been working on. When he got to the office Monday morning he read over the listing of all the sexual-assault victims from the last year, but the name wasn't on it. He was trying to decide where to look next when Ann walked up to his desk. 'You're not going to believe this,' she said.

He looked up, surprised at her uncharacteristic informality and verve.

'This is definitely not a textbook case. Do you know where I found T. Paris?'

He shook his head.

'SPO.'

So that's where he knew the name from. He sat back and thought about it; did that make Terry's behaviour over the weekend more or less suspicious? He had no way of knowing; he didn't have enough information. Maybe the two of them were having a relationship. As he thought about it, he realized it didn't have to be his call. It was time to bring Vince in. He flipped through his Rolodex for his friend's number, but decided it wasn't something he wanted to do on the phone.

'Let me lay it out, and tell me how it sounds to you,' he said when he was seated in front of Vince's desk. 'I told you we were looking for a department connection with this Roulette guy, well, I think we

271

have something. One of the victims says she saw her attacker get into a gray hatchback in front of her building immediately after the attack. Turns out a ticket was issued to a gray Toyota in front of that address on the same day.'

Vince was watching him, not talking, his eyes saying, Yeah, OK, so what's it got to do with me? a hint of a challenge in the set of his jaw, as if he knew what was coming.

'The thing is, the owner of the car is one of yours. Terrance O'Hanlon.'

Vince couldn't contain a laugh. 'Him? You gotta be kidding. The guy's a pussy.'

'I'm not here for my health, Vince. You know I wouldn't bring this to you unless I really thought we had something.'

'You got shit, that's what you got. What, are you a rapist these days if you get a ticket?'

'The guy comes from Long Island not far from where that college girl lives. The rapist uses a .38 Colt, which was also the murder weapon. State records indicate O'Hanlon owns a .38 Colt. And he fits the general description.'

'What description? I read the papers. Every witness says something different.'

'There's another thing. We've been watching him. Saturday I tailed him myself. Twice in one day he goes to the same apartment at 65–44 Saunders Street. He hangs around, rings the buzzer, hangs around some more. This is the afternoon. Then he goes back eleven o'clock at night. Again no-one's there. And he's not acting like someone just making a friendly call.'

'You get the name?'

Joe nodded. 'Tina Paris.'

Vince stared at him. 'So they work together. Who knows what else they do. I don't keep tabs on my investigators after hours.'

'I don't know, it didn't look like that. At the very least, I think she has a right to be informed. We've got to follow every lead, you of all people know that. If your guy is not the one, let's prove it. But let's do it fast. I'm scared of what's going on out there. This guy's a lit fuse. He's not going to stop.'

Vince looked out the window. There were times when he hated this job, the responsibility and all the shit that went with it. Usually his panoramic view of river and sky offered solace; it reminded him he was on top, that he rarely had to take orders. There was nothing to cheer him today. The sky was heavy with the promise of rain, and a low-lying fog blurred the line between water and land. He looked back at Joe. 'OK, what do you need?'

'If we can establish his whereabouts during the time of the murder, and on the days of the last couple of rapes, maybe we can clear him.'

'I'll have to call his supervisor.'

'Can he be trusted?'

'Bud Ryan.'

'He's here? You're stealing all of our good ones.'

Vince buzzed Stacey and asked her to bring Bud in.

'Jesus Christ,' was all Bud said, when he had been given the rundown.

'I understand you've been working closely with O'Hanlon,' Joe said. 'Do you have any idea where he was last Sunday, the twenty-fifth of October?'

'He wasn't working that day, that's all I know.'

'What about the nineteenth of October.'

Bud looked at the calendar on the wall. 'That was a Monday. I'm not sure, maybe that was the day Terry didn't come in. Sometime that week he took a personal and I went out on a tail with Tina.' He turned to Joe. 'Why don't you give me a list of all the dates you need, and I'll check them out.'

Joe nodded. 'I'll get it to you by this afternoon. We're going to continue to keep an eye on him.'

'Let's work together on this one. I'll make Bud available for whatever you need.' Vince's voice was strained. The three men stood up and shook hands.

'We could be wrong,' Joe said. 'I hope we are.'

Chapter Twenty-three

We all knew what 'take a trip' meant, at least we assumed we did. But I couldn't help thinking there might be a point in taking Calvert literally. There are a lot of ways to go on a trip, both the temporary and permanent kind, but I decided to focus on the airports. It was really the car I was looking for, and buses and train stations in New York did not provide parking-lots. I hoped Vince was wrong about the car because searching for the Bonneville was the only thing I could think of to do. In my gut I felt it was the key, but maybe that was just my way of telling myself what I wanted to hear. After Auletta spotted me at the El Caribe, Calvert would be more on his guard than ever, and the chances of a surveillance picking something up were less than slim. The SNU still had a man in there, and Collins had promised to let me know if he heard anything, but I couldn't sit around the office waiting for the case to solve itself.

The rap sheet for Carlos Perales, the registered owner of the vehicle, had listed five street names, includ-ing Gato, confirming my hunch and giving my badly bruised ego a lift. He had been arrested for possession of drugs, burglary, and auto theft. Out of sixteen arrests, three had resulted in convictions. He had done some time but was currently out and off parole. I had called Muñoz yesterday when the report came in, and he agreed to check out the address. The canvass of the neighborhood around Mom's hadn't turned up anyone who had seen anything, at least not anyone who was willing to talk, and he was glad to have something useful for his team to do.

Muñoz turned out to be the perfect person for the assignment. Gato had been living with an aunt who said she hadn't seen him in a long time. Grateful to be communicating in her native tongue, she poured forth her worries about her nephew, who was always in trouble. She had been afraid to contact anyone about his disappearance. The last day she saw him was 24 October. The day Bud and I followed Calvert in the Bonneville was the twenty-sixth, the Monday after the search at Mom's. If Calvert had pegged Gato as the weak link in his alibi, the search could have made him nervous enough to take action. By the time we tailed Calvert in the Bonneville, Gato was probably already gone.

I had already checked for the car on the streets in Gato's neighborhood and around Calvert's apartment. I had driven up and down the blocks around Mom's and even tried the area around the Ninth Precinct. Calvert could have abandoned it on any street in the city, but people have a tendency to stick with their usual haunts. Unless they have a strong motivation. Maybe Calvert wanted to foster the idea that Gato really had gone somewhere. Instead of just dumping the car, he might be using it as a decoy. If the trip was a metaphor, it might be one Calvert was continuing to play out.

Before taking off for the airport, I put in a call to Collins to see if he had any news from the El Caribe or any word on Sweet Thing. When I mentioned where I would be, he said he would be on a surveillance at Kennedy. 'There's a pretty good diner on 150th Avenue right off Rockaway Boulevard. A handy place to grab a burger and take a break. Maybe I'll see you later,' he offered.

While I waited for the elevator, I was musing on the

possibility that Collins was putting out feelers. As the doors opened Vince stepped out and then surprised me by getting back in when he saw me.

'Was O'Hanlon working with you on Saturday night?'

The question and the setting both put me off balance. 'It was Mickey, it's in my report.'

'Not that I want to know all the dirt that goes on outside this office, but are you and Terry spending time off-duty?'

'Vince, are you smoking some funny cigars?'

'Can you think of any reason why he would be hanging around your apartment house?'

'What the hell are you getting at?'

'Remember I told you Sex Crimes thinks the Roulette guy might be someone in the system . . .'

I nodded. The elevator stopped. We stepped out into the lobby, and I followed him to an empty corner by the front window.

'Now they have reason to believe that Terry could be implicated in at least one of the rapes.'

I checked the expression in his eyes to see if he was joking.

'I know it's hard to believe. We don't know where it's going but I want you to know he was around your neighborhood Saturday night.'

It took me a while to digest the information. 'What do you mean, around my neighborhood?'

'In your building. Around five, and then later, after eleven.'

I thought about how strange Terry had been lately. 'You know, Vince, I was going to talk to you about him. The other night when we were tailing Calvert, he was really weird. He came in late again, really hung me up, and then he wouldn't talk about it. He acted like he was at war with someone. I hear a lot of things from guys out there, blowing off steam and stuff, telling me

277

their troubles, but this was different. There's something seriously off about the guy.'

'I had to suspend him about his absentee record anyway, so we sent him home. He doesn't know they suspect him yet. I'm not sure there's anything to it, but keep your back covered. Where are you off to?'

'Routine investigation.'

'Routine, my ass. Don't do anything stupid, like going undercover alone again. Bud is on the case, so if you see Terry you can contact either one of us, but don't tell anyone else in the office.'

'OK.'

'I'm serious. Watch your ass.'

I left the building, my head spinning. Terry had been acting peculiar, but the idea of him as a rapist and murderer was hard to swallow. Still, if you learned anything in my job, it was that people rarely were what they seemed, and all too often it turned out that being in policing was the perfect cover for committing a crime. It was impossible to know what to make of it; the idea that Terry had been at my place was too bizarre to be frightening. I wanted to believe there was some rational explanation. I hadn't known Terry a long time, but all other things aside, he was one of us.

Suddenly I thought about Maddy, ashamed that the last time I had tried to call her I had only been thinking about myself. She had been so frightened the other night; if there was a serious suspect who wasn't one of her dates, she had a right to know. I decided to try her from a pay phone. This time she picked up on the second ring.

'How are you doing?' I asked.

'Fine, if you don't mind five chains on your door.'

'I think I have some good news. They're on to something strong, and it has nothing to do with you.'

'Are you sure?'

'You know I can't get into it, but trust me on this.'

'You mean I can cancel my appointment with the plastic surgeon?'

'Yeah, but don't take any candy from strangers until we know more.'

'I'm on a diet anyway.'

'Well, stick to it.'

'You know me, a pillar of strength.'

'That's no joke.'

There was an awkward silence; Maddy was always embarrassed by compliments, even from me. 'That was a weird fax he sent the *Post*,' she said finally.

'Reminds me of the Son of Sam and all those letters he sent bragging about his victims. Creepy stuff.'

'Weren't you involved in that case?'

'Not till after Berkowitz was in jail. The SPO investigated the corrections officer who sold that picture to the Press. Remember the one? "Sam Sleeps." He snuck up on Berkowitz during the night and got paid five thousand dollars for one shot. A bit of an abuse of the office, you might say.'

'Pretty weird what humanity will pay to see pictures of.'

'I guess it was the idea that he shot all those people, but when he went to sleep he looked just like everybody else. As if rapists and murderers look any different from the rest of us.'

'Life would sure be simpler if they did.'

I laughed. 'Yeah, and we'd both be out of jobs.'

'How's your big case doing?'

'What is it you always say, if I didn't have bad luck I wouldn't have any luck at all.'

'If you need a shoulder, the Crisis Center is always open.'

'I know, I appreciate it, but I've just got to work it out. You take care of yourself.'

'I will.'

'No dates yet.'

'You think I'm crazy?'

I decided to start with La Guardia. Of the three airports in the New York area it was the closest and the easiest to get to from Calvert's apartment in Brooklyn. I drove out after work, just a hairbreadth ahead of the worst rush-hour traffic. There was a good view of two of the public parking-lots from the approach off the Grand Central Parkway. They were practically empty, and the same was true of the three on the other side of the 102nd Street Bridge entrance. I drove by on the service road surveying each lot. It was still light enough to see that there were no green Bonnevilles, so I was spared having to enter and pay each time. The parking garage was a more likely location and I pulled up the ramp, took a ticket, and slowly made my way around the levels. Indoor parking was much more popular, and the garage was almost full. As I reached the third level I saw a dull green boxy shape against the far wall and had a moment of hope, but when I got close to it, it proved to be a Chevy Impala.

I drove back down the ramp and handed my ticket to the guy in the booth at the bottom. I hadn't been in there ten minutes but the minimum was almost ten dollars with tax. I asked for a receipt and promised myself I would do my expense report on time. This could be an expensive expedition.

By this time the rush-hour traffic out to the Island had caught up with me, and it took almost an hour to get to Kennedy, plenty of time to build up my expectations – and an appetite. I thought about that diner Collins had mentioned, but I had a hunch about Long-Term Parking that had been growing all during the drive. If Calvert was playing with metaphors, what could be more perfect? I took the airport exit off the Van Wyck and followed the convoluted signs, which seemed to take me back past the same spot several times, to the Long-Term Parking-Lot. By the time I got there I felt like I was on another planet, or at least at another airport. It was at the far north-west corner, past the Federal Customs Building, down a narrow unpromising road, sandwiched between a murky canal and an expressway, and presided over by a couple of huge blue oil tanks. There was a gate and a tollhouse, but I couldn't believe I had come to the right place. The entire lot was empty. Not a car was in sight anywhere. I backed up, turned around, retraced my route and followed the signs all over again, only to land in the same location. I was too annoyed and discouraged to face the other lots without a break and made my way to Rockaway Boulevard.

The diner was easy to spot, one of those Greek jobs with the classic rectangular shape and a fake stone façade, sort of like a poor man's Roma. As I pulled into the lot I saw Collins's car parked near the front steps. I parked a couple of spaces over and couldn't resist the impulse to check my hair in the rear-view mirror before I got out. There was no denying that since I'd met Jeff I'd thought about him a lot, though not always positively. But what had made me so angry at first, what I saw as vanity and macho posturing, had come to seem, if not endearing, at least well earned. There was an honesty to Jeff and to his stance in the world that was becoming more and more appealing, especially after the dishonesty of Steve's smooth, easy-going manner. All that tenderness and caring that promised everything and gave nothing had come to seem like cruelty in the end. Even the bluntness of Jeff's anger and annoyance seemed preferable to the deceptive calm of life with Steve. And it was an anger I could understand, it had to do with the job, with his beliefs, with what he knew he was up against – it was an anger born out of commitment.

Since joining the SPO, I had avoided getting involved with men in the Department – too much conflict of interest, and most cops were too chauvinist and too one-dimensional anyway to appeal. But now I thought maybe I was wrong, maybe I was looking too much at the surface, maybe only someone in policing could understand what I was up against. Or maybe all this was rationalizing for the way I liked the humorous glint in his eye, the offhand way he flashed his smile, and that air he carried of alert animal energy. I thought about the way his Caribbean-blue eyes changed to an ominous pewter when he was angry and flashed with sparks of pure cobalt when he grinned, and it shocked me to realize that with everything else I had on my mind, I had taken the time to notice so much.

I pushed open the glass door of the diner and looked around. Most of the seats at the counter were taken by truckers and men in coveralls and blue-collar uniforms. A few of the booths were occupied by couples. In the far right corner, a slim, light-haired man in a tweed sports jacket sat with his back to me. I realized it wasn't Collins before I reached him, but he must have heard me coming because he turned around. 'Oh, Hal,' I said, blushing stupidly. 'I thought Jeff was here.'

'Don't look so disappointed.'

'I'm not,' I said, getting more flustered. 'I just thought that was his car in the lot.'

'It was.' His tone had a caustic edge, but his eyes registered amusement, not unlike Jeff's really, but paler and cooler, like bleached denim. 'Jeff's back at the location. My turn for the coffee run. Have a seat.'

'I can't, I'm on a job myself. I just thought I'd say hi and find out if he learned anything new from the El Caribe.'

'Not that I know of, but I'll tell him you were here.'

'Thanks.' I started to retreat.

'Been under any cars lately?'

I smiled weakly in answer to his broad grin. I couldn't get out of there fast enough; I hadn't felt that idiotic since junior high.

Parking-Lot 2 was the largest. I took a ticket at the gate and drove up and down the rows. It was almost full, the cars parked together tightly, and the only way I could be sure I wouldn't miss the Bonneville was to drive by each one. This was turning into a long, frustrating night. When I was satisfied the Bonneville wasn't there, I paid my four dollars, exited, drove on to the airport road, and followed the signs to the next lot, number 4. Four was closest to the international airlines, and to TWA and National. A likely location, but like 2, it yielded nothing. Next was 5, which abutted British Airways. It was smaller and didn't seem as promising. I almost decided to skip it, but I couldn't have been more wrong about Long Term so I entered and drove around twice to be sure.

I exited, paid another four dollars, followed the numbered colored signs through a few more loops, and reached Lot 3, which was the parking garage. My pulse started to race as I began the slow ascent. I wanted, I needed, the Bonneville to be here. I drove as slowly as I could and still maintain a forward motion and stopped every few minutes to be sure I didn't miss anything. I paused by every car that was even remotely similar to the Bonneville. Very few cars were of that vintage and shape, even fewer were the same color. I was beginning to doubt my memory of what I was looking for.

The garage was immense, with three sprawling storeys. It took me well over an hour to cover it at that pace, and when I got to the top and made the final circuit I was ready to scream in frustration. There was no green Bonneville. I pulled over into an empty space, got out and looked over the side at the circling traffic and airport runways beyond. The air was heady with that weird, unique New York airport mix of jet exhaust, carbon monoxide, ozone, and salt spray. Everything throbbed. A kind of vicarious excitement filled the atmosphere from the sheer pulse and whine of the planes taking off and landing, the knowledge that there were so many far-flung places to go to and come from. It had nothing to do with me, this strength, this energy, this lust for motion, but it filled my lungs with an elixir better than oxygen.

I got back in the car with renewed determination. There was still Lot 1, the first, but because of the routing of traffic, my last. Maybe I should have started there. I drove toward the exit ramp, moving slowly, about to shift gears, when I noticed something out of the corner of my eye: a dark shape parked in the shadow by the elevator shaft. I stopped, backed toward it. Dark green, big square trunk, no chrome fins. The numbers on the plate were scratched and obscured, but they matched. I got out and walked around to the front. There was no doubt about it. A forest-green 1964 Bonneville. I was so excited I reached out to try the door handle but stopped myself in time.

The nearest phone was across the road in the United Airlines building. I called Bud. He said it would take about forty minutes to get there. I went back into the garage, turned on the radio, and watched the car until Bud arrived with a big smile and a thermos of coffee. I trusted Bud's intuitions even more than my own, and I was thrilled to see he was almost as excited as I was. He had followed protocol and contacted Muñoz, who called CSU and also made arrangements with the local precinct. Together we waited for the team that would tow the car and start the work. It was one of the longest half-hours of my life. The guys finally arrived, rigged up the car, and we followed them to the One Hundredth in Howard Beach.

CSU dusted the doors, the mirrors, the trunk, and

the front near the hood latch – all the places an owner or driver might leave prints. Muñoz showed up while they were at it and stood a little apart from Bud and me to watch. He had been polite, as always, since the session in Vince's office, but he wasn't the type to forget easily. When the print guys were done, Eli Umansky, the CSU supervisor, came up to Bud. 'What do you want us to do now?'

'Let's open it up,' I said, before he had a chance to answer. It was my case. I'd found the car, I'd directed the team in the garage, but of course he had to go to the nearest likely male. I was pissed. I walked up determinedly, Umansky right behind me, and opened the driver's door. There was a clatter and I immediately stepped back. A couple of small objects had fallen to the ground. I took a piece of paper from the pad I was carrying, knelt down, and scooped up a single key and an empty crack vial. A forensic officer picked them off the paper with tweezers and placed them in evidence bags. I stood back and the team took over to do their work.

They dusted the wheel, the visors, the mirror, the knobs on the radio, the lighter, the handles. They combed the inside of the car, checking behind visors, under cushions, in the glove compartment, under the mats. The car seemed to be pretty well cleaned out. It was almost midnight. 'You've been at it for sixteen hours,' Bud said. 'I can finish up here.'

'I'll hang around a little longer,' I answered. I was still hoping for something more conclusive. They finally finished with the interior of the car and jimmied the lock of the trunk. A blue vinyl gym bag rested next to the spare tire. The bag was dusted for prints and then carefully opened. Inside, underneath a rolled-up pair of pants and a dirty T-shirt, was a Glock 9mm semi-automatic pistol.

Chapter Twenty-four

Joe fielded his fiftieth call of the day and was surprised to hear Vince Bruno's hoarse, commanding voice.

'You got anything solid on O'Hanlon yet?'

'We're still working on it.'

'Piss or get off the pot. I can't suspend him indefinitely.'

'In a case like this, it's not so simple.'

'C'mon, Joe. First you come in here telling me he's your guy. Bud goes through his work schedule and there's nothing to eliminate his presence at any of the attacks.'

'The photo ID wasn't conclusive. The only rape victim who picked him out had over a year to forget her attacker's face.'

'We know the perp changes his appearance. Bring the guy in for a line-up. You can put glasses on, change the hair. Maybe you'll jog some memories. Seeing the guy in the flesh is a whole different ball game.'

'And if we don't get an ID, we lose him. A serial killer is a touchy beast. Usually above average in intelligence. Extremely cunning and, at times, capable of extraordinary control. If he senses he's close to being caught, he could go underground, stop for a while and resurface at another time, maybe in another location, starting the whole cycle over and making it that much more difficult to put the pieces together.' He sighed. 'It's a tough call, but I don't want to tip him off until I know we have enough to convict.'

'It's out of my hands. MacCallister had to be brought

in on this. He blew a gasket. The reputation of the office is at stake. He wants it cleared up. We're going to bring Terry in.'

'Vince, I can't let politics get in the way. I battle that stuff around here all the time.'

'It's not my call. I don't want to blow this any more than you do. But if MacCallister says do it, we do it. I told him it's your case, you've got to be in on it. Bud'll swing by your office in a few minutes, so the two of you can pick him up.'

Joe didn't like it; he wasn't ready – but he knew the system. He had to work with what he had. He called Ann over and asked her to put together a line-up and to start calling in the victims. Maybe one of them would pick O'Hanlon out. Then he radioed the surveillance team to tell them he would intercept. By the time Bud arrived he was waiting downstairs.

After a cursory greeting they rode in silence out to Lake Success. 'I know you don't want to hear this,' Bud said after a while, 'but I'd hate for him to be your man.'

'You and I combined have about sixty years on the job, between us we've seen a lot of stuff go down. I don't know about you, but I can never understand how one day you're a cop, the next day you're an animal.'

'It happens, much too often, but we still don't know what we have here.'

As they approached Terry's street, Joe radioed the team to say they were in the area. An officer advised that O'Hanlon had just left his residence. They were about to turn onto Birch Hill Road to O'Hanlon's complex when they saw him pull out onto Lakeville and turn toward the Long Island Expressway. Bud made a quick U-turn. 'I'll just pull him over.'

'Looks like he's heading in. Why don't we let him go, see where he takes us.'

Bud shrugged his assent and hung back as Terry

led them on to the expressway. They followed him as he made his way into the city through the Midtown Tunnel and on to Second Avenue.

'He's changing his pattern. We've been tailing him for over a week and this is the first time he's come into Manhattan.'

'He's headed downtown, maybe he's going to the office.'

He took a right on Houston, and when he started slowing near Thompson, Moskowitz visibly stiffened. 'He's never returned to a location before, but we're headed straight for the Levenson girl's place.'

There were no spaces in front of the building. Terry seemed oblivious to their presence as he pulled around the corner and parked at a meter on La Guardia. They hung back as he got out of his car, locked it, and walked briskly around the corner. 'I'm too old for this shit,' Joe said, jumping out of the car before Bud had come to a full stop. Terry was already inside by the time they sprinted into the lobby. They pushed past a delivery boy who was rolling his Grand Union cart out the door, and headed for the stairs. It had been a long time since either man had faced this kind of exertion and they were panting heavily by the time they reached the fourth floor. As they pulled the hall door open, they heard another door close down the corridor. The two men exchanged glances, drew their guns in unison, and rushed up to Denise Levenson's apartment.

'Police, open up,' Joe called, pounding loudly. They flattened themselves on opposite sides of the frame as they heard the lock turning. The door opened and Denise stepped out, barefoot, in jeans and a T-shirt, her eyes wide with surprise.

'Where is he?' Joe asked. He barely heard her say 'Who?' when the door to the left of them opened as well. 'Oh, shit,' he said, when he realized it was Gordon Jaeger's apartment.

'What's going on?' Gordon said, recognizing Moskowitz immediately.

'We think he's in the building,' Joe said, starting to explain. He was looking past Gordon's shoulder into the apartment when Terry came out of a room in the back and walked up to the door. 'Is something wrong, Gordie?' His tone was concerned and perplexed. Nothing in his stance seemed even remotely threatening. Then he noticed Bud. 'Ryan, what are you doing here?'

'We were chasing a subject,' Bud stammered, looking from one man to the other and lowering his gun. 'We thought he came this way.' Color was rising up from Terry's collar, tinting his face scarlet. 'Looks like we made a mistake.' He nudged Joe's elbow. 'Sorry,' he said, 'forget it ever happened.'

Terry just stood transfixed as the two older men started backing away.

Chapter Twenty-five

It was Thursday night when I found the car. I had to endure a tense, nerve-rackingly empty weekend, praying we now had the evidence we needed and contemplating the wasteland of my private life. We still didn't have a body, I had no information on Lenora, but for once I accepted the fact that there was nothing I could do but wait.

Bud called on Saturday to fill me in on developments with Terry. He wanted to let me know Terry was no longer a suspect in case I was worried about those reports of him stalking my apartment, but I also think he just needed to talk. He described how he and Joe Moskowitz had almost picked Terry up, and said they both felt like shit. For once he didn't try to soften his language even for me. He couldn't get over the fact that they were going to bring the guy in on the basis of a parking ticket, and all he was doing was visiting a friend. That it was a male friend made it even worse. Terry's private life would have been exposed, his career ruined. We both knew he had good reason for keeping his homosexuality secret: to a lot of guys in policing, including a lot of the brass, being gay is right up there with major crimes. Not as bad as murder, maybe, but probably worse than rape. And in view of his strained relationship with his girlfriend, Sarah, it was apparently something he was just coming to terms with himself. It occurred to me that Terry had probably been looking for me Saturday to apologize for his behavior on our surveillance, or maybe he just needed to have that talk. As soon as someone became a suspect, everything they did seemed suspicious.

I thought about calling Maddy after I hung up with Bud, but why burst her bubble? I knew she was being careful. Knowing the rape investigation was back to square one wouldn't help anything; it would only fan her fears.

The reports were ready on Monday. I picked them up on my way to the office. The search of the car didn't give us everything we wanted, but almost. Firing tests confirmed that the bullets extracted from the wall of Mom's card room were fired from the gun found in the trunk. The gun had been wiped clean, but two sets of Calvert's prints had been lifted, a clear set on the steering wheel and a partial on the key that had fallen out when I opened the door. Gato's prints had been found on the visor and crack vial. The prints on the other surfaces had been too smudged to be identified.

We now had physical evidence connecting Calvert to the car where the murder weapon was found, but the connection was still circumstantial. His prints on the gun would have been an easy conviction, but at least we were getting closer. In the afternoon, the property room delivered a cigar box containing an assortment of small objects removed from the car. I cleared a space on the top of my desk and took each item out. The key, a grease-covered ballpoint pen, a couple of dog-eared matchbooks, a pencil stub, a set of Allen wrenches, a couple of screwdrivers. A meager and pathetic group of articles, the leavings, apparently, of a meager and pathetic life. And yet I couldn't repress a feeling of excitement as I looked at them.

I picked each item up, studied it carefully, and replaced it. The key, of course, was the most interesting. It was a chrome key with a hexagonal top. The name S. Parker was embossed on one side with the words

TRADE MARK along the angles at the top. SP-00560 was printed on the other side, with the words BRASS PADLOCK. A basic padlock key. I would put in a call to the company to see where the locks were sold, but I didn't have much hope a purchaser of such a common item could be traced. And where was the lock the key opened? The key was the key, but what was it the key to? It seemed strangely fitting that the letters SPO should appear on it, though I could see it signified nothing more than a serial number and the initials of the company that made it. I felt like a child caught in a nursery rhyme – Alice through the looking glass – I hoped it was more than a bad pun.

I put the key aside and concentrated on the rest. The pencil was too chewed up to be useful, the matchbooks were the generic kind. I opened each one and held it under the light, searching for writing, scratching of numbers, any fragments of communication, but there was none. The wrenches and screwdrivers were handy for picking the locks but revealed nothing about their owner. That left the pen. It was almost totally covered with some greasy residue, possibly mechanic's grime, that had been either deliberately wiped with a rag or smudged during use. I twisted it under the light. It was the kind of cheap pen businesses had imprinted with their names and addresses, and I could just barely make out some letters under the grease. I placed it back on my desk and rummaged in my top drawer for my magnifying glass.

The first letter looked like an *R*. The next few were completely obliterated, but then I could make out an *n*, then something smudged that looked like it might be a *p* or maybe a *b*, and an *o*, and then another letter I couldn't read. The second line began with an *M*. I was struggling to make out the rest, holding it close to the light, squinting at the little scratchings left, when a folder landed on my desk. I jumped back and turned to see Jeff Collins grinning a satisfied little-boy grin at my alarm. 'Everything we know about Alvin Decker, a.k.a. Sweet Thing.'

'You traced him?'

'Our man in the El Caribe fingered him. That's the good news.'

'The bad?'

'He's gone. Left the city as far as we can tell. We'll keep looking, though, in case he resurfaces.'

'Calvert must have put the word out.'

'That's the way we see it.' He sat down in the chair next to my desk and surveyed my little arsenal of junk. 'Sorry I missed you the other night,' he said. 'I hear you struck gold.'

'Almost,' I said. 'The murder weapon with no prints. A key to god knows what, a pen with most of the letters scratched off.'

'Slim pickings,' he said and laughed.

I saw Bud coming toward us out of the corner of my eye. He stiffened noticeably when he saw Jeff. 'Detective Collins.' He nodded at Jeff, glanced over at me and looked away. 'I thought you had an aversion to the SPO.'

Jeff stood up. 'Thanks for reminding me.' He turned back to me. 'Catch you later, Tina,' he said, and walked out.

The S. Parker company confirmed what I thought. They had delivered fifteen hundred padlocks to the New York area during the last two years, over five hundred had the same style number and they had gone to over a hundred hardware, housewares, and miscellaneous stores. I told the clerk to send me a list of the customers who had sold this particular model and thanked him for his trouble. Then I went back to studying the pen. '*R—npo—M—St—e.*' Not much to go on. The pen itself seemed to be a multicolor stripe. I tried to think what kind of things would be locked with a padlock. Bicycles with padlocks were everywhere in the city, but I didn't think that was what we were looking for in this case. Anything you could close with a chain – a freezer. If that's what the lock was to, I was no closer to learning where it was.

I was sitting at my desk, Mickey opposite me, on the phone as usual. He watched me holding the key, turning it in my hand, viewing it from all angles. 'It's the key to Nydia's chastity belt,' he said when he hung up.

'Yeah, right.' Then I remembered something I had heard a while ago. 'Hey, Mickey, you know why more women than men have hemorrhoids?'

'You must be kidding?' He ran his hand through his wild hair in a vain gesture to smooth it down.

'C'mon, why do you think?'

His expression was skeptical; I never told him jokes. He was definitely curious, though.

'I don't know, tell me.'

I leaned back in my chair and smiled. 'Because men are the perfect assholes.'

There was always a point when a case either came together or fell apart, and with the Calvert investigation I knew this week was it. My satisfaction at finding the car and the murder weapon and my obsession with solving the mystery of the key had temporarily distracted me from the problem of Lenora. I still had to locate my main witness. My buddy at the Postal Inspector's office hadn't come up with an address. Apparently she wasn't yet having her mail forwarded. Maybe she hadn't actually moved. Maybe she was just staying with a friend or relative and having her mail picked up. But if she wasn't planning on moving, why had she packed all those boxes? Maybe the boxes had nothing to do with anything, or maybe she had been planning to put her stuff in storage so she could take off at a moment's notice. It didn't seem likely, but it was certainly possible. The city was full of those storage places. You saw them advertised all the time.

I was staring at her file, trying to decide what to do next, when I thought about the key. It was so obvious I couldn't believe I hadn't thought of it before. Moving. Storage. Maybe the key was to a lock on one of those storage rooms. Or did they have regular locks like doors? I could call some and find out. I hefted the NYNEX Yellow Pages onto my desk, turned to Storage, and just on the off chance that the pen was related, flipped to the Rs. There it was, a full-page ad. Rainbow MiniStorage. *Self-Storage*, the copy read. *Safe, Private, Month-to-Month Rentals, Your Lock, Your Key*. I stopped only long enough to tell Bud where I was going, grabbed my coat and was out the door.

Rainbow MiniStorage was a converted eight-storey warehouse at the river's edge in Fort Greene, not far from Calvert's home. The office was up a flight of steps by the loading ramp. I showed the clerk my ID and asked if they had a space rented to Edward Calvert. She went into the back room, conferred with her boss, who apparently told her to cooperate, because she came back and started going through her files. After a few minutes she said there was no-one by that name listed.

Shit, I thought, what now? He could have used a different name, but what? Then it hit me. That slick bastard. 'Try Carlos Perales,' I said. She went back to her file and quickly returned with his card. I asked if I could see it. Gato had rented an eight-by-ten room on 18 September, the day after the shooting, and paid six months in advance. The address listed was the apartment he shared with his aunt. I stared at the card so long the clerk asked me if something was wrong. 'Everything's fine,' I said. I was like a person in the desert who finally found water but couldn't believe it wasn't a mirage.

I rummaged in my bag for photos of Calvert and Gato and showed them to the clerk. She said they didn't look familiar. The boss came out of the office and took a look and then passed them to a porter who was wheeling a large metal dolly outside. No-one remembered seeing either one. 'You know how many people come through here in a week?' the boss said with rhetorical bravado, handing them back.

'Actually, I don't,' I said under my breath, and then asked if I could see the room. He directed the porter to take me up in the elevator.

The space was on the fourth floor. We rode up in silence and I followed him to room 413. I hadn't brought the key with me, although I could have signed it out. Even in my excitement at making the connection I knew I had to be cautious – if the body was here I wanted everything to be done by the book. The porter led me down a long hallway past a stack of boxes. 'I gotta put these on the elevator,' he said. 'The room's over there.' I continued past several more rooms until I came to 413. It had a metal door secured by a padlocked hasp. I didn't touch the lock, but I looked at it closely enough to see the logo 'S. Parker' stamped on its side.

I went downstairs to put in the call to Bud. I knew this was it; I had to get back upstairs and watch the room. But I had a tremendous urge to call Jeff Collins. I wanted to share the excitement with him. He wasn't, strictly speaking, part of the investigation, but after Mom's and the El Caribe it seemed he belonged. I dialed the number. 'They ain't here,' the guy who answered the phone said. When I asked if there was any way to reach Jeff, he said they were 'out in the field', and asked if I wanted to leave a message. I didn't.

The entourage arrived less than an hour later – Bud, Muñoz, the forensics guys, Eli Umansky from CSU.

'We could be having an affair with all the time we're spending together,' he said when he saw me.

Forensics dusted for prints and then Bud handed me the key. They all stood back a little and watched while I fit it in the lock. It turned easily. I pulled the prongs free and slipped the lock from the hasp, handing it to Umansky, who put it in an evidence bag. Everyone was quiet. For once there were no wisecracks. I flipped the latch back and pulled open the heavy metal door.

The smell was like ether. Pungent and sweet. It seeped toward us like a genie oozing out of a bottle. For a moment nobody moved. Against the back wall was a large white chest-type freezer. It was the only object in the room. Bud and Umansky stepped around me and went in. They didn't ask my permission or suggest I join them, and for once I had no desire to complain. Something in their demeanor made it clear they weren't one-upping me or being patronizing. Both of them had enough experience with homicides to know what they were likely to find. They were sparing me something I didn't need to see out of consideration and respect. I had done enough. I didn't need to prove how tough I could be.

I watched from the door as they opened the freezer. This time the stench hit me like a tidal wave. Bud held his handkerchief over his nose and looked in. 'I think we've got him,' he said, turning quickly away.

Chapter Twenty-six

Janice Smithson was her name. Almost two weeks to the day before he saw her again. He walked into the lounge one evening and there she was, perched on her stool at the bar, wearing her little outfit. He watched her for about fifteen minutes, glancing in her direction from time to time, careful not to stare. Nothing blatant. Nothing threatening. Just a little friendly interest. He didn't know if she remembered seeing him from the time before, but it didn't matter. If he played it right, she would come to him. He just had to keep cool, stay relaxed. Everything would work, as long as he would let it happen. Everything had changed, but nothing had changed really. He just had to trust in fate, trust in himself, keep his vision pure, not get distracted.

He made his move as she got up and was about to walk by. 'You on a stopover?' he asked, just as he had imagined he would. She nodded. 'I thought maybe that was it. Let me buy you a drink, or better still, dinner.' She started to interrupt him, getting ready to refuse. But after the merest hesitation, he went on, infusing his smile with just a hint of entreaty. 'C'mon, don't say no. I hate to eat alone, especially when there's such an attractive alternative.'

He didn't know if he had gone too far with this dinner bit, he hadn't planned on saying it, but she smiled and he took that as a yes, picked up his glass, and led her to a table against the wall. It didn't take long to find out what he needed to know. She had flown in on a Braniff flight from London, had the weekend off, and was flying out Sunday night. She had booked a room with a friend who was coming in on a midnight arrival from Amsterdam.

He smiled and watched her as she chatted about her flights to Europe and her favorite cities. He hardly had to say a thing as she twittered her way through dinner, thinking he was so damned charmed, as if he were no better than those dodo businessmen she passed out overpriced drinks and cheap snacks to on the plane. He found himself relaxing into it, his pulse steady, his palms perfectly dry.

He had never had such a long preamble before. Usually he didn't even know their names till it was over. She sipped wine, growing warmer and more relaxed under his bemused gaze. The effort of keeping up the pretense would be amply rewarded later when the truth dawned and he watched her confusion turn to disbelief and then to shock. He didn't rush it; he wanted her at ease until the last second.

By the time dinner was finished the invitation to her room was a mutual assumption. They walked together to the lobby, where he excused himself and went to the men's room while she picked up the key at the desk. It was enough to be seen by the waitress; he didn't need to be examined by the desk clerk as well. Not that he had anything to worry about. He studied his face in the mirror, combing his hair. The man looking back resembled him, but was not him. The effect he had created was good, excellent, in fact. Exactly what he wanted. The composite in the paper was way off. For all the hysteria in the Press, the cops were no closer to nailing him than before, but then, he had worked to make their job difficult. Doing undercover had been excellent training – maybe he should let them know sometime just how useful his training had been. Put out some tips to would-be criminals – try being a cop first. He laughed. Maybe he'd do it in the next fax.

As he walked back down the hall, it occurred to him she might not be there. Something might have spooked her; her woman's intuition might have come into play; she might have decided she was better off alone. But he was confident he had let nothing slip. It was Friday, 13 November, and she would be the thirteenth. He wasn't superstitious. He didn't believe in bad luck, and it wasn't any of that satanic shit. He wasn't into anything like that. It wasn't that the numbers were magic, he just liked the fatedness of it. And the going against the grain. She would be the best one yet.

He smiled at her warmly as she fidgeted with the key going up in the elevator, but as soon as they had stepped inside the room he turned serious. He took his driving gloves out of his pocket and used them to hold the plastic 'Do Not Disturb' sign as he slipped it onto the outside knob. Then he closed and bolted the door and put the chain on. When he turned back to her, a look of vague confusion had clouded her eyes.

'A little too fast for you?'

She shrugged and nodded at the same time. Not wanting to believe his transformation. 'How about this?' He moved close, speaking right up into her face, leaning into her, bullying her with his body so that she had to step backward toward the bed.

'What are you doing? What's going on?'

'What the hell do you think is going on?' Suddenly he was angry. This had taken long enough. He pulled the gloves on.

'I thought we were having a good time.' Her confusion hovered on the cusp of fear. She simply couldn't make the transition from what she thought had been happening to this new reality.

He continued pressing her backward toward the bed, and when she was close enough he grabbed her shoulders and pushed her down. She tried to leap up and at the same time lunge to the right toward the telephone, but he caught her arm, grabbed the phone, and pulled it out of the wall. She jerked away from him, ran around the other side of the bed, looked wildly for something to use as a weapon, and picked up a lamp. Then she realized she couldn't throw it and tried to yank the plug out of the socket by tugging on the cord. It distracted her for just a second as she turned to look at it, and by the time she turned back the gun was pointed straight at her head. She opened her mouth and closed it without a sound.

She was quick and agile, he had to give her that. But it wouldn't do her any good. He was sick of this shit.

'You'd better put that down now.'

Their eyes locked briefly and she replaced the lamp on the table.

'Now why don't you come back over here? Nice and close.'

She walked slowly, each step deliberate, taking as long as she could. When she was in front of him, he took the muzzle of the gun, stroked her cheek with it, and used it to gently lift her hair behind her ear. She stood straight, her jaw set in anger and defiance. Only the tremor in her limbs gave her away.

'You think you're hot shit, don't you? Janice Smithson, in from London.' She didn't move. With his free hand he grabbed the front of the tailored blouse under her jacket and ripped it open. 'Get this stuff off. All of it. And make it quick.' She hesitated a second, then slowly removed her jacket.

He cocked the gun. All it took was the sound.

She slipped out of her shoes. She unzipped her skirt and stepped out of it, and then undid the buttons that were left on the blouse. Underneath she had on a slip and then panty hose and a bra. It wasn't until she was almost naked that her lower lip started to quiver and she began to cry.

That was better. He removed his own jacket and placed it neatly on the other bed behind him.

'We need to play a little game,' he said.

She shook her head slightly from side to side. A pathetic little-girl gesture of refusal. Suddenly he felt his body swelling. He grabbed the nape of her neck and forced her down into a kneel. 'Open the zipper,' he said. She didn't move. He put the gun to her temple and she quickly unbuckled his belt and pulled down the zipper. He let go of her neck and released himself.

'Ever suck one of these?'

She shook her head. He laughed, pushing her face down until her lips were pressed against him. A shudder rocked his body. 'I should shove it down your throat, you stupid cunt.'

She tried twisting her head away and he pulled back the hammer. 'So innocent. What are you more afraid of, a dick or a gun?' When she opened her mouth to answer he shoved the barrel in. 'Eat this,' he said. Her pupils widened in terror as her eyes darted wildly around the room. 'Looking for a way out? There's no way out, only more ways in.' He started to laugh harder; his joke seemed inordinately funny. And she looked so stupid – helpless and stupid. 'To fire or not to fire: that is the question.' He pulled the hammer, cocking the gun, listening for the first click, waiting for the thrill of anticipation to hit him, but it didn't come. Something wasn't right. He released the hammer and withdrew the gun.

It was her fault. He pulled her up by the arm and threw her back on the bed. She was coughing and shaking with fear, but her eyes followed him like a cornered rabbit. He didn't trust her. He would have to tie her up. He grabbed her panty hose off the floor, ripped into the nylon with his teeth, and tore it apart. Taking the longest piece, he used it to tie her wrists together, binding them and then wrapping it around her waist and tying them down in front of her, doing it quickly, keeping the gun ready. But she was apparently too terrified and confused to resist. He tied the second piece securely around her mouth. It made an excellent gag. He thought he had everything secure, when suddenly she started kicking, putting all her strength into it, flailing her legs in the air. He grabbed one ankle and twisted it hard.

Her fighting made him furious at the same time that it jolted him with desire. He knelt over her, wrenching her ankle outward while pressing his knee down on her other thigh, forcing her legs apart. He stared at her exposed body and knew exactly what he had to do. 'I bet you've had a lot of different dicks in there, but you've never had one like this.' He shoved the gun up inside her, grabbing her tied hands and crushing them against his crotch. His gasp of pleasure matched hers of pain. Kneeling above her, rubbing himself fiercely against her hands, he was mesmerized by the sight of the hard, shiny barrel disappearing into her darkness. It was too much. His temples throbbed; he couldn't seem to breathe; he thought he would pass out. And then it was over in one explosive, agonizing rush. He hadn't even cocked the gun. He pulled it from her and collapsed on the bed.

She rolled away, drawing her knees up, pressing her head into the crumpled spread. They lay that way for what seemed like a long time, each in their own world. After a while he became aware of the bed moving and realized she was sobbing. It was no good; he had lost control. The game hadn't changed; he had changed. He had to get back to it, to make things right. He stood up, straightened his clothes and ran a comb through his hair. Then he looked back at her. She looked pathetic, her body pale and deflated like a wounded doe. Let her go, a small discordant voice within him said. He picked up the gun. He had to put her out of her misery, complete the kill. It was all there was left to do.

But he had to play by the rules. He opened the barrel and checked the bullets. The five hollow points sat neatly in their chambers. Russian Roulette! He would give them the real thing this time – only one empty round. He studied the bullets for a second and then snapped the cylinder closed. The sound echoed in the quiet room and made her turn her head. It was strange, he had almost forgotten she was still alive.

She looked at him, not comprehending. He spun the cylinder. 'Life or death,' he said, 'it's all in a twirl.' He knelt astride her again, holding down both legs this time, and put the gun to her head. He pulled back the hammer and pressed his finger on the trigger, gently at first and then harder as the resistance increased. This was one of the things he liked about the Colt, the way the trigger stacked up to a clean, hard, satisfying break. When the blast came he jumped immediately back and turned away.

He looked around the room, disoriented, unsure of what to do. He was so tired. He turned off the light and sat down in the single chair. He needed to pull himself together, get hold of his thoughts, regain control – of himself, of the game. Maybe it was time for a message, tell them what he had done, taunt them with it. Warn them. He started to compose it in his mind; he wanted to make it good. There would not be many more. He could sense that in the quickening of everything – a turmoil in his blood, in his brain – that was compressing time. He was moving toward it – something big. He didn't know what it was exactly, something special. Different. Twice now he'd gotten too caught up. It was no good blaming himself, it must be a sign. It was time to up the ante. Look for a prey worthy of himself – a prey that would require all his skill and keep him focused.

Suddenly he remembered the room-mate. Janice hadn't been frightened when she told him about the other stewardess; he didn't think it was a ruse. He could wait, do her too, but all his senses were telling him he needed to get out of there. He was breathing too hard, the back of his neck felt clammy, he needed some air. He took a sheet of hotel stationery from the table drawer, ripped off the name at the top, and printed his message. Then he picked up Janice's purse, took out her wallet, flipped through the bills and pulled out a twenty, enough for the fax. He looked in the mirror and, on an impulse, grabbed her lipstick and scrawled a large number 13 on the glass.

No-one saw him in the hall or on the staircase or in the parking garage. The nearest fax machine that would be available at this hour was probably in the International Arrivals Building. It took him only a few minutes to drive there on the airport road. He pulled up in front, put his police insignia on the visor, left the car, and calmly approached the sliding doors. He strode in purposefully, located the machines, took the paper from his jacket pocket, and positioned it for sending.

To the NYPD

Two down now.
How many more?
I'm going after bigger game.
The Captain should be proud.
Stop me if you can.

I'M ZEROED IN.

Chapter Twenty-seven

Now that we had a body, it was imperative to find Lenora. I had previously subpoenaed her phone records to see if there was a history of calls between her and Calvert, and now I went over them again. One number cropped up continuously. It was listed in the reverse directory under the name of Viola Marsden DeWitt in Co-op City in the Bronx. A little more research revealed that Lenora had given Viola's name to the Housing Authority as her nearest relative when she rented the apartment. I decided to drop in on Viola at dinner-time; I didn't even consider calling first. If Lenora was staying there, I didn't want to give her the opportunity to skip for good. I ran the situation by Wing, and he prepared a subpoena in case it appeared Lenora was going to be unwilling to testify after all.

The Bronx was not my usual beat. I worked all the boroughs but hadn't had a case there in years. The huge, bland, monolithic towers of the Co-op City development dominated a barren, desolate landscape of empty lots, gas stations, and two-storey row houses in the outer reaches of the city. There were no adjacent shopping areas, no cafés or friendly neighborhood bars, no movie houses or interesting little shops for browsing, no store windows to stroll by – no street life at all. The towers, and the 'city' they created, were as self-contained as a prison. The buildings were taller, cleaner, better maintained and appointed than the projects, but they shared the same soul-destroying insularity.

I drove around Co-op City Boulevard until I found Carver Loop and located the right tower. Viola's apartment was on the third floor, where presumably the prices were lower and the views not as good, but what the upper floors had views of except each other was difficult to imagine. I waited outside and entered the lobby behind a mother too busy with kids and bicycles to question me as I slipped in the door beside her, so when I rang Viola's apartment bell it was a complete surprise. A woman's voice answered immediately, calling out, 'Who's that?' in harsh tones. 'It's Tina Paris,' I stated loudly through the door. 'I'd like to talk to Lenora.' There was a moment of silence and then I could hear a different voice coming from the back of the apartment. 'Lenora,' I called, 'I need to see you.' I hated screaming through the door, but I couldn't afford to be turned away. There was a murmuring of voices, which quickly took on an urgent cast. Then a door slammed somewhere in the apartment, and I heard footsteps approaching on the uncarpeted floor. The door remained shut, however, and whoever was on the other side was quiet. 'Lenora, if that's you, please let me in. I can't leave until we talk.'

'How'd you find me?' she asked, opening the door. She looked thinner than I remembered, even more worn down and bedraggled than when I first visited her back in Brooklyn.

'Don't worry,' I said, 'I haven't told anyone where you are, not even my boss.' She didn't respond. Her stance as she blocked the doorway conveyed a kind of stubborn inertia. 'I don't think we should talk in the hall, do you?' She moved aside to let me in without a word.

I hadn't allowed myself to think about what I would say before I came, but now I could see it would be even harder than anything I might have imagined. I looked around the apartment, trying to think of a way to break through the passive resistance created by her anger and lethargy. The subpoena was definitely a last resort. I turned back and looked into her eyes. The defiance, the pride, the crazed determination were gone, replaced by the blankness of despair. I looked away and focused on a montage of framed family photos on top of the TV. Lenora stood in one with a handsome uniformed dark-skinned man, a younger Kari in his arms. 'That must be Danny?' I said.

Her eyes followed mine to the picture. Without answering she walked up to the TV, picked up the photo, and turned it face down. 'What do you want from me?'

'I thought we had a deal. I thought we were going to work together.'

This brought a contemptuous laugh. 'Where'd this "we" come from? There's you and there's me and I don't see you losing everything you got.'

'Look, I know how you feel. I know this case is hard on you.'

'You don't know nothin'.'

'Lenora, I tried to help you. I said I would get your phone number changed.'

'That don't mean shit and you know it.'

She was right, but somehow I had to get her back, to touch the part of her that wanted to help. I had never heard her sound so hard or so angry. 'Calvert is just going to keep on hurting people unless we stop him. I need you to help me do that.'

'I can't play cards, can't even go to the social clubs any more. Can't even walk around my own neighborhood. No-one talks to me. When I go to the store they don't even look me in the eye.'

'I'm sorry people are treating you that way, but you're playing right into his hands by walking out.'

'I should never have told you he beat me. I was stupid

to mess things up. So what if he shot some chump. It was none of my business. I should have kept my eyes closed and my mouth shut.'

'But you didn't. Something told you it was right to call us. I know it's scary, but you did the right thing.'

'Let me tell you something, then you tell me about the right thing. Last Thursday I go to pick up Kari like usual, only when I get there I can see he's all upset. So I ask him what happened and he tells me this big cop came to school and took him out of class. "Tell your momma Eddie was here, and if she don't chill I'm comin' back, and then you and me are goin' on a trip far away and she won't be seein' you no more." He's sayin' this to my boy right in the school, like he don't care what anybody think, like he can do anything. I didn't let Kari out of my sight after that. Didn't let him go out to play, or take him to the babysitter. Didn't let him go back to school. I scraped together what I could and borrowed the rest from my sister and sent him to his father in Texas.'

'Shit,' I said. 'Why didn't you call me? I would have had Calvert picked up on harassment charges immediately.'

'Cause you ain't got no juice and you don't give a shit. You think you're something special, telling me you're different, but you're not. You got your job to do and if it messes up someone's life, too bad. Wrap up this case, then move on to another one, right? Find another sucker who falls for your bullshit line about doin' the right thing. You caused me more trouble than Eddie ever did. I don't even know why I'm talkin' to you. You don't mean nothin' on the street and you don't mean nothin' in this apartment neither.'

'I'm sorry, Lenora, I really am. I never wanted to hurt you.'

'Yeah, well, what people want and what they do is two different things.'

I was devastated by what she said; I had no answer.

'At least I don't have to worry about dying no more. I died when I put Kari on that plane.'

Her words pierced through whatever professional armor I had left. I didn't want to admit it, but everything she said was true. I hadn't been thinking about her as a person. She was my witness, someone to coddle along until she testified and gave me what I wanted. I had been more irritated than concerned at her hysteria and threats of suicide. I forced myself to look at her. Her defiance had energized her, given her some of her life back, but it was a sad testament to me that that was all she had left. All that stuff I told myself about defending the 'little people' was just so much bullshit if the little people were the ones that got hurt. Here she was without her son, without a home, and what was I really after? I wanted to put Eddie Calvert behind bars, sure, but what good was that if I had to steamroll over innocent lives to do it? She had my number, all right, and there was nothing I could say or do to change anything. I turned away and walked over to the window, pulled the beige drapes aside, and looked out at the blank vista of the building across the courtyard. The last thing I would ever do now was use that subpoena.

'I'll let my prosecutor know that you are withdrawing from the case,' I said. 'I'll tell him I couldn't find you and that you left me a message to that effect.' I let the curtain drop and without looking at her walked toward the door.

'What are you gonna do about Eddie?'

'I'll get the son of a bitch another way,' I said. 'We found Slick's body, we have a good case.' I reached for the doorknob but turned to her before I opened it. 'You're right about me and the system, Lenora. You'll never know just how sorry I am for what you're going through, but I have to go after him.'

'My sister says you did me a favor getting me out of that life.'

'I always figured you had more going for you than that.'

'When are they gonna testify against Eddie?'

'The grand jury will be sometime next week.'

'They don't need to know where I am, right?'

'I already said you're not part of it any more.'

'Maybe I'll be there, as long as nobody knows where to find me or my son except you.'

'Lenora, I appreciate what you're saying, and I think you mean well. But I can't take much more of this. Don't tell me you're in unless you mean it once and for all.'

'I don't know . . . I mean, Eddie doing what he did, it's not your fault.' She had tears in her eyes. 'He don't belong out on the street, that's for sure.' She took a piece of paper from a phone table by the door and wrote something. 'Here's my sister's number. If anyone but you calls or comes here I'm out. Otherwise I'll do it. Just call me and tell me when.'

She held out the paper and our eyes caught. Hers were bright again, infinitely sad but alive with warmth. I didn't know what I had done to change her feelings but I knew I would think about the things she'd said for a long time. I wanted to hug her, but all I could do was squeeze her hand and hope she understood.

We prepared for the grand jury the rest of the week. By the time Charlie Wing had me on the stand I had just about memorized my reports, and I answered the hundreds of questions he threw my way with only an occasional glance at my notes to verify specific times and dates. The twenty-three jurors stared blankly as Wing had me walk them through my investigation. I detailed everything, from Lenora's first phone call to the search at Mom's and the ultimate discovery of

Slick's body, with the dispassionate objectivity of a senior surgeon describing a procedure to a class of interns. The sequence of names and dates and events laid out the case but it didn't begin to tell the story. The emotion – mine, everyone else's – was missing. The members of the jury had to render a decision, but they would never understand the road I had traveled from the first hysterical phone call to that methodical presentation of the evidence.

There is no defense rebuttal at the grand jury since the purpose is to determine if there is enough evidence to hold a trial. The show is run strictly by the prosecution, so I didn't have to face any cross-examination. That would come later. It was sort of like sparring with your trainer before the real fight.

My hours of testimony over, I left the room and went immediately back upstairs to my desk. I would have liked to meet Lenora and offer some encouragement but knew it wasn't a good idea for me to risk being seen talking to other witnesses. The hearings lasted until three-thirty the next day, and when it was over Charlie came up to fill me in. I knew just by looking at his face it had gone our way.

Lenora had come through fantastically, he said, repeating her story exactly as she had given it first to me and then to him, but her nerves had gotten the better of her, and he saw tears she didn't want to acknowledge forming lines down her cheeks as she left the room. The corroboration offered by Money's testimony helped to nail down the murder, and also substantiated Calvert's sale and use of cocaine during the card game and at other times in his bar. Money had managed to be more coherent than might have been expected, having been through over a month of detox, but how he would hold up under cross at the trial was anybody's guess.

The only real surprise at the hearing was Auletta. Her hostility had been established, but Charlie was unprepared for the form it took. The whole thing was a frame-up, she claimed. Lenora had been Calvert's old lady and when he dumped her she got furious. She tried to get money out of him, and when he wouldn't cough up she invented the story about the killing to get even. It was a blatant plea for sympathy from Calvert, and Charlie eyed the jury while she talked to gauge if they were buying it. A few of the men nodded in apparent agreement with the specter of the wronged woman doing her man dirt, but it didn't seem to affect their judgment in the end. The indictment came down with Calvert facing a multitude of charges ranging from Murder 2 to Reckless Endangerment 1, Assault 1, and Possession and Sale of a Controlled Substance.

'We did it, Tina, he's going to do hard time on this.' The grin on Charlie's usually placid face made him look impish. My smile was just as wide. 'I already called the state Department of Criminal Justice Services to tell them that an arrest of a cop was going down,' he said. 'They'll expedite his prints and paperwork as soon as we put them in.'

We were over the first hurdle, but we had a lot of work to do before the real celebrations. 'The boss is arranging for the arraignment to go before Judge Brock,' Wing said as he got up to leave.

'IAD will handle the booking, but I'm catching the arrest,' I told him.

'You earned it.'

'Thanks.'

After Wing was gone, I called Muñoz and we went over the arrangements. He wasn't thrilled I would be taking the collar, but the arrest would still be a plum for his division. As Calvert's arresting officer, I would be there when he surrendered, but a lot of the glory would go to IAD.

I arrived at the IAD headquarters building in Brooklyn Heights at eight forty-five. They made their home in a decrepit former precinct house that was now surrounded by gentrified co-ops and remodeled brownstones. Several reporters had already taken their place in the dingy lobby. I joined Muñoz, who was standing with some of the investigators who had helped with the search at Mom's.

All conversation ceased as we watched Calvert enter with his attorney, Marcus P. Lambert. Then I heard a loud whisper coming from one of the IAD guys. 'This is going to be a fucking circus.' Several others tittered. He was referring to the man Calvert had chosen to represent him. Lambert was notorious for zeroing in on the political angle of each case or creating one if necessary. He had a gift for turning the criminal into the victim and for rallying the community with his impassioned oratory. His clients weren't just innocent, they were persecuted by the system, and it was his duty not only to exonerate them but to lambaste the system while doing it.

Calvert was quickly whisked off to Muñoz' office, where I read him his rights. Muñoz requested his gun and shield and then printed and papered him. It took a couple of hours for the process to be completed, and then Muñoz and I took him over to the Kings County Supreme Court Building, where Wing met us at the courtroom. Usually a prisoner awaiting arraignment would be put in the holding pens in the basement for hours and sometimes days. Calvert, like all our prisoners, was spared that indignity. This did not improve his mood or behavior, however. Denied the usual outlets of the bully, he resorted to a series of adolescent antics in an attempt to make each step in the process as difficult as possible. He hurled insults at the officers who processed him, refused to stand still for the photo shoot, and would not leave the car when we arrived at the court until I threatened him with a stay at Riker's.

The arraignment itself took all of ten minutes. Judge Brock read each of the charges against Calvert, he pleaded innocent to each one, and the lawyers presented their arguments concerning bail. Lambert fought for Calvert to be RORed, released on his own recognizance as a member in good standing in the community and an officer of the law. Wing argued eloquently against such a decision, stressing the serious nature of the crimes, and requested a bail of $250,000.

Bail was set at $100,000. Lambert presented a bond and Calvert was temporarily free. With his long history of harassing witnesses, I can't say it made me comfortable. But Wing was determined to press for a speedy trial, and at least we had won the first crucial round. Before long, I would see Calvert behind bars.

It was three days later when I was called into Vince's office. Muñoz and Charlie Wing were seated pretty much the way they were a month ago when this case was just getting started. Bud was off on a special assignment. In spite of the indictment, the feeling emanating from the group wasn't much different than it was then. 'Who died?' I asked, looking at the glum, tense faces around me.

'Something important has come up,' Vince said. He was looking at Charlie Wing. Charlie's face, his whole body, was tightened with an air of compressed tension I had never seen in him before. 'There's a problem with the evidence,' he said.

'That's ridiculous,' I blurted, reacting instantly. 'We did everything by the book. We were super careful with this one.'

'The key,' he said. 'It dropped on the ground.'

'That's right. I opened the door and the key and a used crack vial fell out. I scooped them up with a piece of paper. I never touched either one. Umansky from CSU was standing right there. He saw the whole thing.'

315

'Nobody's saying you touched it.'

'What then?'

'Lambert's claiming you planted the evidence. He's made a motion to have the case dismissed. Fruit of the poisoned tree.'

'That's total bullshit. He'll never make it stick, Umansky was right there.'

'I've been over it with Eli. He was standing behind you when you opened the car door. All he saw was the objects falling to the ground when the door opened. He can't honestly testify that he saw them fall out of the car.'

'This is insane.' I looked at the faces of the men staring at me around the room. 'You know I would never tamper with the evidence.'

'It isn't a question of what we know,' Muñoz said, 'it's what Calvert's lawyer can make a judge or a jury believe.'

'Fanatic lady investigator has it in for poor beleaguered black cop,' Wing went on. 'She's been after him for years. Can't get a conviction so this time she frames him, plants the crucial piece of evidence. The only piece of evidence that directly links him to the crime. That's the way he's going to play it. He's been setting it up from day one.'

'You're kidding me, right?'

'The key and the vial were in your hand, maybe held in a pocket with a hole in it. You simultaneously opened the door and let them drop. The vial was just a decoy, of course.'

I looked at Vince. He was squeezing the grip strengthener tightly in his left hand, then he released it and squeezed it with his right. He kept it up, moving it abstractedly from hand to hand as he talked. 'The problem is, it could have happened,' he said, 'and there's no way to prove it didn't.'

'I've read and reread the reports,' Wing said. 'I've

talked to everyone who was at the scene. There's no-one whose line of vision allowed them to see either your hands or the objects actually emerging from the car.'

My mind raced wildly, trying to absorb the impact of what was being said and at the same time muster a defense against it. Then it hit me. 'OK, wait a minute. Let's say I am this fanatic you're talking about. Let's say I wanted to plant a piece of evidence with Calvert's print on. Where would I get it? And not just anything with his prints, but the key to the storage locker where the body was found?'

'You're not gonna believe this one,' Vince said. 'Calvert is prepared to testify that he saw a woman fitting your description entering the Ninth Precinct when he was coming out at the end of a shift. That you bumped into him and dropped a key on the step and that he bent down and picked it up and handed it back to you. As for it being the right key, Lambert claims you could have changed the lock after you got to the storage place. Clients supply their own padlocks. The porter who took you up in the elevator said he went off to move some boxes and doesn't know what you did when you got to the room. He can't swear the lock that was on the door when forensics came is the same one that was there originally.'

I glanced at Muñoz. His eyes betrayed a certain relish, but whether it was at the chutzpah behind this invention or the way the tables were being turned on me wasn't clear.

'C'mon now, what jury would ever buy that? It's totally outrageous.'

'You're right, you're absolutely right,' Wing said. 'And if the jury is made up of twelve reasonable people with no axe to grind, it will be pretty near impossible to convince them this fairy tale has any merit. But Lambert is going to play the racial angle to the hilt.'

I thought about the grandstanding at the arrest and

the allegations of harassment Lambert had been making in the papers, and knew Wing was right about that. 'So what are you telling me?'

'We're going to bargain it out.'

'To what?'

'Assault and possession.'

'But we've got the guy on murder.'

'All of the evidence except the key is circumstantial.'

'We've got two witnesses.'

'Auletta is sticking to her story that Lenora Terrell is a jilted woman. Gives Lambert a regular little female vendetta against poor Calvert to play with. As for Money, would you convict someone on Money's say-so? He just doesn't read as a credible witness.'

'All Calvert's lawyer needs is one juror with reasonable doubt,' Vince said.

'I think we can make the Terrell assault stick,' Wing went on. 'And Lambert will probably go for the possession charge to avoid a full-scale drug investigation.'

'He'll be out in eighteen months.' I was incredulous. I couldn't believe this was happening, that they meant what they were saying.

'I've been over it with MacCallister. It's already been decided.'

'This is just unbelievable shit and you know it, you all know it.'

'This is real life,' Vince said.

'And I'm pie-in-the-sky, is that what you mean?'

Vince's tone turned conciliatory, fatherly. 'You want justice, you want to put the bad guys away. We all want that.'

I wanted to puke.

'At least he'll be off the job,' Wing said quietly.

'Yeah, well, maybe I will, too.' I couldn't stand another second of this. I pushed my chair back with as much energy as I could muster, sending it crashing backward behind me as I stormed out.

Chapter Twenty-eight

The news of the flight attendant's murder hit Joe in the gut like a second ulcer. He had been so sure the parking ticket was that perfect little piece of evidence the suspect overlooked, every cop's dream. Now, with another victim on his hands, he was back to zero. He kept trying to think if he'd missed something in his zeal to nail O'Hanlon. It was bad enough to have been so wrong; he could never forgive himself if he had overlooked something in his pigheadedness that would have saved a woman's life.

The Press had been blasting pictures of Janice Smithson and her bereaved family on the front pages every day, and the switchboard was on overload fielding calls from irate citizens wondering why the police couldn't do their job and offering useless and time-consuming 'tips'. There was only one thing to do. He planted himself at his desk and once more waded through the pages and pages of reports on all the related cases. He was still convinced the killer was in law enforcement. He put in to the computer and came up with seventeen police officers convicted of sex offenses in the last five years. Potentially promising, but they all turned out to be dead ends. Most were ruled out by appearance alone. A few had done time and moved out of the area, a couple were still inside, and none carried the same type of gun, or had an MO that even remotely matched the Russian Roulette rapist's.

Extensive interviews had been conducted with the staff of the International Travel Lodge after Janice's body was discovered, and no-one had seen or heard anything. It seemed incredible, except that it fit the way this guy usually worked. Somehow he managed to be totally innocuous until it was too late. When the phone rang for the twentieth time in an hour, Joe groaned. There didn't seem to be any good news these days.

'That drawing of yours is all wrong,' a brassy female voice announced on the other end.

'Really?' He had heard this one before. But when she identified herself as Veronica DeFalco, one of the waitresses on duty at the Travel Lodge the night of the murder, he immediately perked up. He recognized the name from the list of employees. She had gone away for a few days, she said, which explained why she had not been around during the interviews. Joe arranged to meet her at the hotel bar in an hour.

'Call me Ronnie,' she said, extending a soft pink hand as Joe approached. She seemed to know exactly who he was. She continued setting up the bar for happy hour, inviting him to make himself comfortable.

'How come you're so sure the composite is wrong?' he asked as he pulled up a stool.

'I served them all night, that's how come I know. Him and the girl. Real pretty. Classy, you know? When I saw that picture in the paper I couldn't believe such a thing could happen to her.' She described seeing the two of them talking by the bar and then going over to the table. 'It was a pickup, sure. But I didn't blame the girl. He was a real looker. Smooth, too. I've seen him around here before. Comes in with another cop late at night sometimes.'

'What makes you think they're cops?'

She paused, her head cocked, and thought about it. 'Don't know, really. Maybe it was the way they talked, maybe I heard something. I don't actually remember anything particular. I just always figured them for cops. Weren't pilots, pilots act different. Weren't traveling salesmen, that's for sure.'

He pulled out a copy of the drawing and put it on the table. 'So what's wrong with it?'

Again she cocked her head, considering. 'Hard to say exactly. Hair's different for one thing. Darker. Something about the mouth, and the eyes.' She shrugged, giving a laugh, at a loss to explain what she meant. 'One thing I know, though. This guy had a scar. Tiny, not more than a half inch, right below his eyebrow.'

'You sure? None of the other witnesses ever mentioned a scar.'

'Could be they didn't notice it. It was real small, just a tiny red line. I got real good eyesight. Too good, my mom says, makes me too critical. I could pick out a pimple on the butt of an elephant. That's what my mom says, anyway.'

Joe laughed. For the first time in days he felt like laughing. This was a new piece of information, just maybe it would open things up. He asked her to come back to One Police Plaza with him and work with the sketch artist, help them put together a composite that *did* look like the guy she saw with Janice Smithson on Friday night.

Bud Ryan was sitting in Moskowitz's office when the new composite was finished. Joe pinned it up on the bulletin board in front of his desk and they went back to discussing the reports they were reading, but Bud's eye kept being drawn to it. He kept thinking it looked familiar, but he just couldn't put his finger on who it reminded him of. He had become involved in the case because of the O'Hanlon business, and now he was reading all the victim and witness statements as a kind of *ex officio* adviser. With all the indications of involvement by a law-enforcement officer, it had been decided that an SPO presence in the investigative team was not unwarranted.

Bud had read all the reports through once and was now going over them again. Something caught in the back of his mind like a hangnail on a sweater, but he couldn't quite think what it was. There were connections he knew he was on the verge of making if he could only find them. He was going through the file from the college-girl rape when it hit him. Didn't the victim say something about 'slim pickings'? He leafed through to the end of her description of the incident and there it was. The rapist had gone through her wallet, taken the money, and said, 'Slim pickings.' Oddly, she had remembered this, when she was still unable to recall so much of the incident. It was a peculiar, old-fashioned phrase, highly contemptuous under the circumstances. But he remembered having heard it recently somewhere else.

He looked at the other composite on the wall next to the new one. Any guy who could make himself look so different each time was a real chameleon. It had to be someone who was used to altering his appearance, who knew what a big difference a small change could make. And then it hit him. Someone who did undercover. He looked back at the new composite and suddenly it was like he was seeing it for the first time. He knew exactly who it looked like – who it was.

He thought about the phrase and when he had heard it before. He had been walking by Tina's desk. Jeff Collins had been sitting next to her, surveying the articles taken out of Gato's car, and as he looked them over he had laughed and said, 'Slim pickings.'

He tried to picture Collins's face. Did he have a scar? He didn't usually look at the guy that closely. He thought about the time Collins met them for the search at Mom's. He pictured him standing outside in the sunshine, leaning insolently against his car, and yes, he did have a scar under his right eyebrow. Small but noticeable, just like the police artist had drawn it.

'Joe. Are you sure the Levenson woman said "gray hatchback"?'

'You've got the reports, it's in there.'

'What would you say to a silver Trans Am?'

There was silence while Joe considered the implications of what Bud was suggesting. 'You mean maybe it wasn't even Terry's car Denise saw?'

Bud nodded.

Joe thought about it some more, letting the concept sink in. There was nothing to rule out the presence of another gray car on the street, he just hadn't thought of it. 'To a woman, looking from four floors above? Could be,' he said finally.

'I think I've got your man.'

'Not one of yours?'

'No. Works for SNU. Jeff Collins. A real hot dog. I should have made the connection. I don't know how I missed it. You think you've seen it all, but it's hard to think of a psycho like that being a cop.'

'Tell me about it.'

'Wasn't there something in the last fax about a captain?'

'Yeah.' He quoted, ' "I'm going after bigger game. The Captain should be proud." '

'If I'm not mistaken, Collins's father is a captain on the force. I don't know what precinct.'

'I've heard of Captain Collins,' Joe said. 'Are you sure about this?'

'Absolutely.'

'Boy, this is gonna be a tough one for him.' He sat for a few minutes, shaking his head. Then he roused himself to action. The important thing wasn't who got hurt, but that the killer was stopped. 'I'll call over to SNU and get a photo, see if we can get Collins ID'd by one of the girls. As soon as one victim nails him, we'll bring him in.'

Bud reached for the other phone. 'There's someone else I've got to call.'

Chapter Twenty-nine

I left the office and drove home in the Chevy, wishing I was in the Z out on a nice empty highway. I pictured Nevada or Texas, anything far away from here, from the office and everything to do with it. As soon as I got in the apartment I pulled off my work clothes and hopped in the shower, but I couldn't wash away this day or my anger at everything that had happened. I tried not to think about it, but couldn't think about anything else. I was furious that they wouldn't fight harder to hang on to the case and furious at the system that set things up so that a smart-ass lawyer could get away with such blatant bullshit.

It seemed incredible that everything could hang on something as inconsequential as where I was standing in relation to everyone else when I opened the car. And, of course, I *had* to be the one to open it. Little Ms *Machette* asserting herself. At the SPO we saw a lot of cops and judges and DAs that abused the system, but we had no equivalent defense against lawyers and defendants who abused it for their own purposes. I put on a clean pair of slacks and a nice silk blouse I would never wear on the job, poured myself a stiff Scotch on the rocks, and stared into the pale amber liquid, wondering what the hell I was doing in this line of work.

I sat at the dining table, waves of anger and frustration washing over me, and knew if I sat there any longer I was going to cry. If there is anything I hate, it's someone crying in their beer – or Scotch. I thought about calling Maddy, but I knew she was on her shift, and it wasn't something I could see talking about over the phone. I wasn't sure I wanted to talk about it at all. Not yet anyway. Lenora was the one I ought to call, but how the hell was I going to face her after everything she had been through to get to this? I couldn't even begin to think of dealing with it.

The scenario at the precinct garage kept playing over in my head. I had been so careful every step of the way with this one, and then a simple act that was perfectly natural and legal and ordinary under the circumstances backfired in this crazy way. How could I know that everyone was standing behind me and couldn't actually see the door opening? How could I know anything would fall out? I couldn't, but that didn't console me in the least.

Aside from Maddy, the only person I really wanted to talk to was Jeff. I kept remembering his comment about cases he'd blown that night after the El Caribe. Some day he would tell me about them, he had said. Well, this would be a good day. I dialed the SNU. The desk officer answered. When I asked for Detective Collins he said to hold on, and I heard him call out, 'Hey, Hal, you know where Jeff is?'

'He's out in the field,' he said when he came back to the phone. 'Can I take a message?'

'This is Tina Paris,' I said. 'If he calls in, tell him I would really like to talk to him.' I gave him my home number.

I was more disappointed than I should have been; the guy was hardly ever in when I called him, but this was not a time when logic about anything was much help. I sat looking glumly at the phone, and at the Scotch in front of me. This was not how I wanted to spend the night. I stood up, grabbed a jacket and the key to the Z and started toward the door. Then I stopped myself. Like any other law-enforcement officer I was supposed to carry my gun even when I was off duty. I didn't want to be reminded of anything to do with the job, but those were the regulations. I remembered the conversation I'd had with Maddy about 'packing' and thought that with all the nut jobs out there it probably wasn't such a bad idea. I went to the closet and took out my ankle holster and put it on.

Walking through the living-room I looked at the phone one last time and knew I couldn't go out without calling Lenora after all.

'Lenora, I'm sorry,' I said, when she picked up the phone.

'Did something go wrong?'

'Everything's screwed up. I screwed up, and you deserve better.'

There was silence on the other end of the line as she waited for me to explain what had happened. 'There were problems with the evidence. Calvert's pleading guilty to the assault and some possession charges. The best we can get is eighteen months.'

'I testified like you wanted, didn't they believe me?'

'I'm sorry, Lee, that's what we've got. At least he'll be off the street for a while and off the job.'

'I knew I was wastin' my time. You were dreamin', you thought they were gonna get him. You were just foolin' yourself. Foolin' me, too, but mostly yourself.'

'I'm sorry,' I said again. There was more I could have told her, but nothing else of any consequence I could say.

I got in the Z determined to put it out of my mind, at least for one night, and drove out toward Kennedy at speeds that were definitely not legal. I hadn't exactly admitted to myself why I had taken that direction, but let's face it, it wasn't because I wanted to park on the overpass and watch the pretty lights. I needed some consolation, and I was getting hooked on the guy's sweet knowing smile and on those unnervingly vibrant, penetrating blue eyes. But when I got to the diner on Rockaway Boulevard I was in for another disappointment. There was no silver Trans Am in the parking-lot. I pulled up anyway and went inside. It was early. He might still come by. And anyway, I hadn't had a thing to eat since breakfast. The waitress presented me with one of those giant plastic-laminated menus with as many different items as characters in a Russian novel – all made fresh daily of course.

I perused it for a long time, flipping from the Greek to the Italian to the American section and back again, figuring the merits of a souvlaki platter over a bacon cheeseburger, but nothing appealed to me, and in the end I ordered a Scotch on the rocks with a side of onion rings.

I was on my second Scotch when Jeff came in. 'I got your message,' he said, sitting down. 'I hoped you'd be here.'

He surveyed the congealed pile of cold rings on my plate. 'I guess they weren't any better than Junior's.' His tone was full of ironic good humor.

I shrugged. 'I couldn't even taste them.'

He raised his eyebrows – my mood was coming through loud and clear. 'It's the goddamned case.' I had convinced myself I didn't want to talk about it, but now I spilled the whole story before he even got a chance to order.

'Tough break,' he said when I finished.

I couldn't believe it; I had been counting on him to understand. 'Don't be too generous with the sympathy,' I snapped.

'Hey, I'm on your side. I came here looking for you, remember?'

'Well, "tough break" just doesn't cover it. It sucks. That bastard is going to be out on the street in a year.' He looked like he was about to say something philosophical. 'And don't give me any crap about how I get too involved. I am involved, I want to be involved, that's why I signed on for the stupid job.' He nodded and had the sense to keep quiet. 'There was no tainted evidence in this case. I was really careful. It's a rotten deal.'

'Yeah, you're right, it is. And I'm sorry. You deserve better.'

'That's what I told Lenora.' I stared at the table, my mouth set. 'The city deserves better.'

Jeff shifted uncomfortably in his seat, watching me. 'I didn't mean to be flip,' he said after a few minutes. 'I've been having kind of a hard time of it myself. I think my boss and my ex-wife are having a contest to see who can make my life more miserable.' He gave a little, self-deprecating laugh. 'We both need to forget all that for a while.'

His expression was open and encouraging, but also ironic. He had a way of undercutting his own pretensions, of making everything seem a little like a joke, that I found both intriguing and infuriating – maybe it was too much like what I did myself. But he really was a sweet guy, and I had really wanted to see him. Dumping my frustration on him wasn't being fair to him or to myself. 'I'm the one who flew off the handle,' I said. I let myself return his warm gaze. 'I'm glad you're here. I had to see you. I couldn't think of anyone else I wanted to call.'

We stared into each other's eyes. Then he reached out as if he was going to take my hand, but hesitated and just gently grazed it with his. 'Let's get out of here. I know a nice place out at the beach near Brightwaters. Candlelight, waves lapping, it'll do us both good.'

I nodded, then decided I had better check my machine before we left. There was only one message, from Bud, asking me to call him immediately. It was too late to get him at the office so I tried his home number. His wife, Evelyn, answered. He wasn't there and she had no idea what it was about.

'I wonder if it has something to do with the Calvert case,' I said, reporting it to Jeff. 'Maybe he's gotten Vince and Wing to change their minds.'

'Hey, c'mon,' he said, 'I thought we were going to forget about work for a while.'

I laughed. 'You're right. I promise. No more.'

The Trans Am and the Z were parked side by side in the lot, looking like bionic lovers in some weird sci-fi sitcom. 'His and hers,' Jeff said with a laugh, making the same connection.

I walked up to the Z. 'Let's take mine. I need to drive.'

'You sober?'

I nodded.

'OK. One of the guys can pick my car up later. Let me just get something.' He lifted the hatch, took out an attaché case and put it behind the passenger seat of the Z.

I picked up the Southern State off Rockaway and felt myself relaxing as I drove east on the tree-lined parkway. Jeff and I were both quiet, thinking our own thoughts, the silence enhancing the electricity that was starting to crackle pleasantly between us now that we were alone together for the first time, not as two cops but as a man and a woman. After a while I turned on the radio to hear the news. There was a bulletin about the murder that had occurred out by Kennedy. 'According to the Department spokesperson Sergeant Maddy Keitel, there has been a break in the Russian Roulette murder cases,' the announcer began. Jeff leaned forward and switched it off.

'That's my friend Maddy,' I protested.

'It's bullshit. If they knew who it was they would have picked him up.'

'Maybe they have.'

'I thought we were going to forget about the job and be real people for a while.' He sounded irritated but then he softened his voice. 'Just you and me.'

The restaurant was a nice mix of casual and intimate, with bleached wooden tables, fishnets on the walls, and a wonderful view of the little harbor on the South Bay. Jeff ordered a California Chardonnay from the wine list, the waiter opened it with a flourish, and I smiled as we clinked glasses, starting to enjoy myself. Maybe I was right about this guy, maybe he *was* several cuts above the usual chauvinist thug the Department attracted.

The dining tables were separated from the bar portion of the restaurant by a paneled wooden divider, which gave the diners privacy but didn't cut off the view of the bar and the TV above it. Our table overlooked the water so I didn't spend much time facing the other direction, but as we were finishing our main course there was another news bulletin about the airport murder that caught my eye. Apparently a new witness had come forward and supplied police with a description of the man believed to be the killer. 'Luck ran out for the young flight attendant at the International Hotel on Friday the thirteenth,' the newscaster intoned, 'but maybe luck is running out for her killer as well.' Authorities were convinced that the killer was the Russian Roulette rapist. 'The man is known to alter his appearance,' the anchor went on, 'but he is believed to be approximately six feet tall, of medium build, with light-brown or blond hair and blue eyes. There is a small scar over his left eye.' A new composite, based on the latest information, was flashed across the screen.

I glanced at the drawing and then happened to look over at Jeff. The resemblance was so shocking I choked on the swallow of wine I had just taken. I looked at the picture again. Not a perfect likeness, but a good one, as if some slightly inept amateur artist had done his portrait. The network moved on to a story about the local Thanksgiving food drive. I looked back at Jeff, who was downing the last of his roast beef, oblivious to what was on the TV behind him, and told myself it was ridiculous. There couldn't possibly be any connection. I ate a few more bites of my lobster Newburg, trying to forget about it, but then my eye was drawn to something I had never noticed before, the half-inch scar that was clearly visible just below his eyebrow.

It was no longer possible to eat. I kept looking at the scar and then forcing myself to look away. What do I really know about this guy? I asked myself. That he's a cop and a good one. That he has a nice way about him and can be charming if he wants to be. Not much more than that. What did I know about the killer? I ran over the newspaper articles in my mind and thought about what Vince had told me. I knew he was suspected of being a cop, and that he gained entry by establishing some initial rapport with his victims. Jeff could certainly muster the charm to do that, but that was hardly conclusive. I tried to remember exactly what Vince had said. Believed to be in law enforcement, I thought it was. That covered a lot of men, hundreds of whom fit the general description. My God, they were going to pick Terry up, and he and Jeff hardly resembled each other at all. But that, I had to remind myself, was before the latest murder, before the new composite.

I took a sip of wine and tried to go back to my dinner, but my eye kept returning to that scar even while my brain tried to reason the connection away. What I really needed was a test. Something to prove it couldn't be him so I could forget about it once and for all.

Jeff noticed the odd expression on my face and asked if anything was wrong. 'I keep thinking about Calvert,' I said. 'I can't get it out of my mind.' It sounded lame, but I couldn't very well tell him the truth, although part of me just wanted to ask him outright. I wished the composite was still on the screen so I could say, 'Hey, Jeff, isn't it amazing how that new composite looks like you?' and have him turn around and look at it and then laugh it off in a way that would be totally, incontrovertibly convincing. What I needed was a handle, some way to approach it. Then the phrase 'luck ran out on Friday the thirteenth' came back to me. That was the day I had found Slick's body.

'I know we agreed we wouldn't talk about work,' I said, trying to sound casual, 'but I keep thinking about how excited I was, how sure I was that everything was falling into place, that I was nailing Calvert at last. And then they pull this. The day I found Slick's body in the storage place I was flying. It was Friday the thirteenth, and I thought, Boy, that's weird, because it's my lucky day. I even tried to find you to help celebrate, but your office said you were out in the field. I guess you were at the airport again.'

'Did they tell you that?'

'Not in so many words.'

'Hey, I was nowhere near that place that night.'

'So you have guys in the office covering for you, huh?'

He cocked his head and gave me a look. 'You know, that's just the way Nancy used to sound.'

'What do you mean?'

'When she thought I was playing around. That same damned suspicious tone of voice.'

I tried to laugh it off. 'You *are* pretty hard to find.'

'Listen, if I didn't want to be found, you would never find me.'

I stared down at my plate, more confused than ever. Was Jeff trying to cover something up, or was he just bristling at what seemed like premature possessiveness on my part? I got up, excused myself, and went to the ladies' room. There was a phone in the hall, and

I thought I should probably give Bud another call, but as I approached, someone came out of the men's room and picked up the receiver. When I came back out he was still chatting. I stood a few feet away, trying to gauge how long he would be on. It was definitely a conversation that was winding up rather than down, so I went back to the table.

'I'm sorry I said that stuff about Nancy,' Jeff said when I sat back down. 'You're nothing like her. I'm really not such a hard case. There's just a lot of pressure at work right now. But there's no excuse for taking it out on you.' He reached for my hand. 'I've been waiting to be alone with you for a long time. I don't want to blow it.'

I smiled uneasily. Was he this sweet guy with an appealing overlay of macho reserve and a sexy undercurrent of animal energy, or was he someone terrifying and dangerous under a mask of normalcy? Then I thought, This is ridiculous, I'm just panicking. It's just like the Son of Sam; everyone I saw I thought was the killer.

'Ever been to Heckscher State Park?'

I shook my head.

'Let's go. Take a walk on the beach. It'll help take your mind off things.' He gave me a tentative, beseeching, little-boy smile I couldn't resist.

As we approached the car Jeff put his hand out for my keys. 'You're too tired,' he said when I hesitated. 'Let me drive.' I didn't know what to do. My police side said, Be cautious, don't do it, but the woman in me was ready to acquiesce. He came up and pulled me toward him. The kiss he gave me was warm and sweet and sensual, and guaranteed to make me forget my doubts.

We got onto the Montauk Highway going east toward Islip, driving with the windows open, in spite of the November chill, to enjoy the fresh salt air. Jeff looked thoughtful. 'I have a confession to make,' he said after a few minutes. There was nothing in his tone to indicate it was the kind of confession I dreaded. 'I really was at the airport on the thirteenth.'

'Why didn't you say so before?'

'There are some things I just don't want you to know about that night.'

'Then why are you telling me now?'

'Because it doesn't matter any more.'

He was silent after that. I looked over at his face, trying to read his expression, but he was looking straight ahead. Though meant to be reassuring, his comment had started another storm of doubt, and I had to ask myself my original question again. What *did* I really know about him? The fact that I was attracted to him meant nothing; the papers claimed that several of the rape victims were attracted to their attacker at first. My attraction was just muddying up the waters, making me less rational. Why should there be anything I wasn't supposed to know about that night? I couldn't think of an answer, not if Jeff was who he appeared to be, the man I wanted him to be. And what could 'it doesn't matter any more' possibly mean. The whole business sounded ominous. It was impossible to put a positive spin on it. My mind raced madly in circles.

It was time to calm down, to deal with this as Tina Paris, investigator, and stop letting my emotions rule. We were approaching a gas station up ahead. I looked at the gauge. We had about a quarter of a tank. 'Maybe we should stop for gas,' I said. 'There probably won't be anyone open later.' He glanced at the gauge himself and then pulled in.

'I think I'll try Bud again,' I said, jumping out before he could protest. He got out himself to pump the gas without comment. There was a small convenience store. The phone was on the wall around the corner from the entrance. I decided to call my own machine first in case he had left a new message. 'Tina, this is Bud. I need

335

to speak to you immediately. This is urgent. Leave a number and location where you can be reached. We need to find Collins.'

My eyes were immediately drawn to the figure of Jeff standing by the car. What was this all about? Suddenly he looked like a total stranger. I rummaged in my purse for some more change and called Bud, but his machine answered. I gave my location and current destination, replaced the receiver and went back to the car, frustrated and confused.

Jeff was just putting the gas cap back on. 'Need anything?' he asked as he went inside to pay. I shook my head. He didn't ask what Bud had said, but didn't seem the least perturbed I had called him, either. It didn't seem possible that anyone who had killed two women and raped several more could seem so relaxed and unconcerned now. But I knew that didn't really mean anything. I thought about Bud, what a cautious person he was. There was no way he would leave that kind of message lightly. I was forgetting the things he had taught me about the duplicity of surfaces and not being deceived by the appearance of things. Once again I tried to piece together everything I knew about Jeff. There was no denying it, there was nothing that ruled him out. And I was being so stupid, so deliberately blind. If I were in the same situation in an undercover I knew what I would do. If I was wrong about Jeff, I had to be prepared. I reached down to my ankle holster to take out my Smith & Wesson and put it somewhere more accessible before he returned from the store.

I was still leaning down when the driver's door opened. I looked up, startled, and stuck the gun quickly in the back of my waistband. I didn't know what to think; I knew Jeff hadn't come out yet. It took a second to register that the man looking down at me was Hal. When I'd seen him in the diner his hair was blond; now it was darker, obviously colored brown, and slicked back in a way that made him look both harder and more sophisticated. The sight of him infused me with a feeling of foreboding I couldn't explain. A cold sweat crawled up my back.

'Scared you, didn't I?' He got in and closed the door.

'What are you doing?'

'Haven't you figured it out yet?' He glanced toward the glass door of the store, where we could see Jeff standing by the cashier.

'Oh, God. You mean it's true?' It was like being punched in the stomach. 'I just couldn't believe it.'

'Yeah, we couldn't either.' He turned on the ignition and backed out of the space. 'We've got to get you out of here. You're his next.'

As we pulled out I noticed Jeff's Trans Am.

'You came in his car?'

Hal nodded. 'I picked it up at the diner; I knew that's where he'd go to track you. But he won't be able to follow us. I've alerted the local authorities.'

I was so stunned I couldn't put it all together. I looked out of the window and saw Jeff emerging from the store. A pair of Suffolk County Police Department squad cars pulled in at the same moment and came to a screeching halt. Two officers jumped from each car and approached him. I was still close enough to see the stunned expression on his face. As they moved toward him more aggressively, I saw him look around the lot, notice his car, and then do a quick scan, looking for mine. Then he noticed us pulling away. I turned all the way around to watch out the back window. I couldn't read his expression any more, but as Hal pulled around the corner I heard him scream my name. He bolted in our direction but got maybe two steps before the four officers converged on him, dragging him to the ground. My instinct was to yell for Hal to stop so we could help him. I still hadn't processed what was going on. In my mind he was still the guy I was falling in love

337

with, not the Russian Roulette murderer. They were pulling him up, his hands cuffed behind his back, and then I couldn't see any more.

I turned back to face the road, trying to put it all together. Hal was driving fast and I realized I had no idea where we were going. 'We set up a base at the Starlight Motel on Sunrise,' he said, reading my mind. 'It's just up ahead.'

'That must be what Bud was calling about.'

'I don't know about the calls, but he should be waiting for us at the motel.'

The motel was a small, old-fashioned clapboard affair, one storey with the rooms arranged in a U shape. There were only a few cars in the lot when we pulled up. Most of the others must not have arrived yet. It didn't occur to me to ask Hal how he knew Jeff was after me, or how he knew where to find us. I was relieved he had gotten there in time, but I still couldn't absorb the fact that this was all happening.

When he put the key in the lock without even knocking first, I should have realized something was wrong. He opened the door and stood aside for me to walk in. It was a small room with one double bed, a couple of bedside tables and lamps, a TV, and a single chair. The light by the TV was already on. The door to the bathroom was open and I walked in far enough to see there was no-one inside. 'Where is everybody?' I asked, turning back to Hal.

He was leaning with his back against the door, a brazen, calculating expression transforming his face. 'You know you really disappointed me. I thought you'd be different, more of a challenge. The night we picked you up in that parking-lot I thought you might give me a real run for my money. But you're as dumb as the rest of them. You cunts are all alike.'

He started moving toward me. I backed away instinctively as my mind vainly tried to make sense of what he was saying. Hal! Was he the rapist? What about Jeff? He let me get as far as the bed before pulling his gun. 'I know you have a little pea shooter tucked away. An ankle holster on your right leg cause you're left-handed. I want you to reach down and take it off, leave the gun in it. Do it real slow.'

He kept coming toward me as I reached down and pulled the holster off. As he got nearer I flung my arm up and out, heaving the stiff leather into his face and grabbing for the gun at the back of my waist, but he was faster than I was. Plucking the holster out of midair, he swung his arm back and hit me across the side of the head, tumbling me onto the bed.

'You think you're real cute, don't you?' He dropped the holster, held down my arms and climbed astride me, pinning my legs with his thighs. 'Where's the little pea shooter? Where did you stick it?' He chuckled to himself as he stared down at me, contemplating his next move. 'I guess we'll have to take off some of these clothes to find out.' He pulled my jacket off my shoulders, using it to pin my arms. I kept looking at his face. There was no scar. It didn't make sense, but it no longer mattered. My mind had switched into survival mode. I watched every move he made with a heightened intensity, all my senses operating on a pure, instinctual level. He had me immobilized, but the important thing was not to give up. All I needed was one brief second to gain an edge, one sliver of time when he let down his guard.

But I couldn't control all my reactions. When he took the long barrel of his Colt and stroked the side of my face, I gritted my teeth but couldn't prevent myself from twisting away. He grabbed my chin and held it. 'What's the matter? I'm not good enough for you? Too hot for our star narc to look at anybody else. Funny though, a lot of people say me and your boy Collins look alike. That's what gave me the idea.' He ran the muzzle of the gun down my neck and chest to the opening of my blouse, slipped the barrel between the buttons, gave a good pull, and ripped it open. 'I like that, no bra,' he said, as he tore the silk aside, exposing my breast. 'I've been watching you. You think you're a hot little number, don't you? A hot little cop with a hot little gun tucked away somewhere.' His laugh raised goose bumps over my whole body. It was the coldest human sound I had ever heard. He began to fondle my breast with his free hand. Tears of anger and humiliation filled my eyes. I was furious with myself; I hated to give him the satisfaction.

'I'm going to enjoy this,' he mused, pulling open another button. 'When I saw you standing in that diner last week everything just clicked. There you were, all embarrassed, looking for Mr Goodboy, the perfect decoy – the perfect victim. I just needed one clear identifying mark to clinch it, and then I thought of the scar. When this is all over I'll walk away and watch your pretty boy do the time. Too bad you won't be here to see it.'

His reverie gave me the opportunity I needed. He was so busy congratulating himself he didn't notice as I wriggled my right elbow out of the sleeve far enough to reach behind me and get hold of the handle of my revolver. I knew I had only one chance. I took a deep breath, gathered all my strength, and heaved him up as I pulled out the gun. There was no time to aim, and I had no control with my right hand anyway. I fired as soon as my hand was free and pointed in his general direction. He cried out in pain as the bullet grazed his right arm, jumping away and dropping his gun.

I was on my feet with the Smith & Wesson pointed at his head before he knew what had happened. 'Get up, you bastard! I ought to shoot your fucking nuts off.'

I moved around the bed toward him, kicking the Colt under the bed from where it lay on the floor. The phone was on the night table behind him. We both eyed it at the same time. I knew he was figuring the odds on a successful leap to pull it out of the jack. 'Away from the bed,' I said. 'I want you up against the wall.' I could feel his body building resistance. 'If I see one muscle move I'll shoot. Don't think I won't.' When he was up against the wall by the TV I backed around him toward the phone. I held the receiver against my shoulder and dialed 911. I kept the gun pointed; my eyes never left him for one second.

It took several rings before I had a connection. 'This is Tina Paris. I'm an investigator with the state Special Prosecutor's Office. I'm at the Starlight Motel on Sunrise Highway. I need police assistance. I have a subject in custody who is wanted for the Russian Roulette rapes and murders. Get some cars out here forthwith.' The person at the other end started questioning me. I had no time to argue. 'Just do it,' I said and hung up.

'Call an ambulance, I'm bleeding,' Hal moaned, cradling his arm like a woman with a baby.

'Shut up or I'll shoot.'

'You know you can't kill me. You're not cut out for it. You couldn't even kill that skell on the roof, you're not going to kill a cop.'

We watched each other intently, our eyes locked. Suddenly he threw his arm out, smashing the lamp next to the TV and plunging the room into darkness. He dove onto the floor. I fired as he rolled behind the bed, dropping down on the other side. He grappled for his gun, found it, and fired over my head. We both lay there panting in the dark like cornered animals, the world narrowed to nothing but each other's presence. I heard him crawling into the bathroom and started easing myself around the bed. Then I heard the glass breaking. By the time I got to the bathroom he had gone out the window, and I immediately backtracked to the front door. I opened it cautiously and looked in both directions but didn't see anything. Slowly, my body pressed against the building, I started moving toward the corner. I took a deep breath and stepped around, my gun ready. He had disappeared.

There was a wide driveway around the building, and beyond that a scrubby border of bushes and trees. I peered out but could see nothing beyond the arc of the motel lights. Carefully, I made my way up to the broken window and looked into the bathroom from the outside in case he had somehow gone back that way, but he wasn't there. I turned back to the wooded area and was vainly peering into the shadows when I heard a car starting out front. I automatically turned and started to run around the side of the building, knowing as I ran that it was a mistake, that I had to be more cautious. It didn't even sound like my car. I turned to look at the room and saw the glint of Hal's gun in the open doorway. I just kept running – motion was my only hope – and somersaulted behind the nearest car in time to hear the blast as Hal fired. I lay there winded, and as I tried to get my bearings I heard another engine and knew this time it was the sound of the Z revving up.

I stood and watched as Hal squealed onto the highway and then noticed the Cadillac Seville, pulled over to the side, idling. The occupants were probably too shocked by the shots to move. I rushed up, flashed my shield, and told the startled couple I was requisitioning their Caddie. 'Now,' I yelled as they stared at me in disbelief. They wouldn't forget this little rendezvous for a long time.

Hal had the advantage in the Z but I had lucked out with the Seville – what it lacked in handling it made up for in power. It only took me a couple of minutes to pick him up. Sunrise became a two-lane after about a mile. He stayed on it past Edwards Airport until he could see he wasn't losing me and then made a sudden sharp left on to Vet's Highway. The Caddie skidded in the curve and I almost lost it but straightened out in time and started gaining again. Hal took another turn on to a back road, and I knew the Seville would be no match for the Z under these conditions. The skid had reminded me of the Z's one weird quirk, however. If I could force Hal into a sharp right at the speeds we were going, he would lose control before he knew what was happening.

He almost got away from me a couple of times, but I kept up the pressure as best I could, flooring the Caddie. And then I saw my opportunity. We were moving into a tight right curve and up ahead was a bridge where the road we were on went under the highway. I had to force him to take that right hard. I pressed my foot on the accelerator so fiercely that I thought it would burn a hole through the rocker panel. The Caddie jolted forward, nipping at Hal's tail. He floored the Z going into the right turn, the wheels locked, the Z went into a spin, did two complete turns, and sideswiped the stone abutment, coming to a halt under the bridge.

I pulled up, the nose of the Caddie blocking the Z, and cut the engine. There was something dripping under the Z's front end, but otherwise there wasn't a sound. I peered out the window but couldn't see Hal anywhere.

I got out, pulled my gun, crouched down behind the Seville in case Hal was out there somewhere waiting to take potshots, and inched around to where the Z had crashed. Nothing was moving anywhere. I approached the driver's-side window cautiously, figuring Hal must have hit his head on impact, expecting, and hoping, to see his unconscious body. There was no-one inside. The sight of the empty seat gripped me with a feeling of absolute dread. The hair on the back of my neck stood up, as if I was confronting something beyond the human – something supernatural. I had to force myself not to panic. I looked in the car, searching for an explanation and saw that the impact had ripped the door on the passenger side clean off, allowing Hal to get out before I had even pulled up. Now my panic took on another dimension. My eyes darted frantically around. The lights of both cars were still on, creating areas of blinding brightness and strange elongated shadows. My whole body was clammy with fear.

Suddenly, something grabbed my ankles. Before I had a chance to scream I was flat on my back. The impact knocked the breath out of me and sent my gun flying. I couldn't muster the strength to fight or get away as Hal pulled himself toward me from his hiding place under the car. He managed to crawl out, kneel above me, raise his gun, and take aim. In an act of sheer desperation, I grabbed on to the cylinder, grasping it as hard as I could. As long as I held on to it, he couldn't cock it to fire. He beat at me with his other hand, momentarily loosening my grip, forcing the hammer back with an ominous click. 'Who the hell do you think you are, you stupid bitch?' he screamed in frustration. 'You think you can stop me?'

I grabbed the cylinder with both hands now, mustering all my strength. He pulled my hand along with his so the gun was aimed at my temple, struggling to set me up like one of his victims, but I wouldn't let go. He couldn't hold the gun steady or completely cock it to fire. Then he grabbed my hair and banged my head against the ground. The pain was blinding. I gritted my teeth and hung on, but my grip was loosening. I heard the second and third click as the cylinder rotated into place. Absolutely desperate now, I wedged my thumb between the hammer and the breech block. The firing pin pressed into my flesh as he pulled on the trigger. But with my thumb there, the gun couldn't fire. He pulled in harder and the sharp metal pin pierced my finger through to the bone. My scream startled both of us. Rousing reserves of strength I didn't know I had left, I forced his arm out, swung it around and hit him with the butt of the gun across the nose. He yelped in pain and pulled back. I yanked his arm again, hitting him on the side of the head this time, knocking him onto the ground.

I instantly grabbed the gun, leapt up into a kneeling combat position, and moved just far enough away so he couldn't grab at me, the gun at arm's length, straight out in front and pointed directly at his head. 'I want you alive, but move and I'll fucking kill you,' I screamed, gasping for breath.

I had no cuffs with me and needed him in a less threatening position if I was going to hold him until help came. 'I want you face down with your arms folded underneath you.' He didn't move.

'Do it.' He just looked at me. I pulled the hammer back to the first click.

'Shoot, why don't you?' His voice was high pitched with hysterical bravado.

I pulled the hammer a little farther. He laughed. 'You couldn't shoot a rabid fox if it was coming straight at you.'

I pulled the hammer all the way back and the cylinder completed its revolution, clicking into place.

'You fucking cunt. I should have killed you in the motel when I had the chance.'

I moved closer until I had the gun up against his head. He knew even better than I did that the slightest pressure of my finger on the trigger would kill him. We stayed frozen that way like some ancient tableau. The silence stretched around us to infinity, yet encircled us like a cocoon. We were a universe to ourselves. A calm power filled my veins, steadying my heart and clearing my mind. I knew help could not be far behind. I had made that call; they must have realized their mistake with Jeff. They would have brought out all the reinforcements by now. But I also knew I could hold him as long as I had to. I started to read him his rights: 'You have the right to remain silent. Anything you say can and will be held against you . . .' The dull moan of a vehicle approaching from the distance invaded the capsule of our world. I heard it coming closer, nearing the curve, the rumble turning to a deafening roar. As it rounded the bend I glanced up to see a big black Harley whizzing past. It was only a split second of inattention, but it was enough for him to make a lunge for my leg. I turned back and fired point-blank at his head.

Epilogue

After a couple of days in the hospital with two broken ribs and a concussion, I went back to the office to a great homecoming from the guys, a lot of fanfare from the Press, and your basic official debriefing. I was still too blown away by the whole experience and too groggy on painkillers to really enjoy any of it. When Vince called me into his office for a personal pat on the back and then offered me a couple of months' leave, I was happy to take it.

I played my grisly dance with Hal over and over in my mind, appalled at how gullible I had been at some moments, and proud of my quick reactions at others. The important thing, and given the circumstances, the amazing thing, was that I was still alive. I cried with gratitude and relief for weeks whenever I thought about it. But I had killed a man, and I didn't think I would ever see things in quite the same way again. There was a good, strong, healthy part of me that thought: The son of a bitch deserved to die. He killed two women, raped at least ten more, and was unquestionably set on raping and killing me as well. And he was a cop. I remembered when the thought of Calvert in uniform made me sick. The thought of Hal carrying a shield was absolutely unbearable. But another part of me went over the events wondering what I could have done differently, trying to dope out whether there was any way I could have taken him alive.

I don't believe in killing; I hate the fact that the answer to violence is more violence. But I knew it was an ego thing, too. I had this idea that I would get through my twenty years in policing without using my gun. A completely clean tour. I wasn't the only one who carried this ideal; it was the other side of being a cowboy. Some cops counted notches in their belt like gunslingers; some of us wanted to stay pure. It was one of the reasons I went with the SPO in the first place. I knew I wanted to be in law enforcement, and anti-corruption seemed to offer a clean way to do it. But maybe you can't stay clean in a dirty world.

Whenever I thought about taking Hal alive, when I had that image in my mind, I knew I didn't trust the outcome. What if the system had let the monster go? Bargained him down on some technicality the way they did with Calvert? When I looked at it that way, there was no way I could be sorry I pulled the trigger.

The terror I had felt during my confrontation with Hal, and the excitement of the aftermath, certainly dimmed my anger about what went down with Calvert. But I wasn't about to forget. When all the confetti had been swept away, I still had a lot to think about. I heard from the grapevine that Jeff took a leave too. I would have liked to talk to him about everything that had happened, but maybe it was better if we left it alone. He had a lot to handle himself. A partner who not only turned out to be a psycho but tried to set him up to take the fall. And a woman he thought he trusted who was capable of suspecting him of the most hideous crimes a man can commit.

I always prided myself on being a good judge of people, but with Jeff I had really screwed up. I didn't know if he could ever forgive me, or if he would ever want to. With Lenora it was different. By the time we spoke again, she had made her peace with it. When she had had time to think about it, she decided she had done the right thing after all. It helped that the courts gave Calvert the maximum sentence and he was serving a three-year term – more than we had hoped for. He was off the street. But she wasn't scared of him any more, she said. And she thanked me for that. She said watching me taught her you didn't have to be afraid. She had her self-respect now, and no-one could take it away from her again. Her voice was full of strength and pride, and the sound of it was good for my soul. She invited me to come over to her new apartment for dinner with her and Kari, and I'm planning on doing that soon.

Pleased as I am for her, I know she has given me a much greater gift than I have given her. She brought me back down to earth and made me realize how far I had strayed from what I thought my life was about. She restored my faith in the positive side of human nature.

You learn a lot after thirteen years on a job like this. A lot about life, about people, about yourself – usually more than you want to know. You learn a lot about corruption and venality and frailty and human weakness. If you stick to the obvious lessons it'll do you in. It happened to guys I worked with and guys I knew from other departments. Some quit, a lot got divorced, a few got killed, a couple killed themselves.

You can let the negativity get to you and you can get complacent in your cynicism. Sometimes it's like suffocating under a mountain of garbage. You see too many cops whose heads are turned by all the money and drugs lying around for the taking, too many judges in tight with organized crime, too many Mafia lawyers getting paid fortunes to make mincemeat out of your cases and maybe succeeding. Only once in a while does someone come along like Lenora to renew your faith in the courage of ordinary frightened human beings.

As the weeks went by, I thought of walking away, of looking for some other kind of work, but whenever I did I remembered my favorite aphorism: All that it takes for evil to triumph is for good people to do nothing.

It was a shock to discover on my first day back how well the office had been functioning without me. Bud and Mickey and Mel filled me in on the status of current cases. They had kept up with Dandrell and had gotten enough information to obtain a court order for a wire. It looked like something might come of it. I handed Randazzo a story about a car accident, so the door was still open on that one. And we had gotten the Muehler conviction, so there would be one less scumbag on the street for a while. But the surprising news was what had been going on down at the SNU. Apparently Hal had been working a deal with a ring of Dominicans, taking bribes to look the other way when shipments came in at Kennedy, and then skimming the evidence on the busts he did make. A couple of uniforms from the Nine Nine were implicated. IAD and the SPO were both involved in the investigation. I remembered what Jeff had said about something going down at the airport on Friday the thirteenth that he didn't want me to know about, and figured he must have caught on and been afraid I would assume he was involved. I had a lot to make up to him for.

I tried to reconnect, but the guys could see how hard it was.

'Here's something for you,' Bud quipped, plunking a huge stack of files onto my desk. 'Just in case you forgot how glamorous this job really is.'

'The office has a new joker,' I said. But I was grateful. At least reading them gave me something to do.

It was my third day back when Vince waved me into his office. 'Mel and Mickey have been monitoring the wire on Dandrell,' he said. 'Anyone fill you in on that?'

I nodded.

'Good. Mickey just called in with some news. A meet is about to go down with Randazzo, Dandrell, and René Drogin.'

'The mayor's assistant?'

'And closest personal confidant. The tech room's got your equipment ready. Get your ass out there, Paris.' He looked me straight in the eye. 'We need you back.'

I hesitated for only a second before the excitement took over. I hadn't resolved all the philosophical issues attached to the job, but that could wait. I never could resist the thrill of the chase.

THE END

A SELECTION LIST OF CRIME AND MYSTERY TITLES AVAILABLE FROM BANTAM BOOKS

THE PRICES SHOWN BELOW WERE CORRECT AT THE TIME OF GOING TO PRESS. HOWEVER TRANSWORLD PUBLISHERS RESERVE THE RIGHT TO SHOW NEW RETAIL PRICES ON COVERS WHICH MAY DIFFER FROM THOSE PREVIOUSLY ADVERTISED IN THE TEXT OR ELSEWHERE.

☐ 40400 8	A SEASON IN PURGATORY	Dominick Dunne	£4.99
☐ 40321 4	AN INCONVENIENT WOMAN	Dominick Dunne	£4.99
☐ 40485 7	ALL THE LONELY PEOPLE	Martin Edwards	£2.99
☐ 40486 5	SUSPICIOUS MINDS	Martin Edwards	£2.99
☐ 40693 0	I REMEMBER YOU	Martin Edwards	£3.99
☐ 40237 4	FOR THE SAKE OF ELENA	Elizabeth George	£4.99
☐ 17510 6	A GREAT DELIVERANCE	Elizabeth George	£4.99
☐ 17511 4	PAYMENT IN BLOOD	Elizabeth George	£4.99
☐ 40168 8	A SUITABLE VENGEANCE	Elizabeth George	£4.99
☐ 40167 X	WELL-SCHOOLED IN MURDER	Elizabeth George	£4.99
☐ 40238 2	MISSING JOSEPH	Elizabeth George	£4.99
☐ 40845 3	PLAYING FOR THE ASHES	Elizabeth George	£4.99
☐ 17605 6	ONE WAS NOT ENOUGH (NF)	Georgina Lloyd	£2.99
☐ 17606 4	MOTIVE TO MURDER (NF)	Georgina Lloyd	£2.99
☐ 40422 9	THE PASSION KILLERS (NF)	Georgina Lloyd	£3.50
☐ 40627 2	MURDERS UNSPEAKABLE	Georgina Lloyd	£3.99
☐ 40792 9	DEATH OF A CAD	M C Beaton	£3.99
☐ 40791 0	DEATH OF A GOSSIP	M C Beaton	£3.99
☐ 40794 5	DEATH OF AN OUTSIDER	M C Beaton	£3.99
☐ 40793 7	DEATH OF A PERFECT WIFE	M C Beaton	£3.99
☐ 17524 6	THE SPY IN QUESTION	Tim Sebastian	£3.99
☐ 40055 X	SPY SHADOW	Tim Sebastian	£3.99
☐ 40056 3	SAVIOUR'S GATE	Tim Sebastian	£3.99
☐ 40258 7	EXIT BERLIN	Tim Sebastian	£3.99
☐ 40255 2	THE GOLDEN ORANGE	Joseph Wambaugh	£3.99
☐ 17697 8	THE BLOODING (NF)	Joseph Wambaugh	£3.99
☐ 17555 6	ECHOES IN THE DARKNESS	Joseph Wambaugh	£3.99
☐ 40535 7	FUGITIVE NIGHTS	Joseph Wambaugh	£3.99
☐ 40796 1	FINNEGAN'S WEEK	Joseph Wambaugh	£4.99

*My
Naughty
Little Sister's
Friends*

My
Naughty
Little Sister's
Friends

Dorothy Edwards
Illustrated by Shirley Hughes

EGMONT

First published in Great Britain 1962
by Methuen Children's Books Ltd
Reissued 2002 by Egmont Books Limited
239 Kensington High Street, London W8 6SA

Text copyright © 1962 The Estate of Dorothy Edwards
Illustrations copyright © 1962 Shirley Hughes

ISBN 1 4052 0291 2

10 9 8 7 6 5 4

A CIP catalogue record for this title
is available from the British Library

Typeset by Avon DataSet Ltd, Bidford on Avon, Warwickshire
Printed and bound in Great Britain by Cox & Wyman Ltd,
Reading, Berkshire

Contents

1 The Cocoa week-end

When I was a little girl I sometimes went to stay with my godmother-aunt in the country, for the week-end.

My mother would pack a little case for me, and then my godmother would come to spend a day with us and take me back with her.

My little sister was always very interested when she saw Mother packing my case, and she would remember things to go in it, and go and fetch them *without being asked*.

1

She used to ask me questions and questions about going visiting, and when I told her everything she used to ask me all over again because she liked hearing it so much.

I told her about the nice little blue bed that I slept in at my godmother's and the picture of the big dog and the little dog on the bedroom wall. I told her and told her about them.

Then she wanted to hear about the things we had to eat and the things I did. I told her about all the tiny little baby-looking cakes that my godmother made, and about my godmother's piano, and how she let me play little made-up tunes on it if I wanted to.

And she would say, 'Tell me again about the piano,' my little sister would say. 'Tell me again. I like about the piano.'

So I would tell her about the piano all over again, and then I would pretend to play tunes on the table, and my sister would pretend to play tunes on the table too, and we would laugh and laugh.

But, when my mother said, 'Wouldn't you like to go on a visit one day?' my little sister would say, 'I'm not very sure.'

My little sister told her friend Mrs Cocoa all about my goings away, and Mrs Cocoa was surprised to find how much my little sister knew about it, and *she* said, 'Wouldn't you like to go on a visit one day?' as well.

When Mrs Cocoa said this, my sister said, 'I don't think I should mind the visit but I shouldn't like the long-way-away.'

My little sister said, 'I should like to sleep

in a different bed with a different picture on the wall and eat different dinners and play the piano, but I don't think I should like to go a long way to do it.'

You see my godmother-aunt did live quite a long way from our house, and my little sister was rather frightened to think what a long way it was.

Now kind Mrs Cocoa thought about what my little sister had said, and the next time she heard that I was going to stay with my godmother-aunt, she said to my little sister, 'How would you like to go away for a week-end, too? How would you like to come and stay with me?'

Mrs Cocoa said, 'You can sleep in my little spare bedroom and eat all your dinners and things with Mr Cocoa and me, and you won't be a long-way-away, will you?'

Wasn't that a lovely idea for clever Mrs Cocoa to have had? Mrs Cocoa lived next door to us, and my little sister knew her house very well, but she had never slept there and had all her dinners and things there, so it would be a real visit, wouldn't it?

My sister was very pleased. It was just what she wanted: a real visit that was not far away, so she said at once, 'Please, Mrs Cocoa, I should like that.'

So when my mother packed my case she packed one for my naughty little sister as well, and my little sister helped her to fetch things for both the cases.

When my godmother-aunt was ready to go, and I put my best hat and coat on, my sister said she must put *her* best hat and coat on too because she was going visiting just like her big sister.

Now you know there was a little gate that Mr Cocoa had made in the fence between his garden and ours, especially for my little sister so that she could come in to see Mrs Cocoa when she wanted to. It was a dear little gate and my little sister was always using it, but because she was going to visit Mrs Cocoa, she said she didn't want to go through her gate, she wanted to go through Mrs Cocoa's *front door*.

'I'm not Mrs Cocoa's next-door girl,' she said. 'I'm a visitor!'

So my father carried the case for her, and my little sister went down our front garden and through our front gate and through Mrs Cocoa's front gate and *up* her front garden and Father lifted her up so she could knock on Mrs Cocoa's knocker.

My little sister knocked very hard and called out, 'Here I am, Mrs Cocoa; I've come to visit you!' And Mrs Cocoa opened the door, and said, 'Well, I *am* pleased to see you, come in do. You're just in time for tea.'

'Come in, my dear,' Mrs Cocoa said, and Mr Cocoa came out into the hall and said, 'I'll take your luggage, ma'am,' just as if he hardly knew my sister at all! Wasn't that nice?

My little sister said, 'Thank you, Mr Jones.' Not 'Mr Cocoa'. She said, 'Thank you, *Mr Jones*,' in a visitor-way.

Then she kissed our father 'good-bye' and Father said, 'Have a good time, old lady,' and then she was really on a visit by herself.

Mrs Cocoa gave my sister a very beautiful tea with all her best moss-rose tea-set on the table too, and that was exciting because although my sister had known Mrs Cocoa a long time she had never seen the moss-rose tea-set used before.

Then Mrs Cocoa took my sister upstairs to show her where she was going to sleep, and that was exciting too, because Mrs Cocoa had found a bed-cover with flowers and dragons and gold curly things needleworked all over it that my little sister had never seen before and this was on the little bed she was to sleep in.

There was a new picture on the wall too. Mrs Cocoa had told Mr Cocoa about the picture at my godmother-aunt's house, and kind Mr Cocoa had found a picture in a book and put it in a frame specially for the Visit. It was a picture of a singing lady lying in some water with flowers floating on it. Mr Cocoa said he liked the picture because the flowers and bushes and things in it looked so real.

My little sister liked the picture too. She said she liked it because the naughty lady hadn't taken her dress off, and she was wet as wet. She liked to have a picture of a naughty wet lady to look at, she said.

Weren't the Cocoas kind to think of all these nice surprises? Mr Cocoa said, 'We haven't got a piano, but I've got something else here that ought to keep you out of mischief.'

And do you know what he had? It was a musical-box! It was a little brown box with a glass window in the top, and at the side of the box there was a key. When you turned the key a little shiny thing with holes in it went round and round – you could see it through the glass window, and a pretty little tune came out of the box that Mr Cocoa said was called 'The Bluebells of Scotland'.

If you want to know what it sounded like perhaps you can ask someone to hum it for you.

Mr Cocoa showed my sister how to wind the musical-box and then he said she could play it whenever she liked. And she did play it – lots and lots of times while she was visiting.

My sister stayed with the dear Cocoa Joneses all that week-end and had a lovely time with them. She slept in the little bed and ate Mrs Cocoa's dinners and things and played the musical-box and went for walks with Mr Cocoa while Mrs Cocoa had a rest, and it was all very strange and pleasant.

But, do you know, my little sister NEVER ONCE CAME BACK HOME. She never even knocked on the wall to our mother! Not once. Mother said she saw my little sister playing in Mrs Cocoa's garden, and she watched her going off for walks, but my little sister didn't even look at our house!

She was really being away on a visit.

When the week-end was over, Mrs Cocoa packed her case for her, and Mr Cocoa took her home by the front door to show that she had been away.

When my little sister saw me again, she didn't ask about *my* visit – oh no! She told me instead all about her visit to the Cocoas. She told me about the dragon and flower bed-cover and the naughty lady picture, and she said, 'There wasn't a piano, but I played another thing.'

My little sister couldn't remember the name of the musical-box though, so she said, 'I played a la-la box', and she la-la'd all the 'Bluebells of Scotland' tune for me without making one mistake. Wasn't she clever?

2 My Naughty Little Sister and the guard

Do you like trains?

When I was a little girl I didn't like trains at all; but my little sister did. I thought that trains were horrid and noisy and puffy and steamy but my little sister said they were lovely things, and when she saw one she waved and waved and shouted and shouted to it.

Well now, one day a kind aunt wrote to our mother to ask if my little sister would like to go and stay for a week-end. All by herself.

Not with my father or mother, or even with me, but all by herself like a grown-up lady!

My mother said, 'I don't think she's old enough,' and my father said, 'I don't think she's good enough,' and I said, 'She'll be too frightened.' Because, if you remember, she *had* been frightened about visiting people.

But my little sister said, 'I should like to go and stay for a week-end all by myself. I *am* an old enough girl, and I am not a frightened girl any more. I want to go!'

My mother didn't say anything and my father didn't say anything and I didn't say anything, and my little sister knew why that was, because she said, 'I'm not a good girl now, but I will be good as gold if you will let me go.'

So my father and mother said they thought she might go if she *was* as good as gold. So my little sister was good. She was quiet and tidy and whispery all the week and when the week-end came she *did* go away. All on her own.

This is the exciting thing that happened to her.

Our kind aunt lived quite a long way away, and my little sister had to go on a train *all by herself*.

Wasn't that exciting? All by herself. She had a little brown case with her nightdress inside, and her slippers and her dressing-gown and her best dress for Sunday and all the things she had taken to dear Mrs

Cocoa's. My little sister carried Rosy-Primrose under her arm, but of course Mother carried the case to the station for her.

'Auntie will meet you at the other end,' Mother said. 'So she will carry it to her house for you.'

'I hope Auntie won't forget to look for me,' said my little sister, 'because I don't think I could open a train door all by myself.'

'That's all right,' our mother told her, 'I'm going to ask the guard to keep an eye on you.'

My little sister was going to say, 'What guard?' and ask questions and questions, but she knew that Mother was in a hurry to get the ticket.

When she got to the station she was very excited. She *wanted* to fidget and climb on all the parcels and run along the platform and peep at the man who puts the parcels on the weighing machine. But she didn't. She remembered about being good as gold. Wasn't she sensible?

When the train came in, she didn't rush about or fuss, she walked nicely down the platform beside Mother to where the guard was standing, and when Mother stopped to speak to the guard my little sister didn't talk at all. She just stared at the guard because he was such a big beautiful man.

The guard had a big red beautiful face and a big fluffy black moustache and a golden glittery band on his cap and a silver glittery whistle round his neck and two beautiful flags – a red one and a green one under his arm. He gave my mother and my little sister a most pleasant smile.

'I am going to put this little girl in the end carriage, Guard,' our mother said, 'and I wonder if you would be kind enough to look after her ticket for her, and see that she gets off at the right station?'

The guard smiled very kindly then at my little sister. 'She is a very little girl,' he said. 'Is she a good child? If she is, she can come in the guard's van with me for the journey.'

My little sister thought she had better say something, because she thought how nice it would be to travel in a real guard's van with a real guard, almost as nice as travelling with the engine-driver and not nearly so hot and coaly. She said, 'I am not always a good child. But I am being very good *this week*!'

So the guard said, 'That's good enough for me. In you go then,' and my sister climbed up into the guard's van.

He said, 'Sit on my little seat in the corner there.' And although it was rather a high little seat my little sister managed to climb on to it while the guard put her little case into the van, and picked up some parcels from the platform and put them in too.

Then the guard took his green flag, and blew his whistle, and Mother called out, 'Good-bye, give my love to Auntie,' and the train started to move. The guard jumped in quickly and shut the door. And they were off!

What a very nice man the guard was! He talked all the time to my little sister. He showed her a lantern that made red and green lights, and let her look at some sheets of paper with lines and printing on them that he said he had to write on every day. He lent my sister a pencil and let her scribble on the back of one of his pieces of paper, but it was very difficult because the train was so bumpy, so he gave her an apple to eat instead.

Each time the train stopped at a station the

20

guard jumped down and took in parcels and sacks and put other parcels and sacks on to the platform. Sometimes there were railway porters waiting for the van, with trucks full of luggage, and they stared at my sister and asked the guard who she was. 'Oh, she's my new Mate,' the guard said, and my little sister felt proud as proud.

At one station the guard took in a big basket full of chickens, all looking out in a very pecky way. But the guard told my sister they wouldn't really hurt anyone. 'I often bring chickens,' he said, 'and ducks and dogs and cats.'

He said that one day he took a very growly dog that grumbled all the time. 'I was glad to see the back of him,' the guard said.

Then he said, 'Yes, I've looked after a lot

of animals since I've been on the Line, but you are the first little girl.'

My little sister liked to think that she was the first little girl to travel with the guard, and she said, 'If you have any other little girls to mind you'll be able to tell them about me.' And the guard said that he certainly would.

At last they came to the station that was near our aunt's house, and there was Auntie herself and two of our cousins as well, all waiting for her, and all so happy to see my little sister.

'There's Auntie!' my sister said, and she jumped up and down with excitement as the guard began to open the door.

But she remembered to be a polite child even though she was excited, and before she went off she shook hands with the guard and said, 'Thank you for having me,' – just like a party – 'thank you for having me.'

And the guard said, 'It has been a real pleasure,' and when the train moved off again, he stayed by his window so as to wave to my little sister and she waved to him. How our cousins stared to see a guard waving from his guard's van window at my little sister.

So my little sister stayed with our auntie for a week-end and she wasn't naughty once. On Monday when she came back home Auntie came with her, because she wanted to come for the day to see our mother, so my sister didn't travel in the guard's van that time; but she remembered all about it, and when she and Bad Harry played trains in the garden she said, 'I must be the guard because I know all about it.'

And she did, didn't she?

3 Bad Harry and the milkman

Long ago, when my sister was a naughty little girl and not a grown-up lady, she had a friend called Harry. Harry was a naughty boy, so he and my sister were very good friends.

Harry and my sister were very noisy when they played together. If they saw anything funny they would laugh and laugh and roll about on the ground, and they always laughed at the same time at the same thing.

And when my sister was cross, Harry was cross, and when she was stubborn he was stubborn too, and when she said: '*I* want that!' about something, Harry always said: 'You can't have it, because *I* want it.'

My sister would shout, 'Give it to me at once!' and Harry would shout, 'No'.

Then my sister would jump up and down and say, 'Bad Harry' over and over again. 'Bad, bad, Harry!'

Then she would pull his hair, and he would pull her hair and they would hit each other in a very unkind way, until our mother came out and grumbled at them. Then they would stop fighting.

But they went on being friends just the same.

But when Harry came to our house or she

went to Harry's house, she had to say 'Bad Harry' so many times that we called him Bad Harry in the end, and he really was, bad as bad. Oh dear.

They were cross good friends, weren't they?

Well now, when my sister and Harry were very small, they didn't come visiting each other on their own. Our mother took my sister to Harry's house, and Harry's mother brought him round to see us, and as our mothers were busy women they couldn't always be walking round to each other's houses, so there were some days when Harry and my sister couldn't see each other and they didn't like that at all.

One day, when it was cold and snowy, Harry's poor mother wasn't a very well lady, and she couldn't go out, so Harry had to stop at home and not see my sister, and he didn't like that.

Harry stood and looked out of the window, and saw the snow coming down, and everything looking very white and pretty, and he thought of all the lovely games he could have in the snow with my sister.

He thought of making snowballs and throwing them at her, as he'd seen the big boys making snowballs and throwing them at their friends, and he thought of them making a funny old snow-man with a pipe like a picture in one of his books. He thought of all sorts of nice games in the snow.

Then he got very cross and miserable in case the snow should melt before he could play with my sister again.

Then Harry had a bad idea (not a good idea – a *bad* one). He thought he would put on his coat and hat and go and visit my sister all on his own.

What a very bad Harry.

The next-door lady who had come in to

make Harry's breakfast had gone home for a little while, and his mother was fast asleep in bed upstairs, so there was no one to ask.

Bad Harry went and fetched his coat and put it on. He wasn't good about buttons then, so he left it undone.

He found his woolly cap and he put it on. He forgot his gloves, and his leggings and his shoes. He *was in such a hurry*.

He opened the front door, and off he went in his bunny-slippers down the path and out into the snow. He *was* excited; he hurried to get to our house to play with my sister.

The snow fell and fell. It was swirly and curly and cold and it blew into Harry's face, and it crunched under his bunny-slippers, and he thought it was very exciting.

Now all the people who lived in Harry's road had very kindly swept the snow from the pavements in front of their houses so it was quite easy for Harry to get along, but when he turned the first corner, he came to a road where the people hadn't been so kind and thoughtful about clearing the pavements, and soon his little bunny-slippers were quite covered up when he walked.

And his feet got wet and cold.

The wind was blowing down that street too, and it threw the snow into Harry's face in a very unkind way, and Harry suddenly found that his fingers were cold too.

His feet were cold and his fingers were cold, and he hadn't done his coat up so he was all cold. Cold as cold.

And because he was only a little boy then, Harry did a silly little boy thing. He stood quite still. He opened his mouth and he started to cry and cry.

Now, we had a very nice milkman who came to our house. He was a great friend of my little sister's. This milkman had an old white horse and a jingly cart and when he came down the road he would call out 'MILK-O! M-I-L-K-O!'

Like that, and when he came to the door he would sing, 'Milk for the babies, cream for the ladies! M-I-L-K-O!' He was a nice milkman.

He was *just* the person to come along with his white horse and jingly cart and find poor Bad Harry crying because he was cold.

Down the road he came, jingle jingle

rather slowly because of the snow on the road, and his old white horse walking carefully, carefully. And he saw Harry.

He saw cold Harry crying so he said, 'Wo-a there,' to his old white horse, and the milk-cart stopped and he got down and said, 'Why, you're the little chap who plays with young Saucy down the next street.'

When the milkman said 'young Saucy down the next street' he meant my sister because he always called her that (although it wasn't her name of course).

When the nice milkman saw how cold poor Harry was, and how miserable he was, he put him into his milk-cart and wrapped him up in a rug that was on the seat, and because he didn't know where Harry lived, he took him round to our house, which wasn't very far away – only round the next corner after all!

Now my sister was standing by *our* kitchen window being as cross as cross, and wanting to play in the snow with Harry, when she saw the milkman stopping at the gate.

She was very surprised when she saw him lift a bundle in a rug out of his cart and carry it up our path, so she ran to the door with Mother to see what it was all about.

When they opened the door they heard Harry bellowing and crying because he was so cold, and Mother thanked the milkman for bringing him and took him in quickly to warm by our fire.

Poor Harry! Mother rubbed and rubbed him and gave him hot milk and made him

sit with his feet in a bowl of hot water, until he stopped crying and told her that he had come round *all on his own*.

My sister *did* open her eyes when she heard this! On his own!

Mother told Harry that he had been *very naughty*. She said his mother might be very, very worried, and she sent me round at once to tell Harry's next-door lady where he was.

My sister stared hard at Harry when our mother told him he had been naughty and that his mother would be worried. When our mother scolded Harry he began to cry again, and this time my naughty little sister cried as well.

And they made so much noise that Mother forgave Harry and fetched him a biscuit, and he stopped crying.

My sister stopped crying too and Mother gave her a biscuit, and they sat quiet as quiet until I came back with Harry's shoes and some dry socks and leggings for him to put on, so that I could take him home again.

I told him that his next-door lady had said that his mother was still asleep and if we hurried we could get back before the poor not-well lady woke up.

So Harry hurried back with me and he was home again before his mother could wake up and worry.

Next day it was even more cold, and when the milkman came my sister saw that he had put some funny little red-woollen bag things on his horse's ears.

She said, 'Why has your horse got those funny bag-things, milkman?'

And the nice milkman laughed and said, 'In case we have to pick up that bad friend of yours again. He yelled so much he made my horse's ears twitch. He might give her ear-ache next time.'

And my sister looked very good, and she said in a very good quiet voice, 'I'm afraid Harry is a Bad Boy.'

4 The very old birthday party

Long ago, when my sister was a naughty little girl, we had a very old, old great-Auntie who lived in a big house with lots of other very old ladies and gentlemen.

Our mother used to go and visit this old Auntie sometimes and she used to tell us all about her. Then, one day our mother said, 'How would you like to come with me to visit Dear Old Auntie?'

Our mother said, 'She is going to have a birthday party next week, and I think it would be very nice if you little girls could come to it. You see it is a very special party because old Auntie will be one hundred years old.'

One hundred years! That is very, very old. You ask some big person to tell you how old that means.

Well, *I* knew how old a hundred years was, so I said, 'Good gracious, what an old lady!'

My sister didn't know how old it was then because she was so little, but she said, 'Good gracious' too, because I had.

'She is a very sweet little old lady,' our mother told us. 'Everyone likes her. The lady who looks after all the old ladies and gentlemen says that Dear Old Auntie is the *pride* of the Home.'

Wasn't that a nice thing for our old Auntie to be? The pride of the Home. We thought it was anyway, and we were very pleased to think that we were going to visit such a dear old lady on her one hundredth birthday.

Well now, when the birthday came, we were both very excited. We wore our best Sunday dresses and looked very smart girls.

Our mother had told us that we might take some money from our money-boxes to buy a present for our Dear Old Auntie in the Woolworths shop. Our mother let us choose our own presents too. I bought our Dear Old Auntie a nice little white handkerchief with blue flowers on the corner. It took me a long time to think what to buy.

But my little sister didn't think at all. She

knew just what she wanted. She said, 'I am going to buy one of those glassy-looking things with the little houses inside that make it snow when you shake them.'

My little sister had been to the Woolworths shop with Mrs Cocoa, so she knew all about these glassy things.

Do you know about them? They are very pretty.

I thought it was a silly thing to give to such a very old lady, but my naughty little sister said, 'It isn't silly. I would like one of those glassy things for *my* birthday!'

And she said she wouldn't buy anything else, so our mother took her along to the toy-counter and let her pay for one of the glassy things with her own money.

So, when we went to visit the Birthday

Old Lady we had some nice presents for her. I had the handkerchief and my sister had the glassy thing with the snow inside it, and Mother had a box of sweeties from my father, and a nice woollen shawl that Mrs Cocoa Jones had kindly knitted from some wool that Mother had bought.

Wasn't she a lucky old lady?

My sister and I had never been to an old people's Home before, so we were very quiet and staring when we got there.

There were so many old people. Dear old ladies and dear old gentlemen all with white hair and smiling faces, and they all talked to us and waved to us and shook hands with us in a very friendly way.

And we smiled too. My sister smiled *and* smiled.

The lady who looked after the old people was called Miss Simmons and she was very kind.

'We are all very glad to see such young people,' she said to my sister. 'Do you know I don't think we've ever had anyone quite as young as you before?'

My sister was very pleased to think that she was the first very young visitor, and she did something that she sometimes did to Mr and Mrs Cocoa Jones. *She blew kisses.* She was being nice.

Our dear old great-auntie was sitting by the fire in a big chair, and when Miss Simmons took us over to meet her, she was very pleased to see us.

What a very little old wrinkly pretty lady our old auntie was! She had a tiny soft little voice and twinkly little eyes and she took a great fancy to my naughty sister at once. She asked her to sit next to her. Wasn't that a nice thing for my sister to be asked to do?

The old Auntie was very pleased with her presents. She put the shawl on straight away, and she put my handkerchief into her sleeve straight away too. But when she saw what my sister had brought she clapped her hands together in a funny old-lady way and she said, 'Well-well-well. What a lovely treat! I haven't seen one of these since I was a little girl. I saw one in another little girl's house and I always wanted one. Now I've got one at last!'

And the dear old lady shook up the glassy thing and made the snow fall on to the little house, and then she shook it again and made the snow fall again. She did it so many times that we knew how very pleased she was.

'Just fancy,' she said, 'I wanted one when I was a little girl like you, and I've got one today on my hundredth birthday.'

Miss Simmons said, 'I see you have a box of sweeties too. But I don't think you had better eat them yet. We have a birthday cake with one hundred candles for you to cut and a very nice birthday tea. It would be a pity to eat sweeties and spoil your appetite.'

Now my sister had heard Mother say that

sort of thing to her but she was surprised to think that people had to say such things to old ladies, and she stared rather hard at her Dear Old Auntie.

And what do you think? When kind Miss Simmons went off to see about the birthday tea, old Auntie opened her box of sweeties, and gave one to me and one to my sister and then she ate one herself!

And she laughed and my sister laughed.

When Miss Simmons came back and saw what old Auntie had done she shook her finger at her. 'You are a very naughty old lady,' Miss Simmons said.

Then Miss Simmons looked at the hundred-years-old lady, and my bad little sister, both laughing together and she said, 'Goodness me, you can see you are relations. *You both look alike!*'

And do you know, when I looked, and Mother looked, at the naughty old lady and my naughty little sister, we saw that they did!

5 The cross spotty child

One day, a long time ago, my naughty little sister wasn't at all a well girl. She was all burny and tickly and tired and sad and spotty and when our nice doctor came to see her he said, 'You've got measles, old lady.'

'You've got measles,' that nice doctor said, 'and you will have to stay in bed for a few days.'

When my sister heard that she had measles she began to cry, 'I don't want measles. Nasty measles,' and made herself

49

burnier and ticklier and sadder than ever.

Have you had measles? Have you? If you have you will remember how nasty it is. I am sure that if you did have measles at any time you would be a very good child. You wouldn't fuss and fuss. But my sister did, I'm sorry to say.

She fidgeted and fidgeted and fussed and cried and had to be read to all the time, and wouldn't drink her orange-juice and lost her hanky in the bed until our mother said, 'Oh, dear, I don't want you to have measles, I'm sure.'

She *was* a cross spotty child.

When our mother had to go out to do her shopping, kind Mrs Cocoa Jones came in to sit with my sister. Mrs Cocoa brought her knitting with her, and sat by my sister's bed and knitted and knitted. Mrs Cocoa was a kind lady and when my little sister moaned and grumbled she said, 'There, there, duckie,' in a very kind way.

My little sister didn't like Mrs Cocoa saying, 'There, there, duckie,' to her, because she was feeling so cross herself, so she pulled the sheet over her face and said, 'Go away, Mrs Cocoa.'

But Mrs Cocoa didn't go away, she just went on knitting and knitting until my naughty little sister pulled the sheet down from her face to see what Mrs Cocoa could be doing and whether she had made her cross.

But kind Mrs Cocoa wasn't cross – she was just sorry to see my poor spotty sister, and when she saw my sister looking at her, she said, 'Now, I was just thinking. I believe I have the very thing to cheer you up.'

My sister was surprised when Mrs Cocoa said this instead of being cross with her for saying 'Go away,' so she listened hard and forgot to be miserable.

'When I was a little girl,' Mrs Cocoa said, 'my granny didn't like to see poor not-well children looking miserable so she made a get-better box that she used to lend to all her grandchildren when they were ill.'

Mrs Cocoa said, 'My granny kept this box on top of her dresser, and when she found anything that she thought might amuse a not-well child she would put it in her box.'

Mrs Cocoa said that it was a great treat to borrow the get-better box because although you knew some of the things that would be in it, there was always something fresh.

My little sister stopped being cross and moany while she listened to Mrs Cocoa, because she hadn't heard of a get-better box before.

She said, 'What things, Mrs Cocoa? What was in the box?'

'All kinds of things,' Mrs Cocoa said.

'Tell me! Tell me!' said my spotty little sister and she began to look cross because she wanted to know so much.

But Mrs Cocoa said, 'I won't tell you, for *you can see for yourself.*'

Mrs Cocoa said, 'I hadn't thought about it until just this very minute; but do you know, I've got my granny's very own get-better box in my house and I had forgotten all about it! It's up in an old trunk in the spare bedroom. There are a lot of heavy boxes on top of the trunk, but if you are a good girl now, I will ask Mr Cocoa to get them down for me when he comes home from work. I will get the box out of the trunk and bring it for you to see tomorrow.'

Wasn't that a beautiful idea?

Mrs Cocoa Jones said, 'I haven't seen that box for years and years, it will be quite a treat to look in it again. I am sure it will be just the thing to lend to a cross little spotty girl with measles, don't you?'

And my naughty little sister thought it

was just the thing indeed!

So, next morning, as soon as my sister had had some bread and milk and a spoonful of medicine, Mrs Cocoa came upstairs to see her, with her grandmother's get-better box under her arm.

There was a *smiling* spotty child waiting for her today.

It was a beautiful-looking box, because Mrs Cocoa's old grandmother had stuck beautiful pieces of wallpaper on the lid and on the sides of the box, and Mrs Cocoa said that the wallpaper on the front was some that had been in her granny's front bedroom, and that on the back had been in her parlour. The paper on the lid had come from her Aunty Kitty's sitting-room; the paper on one side had been in Mrs Cocoa's mother's kitchen, while the paper on the other side which was really lovely, with roses and green dickey-birds, had come from Mrs Cocoa's own bedroom wallpaper when she was a little girl!

My sister was so interested to hear this that she almost forgot about opening the box!

But she did open it, and she found so many things that I can only tell you about some of them.

On top of the box she found a lovely piece of shining stuff folded very tidily, and when she opened it out on her bed she saw that it was covered with round sparkly things that Mrs Cocoa said were called *spangles*. Mrs Cocoa said that it was part of a dress that a real fairy-queen had worn in a real pantomime. She said that a lady who had worked in a theatre had given it to her grandmother long, long ago.

Under the sparkly stuff were boxes and boxes. Tiny boxes with pretty pictures painted on the lids, and in every box a nice little interesting thing. A string of tiny beads, or a little-little dollie, or some shells. In one box was a very little paper fan, and in another there was a little laughing clown's face cut out of paper that Mrs Cocoa's granny had stuck there as a surprise.

My sister was so surprised that she smiled, and Mrs Cocoa told her that her granny had put that in to make a not-well child be surprised and smile. She said that she remembered smiling at that box when she was a little girl.

Mrs Cocoa's old granny had been very clever, hadn't she?

There were picture postcards in that not-well box, and pretty stones – some sparkly and some with holes in them. There was a small hard fir cone, and pieces of coloured glass that you could hold up before your eyes and look through. There was a silver pencil with a hole in the handle that you could look through too and see a magic picture.

There was a small book with pictures in it – oh, I can't remember what else!

It amused and *amused* my sister.

She took all the things out carefully and then she put them all back carefully. She shut the lid and looked at the wallpaper outside all over again.

Then she took the things out again, and looked at them again and played with them and was as interested as could be!

And Mrs Cocoa said, 'Well, I never! That's just what I did myself when I was a child!'

When my sister was better she gave the box back to Mrs Cocoa – just as Mrs Cocoa had given the box back to her granny.

Mrs Cocoa Jones laid all the things from the box out in the sunshine in her back garden to air them after the measles. She said her grandmother always did that, and because Mrs Cocoa's granny had done it, it made it all very specially nice for my little sister to think about.

After that, my sister often played at making a get-better box with a boot-box that Mother gave her, and once she drew red chalk spots on poor Rosy-Primrose's face so that she could have measles and the get-better box to play with.

6 My Naughty Little Sister and the sweep

One morning, when I was a little girl and my naughty little sister was a girl littler than me, we went downstairs to breakfast and found everything looking very funny indeed.

The table was pushed right up against the wall, and the chairs were standing on the table and they were all covered over with a big sheet. The curtains were gone from the window, and the armchairs and the pictures and the clock and lots of other things. All gone!

My little sister was very interested to see all this, and when she looked out of the window, she saw that the armchairs and the pictures and all the other things were piled up in our back garden. My little sister *did* stare.

Clock and pictures and armchairs in the back garden, and things covered up with sheets, no curtains! Wasn't that a strange thing to find? My little sister said, 'We have got a funny home today.'

Then my mother told us that the chimney-sweep was coming to clean the chimney and that she had had to get the room ready for him. My naughty little sister was very excited because she had never seen a sweep, and she jumped and said 'Sweep,' and jumped and said 'Sweep,' again and again because she was so excited. Then she said, 'Won't we have any breakfast?'

'Won't we have any breakfast?' said my hungry little sister, because the chairs were standing on the table. And Mother said, 'As it is a lovely sunny morning you are going to have a picnic breakfast in the garden.'

Then my little sister was very pleased indeed because she had never had a picnic breakfast before.

She said, 'What shall we eat?' and my mother told her, 'Well, as it is a special picnic breakfast, I have made you some egg sandwiches.' Wasn't that nice? Sandwiches for breakfast! There was milk too, and bananas. My sister *did* like it!

We sat on the back doorstep and ate and ate and drank and drank because it was so nice to be eating our breakfast in the open air.

Then, just as my little sister finished her very last bite of banana, a big man with a black-dirty face came in the back gate and Mother said, 'Here is the sweep at last.'

Well, *you* know all about sweeps, but my little sister didn't, and she was so interested that my mother said she could watch the sweep so long as she didn't meddle in any way. My sister said she would be very good, so my mother found her one of my overalls, and tied a hanky round her head to keep her hair clean, and said, 'Now you can go and watch the sweep.'

My little sister watched the sweep man push the brush up the chimney and she watched when he screwed a cane on to the brush and a cane on to that cane, and a cane on to that cane, all the time pushing the brush up and up the chimney, and she stayed as good as good. She was very quiet. *She didn't say a thing.*

She was so mousy-quiet that the black sweep man said, 'You are quiet, missy, haven't you got a tongue?'

My sister was very surprised when the sweep asked if she had got a tongue, so she stuck her tongue out quickly to show that she had got one, and he said, 'Fancy that now!'

Then my little sister laughed and the sweep laughed and she wasn't quiet any more. She talked and talked until he had finished his work.

Then my sister asked the sweep what he

was going to do with all the soot he had collected and he said, 'I shall leave it for your father to use in his garden. It's good for frightening off the tiddly little slugs.'

So, when the sweep man went away he left a little pile of soot in the garden for our father. My sister was sorry when he went away, and she asked my mother lots of questions. She wanted to know so many things that Mother said, 'If I answer you now I'll never get the place straight, so just you run off and play like a good girl, and I will tell you all about soot and chimney-sweeps later on.'

So my sister went off, and Mother cleaned up the room and brought in the chairs and hung up curtains and did all the other tidying up things and all the time my sister was very quiet.

There had been lots of things my sister had wanted to know very badly. One thing she had wanted to know was if there was soot in *all* the chimneys. She wondered if there was any soot in her own bedroom chimney.

She went upstairs and looked up her chimney but she couldn't see because it was too dark up there.

It was very dark and my sister probably wouldn't have bothered any more about it, only she happened to remember that there was a long cane on the landing with a feather duster on the top, that Mother used for getting the cobwebs from the top of the stairs.

Yes, I thought you would guess. The cane was very bendy and it wasn't difficult for a little girl to push it up the chimney.

Have you ever done anything so very silly as this? If you have you will know how dirty soot is. It's much dirtier than mud even.

My silly sister pushed the feather duster up her bedroom chimney and a lot of soot fell down into the fireplace. It was such a lot of soot and it looked so dirty that my little sister got frightened and wished that she hadn't done such an awful thing.

She couldn't help thinking that Mother would be very cross when she saw it.

So she thought she had better *hide it*.

You will never guess where that silly child tried to hide the soot. IN HER BED.

Yes, in her own nice clean little comfortable bed.

I'm glad to think that you wouldn't be so silly.

My sister made such a mess carrying the soot across the room and touching things with her sooty fingers and treading on the floor with sooty feet that she didn't know what to do.

She saw how messy her bedroom was and she was very, very sorry; she was so sorry that she ran right downstairs to the garden where Mother was shaking the mats and she flung her little sooty arms round Mother's skirt, and pushed her little sooty face into Mother's apron, and she said, 'Oh, I have been a bad girl. I have been a bad girl. Scold me a lot. Scold me a lot.' And then she cried and cried and cried and cried and *cried*.

And she was so sorry and so ashamed that Mother forgave her even though it made her a lot of extra work on a very busy day.

My little sister was so sorry that she fetched things and carried things and told Mother when the sheets were dry and helped to lay the table for dinner and behaved like the best child in England, so that our father said it was almost worth having her behave so badly when she could show afterwards what a good girl she really was.

Our father was a very funny man.

7 My Naughty Little Sister is very sorry

A long time ago, when I was a little girl with a naughty little sister, a cross lady lived in our road. This cross lady was called Mrs Lock and she didn't like children.

Mrs Lock didn't like children at all, and if she saw a boy or girl stopping by her front gate she would tap on her window to them and say, 'Don't hang about here,' in a very grumbling voice.

Wasn't that a cross thing to do? I will tell you why Mrs Lock was so cross. It was because she had a very beautiful garden outside her front door and once some boys had been playing football in the roadway, and the ball had bounced into her garden and broken down a beautiful rose-tree.

So when Mrs Lock saw children by her gate she thought they were going to start playing with footballs and damage her garden, and she always sent them away. Sometimes she came right out of the house and down to the gate and said, 'Go and play in the park – the roadway is no place for games,' and she would look so fierce and cross that the children would hurry away at once.

There was another reason too, why Mrs Lock was so cross. You see, she had a beautiful smoky-looking cat, and one day a nasty child had thrown a stone at the cat and hurt his poor leg, so if Mrs Lock saw a boy or girl stroking her smoky-looking cat, she would say, 'Don't you meddle with that cat, now!'

What a cross lady she was! But I suppose you couldn't really blame her. It isn't nice to have your rose-trees broken, and it's very, very bad to have your poor cat injured, isn't it?

Well now: one bright sunshiny morning, my naughty little sister went out for a little walk down the road all by herself. It was only a very small walk, just as far as the lamp-post at the corner of the road and back again, but my little sister was pretending that it was a very long walk; she was pretending that she was a shopping lady, stopping at all the hedges and gate-ways and saying that they were shops.

My little sister had a lovely game, all by herself, being a shopping-lady. It was a very nice day, and she had a little cane shopping-basket just like our mother's and a little old purse full of beads for pennies.

First my little sister stopped at a hedge and said, 'I'll have a nice cabbage today, please.' Then she picked a leaf and pretended that it was a cabbage, and put it carefully into her basket. She took two beads out of her purse and left them under the hedge to pay for it.

She went on until she came to a wall; there were two little round stones by the wall, so she pretended that they were eggs and bought them too.

Then she found a piece of red flower-pot which made nice meat for her pretend dinner. She had a lovely game.

Just as she arrived at Mrs Lock's gate, the big smoky-looking cat jumped up on to it and began to purr and purr and as he purred his big feathery tail went all curly and twisty and he looked very beautiful. My sister stopped to look at him.

When the big smoky-looking cat saw my sister looking at him, he opened his mouth and showed her all his sharp little teeth, then he stretched out his curly pink tongue and began to lick one of his legs. He licked and licked.

My little sister was very pleased to see such a nice cat and she stood tippy-toed and touched him. When she did this he stopped licking and began to purr again. He was nice

and warm and furry, so she stroked him,
very gently towards his tail because Mother
had told us that pussies didn't like being
stroked the other way. 'Dear Pussy. Nice
animal,' she said to him.

Now, as my sister was such a little girl Mrs Lock didn't see her standing by the gate, so she didn't say 'go away' to her, and my sister had a long talk with the smoky-looking cat.

She told him that she was a shopping-lady. 'I have bought lots of things,' she said. 'I can't think of anything else.'

When she said this, the cat got up suddenly and jumped right off the gate back into Mrs Lock's garden, and as he jumped the gate opened wide. 'Meeow,' he said. 'Meeow' – like that.

My bad little sister looked through the gate and she saw the smoky cat going up the path. She saw all the pretty tulip flowers and the wallflowers growing on each side, and do you know what she said?

She said, 'That was very kind of you,

Pussy. Now I can buy a nice cup to drink my milk out of.'

And she walked into Mrs Lock's garden. Mrs Lock's tulip flowers were all different colours: red, yellow, pink and white. You know that tulip flowers look rather like cups, don't you?

Yes. You know.

'I'll have a yellow cup, please,' my bad sister said. 'Here's the money, Pussy.'

And she picked a yellow tulip head and put it in her basket.

The smoky-looking cat walked round and round her legs, and his long tickly tail waved and waved and he said, 'Purr' to my little sister who was pretending to be a shopping-lady.

And Mrs Lock saw her from her front window.

Mrs Lock *was* cross. She tapped hard on her window glass and my naughty little sister saw her. Then she remembered that she wasn't really a shopping-lady, she remembered that she was a little girl. She remembered that it was naughty to pick flowers that didn't belong to you.

Of course you know what she did? Yes. She ran away, through the gate and down the road to our house, while Mrs Lock tapped and tapped and the smoky cat stood still in surprise.

My little sister ran straight indoors and straight upstairs and hid herself under the bed.

Mrs Lock came down the road after her, and when she saw my little sister run into the house, she came and knocked at our door, and told our mother all about my little sister's bad behaviour.

My mother was very sorry to hear that my sister had picked one of Mrs Lock's tulips, and when Mrs Lock had gone, our mother went upstairs and peeped under the bed. You see, she knew *just* where her naughty little girl would be.

'Come out,' Mother said in a kind voice, because she knew my little sister was ashamed of herself, and my little sister came out very slowly, and stood by the side of the bed and looked very sad; but Mother was so nice that my sister told her all about the pretending game and the pussy cat, and Mother explained to her that you have to think even when you're pretending hard, and not do naughty things by mistake.

Then she told my sister all about why Mrs Lock was cross. About her rose-tree and the nasty thing that had happened to the smoky-looking cat. And my sister was very, very sorry.

When Mother went downstairs again my

sister had a good idea. She went to her toy-box and she found the beautiful card that our granny had sent her for her birthday. It had a pretty picture of a pussy cat and a bunch of roses on it. It was the nicest card my sister had ever had, but she thought she would give it to Mrs Lock to show that she was sorry.

She didn't say a word to anyone. She went out very quietly down the road to Mrs Lock's gate.

When she got there, my little sister went inside the gate and up the path. The smoky-looking cat came round the side of the house to meet her, but she didn't stop to stroke him. No. She went up to Mrs Lock's front door, and rattled the letter box, then she pushed the postcard inside. She put her mouth close to the letter box and shouted, 'I am sorry I took your flower, Mrs Lock. I am very-very sorry. I have brought you my best postcard for a present.' And then she ran away again. Only this time Mrs Lock didn't tap the glass.

The very next time my little sister went by Mrs Lock's gate there was Mrs Lock herself, pulling weeds out of her pathway, and there was the smoky-looking cat sitting on a gatepost. When the cat saw my little sister he jumped down from the gatepost and said 'purr' to her and rubbed round and round her legs. Then Mrs Lock stood up very straight and looked over the gate at my little sister.

Mrs Lock said, 'Thank you for the card.'

All the time the smoky-coloured cat was purring and rubbing, rubbing and purring round and round my sister's legs and Mrs Lock said, 'My cat likes you. His name is Tibbles. Stroke him.'

And my sister did stroke him, and after that she stroked him every time she went past Mrs Lock's gate and found him sitting there in the sunshine. And although Mrs Lock often saw her stroking him she never said, 'Don't you meddle with my cat,' to her.

AND when Christmas time came Mrs Lock sent my sister a card with robins and holly and shiny glittery stuff on it that was even more lovely than the pussy-cat card.

8 What a jealous child!

When my sister was a naughty little girl she had a godmother-auntie whom she loved very much.

This godmother-auntie was a very, very kind, and very, very pretty young lady. My little sister used to say that she was like a fairy in a book. She had curly gold hair and twinkling blue eyes and she was always laughing and singing.

And she was never cross. She used to have a lovely hat with cherries on it, and one day my greedy sister pulled the cherries off her hat and tried to eat them, and she didn't grumble at all. When she saw the dreadful face my naughty little sister was making when she found that those hat-cherries were full of nasty cotton-wool stuff she only laughed, and said, 'If you'd *told* me you wanted them to play with you could have had them, and then I would have explained that they were not real.'

And when our mother scolded my sister this pretty lady said, 'Don't worry, I was going to put a rose on that hat anyway.'

And the next time she came to see us she *had* put a rose on her hat – a big pink one, and to please my little sister she had brought along a small pink rose for her to wear on *her* hat! 'Only don't try to eat that,' she said, 'because it is made of silk and won't taste at all nice.'

Wasn't she kind?

This beautiful godmother worked in a big sweetie shop in London where they made specially grand sweeties in a big kitchen behind the shop, and she used to tell my sister and me all about how the sweeties were made.

She told us how the sweeties were rolled in sugar and cut with real silver knives and how all the fruity pieces in them came right across the sea from France in wooden boxes, and we were very interested.

She always brought us a big box of sweeties from her shop and they were grander than any sweeties we'd ever seen before. They were in a very smart silky box with flowers on it, and the box was tied up with real hair-ribbony ribbon that our mother always put away in her ribbon box.

When our mother saw the beautiful tied-up box she always said, 'It looks too pretty to open.' But we *did* open it.

And when the box was opened she would say, 'They look too nice to eat.' But we *did* eat them, and Mother always had the first one – and she always took the almondy one in the middle with the green bits sticking out of it, because there was only one of those, and she didn't want my sister and me to be cross about who should have it.

My little sister loved those boxes of sweeties because her godmother-aunt had told her all about the big shop and the place where they were made, and she would be very careful before she chose her sweet, and when she did choose it she would say, 'Tell me about this one, Godma-aunt.'

And she would hear all over again about silver knives and French cherries and men in white caps who twisted the sweetie stuff on hooks and pulled it out and p-u-l-l-e-d it out to make it clear and shiny.

When her beautiful godmother said, 'Pulled it out' she would make pulling out faces and speak in a pulling out voice, she would say, 'P-u-l-l-e-d i-t o-u-t' – like that.

How my sister would laugh. She always wanted to hear about the pulling out of the sweetie stuff when her godmother came to see us.

We were always glad to see my little sister's godmother, she was so very nice. My little sister liked seeing her best of all. She liked to climb on to her godmother's lap and stare at her pretty smily face. She would pat her cheeks and say, 'Sing to me, Godma-aunt. Sing me a funny song.'

And her godmother would sing her all sorts of funny songs until my sister's eyes got all peepy and teary with laughing so much.

Then my sister, who was not a kissing child at all, would hug and kiss her pretty godmother-auntie and say, 'I do love you, you nice lady!'

Wasn't she a lovely godmother to have?

Now, you wouldn't think that anyone could ever be cross with such a dear lady, would you?

You would be surprised to hear that someone shouted at her and said, 'Go away,

I don't want you,' wouldn't you?

I know I was surprised when my sister behaved like that to her dear godmother. But she did. And do you know why? It's because she was an unpleasant, jealous girl.

You see, one day her dear godmother brought a great tall man to see us. She had never brought anyone else before, and my sister didn't quite like it. She liked to have her godmother on her own. She said, 'I'm shy,' and ran and hid her face in Mother's lap, and when Mother told her to sit on a chair and to stop being silly, she sat and stared at her godmother-aunt and the great tall man and looked cross as cross.

Do you know why she behaved like that?

It was because the great tall man liked her godmother-aunt too and it was because her godmother-aunt liked the tall man very much.

My naughty little sister didn't want her godmother to like anyone but her, and she didn't want the big tall man to like her godmother.

She was jealous. And that is a very nasty thing to be, isn't it? What a good thing you aren't a child like that.

My sister pretended that she didn't want any sweeties, and her poor godmother looked quite worried.

'But Albert made some of them,' she said.

Albert was the great tall man.

Our godmother started to tell us all about Albert making the sweeties, but my sister wouldn't listen. She got down from her chair and said, 'I want to go to bed now.'

Do you know that was in the morning, and she hadn't had her dinner. Wasn't she being awkward?

Mother said, 'You behave yourself, you naughty little girl.'

But the beautiful godmother-auntie said, 'Don't be cross with her, I think she's not sure about Albert.'

She smiled very kindly at my sister and said, 'You must like Albert, duckie. Albert and I are going to get married very soon and we shall be living in a dear little house and you can come and stay with us.' And she came over to my sister in a kind way.

When my sister heard this, when she heard that the great tall man and her pretty godmother-aunt were going to be married, she was so cross that she said what I told you.

She said, 'GO AWAY. I DON'T WANT YOU.'

She said, 'I don't want you and I don't want that great tall man. You can go away now.'

Oh dear! Our mother was cross! But what do you think? That great big tall Albert man started to laugh, and he had such a loud roary laugh that my sister forgot to be jealous and stared at him.

When Albert laughed my sister's godmother began to laugh too, and they made so much noise that our mother began to laugh as well, and so did I – you never heard so much laughing.

Then that funny Albert man got up and

opened a big bag that he had brought with him, and he took out a big, wide saucepan. Then he took out a bag of sugar and some butter and some treacle stuff in a tin. He was laughing all the time he did it because my sister was staring so much!

He took these things out to our mother's kitchen and he began to cook all the sugar and stuff in his saucepan. He didn't say anything, he just cooked.

No one had ever done a thing like that in our house before, so my sister went on being not jealous, and went out into the kitchen to see what he was doing instead.

When Albert saw my sister looking at him he put his hand into his bag and took out a white hat and *put it on his head*.

And he cooked and cooked and stirred

with a spoon and cooked until all the sugar-butter-treacly stuff began to smell very nice indeed.

Then Albert took the saucepan off the stove, and did another funny thing.

He took the towel off the hook behind our kitchen door, and he wiped the hook very clean with our mother's dish-cloth and dried it beautifully on the tea towel.

My sister's eyes said 'O' 'O', she was so astonished.

Then, all of a sudden, Albert took the warm sticky stuff out of the saucepan and threw it over the hook.

Then he got a hold on the end of it and he p-u-l-l-e-d it and he p-u-l-l-e-d it. Then he twisted it up and he threw it back over the hook and he p-u-l-l-e-d and p-u-l-l-e-d it again, quick as quick.

It was just like my sister's godmother had told us. And it wasn't in the shop-kitchen either, it was in our own mother's own kitchen.

Albert pulled that stuff until it was clear and then he took it off the hook, quick as quick! It was all long and twisty.

It was a beautiful thing to do, wasn't it?

Albert didn't speak to my sister, he just spoke out loud to himself; he said, 'I wonder if it tastes all right?'

He got a hammer and began to break the long twisty piece of toffee-stuff. When he did this, a piece jumped right off the table and fell by my sister's foot.

Our kitchen smelled so nice and the sweetie looked so nice, that my sister picked that piece up and popped it into her mouth and it was *quite delicious*.

Now she wasn't jealous at all. She was proud. She was proud to think that she knew such a clever man. 'It is very, very nice, Albert,' she said. 'You are very clever.'

Then she laughed and Albert laughed, and Albert let her put his funny white cap on, and her godmother lifted her up so that she could see herself in the glass wearing the white cap, and everyone was very happy.

My sister looked at her lovely smiling godmother and the great, tall, clever Albert and she said, 'I don't mind Albert being my godmother-uncle after all.

9 The smart girl

One day, when I was a little girl and my little sister was sometimes naughty, the Mayor of our town invited us to a children's garden party. Bad Harry was invited too, and so were all the other children who lived near us.

When Mrs Cocoa heard that my little sister was going to the Mayor's party she was very pleased because she loved my bad little sister very much, and so she made her a beautiful party dress to wear.

Mrs Cocoa said that she had some nice material called Indian muslin in her drawer that would be just the thing for a party-dress.

The Indian muslin was all white with little white needlework flowers all over it. Mrs Cocoa made it into a dress for my little sister, and when it was finished she put a pink ribbon round the middle of it, and pink bows on the sleeves, and she made a frilly petticoat to go underneath it; and when my little sister tried it on she looked just like a beautiful new doll straight out of the box.

Bad Harry was there when my sister tried her dress on and he opened his eyes very wide.

'Nice,' said Bad Harry. 'You *do* look nice.'

And he said, 'Nice and nice and nice,' to show my sister how very smart he thought she looked.

My little sister didn't say anything. She just stood on the table and looked at herself in the mirror over the mantelpiece and was so very pleased she couldn't talk at all.

She was quite quiet until dear Mrs Cocoa said, 'Don't you like it?' Then she spoke. She said, 'Oh, Mrs Cocoa, I am just like a fairy. I think I must take it off quickly before it gets dirty.'

That was a surprising thing for my little sister to say, for as a rule she didn't mind being dirty a bit.

When our mother had taken the dress off for her, my funny sister ran to Mrs Cocoa and hugged her and kissed her and said, 'Dear Mrs Cocoa, I love my smart dress. I love it very much. *I love me in it, too.*'

She wouldn't hug Mrs Cocoa while she had the dress on, because she was afraid of spoiling it. Wasn't she funny?

Before the party day my little sister often went upstairs and asked our mother to let her peep into the wardrobe and see the Indian muslin dress, but she didn't want to try it on again, she wouldn't even touch it. She said she wanted it to be absolutely beautiful for the party. Wasn't she a strange child?

When the party day came, and she saw me getting ready to go, my little sister said, 'Mother, I will wear my smart dress *now*.' And she stood straight and good on a chair while Mother washed her, and straight and good when she was dressed, AND straight and good when her hair was brushed, because she wanted to look just like a fairy.

Bad Harry came to call for us. 'Come on, come on,' he said, because he was impatient, but my little sister would not hurry. She said,

'Good-bye' to our mother in a very quiet voice, and she took my hand like a good girl and walked along very neatly in her white shoes, not scuffling the dust or anything!

Mrs Cocoa came to her gate to see us off and my sister waved her hand to her. 'I can't kiss you, Mrs Cocoa,' she said, 'because I am all neat and nice,' and although Bad Harry said, 'Hurry! Hurry!' and ran ahead and back again and again she still walked very nicely and slowly with me.

At last we came to the Mayor's Garden Party place. It did look grand! The Mayor had hung lots of little coloured flags all round his garden, and the big gates were open and a band was playing, and we could hear Punch-and-Judy noises and see stripy tents inside. Bad Harry was so excited that he just dashed ahead of us, and would have gone in on his own, if the gate man hadn't asked for his invitation card that I was carrying for him!

There were a lot of people crowding round the gate watching the children going to the party, and one lady said, 'Oh, the little duckie,' when she saw my neat and nice sister, and my little sister felt very proud. But she didn't turn her head, and she didn't let go of my hand, because she wanted to look as fairy-like as possible!

The Mayor had made a lovely party for us. We soon found that the stripy tents had all sorts of interesting things in them. Things that you could do without paying for them. It was just like a lovely *free* fair!

There were hoop-la's and magic fish-ponds and swings and pony-rides and Mr Punch and a conjurer, all as free as free. There was even a coconut shy, and we saw some of the bigger children throwing balls at the coconuts.

Wasn't it kind of the Mayor? We saw him walking in the garden with a gold chain round his neck, and he smiled at us and asked if we were having a good time. We said, 'Yes, thank you,' and he said, 'Good. Good.'

And we were enjoying ourselves. At least I was. And Bad Harry was. But my little sister didn't seem to be enjoying it very much at all. You see, she was afraid of spoiling her smart dress, and when the gentleman with the roundabouts said, 'Come on now, who wants a ride?' she couldn't say 'Me! Me!' because she wanted to look smart and she was afraid she might get her dress dirty on the roundabouts; and when the fish-pond young lady said, 'Come and fish for a magic prize,' she said, 'No, thank you, I might get wet!'

Bad Harry fished and he won a tin whistle, but, although she wanted a tin whistle very much, she wouldn't fish, oh no!

When we went to see Mr Punch she stood at the back of the crowd because of her sticking out dress, and she was so far away that when Mr Punch smacked his baby, she didn't hear the nice man by the Punch show saying, 'It's all right, children, he isn't really hurting it, you know!' and so of course she cried, and then she had to stop crying because she might make her Indian muslin dress all teary.

Bad Harry got quite cross at last and he said, 'Why did you wear that silly old dress?'

My sister said, 'It's not silly. It's smart.'

And Harry said, 'It's smart *and* it's silly if you can't do anything in it.'

My little sister said, 'I want to be smart.'

Then Bad Harry said, 'Well, if you keep on being smart like that you won't be able to have any of the Mayor's nice tea that the ladies are putting on the tables in that big tent over there. It's a very nice tea,' Bad Harry said. 'There are lots of cakes and jellies. I know because I've just been over there to look.'

When my little sister heard about the tea and the jellies and when she thought about the roundabouts and the fish-pond she began to feel quite sorry. But she didn't want to spoil her smart dress.

She thought and thought. She saw the other children running about and sliding on slides and eating ice-cream and throwing balls at coconuts, and then she had a funny idea.

Very, very quietly she walked away from the fair-place and round behind some bushes where no one could see her. I didn't notice her go, because Bad Harry and I were trying to throw rings over some hooks on the hoop-la stall.

When I *did* find that she had gone, I was very worried, especially as a big gentleman in a red coat began to bang on a tray and call out, 'Now, children, line up, and we will go in to tea.'

I must say I didn't want to have to go and look for my sister just at tea-time. I thought that the other children might eat all the cakes and jellies and things before I found her, and I wouldn't like that much.

But I *had* promised to look after her, so I

began to ask people if they had seen her.

I was just asking a lady, when I heard everyone burst out laughing.

All the boys and girls laughed, and the roundabout man, and the Punch man and the fish-pond lady, and the Mayor and Bad Harry. They laughed and laughed and laughed.

They were laughing at my naughty little sister!

What do you think she had done?

She had got so tired of being careful of her beautiful dress that she had gone behind the bushes and *taken it off*. I don't know how she managed on her own – but she did.

She had taken off her dress and her lovely frilly petticoat and had put them very carefully over a garden seat, and out she jumped, her old noisy jumping self again, skipping up and down in her little white vest and her little white knickers! And she was laughing too.

'*Now* I can have swings, and fish-ponds, and roundabouts and a *big tea*,' she shouted. 'Now I can be ME again.'

She was very pleased with her good idea.

'I shan't spoil my beautiful dress now,' she said. 'Aren't I a clever girl?'

What would you have said if she had been your Naughty Little Sister?

10 My Naughty Little Sister is a curly girl

There was a little girl called Winnie who used to come and see us sometimes when I was a little girl with a naughty little sister.

This girl Winnie was a very quiet, tidy child. She never rushed about and shouted or played dirty games, and she always wore neat clean dresses.

Winnie had some of those long round and round curls like chimney-pots that hung round her head in a very tidy way, and when Winnie moved her head these little curls jumped up and down. Mother told us that these curls were called *ringlets*.

One day, when Winnie and her mother were spending the afternoon at our house, my sister sat staring very hard at Winnie's ringlets, and all of a sudden she got up and went over to her and pushed one of her little fingers into one of Winnie's tidy ringlets.

Then, because the ringlet looked so nice on her finger, she pushed another finger into another ringlet.

Now, if anyone had interfered with *my sister's hair* she would have screamed and screamed – she even made a fuss when our mother brushed it – but Winnie sat still and quiet in a very mousy way, although I don't think she liked having her hair meddled with any more than my sister would have done.

Winnie's mother certainly didn't like it, and she said in a polite firm voice, 'Please don't fiddle with Winifred's hair, dear, the curls may come out.'

Then Winnie's mother said to our mother, 'They take such ages to put in every night.'

When Winnie's mother said this, my funny sister thought that the curls would come right out of Winnie's head if she touched them too much. And she thought that Winnie's mother would have to pick all the curls up and put them back into Winnie's head at night-time. So she stopped touching Winnie's hair at once, and went and sat down again.

She didn't think she would like to be Winnie with falling-out curls.

My little sister sat looking at Winnie though, in case a curl should fall out on its own, but when it didn't, she got tired of looking at her, and went out into the garden instead to talk over the fence to dear Mrs Cocoa Jones.

'Mrs Cocoa,' she said, 'Winnie has funny curls.'

Mrs Cocoa was surprised when my sister said this, so she told her what Winnie's mother had said about the curls coming out.

Now, Mrs Cocoa was a kind polite lady and she didn't laugh at my little sister for making such a funny mistake. She just told her all about how Winnie's mother made Winnie's curls for her.

Mrs Cocoa told my sister how, when *she* was a little girl, her kind old grandmother had curled *her* hair. She said that her grandmother had made her hair damp with a wet brush and had twisted her hair up in little pieces of rag, and how she had gone to bed with her hair twisted up like this and how, next morning, when her grandmother had undone her curlers she had had ringlets just like Winnie's.

My sister was very interested to hear all this.

'Of course,' Mrs Cocoa said, 'my granny only did up my hair on Saturday nights so that it would be curly for Sunday. On ordinary week-nights I had two little pigtails like yours.'

When my sister heard Mrs Cocoa saying about how her grandmother curled her hair for her, she began to smile as big as that.

'I know, Mrs Cocoa,' she said, 'you can make me a curly girl.'

Mrs Cocoa said that my sister would have to sit still and not scream then, and my sister said she would be very still indeed, so Mrs Cocoa said, 'Well then, if your mother is willing, I'll pop in tonight and put some curlers in for you.'

After that, my sister went back into the house, and sat very quietly looking at Winnie and Winnie's beautiful ringlets and smiling in a pussy-cat pleased way to herself.

She didn't say anything to Winnie and her mother about what kind Mrs Cocoa was going to do, but when they had gone she told Mother and me all about it, and Mother said it was very kind of Mrs Cocoa to offer to make ringlets of my sister's hair, and she said, 'Mrs

Cocoa can try anyway, although I can't think *how* you will sit still without making a fuss.'

But my sister said, 'I want ringlets like Winnie's,' and she said it in a very loud voice to show that she wouldn't fuss, so our mother didn't say anything else, and when Mrs Cocoa came over at my sister's bedtime, with a lot of strips of pink rag, and asked for my sister's hairbrush and a basin of water, our mother fetched them for her without saying a word about how my sister usually fussed.

Now, my sister had said that she wasn't going to be a naughty girl when Mrs Cocoa curled her hair, and she knew that Mother expected her to be naughty and that I expected her to be naughty, so, although she found that she didn't like having her hair twisted up into rags very much, *she was good as gold.*

My sister didn't like having her hair twisted up into those rags one bit. You see, her hair was rather long, and Mrs Cocoa had to twist *and* twist *very tightly indeed* to make sure that the curlers would stay in; and the tighter the curl-rags were the more uncomfortable they felt.

But my sister didn't say so. She sat very good and quiet and she thought about all those lovely Winnie-ringlets, and when Mrs Cocoa had finished she thanked her very nicely indeed and went upstairs with Rosy-Primrose, with her hair all curled up tight with little pink rags sticking up all over her head.

But, oh dear.

Have *you* ever tried to sleep with curlers in

your hair? My sister tried and tried, but wherever she turned her head there was a little knob of hair to lie on and it was most uncomfortable.

She tried to go to sleep with her nose in the pillow but that was most feathery and unpleasant.

In the end the poor child went to sleep with her head right over the edge of the bed and her arm tight round the bedpost to keep herself from falling out.

That wasn't comfortable either, so she woke up.

When my little sister woke up she shouted because she couldn't remember why she was lying in such a funny way, and our mother had to come in to her.

When Mother saw how hard it was for my

little sister to sleep with her curlers in, she said perhaps they had better come out, and that made my naughty little sister cry because she did want Winnie-ringlets, until Mother said, 'Well, if you want curls don't fuss then,' and went back to her own bed.

After that my poor sister slept and woke up and slept and woke up all night, but she didn't shout any more, and when morning came she was sleepy and cross and peepy-eyed.

But when she had had her breakfast, Mrs Cocoa came in to undo the curlers, and my sister cheered up and began to smile.

She sat very still while kind Mrs Cocoa took out the rags and carefully combed each ringlet into shape, and when Mrs Cocoa had finished, and my sister climbed up to see herself in the mirror she smiled like anything.

And I smiled and Mother smiled.

She was a curly girl – curlier than Winnie even, because she had a lot more hair than Winnie had. She had real ringlets that you could push your fingers into!

My sister was a proud girl that day, she sat about in a still quiet way – just like Winnie did, and after dinner she fell fast asleep in her chair.

When my sister woke up she sat for a little while and did a lot of thinking, then she got down from her chair and went round to see Mrs Cocoa.

'Thank you very much, Mrs Cocoa, for making me a curly girl,' my sister said, 'but I don't think I will be curly any more. It makes me too sleepy to be curly.'

'I know why Winnie is so quiet now,' my

sister said, 'it's because she can't sleep for curlers. I think I would rather be me, fast asleep with pigtails.'

And Mrs Cocoa said, 'That's a very good idea, I think. Anyway who wants *you* to look like that Winnie?'